"Sundin displays her usual knack for weaving historical detail into a rousing war drama in this enjoyable launch of the Sunrise at Normandy series. Sundin's lively book combines heart-pounding war action with inspirational romance to great effect."

Publishers Weekly

"The author of *When Tides Turn* kicks off a new wartime series, mixing her usual excellent historical research with fast-paced, breathtaking suspense."

Library Journal

"With a commanding grasp of naval history, Sundin spotlights women in the war effort and immerses readers in the ups and downs of naval missions and military exercises as she leads up to a riveting climax in the waters off Omaha Beach."

Booklist

"*The Sea Before Us* is another deftly crafted gem of a novel by Sarah Sundin and showcases her genuine flair for creating a simply riveting and entertaining read from beginning to end."

Midwest Book Reviews

"Sundin's historical research is second to none."

RT Book Reviews

"With a pitch-perfect balance between history and the fine-tuned elements of story, *The Sea Before Us* stands out as superior in WWII fiction. It's at once engaging, emotional, and a strong series debut. I couldn't put it down—and when it came to the last page, I didn't want to."

Kristy Cambron, bestselling author of *The Lost Castle* and the Hidden Masterpiece series

"Once again Sarah Sundin delivers a powerful World War II story in *The Sea Before Us*. History comes to life through Sundin's characters, who cope with the trials and dangers not only on the fields of combat but also in their personal lives. This great combination of dramatic history and likeable characters will keep you turning pages to find out what happens next."

Ann H. Gabhart, author of *These Healing Hills*

Books by Sarah Sundin

SUNRISE *at* NORMANDY

THREE

The
LAND BENEATH US

SARAH
SUNDIN

Revell

a division of Baker Publishing Group
Grand Rapids, Michigan

Published by Revell
a division of Baker Publishing Group
PO Box 6287, Grand Rapids, MI 49516-6287
www.revellbooks.com

Printed in the United States of America

Library of Congress Cataloging-in-Publication Data
Names: Sundin, Sarah, author.
Title: The land beneath us / Sarah Sundin.
Description: Grand Rapids, MI : Revell, [2019] | Series: Sunrise at Normandy ; 3
Identifiers: LCCN 2019020156 | ISBN 9780800727994 (pbk.)
Subjects: | GSAFD: Love stories. | Historical fiction.
Classification: LCC PS3619.U5626 L36 2019 | DDC 813/.6—dc23
LC record available at https://lccn.loc.gov/2019020156

ISBN 978-0-8007-3775-7 (casebound)

20   21   22   23   24   25   26   7   6   5   4   3   2   1

Presidential Radio Broadcast

6 June 1944

Almighty God: Our sons, pride of our Nation, this day have set upon a mighty endeavor, a struggle to preserve our Republic, our religion, and our civilization, and to set free a suffering humanity.

Lead them straight and true; give strength to their arms, stoutness to their hearts, steadfastness in their faith. . . .

For these men are lately drawn from the ways of peace. They fight not for the lust of conquest. They fight to end conquest. They fight to liberate. They fight to let justice arise, and tolerance and good will among all Thy people. They yearn but for the end of battle, for their return to the haven of home.

Some will never return. Embrace these, Father, and receive them, Thy heroic servants, into Thy kingdom.

And for us at home—fathers, mothers, children, wives, sisters, and brothers of brave men overseas—whose thoughts and prayers are ever with them—help us, Almighty God, to rededicate ourselves in renewed faith in Thee in this hour of great sacrifice. . . .

Thy will be done, Almighty God.
Amen.

President Franklin D. Roosevelt

1

Most men woke in a cold sweat when they dreamed of their own deaths, but not Private Clay Paxton.

Clay crawled through a foxhole, just like in his recurring dream. Bullets zinged overhead, but these were American bullets fired to teach the Army Ranger recruits to keep their heads down.

"Come on, G. M.," he called to his buddy. Gene Mayer might be fast and wiry, but the Californian wilted in the Tennessee humidity.

"Right on your heels, Pax."

Clay slithered out of the foxhole and under rows of barbed wire. His wrestling training kept his movements low, controlled, and speedy, even with full gear on his back.

The soldier to his right cussed. His rifle barrel had gotten caught in the wire.

"Back up, Holman." Clay elbowed his way through the dirt. "Try again. Head low."

Holman cussed again, but a friendly sort of cuss.

Clay cleared the wires and sprinted to the next station in the obstacle course, his respiratory rate fast but even.

He clambered up a cargo net and slapped his hand on the wooden platform that led to the rope bridge over the Elk River.

A boot slammed down.

"Watch out!" Clay yanked his hand away, and he lurched down, barely catching himself.

Bertie King sneered down at him. "No room in the Rangers for a half-breed."

If he wanted Clay to bite, he'd have to use fresher bait than that old worm.

"No room for a half-wit either, King," Gene said. "Let him up."

"What's the holdup, boys?" Sergeant Tommy Lombardi strode over. "King! Get your tail over that bridge. Paxton, Mayer, what are you waiting for?"

King stepped out onto the bridge, muttering obscenities about Lombardi's Italian blood.

Clay puffed out a breath. Nothing stupider than insulting your sergeant.

He hefted himself onto the platform, grasped the two side ropes, and set his boot on the center rope. Angling his feet, he worked his way across.

"Why do you let him talk to you that way?" Gene asked.

Clay shook his head. Not only had he never been the brawling kind, but any fight would be considered his fault, just because his mama was Mexican. "Let's save the fighting for the battlefield."

"You have to put up with this a lot?" Gene asked, his voice low and hard.

"Not as much as you might think." Growing up, he'd had Wyatt and Adler to protect him.

Until that night two years ago when they'd stripped him of his future and cast him into a pit. Showed what they really thought of their half-breed half brother.

Pain and humiliation threatened his balance, and he hardened his chest. None of that mattered anymore. The Lord had given

8

him the recurring dream to show him the way out of the pit, and Clay thanked him once again.

On the far side of the river, Clay ran through the forest, hurdling logs and darting around boulders. Gene's long legs gained on him.

As soon as Clay had seen the notice about the Rangers at basic training, he'd volunteered. Styled after the British Commandos, the US Army Rangers had already seen action in North Africa. In April, the 2nd Ranger Battalion had been activated at Camp Forrest, and now Clay hoped to replace one of the original volunteers who hadn't made the cut.

Clay jogged to a dangling rope and climbed ten feet to the single rope line across the Elk. Hand over hand, Clay swung like a monkey over the green water.

An explosion to his left, and a geyser shot up and soaked him.

He didn't lose his grip or his nerve.

"Do that again, boys," Gene shouted. "Feels good."

It did, and Clay laughed.

On the other side, he sprinted toward a ten-foot-tall wooden fence.

"They don't call me king for nothing." Bertie King straddled the fence and beat his chest like Tarzan. "You girls might as well give up, 'cause they only take the best. Me."

Clay worked wet fingers between the planks and made his way up. Didn't King realize the Rangers wanted men who worked together?

"No stinking Jews." King kicked at Sid Rubenstein's hand.

Ruby dropped to the ground, yelling and swearing.

King threw back his head and laughed.

A mistake.

He lost his balance and toppled backward. With a scream, he cartwheeled to earth and landed hard on one leg.

A crack.

Two years ago, a scream, a fall, and a crack had changed the course of Clay's life. Once again, he scrambled down to help.

King's lower right leg bent at an unnatural angle. The man cussed and struggled to sit up.

"Lie down, Bertie. Stay calm." Clay pressed on the patient's shoulders. "Gene, go get the medic."

Bertie swore at him, insulting his heritage, his paternity, and his intelligence.

"Lie still, or you'll make it worse." Clay unsheathed his knife and sliced the trouser leg open from knee to ankle. "Y'all back up and give him some air. Ruby, Holman, open your first aid kits, get out the field dressings."

"How bad is it?" Bertie said between gritted teeth.

The blood and the angle of the leg made the diagnosis simple. "Complicated compound fracture of both the tibia and fibula—the bones in your shin." The man would need surgery, and he'd be out of the Rangers.

Clay took a field dressing from Ruby and opened it, careful to touch it as little as possible with his filthy hands. Right now stopping the bleeding was more important than sterility, so he pressed the dressing to the bloodiest part of the wound.

"Medics are here!" The circle of men opened.

Two fellows ran up with a litter and medical kits. "What happened?"

Lieutenant Bill Taylor stood behind the medics.

Clay's heart hammered harder than it had running the course. Time to play dumb again. "King here fell off the wall. Reckon he broke his leg."

"What? You should have heard Paxton a minute ago," Holman said. "Talking about fibulas and all. He ought to be a doctor."

He winced and let the medics take his place. "Nah, I ain't smart enough. I just paid attention in first aid class. Y'all should have done the same."

"A medic then." Rubenstein pointed to the men splinting the remnants of Bertie King's leg. "Say, Lieutenant, didn't you say you need more medics in this unit?"

"Very much." Keen eyes fixed on Clay, and Lieutenant Taylor beckoned to him.

No, no, no. Clay trudged over. Medics didn't heave hand grenades into pillboxes like in his dream.

Taylor crossed muscular arms. "We need medics who can handle the physical training. You're doing well here, Paxton. You're the ideal candidate."

If the brass dug into Clay's records, they might learn he'd been top of his high school class, admitted to the University of Texas as a premedical student.

Clay sharpened his gaze. "Sir, I didn't volunteer for the Rangers to patch people up. Doesn't the Good Book say there's a time to every purpose? A time to kill, and a time to heal?"

"It certainly does."

"Well, sir, this ain't my healing time."

The lieutenant grinned. "I can't say I'm not disappointed, but I like your fighting spirit. You're dismissed."

Clay released a long breath. He had to be more careful.

He couldn't allow the shards of his old dream to shred his new dream.

TULLAHOMA, TENNESSEE
SUNDAY, JUNE 13, 1943

Leah Jones studied the poem in her composition book as the bus jostled down the road.

> Between these lines
> Begins a tale
> Of hope, of chivalry beheld.

Beguiles my soul,
Becalms my heart,
And here I find where I belong.

"Is *begins* too mundane?" she asked her new roommate, Darlene Bishop. "*Beget* perhaps? *Bespoke*? No, neither is right."

"Sugar, you need to get your head out of the clouds." Darlene's Southern accent rocked in unison with the bus.

Leah listed more "be" words in the margin. "Librarians are supposed to have their heads in the clouds."

Darlene's bright red lips twisted. "You're working at an Army camp, sugar. These soldiers are wolves, every one of them. If you don't keep your eyes open, they'll eat you alive."

Leah laughed and smoothed the threadbare gray charity-barrel dress that hung on her like a gunnysack. "They won't give me a second glance."

"Nonsense." Darlene's blue eyes narrowed in scrutiny. "When you get your first paycheck, I'll take you to the beauty shop and the dress shop. You won't need much makeup with your dark coloring. Why, we'll smarten you right up."

Leah fingered the curl at the end of her waist-length braid, and a thrill ran through her. Oh, to have things of her own. She couldn't believe the boardinghouse placed only two girls in a room, and she had a bed all to herself.

"That's Gate 1." Darlene pointed out the window.

Cars and trucks and buses lined up at a booth with a sign that read "Camp Forrest." Although the camp had been named for Confederate General Nathan Bedford Forrest, the pine trees framing the entrance still seemed appropriate.

Darlene fluffed her blonde curls. "Remember to stay away from the POW camp. I can't believe they brought over a thousand Germans here last week. Gives me the willies."

Leah shrugged. Since the Allies had captured hundreds of thousands of Germans and Italians after the victory in North Africa, the prisoners had to go somewhere. "I'm sure the enclosure is secure."

Darlene wrinkled her pretty nose. "Oh, fiddle! I forgot to ask for you. I was meaning to find out where the library is."

Leah blinked at her roommate. Darlene had worked at Camp Forrest for a year. How could she not know where the library was? "Miss Mayhew's letter said it was between the service club and the sports arena."

"This is your stop then. That's the service club." She tapped Leah's arm. "If you need me, I'm at the PX at Avenue G and 26th."

"Thank you." Leah slid her book into her canvas schoolbag and squeezed past Darlene.

"Lamb to the wolves," Darlene muttered.

Leah smiled. A lamb could never have survived the orphanage.

She stepped off the bus, and pine-scented heat settled on her. A long two-story white frame building marked "Club 1" rose before her.

Leah passed groups of khaki-clad soldiers who cast sidelong glances that declared she didn't belong.

Oh, there it was. A smaller white frame building, too plain for the splendors it housed. All library buildings deserved to be as glorious as the one in her earliest memory.

A soldier stepped out of the library, as grand as an Indian chief with his strong features and high cheekbones and a complexion even darker than her own. He slipped on a cap over shiny black hair, and his gaze landed on her.

Leah held her breath. She'd been caught staring.

He gave her the same bewildered look the other soldiers had, but then he tipped his head in a thoughtful way and descended the steps. "Pardon me, miss. Are you lost?"

Men never talked to her, and her gaze swung to the library. "Oh no. I'm found."

"I reckon you like libraries." His accent sounded more cowboy than Indian, and he had a nice deep chuckle.

"They're my greatest joy. After the Lord, of course." She didn't think she'd ever seen such dark eyes, yet they shone with warm amusement.

"Glad your priorities are straight, young lady."

He obviously shared them, except . . . "You don't have a book."

He flashed a grin. "A muddy tent is no place for books. I do my reading here."

Leah wrapped her fingers around the fraying strap of her schoolbag. "Maybe I'll see you again. I work here. Today's my first day."

"Oh." With rounded eyes, his gaze swept her up and down, but in a swift way as if he thought it rude. "Then I won't keep you, Miss . . ."

Something about him made her want to tell the whole story of her name and why it wasn't hers at all, but she merely extended her hand. "Leah Jones."

"Private Clay Paxton." He shook her hand with a grip both strong and gentle.

She said good-bye and climbed the steps. Darlene was mistaken about the men being wolves. She obviously hadn't met Clay Paxton.

Once inside, the rich familiar scent enveloped her, of ink and ideas and imagination.

A brunette stood behind a desk to Leah's right, setting books in a stack. She looked up and startled, then gave Leah a curious look. "May I help you, miss?"

"I'm Leah Jones. Are you Miss Mayhew?"

"You're . . . Leah . . . Miss Jones?" Shock and pity and restraint battled for control of her pretty features.

Leah stretched to her full five feet. "Yes, ma'am. Miss Tilletson sent me. I have my papers here." She poked her hand into her schoolbag.

14

"No, no. That isn't necessary. Oh my. Miss Tilletson said you came from the orphanage, but I had . . . no idea."

Shame and grief wound around Leah's heart in equal measure.

Miss Mayhew wore a trim powder blue suit. She inched closer as if afraid Leah might smell or have lice, but the orphanage had stressed cleanliness as a great virtue.

"Do you . . ." She gave Leah a sympathetic frown. "Do you have something more professional to wear? And your hair . . . could you put it up, perhaps?"

Leah's stomach curled up. "This is my best dress, ma'am. But when I get my first paycheck, I'll buy outfits and get a haircut. I promise."

Miss Mayhew's cheeks reddened, and she returned behind the desk and opened a drawer. "You won't be paid until the end of the week. That won't do."

"I'm sorry, ma'am." Her eyes stung, but years of practice kept them dry. "Miss Tilletson and the ladies from church in Des Moines gave me money for my high school graduation last week. They were very generous. Very. They meant for me to buy clothes, but after I paid for bus and train tickets and my first month's room and board, I had nothing left."

"You're working the closing shifts." Miss Mayhew strode to her and held out a ten-dollar bill. "Tomorrow morning, go downtown and buy an outfit or two."

Leah edged back. "No, ma'am. I refuse to take charity ever again."

The librarian pursed her lips. "It isn't charity. It—it's a loan until your first paycheck."

That much money would buy a suit and shoes and a haircut too. "I promise I'll earn it. Every penny."

"I'm sure you will. I've known Miss Tilletson since library school, and she said you were smart and diligent." Miss Mayhew gazed around the room. "I would rather have hired a library school graduate. You aren't qualified to help with cataloging or research or acquisitions, but you can serve as a circulation librarian."

Leah tucked the money into the deepest corner of her bag. "I know the Dewey decimal system, I read all Miss Tilletson's library science books, and I plan to go to library school after I earn the tuition."

Miss Mayhew's smile twitched between pity and disbelief. "Yes. Well. Why don't you set your . . . bag in this drawer, and I'll show you our operations."

"Excuse me, ma'am." A tall blond soldier nodded to Miss Mayhew. "My sergeant told me to read the field manual on service of the 75-millimeter howitzer. Do you have it?"

"Yes, sir." She turned to Leah. "Have a seat, Miss Jones. I'll be right back."

"Thank you." Leah sat behind the circulation desk and set her bag in the drawer—beside a heart-shaped cardboard box with a tag that read "To Myra. Love, John."

Her mouth watered. What would it be like to have an entire box of candy to herself?

She tipped open the lid. She just wanted a look. A smell. About half the chocolates were gone, but a dozen remained, round and glossy, with pretty swirls on top.

Leah's fingers strained for the chocolates, but she closed the box and the drawer. Tonight she'd pretend her father had brought her candy. He'd want her to have occasional treats.

But most of all, he'd want her to find her sisters.

The bookshelves called to her. If she could discover a picture or a snippet of information connected to one of her memories, then she'd know where she came from. And maybe she could find a Greek surname that sounded like her memory.

Ka-wa-los.

When her parents died, she'd only been four, too young to pronounce her name properly.

With a name and a city, she could locate the first orphanage she'd been sent to, the last place she'd seen her twin baby sisters. Every night she prayed that they were safe, that they had each other, and that one day she'd find them.

Only then would Leah belong.

2

Clay laced his hands behind his head to stretch his aching shoulders. It felt good to rest for a day and to know he'd treated Bertie King properly.

In the camp library, he reviewed the medical guide. Cut the clothing away from the wound, stop the bleeding, apply a field dressing. If the medics had been delayed, Clay would have improvised a ring splint. Then after the medics administered a quarter grain of morphine, King could have been transported to the hospital for surgery.

How would Dr. Hill have treated this case? The physician's kind face came to mind, but Clay shoved aside memories of his former mentor back in Kerrville, Texas. Ellen Hill had destroyed that relationship as well. The doctor's daughter had only dated Clay to catch the eye of his older brother Adler. She'd caught it, all right.

Did she ever regret that before she died?

Clay shook his head to clear the pain. Movement behind him, and Clay reached for the newspaper at the table's edge to slide over the book.

It was the librarian, not a Ranger, and Clay relaxed.

18

Not Miss Mayhew. A petite brunette in a light green suit parked a cart by the rack beside him, where newspapers hung over dowel rods like sheets on Mama's clothesline. The woman pulled a newspaper off the rack and set it on the bottom shelf of her cart.

Then she spotted Clay and smiled. "Hello, Private Paxton."

Clay froze. He knew her? Round face, dark eyes, olive complexion, Midwestern accent. Had she transferred from the PX? The mess? He rarely forgot names.

She fingered the curly black hair above her collar, and her smile wavered. "I'm Leah Jones. We met last week on my first day here. I got a haircut and a new outfit."

She certainly had. Last week Leah Jones looked like a twelve-year-old street urchin in a tent of a dress. Now she looked more grown up, almost grown up enough to be a librarian.

Clay broke out in a grin. "Hello, Miss Jones. Don't you look nice today?"

Her gaze darted around. "Um, thank you."

Probably not used to compliments. "How's the job? Do you like working here?"

"I do." Her face shone. "I believe in libraries."

Clay chuckled and leaned back in his chair. "Last week I got the impression you believed in God."

Leah plucked another newspaper from the rack. "I think God would say he believes in libraries too."

She had an amusing way of speaking. "Why do you say that?"

"Think about how the Lord loves words. He spoke the universe into being, and he gave us his word both in written form and living form."

Clay brushed his fingers over the text before him. "Since the Lord knows everything, I reckon that makes him the ultimate library."

"What a glorious thought." Leah clutched a newspaper to her chest and gazed over Clay's head. "Imagine. Even the best-read person on earth knows only a fraction of the information in this library, but the Lord has more knowledge than the Library of Congress."

Her gaze drifted down to him, she lifted a quick smile, and she removed the last newspapers from the rack.

Ordinarily, he'd end the conversation there. Since his remaining time on earth could be measured in months, he didn't flirt with girls. But something about Leah reminded him of a lost puppy in need of a bone and a pat on the head.

"Have you ever been to the Library of Congress?" he asked.

"No, never." She pulled a fat Sunday paper from her cart and laid it over a dowel. "Before I came here, I'd only patronized my school libraries in Des Moines. But when I was little, my parents took me to a grand library that smelled of leather and lemon oil and looked like a starry sky, even by day. I wish I knew where it was."

Clay massaged his sore bicep. "Don't your parents remember?"

Another paper joined its friends on the rack. "My parents died when I was four. I don't remember my name, much less where we lived."

That shoved the air out of his lungs harder than when Ernie McKillop had thrown him to the ground in training the day before. "I'm sorry to hear that, miss."

"Don't be." She smiled as if she were consoling him, and she folded the last paper over the rack. "I never wanted for anything, and the second orphanage, the one in Des Moines, treated me kindly."

He winced. "But your . . . name."

She pulled out the chair across from him and sat. "I do remember my first name. It's Thalia. But the people who adopted me from the first orphanage said it was pagan and foreign, since Thalia is one of the muses in Greek mythology. They called me Leah for short and gave me their last name, Jones. When they left me in Des Moines, the orphanage kept the name."

Clay's jaw sagged. She rattled off the tragedies like most girls rattled off their favorite movie stars.

Leah rested her chin in her hand and smiled toward the bookshelves. "My last name was long and Greek and sounded like Ka-wa-los. Maybe one of these books will tell me. Maybe someday I'll see a name and say, 'That's it.'"

Despite everything bad that had happened to Clay, he had his name and a home and parents who loved him. Leah didn't.

"Listen to me jabbering." She leaned forward. "What are you reading?"

Clay grabbed the newspaper to drag over, but it was too late.

"*Guides to Therapy for Medical Officers*," she read upside down. "Are you a medical officer? No, you're a private. Are you a medic?"

"No . . ." A dozen excuses bounced in his head, each falling flat. Hadn't she told him her long and sorry life story? Clay leaned his elbows on the table and lowered his voice. "Listen, none of the fellows know this, so please don't say anything."

Her brown eyes rounded. "I—I won't."

Clay fingered the pages of the book. "I used to want to be a physician."

"Oh, but then you were drafted."

If only he'd been drafted earlier. "The Army didn't kill that dream. My brothers did."

"Your brothers?"

Clay drew a long breath and rolled his shoulders. "Half brothers. I worked for my daddy for two years after high school to earn my tuition money. I was accepted into the University of Texas, premed, but my brother stole my savings."

Leah gasped. "Your brother? But why?"

Why had he brought this up? He'd never even told Gene this story. Clay shifted in his chair. "Back in '41, my brother Adler's fiancée died in a fall. It was an accident, but Adler blamed our oldest brother, Wyatt, and tried to kill him."

"Oh no. How awful."

Clay rubbed a page between his fingers. "I tackled Adler so Wyatt could escape. Reckon Wyatt feared for his life and wanted money to get away. So he took mine, every penny of it."

"He never paid you back?"

"Haven't seen hide nor hair of him since. Haven't wanted to."

Leah frowned at the medical guide. "And you couldn't afford college."

"Worse. I had to keep working at Paxton Trucking. Adler ran away that night too, and Daddy needed my help."

"He ran away too? Because of his girlfriend?"

"Because of—" Clay almost said, "Because of mine," but Leah was too young and innocent for that sordid tale. "Because he took out his anger on me in the worst possible way. He'll never come home again, and that's for the best."

Leah's gaze grew distant. "I can see why you haven't been able to forgive them."

Clay's chin jerked back. "I've forgiven them."

"You have?"

"Of course. I forgave them long ago."

"I'm glad." She raised a twitchy smile, then glanced over her shoulder and stood. "I should return to work."

"Yeah." Clay's stomach lurched. Of course he'd forgiven them. He'd prayed that prayer more than once in the last two years.

Leah grasped the handle of her cart. "No matter what happened in my life, I could always find one good thing to enjoy—a beautiful word, a sunset, a song. I'm glad you've found your good thing." With a serene smile, she patted the medical book and went her way.

Clay flipped the book shut. Why did *he* suddenly feel like the lost puppy?

3

The saleslady whisked the pile of dresses and suits from over the top of Leah's dressing room door. "I'll take these to the cash register, hon."

"Decadent," Leah said.

"Decadent?" Darlene Bishop's laugh floated over the door. "You only bought four outfits today, including the dress you're wearing home. With the suit you bought last week, that's only five."

Since Leah was accustomed to one church dress, one school dress, and one work dress, five beautiful outfits felt decadent indeed, especially since she could mix components.

She studied herself in the full-length mirror. Never had she owned such a pretty dress, a buttery yellow shirtwaist sprigged with tiny white flowers and leaves the same sage green as her suit, with a scalloped white collar and cuffs, like someone would wear to a summer lawn party in a novel.

It fit so well it made her squirm. She hardly recognized herself with a waistline and calves, much less with lipstick and her hair cut fashionably below her chin.

"Are you finished?" Darlene called.

"Yes." Leah stepped into her beige pumps and grabbed the matching shoulder bag. Maybe someday she'd learn to walk in heels. Most girls her age already knew how, but Leah didn't know what to do with an extra three inches.

Darlene poked around in a basket on top of a circular rack of blouses. "Aren't these cute? Just what you need."

A kaleidoscope of color radiated from the basket—dozens of jeweled pins shaped like flowers and animals and American flags. "They're beautiful."

"Which one do you like?"

The bouquet, and Leah cupped the beauty in her hand. Glass blossoms in every hue adorned golden stems tied with a curling golden ribbon. "Maybe next month. I need to watch my budget."

Her roommate heaved a sigh as if Leah had denied Darlene the pin, and she flounced to the register. "You have a job, sugar. Live a little."

"First I need to live. I have to pay room and board, bus fare, and cafeteria lunches."

The saleslady rang up the purchase with cheery cha-chings from the cash register, and she folded each item in a snowy tissue paper cocoon.

It was all Leah's. What a blessing.

Darlene batted mascaraed eyelashes. "Promise me you'll buy the pin next month."

"We'll see." She still needed an umbrella and a wallet and a pen.

The saleslady smiled at Leah. "That'll be $17.47."

Two and a half dollars under her budget, and Leah reached to open her shoulder bag.

"Shall I ring that up for you too?" The saleslady nodded to Leah's hands.

She uncurled her fingers. The bouquet pin? She'd carried it to the counter? What if she'd dropped it into her bag?

Her heart stopped.

"Oh yes," Darlene said. "The camel-colored suit is divine, but that pin would set it off."

Leah forced her lungs to pump out words, and she handed the pin to the saleslady. "No, thank you. Not today." She fumbled for the bills inside her purse.

What had she almost done? She'd never taken anything from a store before, but then she'd rarely been inside stores. The shopkeepers in Des Moines shooed out the orphans.

This was why.

The saleslady punched keys on the cash register, her lips in a thin red line.

Leah tried to breathe evenly. What sort of things had she taken in the past? Food, for the most part. And lovely lonely things.

Pearl Gunderson's hair ribbon of robin egg blue, forsaken on the playground. An eraser, one of the clever typewriter ones on a wheel with a little brush, abandoned on the floor in typing class. Stella Black's tiny celluloid Kewpie that she always made the villain in her games, left in the mud in Stella's yard. Leah had taken the doll home, bathed her, made her a dress from a handkerchief, and named her Euterpe after the muse of lyric poetry and music.

The saleslady handed her a large pasteboard box tied with string.

Outside in the extraordinary heat and rain, Darlene opened her umbrella. They strolled down West Lincoln past Clayton's Shoes, where Leah had bought her pumps and purse with Miss Mayhew's loan. In the autumn, Leah could buy a second purse and pair of shoes, a set for each season. She still had two shoe ration coupons remaining for the year. How exciting.

"Here's Taylor's Pharmacy," Darlene said as they turned left onto Atlantic. "They'll have umbrellas."

Leah opened the door, setting bells to jangling, and she clenched her fingers together so they wouldn't even think of browsing.

"May I help you?" a middle-aged saleslady called from behind a glass counter, her eyes curved into friendly half-moons.

"Yes, ma'am. I'd like to buy an umbrella."

For the next fifteen minutes, the lady showed her over a dozen, and Leah chose a sturdy one in her price range.

Leah paid for the umbrella. Beside the counter stood a collection bin for the Victory Book Campaign, emblazoned with a red, white, and blue poster stating "Give more books. Give good books." How marvelous it would be to have so many books you could give them away.

Darlene stood just inside the door with four soldiers wearing khaki shirts and trousers and garrison caps. "There she is, fellas. My roommate, Leah. She works at Camp Forrest too."

A tall skinny soldier gave her a lopsided grin. "At the PX? The mess?"

Leah held her breath. She wasn't used to men looking straight at her or talking to her. "At the library. I'm a librarian."

"One of those bookish gals, huh?"

"Yes, sir. I am."

"Sugar, don't admit that." Darlene nudged her. "Not if you want dates."

Leah didn't want dates, but she worked up a smile for her friend.

Darlene shook back her hair. "Leah spends far too much time in the library. She works every night until nine thirty. Then after she closes, she stays an extra hour just to read. All by herself."

To research, but the explanation would be wasted again.

A square-faced soldier with pale blond hair gave her the type of grin Leah had only seen directed at girls like Darlene. "Sounds like you could use a night on the town. How about the four of us, the two of you? Maybe you've got a couple girlfriends."

Darlene set her hand on her hip. "Sure, handsome. I know

plenty of gals. But y'all had better take us somewhere nice. We're plumb tired of the cafeteria."

Leah felt ill. Why, she didn't even know these men, much less how to act on a date. "Not me, but thank you for the invitation."

The skinny soldier crossed his arms. "Got yourself a boyfriend?"

"No. I just . . ." Leah twisted her purse strap and smiled in a way that she hoped would communicate polite regret. "I'm still settling in and getting used to my job."

The black-haired soldier at the end was looking at her chest.

Leah pulled her purse in front of her like a shield.

The man had a notch in his left ear like a tomcat who had been in too many fights. He met her gaze. His eyes were dark and as cold as midnight in Iowa in January, and a shudder ran through her. One of the wolves.

"Any of you fellows have a pen?" Darlene asked.

Two immediately sprang forth.

Darlene uncapped one, took the hand of the blond soldier, and wrote on the back of his hand. "The number for my boarding-house. Ask for Darlene. I'll round up some friends."

He grinned at his hand. "Say, that'd be swell."

"Bye, fellas." Darlene wiggled her fingers in farewell, took Leah's arm, and headed outside. After both umbrellas were raised, they strolled down Atlantic past Sterling Stores and the First National Bank. For once, Darlene was silent.

In front of Couch's, where signs advertised appliance sales and repairs, Darlene stopped and huffed. "What's wrong with you? You could have had a date."

"I don't know those men, don't even know their names."

Another huff and louder. "Sugar, you've got a lot to learn. I'm willing to teach you, but you've got to be willing to listen."

Leah's lips twisted. "One thing at a time, please."

Darlene fell silent, and then she hugged Leah's arm. "A new

job, new clothes, new hairdo. And now that you look cute, men are asking you out. I suppose it's a lot for you."

"It is." She couldn't even imagine herself on a date.

Maybe with Clay Paxton, who was so kind and bright. He also knew tragedy, and she longed to talk with him again.

But not on a date. She wasn't ready, not even with Clay.

4

With his stance and arms wide, Clay hunkered over and sized up Bob Holman. All around, men were throwing each other down into the red dirt. Years of wrestling had taught Clay to take his time and plan his attack. Ideally, he'd make his opponent act first out of impatience.

Holman was tall, with broad shoulders and skinny legs. He'd rely on his upper-body strength, and Clay would use that against him.

"Congratulations, Paxton," Sgt. Tommy Lombardi yelled. "Holman just shot you dead. Don't hesitate. Attack."

Clay opened his mouth to defend himself, but privates didn't do such things. "Yes, Sergeant."

Of course, now Holman was ready. Clay lunged as if he planned to grasp Holman's shoulders. Taking advantage of his lower center of gravity, Clay ducked under Holman's raised arms and off to one side, grabbed him around the waist, and hooked one leg behind Holman's knees. His opponent fell hard, and Clay scrambled on top to pin him.

Victory.

Then two fingers jammed up into his nostrils. Clay jerked back, and in a smooth move, Holman rolled him over and pinned him on his back, knife hand to his throat.

Clay wiggled his nose in pain. "You can't do that."

Holman chuckled. "I can and I did. You heard Knudson—Rangers fight dirty."

With a groan, Clay closed his eyes. Capt. Dean Knudson had fought with the 1st Ranger Battalion in North Africa, but the dirty fighting techniques he advocated went against Clay's training and sportsmanship.

Lombardi leaned over Clay. "This ain't a high school wrestling match with rules and referees. You think the Jerries fight fair? The Japs?"

"No, Sergeant." But that didn't mean a man fighting fair couldn't win.

Lombardi cussed and moved down the line.

"You'll get it, Pax." Holman stood and brushed himself off. "After all, aren't Mexicans hot-blooded?"

"Better not test me on that." Clay got to his feet but left the dirt in place. Of the three Paxton boys, only Adler had a temper—and he was the blondest of the bunch.

"All right, men, gather round," Lieutenant Taylor called.

Clay found Gene and stood beside him in the sloppy circle. Gene's right sleeve hung by a few threads. "More ventilation?" Clay asked.

"Courtesy of Lyons. Man's as tough as his namesake."

Yesterday Clay had gotten the better of Frank Lyons, but any pride in that feat was tempered by today's humiliation.

"A new commander?" Gene flicked his chin toward a major striding into the center of the circle.

Clay snapped to attention and saluted. The 2nd Ranger Battalion had already gone through at least four commanders.

"At ease." The new fellow stood tall and broad chested, and he assessed the motley group of soldiers sweating under the blazing sun. "Men, I'm Jim Rudder, your new battalion commander. I've been sent down here to restore order and get going with realistic training."

With his hands clasped in the small of his back, Clay frowned at the name and the Texas accent. Jim Rudder? He knew that name, but from where?

"I'm going to work you harder than you've ever worked." Major Rudder spoke with the authority of a football coach. "Before you know it, you're going to be the best-trained fighting men in this man's army. Now with your cooperation, there will be passes from time to time. I'll grant as many leaves and passes as I can. If I don't get your cooperation, we'll still get the job done, but it'll be a lot tougher on you. If such a program does not appeal to you, we'll transfer you out."

Clay's question had been answered. James Rudder had coached football at John Tarleton Agricultural College in Texas, and he'd tried to recruit Clay. He winced. Rudder had better not remember him. The last thing Clay wanted was reminiscing.

"Company commanders, take charge of your companies," Rudder said.

That was about the shortest speech Clay had heard from a CO, and he and Gene exchanged a look. Would Major Rudder whip the battalion into shape, or would he fall to the wayside with the others?

"All right, men. Grab your packs," Lieutenant Taylor called. "Twelve-mile speed march, then lunch if you're still alive."

The men grumbled as they trudged to their packs, but not Clay. He liked the conditioning, the drills, the weapons training, and the marches. Every day he felt stronger and more capable. If only that were enough.

Sitting on his cot in the pyramidal tent that evening, Clay peeled off his socks. Only one new blister, and it had already popped.

"What? No blood in your boots? Don't you want to be a Ranger, Pax?" Gene showed off one blood-soaked sock.

Clay chuckled. "Don't rat on me, buddy."

"I won't."

"Bathe your feet well," Clay said. "Dry them thoroughly and let them air out tonight. And don't forget to use foot powder in the morning."

"Yes, doc."

Clay's chest tightened, but how could he keep his mouth shut when he could help someone? "I'm not a doctor. I just—"

"Listened in class." Bob Holman lay on his cot reading a magazine. "Yeah, we know."

The tent flap swung open, and Sergeant Lombardi stepped in. "Listen up, men. Report to headquarters. Major Rudder wants to meet his men one on one."

One on one? Clay would have to be careful to say little and get out fast.

All the fellows groaned as they slipped battered feet into shoes, so Clay's groan went unnoticed.

The six men in his tent filed out into the humid purple dusk and traipsed down the dirt road in Tent City to HQ.

Never one to put off the inevitable, Clay led the pack, and Lombardi let him in first.

In the tent, Major Rudder and Lieutenant Taylor sat on campstools behind a field desk. Clay removed his garrison cap, halted in front of the desk, and saluted. "Sir, Private Paxton reports to the battalion commander."

Lombardi stood to the side of the desk. "Clay Paxton from my section, sir."

"At ease, Private." Rudder had fair hair, light eyes, and a big old Texas smile. "Where are you from?"

Clay clenched his cap behind his back. No getting around that nugget of information. "Kerrville, Texas, sir."

That grin grew. "Kerrville. I've been there. Beautiful country."

"Yes, sir."

"Say . . ." His eyes turned down at the corners. "What was your name again? Clay Paxton?"

Oh no. He did remember. "Yes, sir."

"Well, I'll be." The major slapped his knee. "Kerrville High, class of '39, am I right?"

"Yes, sir." Maybe his memory would stop right there.

"I tried to recruit you. You were a fine linebacker."

Clay forced a smile. "I'm honored you remember, sir."

Rudder wagged a finger. "I also remember you turned me down. What was it again?"

That reason had disappeared. "I needed to work in the family business."

The major frowned. "Top of your class, wanted to study medicine at the University of Texas. As an Aggie, I'd never forget that."

"Medicine?" Lieutenant Taylor asked.

No, no, no. Not that. Somehow Clay kept his face impassive.

Rudder swung his grin to Taylor. "Took a war to do it, but I finally got this kid on my team."

Taylor glanced at Lombardi. "Actually, we were talking about transferring him out."

Clay fought the sagging in his shoulders. Had it gotten that bad? He'd started so well.

"Why is that?" Rudder asked the platoon commander.

Taylor shrugged. "Does great in conditioning, he's a good shot and knows his material. But he overanalyzes, and he's bound by rules. He's a good soldier, but not a good Ranger."

"He lacks the killer instinct," Lombardi said.

Rudder studied Clay, but without the grin this time. "What do you have to say?"

Clay couldn't mention his recurring dream and how it drove him, so he turned his gaze hard and sharp. "Sir, I want to be a Ranger more than I've wanted anything in my life. I can learn. I can do this."

"There's another option, Paxton." Taylor leaned his elbows on the field desk. "Become a medic."

"Sir, I—"

The lieutenant raised a hand to silence him. "You obviously have an interest in medicine. Our medics have to meet the same physical standards as the rest of the Rangers, but they don't have to kill. It's perfect for you."

"Great idea," Rudder said.

"No." Clay sucked in a breath at his breach of military etiquette. "Sir, medics don't fight. I volunteered for the Rangers because I want to fight. I need to fight. Please give me a chance, sir. I can do this."

Lombardi rolled his eyes at Taylor, and Taylor shook his head at Rudder, and Rudder appraised Clay again.

He tried to look tough.

Rudder didn't let up his scrutiny. "As a linebacker, you were fast, strong, smart, and a team player. That's why I wanted you on my team then, and that's why I want you on my team now. I'll give you another chance."

Clay's grin burst free. "Thank you, sir. I won't let you down."

"But you'll need to show some serious improvement, or you're out. Understood?"

"Yes, sir." Clay left the tent, traded a joke with his buddies, and marched back to his tent.

His secret was out. The brass knew about medical school. If he didn't learn to fight dirty, they'd make him a medic.

Clay kicked a rock out of the road. Wouldn't Daddy and Mama like that?

"The Lord didn't make you a killer," Mama had told him when he received his draft notice. "He made you a healer."

Telling his parents about his recurring dream hadn't helped, not even when he'd related how he felt overwhelming peace and joy each time he awoke. How he knew he was meant to die in combat saving his buddies—a good purpose he'd embraced. How the dream was a message from the Lord, a welcome one, assuring him the miserable years in the pit would soon end.

In the Bible, not everyone liked Joseph's dreams either, but they'd come to pass.

Since that talk with his parents, Clay hadn't mentioned his dream to a soul. It was a treasured secret between him and God.

Daddy and Mama would love to see that dream thwarted.

And his brothers? They'd shown him they believed a half-breed didn't deserve fancy goals like going to college or becoming a physician or marrying the doctor's daughter.

His gut burned—he'd have to mine that anger next time they practiced hand-to-hand combat.

Why did Leah Jones's thoughtful little face flash before him? *"I can understand why you haven't forgiven them."*

"Lord, they took everything from me," he muttered. "Let me keep this dream. Don't let anyone steal it."

5

Miss Mayhew parked a cart in front of the circulation desk. "Here are this month's acquisitions for you to shelve."

"What a treasure." Leah leaned over to read the titles, including *The Clinical Recognition and Treatment of Shock.* She'd have to show Clay the next time he came in.

The previous Sunday he'd insisted she call him Clay. Sometimes he visited on weekday evenings too. Although he always looked exhausted from training, he never failed to be cheerful.

Leah sorted the books by category. Darlene had coached her on how to act with Clay, to be friendly but not too eager. She'd also taught Leah some flirtation techniques, but when Leah practiced them, Darlene said perhaps it would be better for Leah to be herself.

Why would she try to be anyone else?

Beside the Army technical and field manuals, plenty of other books enticed Leah to explore. Would any yield clues about her background? Finding those would require serendipity, and one couldn't plan serendipity.

"Good evening, Leah."

She smiled at the familiar Texas twang, grabbed the medical

handbook, and spun around, coaching herself to look friendly but not eager. "Hello, Clay."

He had a friend with him, taller than he, but lankier, with strawberry blond hair and freckles.

Leah hugged the book. Clay had asked her not to mention his medical interests, and she'd honor that.

"Leah, this is my friend Jim."

She extended her hand. "Nice to meet you, Jim."

They both laughed. "It's G. M.," Clay's friend said. "Short for Gene Mayer. We've got to teach this cowboy to talk right."

Clay pointed with his thumb at G. M. "Got to teach Mr. Hollywood here to listen right."

Leah joined the laughter. It felt strange to laugh with men, but very nice.

"Clay isn't as stupid as he looks," G. M. said. "He speaks fluent Spanish."

"Do you?"

"Yes, ma'am." Clay nodded at her. "My mama's Mexican."

"Oh!" That explained his bronze coloring and obsidian hair. "But Paxton . . . your father—"

"As white as the pages of that book. Blond hair, blue eyes, the works."

Why, yes. She studied his features. He'd certainly received excellent traits from each side. "How fascinating."

Clay dipped his chin. "Never heard it called fascinating before."

"It is. I'm a firm believer that our country is richer for the mixture of her various cultures."

"That's Clay, all right." G. M. slapped him on the back. "All mixed up."

"Speaking of being mixed up . . ." Clay pulled a slip of paper from the pocket of his khaki shirt. "We're here to find *Elementary Map and Aerial Photograph Reading*. Field Manual 21-25."

Leah pointed to her right. "All our field and technical manuals are in the second aisle in numerical order. Would you like me to show you?"

"We'll find it. Thanks." A big grin, and Clay and G. M. left.

Behind the circulation desk, Miss Mayhew cleared her throat and frowned at Leah. Yesterday she'd reprimanded Leah for flirting with the patrons, which had rendered Leah speechless. Was having a friendly conversation considered flirting? My, she had a lot to learn.

Leah mouthed "Sorry," loaded her cart again, and pushed it to the fourth aisle, away from Clay and G. M. She picked up a pile of books and searched for the correct locations.

"Hear about the party at the USO on Saturday?" G. M.'s voice filtered through the stacks.

"For Independence Day?" Clay said. "I heard."

"Get a date and join Betty Jo and me."

Leah held her breath, a book suspended midair.

"No, thanks," Clay said.

"How about that Leah? She's pretty cute, and she seems to like you, though I don't know why."

Leah scrunched her eyes shut, dreading both the yes and the no.

"I've told you, G. M. I'm not interested in dating right now, all right?"

"Still—"

"Not interested. Now here's the manual, Mr. Busybody."

Not interested. Leah's arm drooped, but she gave her head a good shake and slid the book into place.

What would she have done if he'd asked her? She probably would have frozen or declined as she had with the soldiers in the drugstore.

She ought to be thankful she'd learned Clay wasn't interested in her before she let herself become infatuated.

But it bruised. Even with a divine camel-colored suit and a cute haircut and makeup, she was still odd and foreign.

MONDAY, JULY 5, 1943

"Assume position!" Sergeant Lombardi yelled.

Clay tossed his shirt into a heap with the other men's. The six Rangers from his tent stepped alongside the twelve-foot log for the morning log drill.

"You take that end, and I'll take the other," he said to Gene. This drill was dangerous, and the other four men had hangovers. Since the USO didn't serve booze at their party, the men had made up for it on the Fourth of July itself.

Clay looked them each in their bloodshot eyes. "Look lively, boys. Y'all can do it."

"Quit yelling." Holman cringed and massaged his temples.

Wait till he heard Lombardi. Clay squatted and wrapped his arms around the log, as fat as a telephone pole and just as heavy.

"Ready!" Lombardi shouted. "Exercise."

With loud grunts, Clay and his buddies hoisted the log waist high and stood. Clay's thigh muscles strained.

Following Lombardi's commands, Clay ducked under the log until it rested on his right shoulder. The other men stayed with him, but with more cussing than usual.

Clay pushed to standing and set his feet wide. With his right arm wrapped around the log, he set his left hand on his hip and leaned to the left. His abdominal oblique muscles made their presence known, and perspiration tickled along his hairline.

The men straightened to standing again. The log lurched to the right, and Clay scooted his feet to compensate. McKillop swore— he must have been the one who stumbled.

"Y'all can do it, boys. All together," Clay said. With both hands he thrust the log overhead. Every muscle in his arms screamed and screamed harder when he lowered the log to his left shoulder. The weight increased—one of the men behind him had messed up.

For the next half hour, they manipulated that log. The drill built both muscle and teamwork, and Clay put his all into it.

At last they set the log down on the dirt, with only a few new scratches on ears and shoulders and hands.

"To the pit," Lombardi called. "Double time."

The men jogged off the parade grounds and along the road.

Gene fell in beside Clay. "Hate picking up their slack when they've got hangovers."

"It evens out. Remember, they picked up our slack when we had dysentery."

"Don't remind me." Gene clutched his stomach as they ran. "Glad Rudder's putting our cooks through cooking school."

"Me too." Major Rudder showed no mercy in training the men. But he'd also moved the Rangers out of Tent City and into real wooden barracks with showers and a dayroom and electric lights. He'd started "gripe sessions," and he listened to the men's concerns and made changes. "Looking forward to good food."

Gene whacked him in the arm. "That's why you should've gone to the USO party."

Clay's shirtsleeves, tied around his waist, slipped, and he tightened the knot as he ran. "I told you. I won't be here long, and I don't want to start something I can't finish." Here in Tullahoma . . . here on earth . . . Gene didn't need to know what he really meant.

"Doesn't mean you can't go out and have fun."

"Come on." Clay spread his arms wide and mimicked the bragging look he'd seen so often. "How could a girl go out with me even once and not fall in love?"

Gene cracked up and punched Clay in the arm. "Yeah, that's likely."

Clay laughed too, but his own words stung. Ellen Hill had been his only girlfriend. In Kerrville, the white girls were put off by his brown skin, and the Mexican girls by his white name. And Ellen? Even after a year together, she'd only had eyes for Adler.

"Still, that little Leah—I bet she'd like a USO party."

Clay swiped sweat from his upper lip. "Nah. She's sweet, but she's too young."

Gene gave him a funny look. "You're not that old. What? Twenty-two? She's got to be at least eighteen."

"Just barely. It's more . . . she's really young inside."

"Yeah? She'll grow up quick around this place."

"Reckon so." It would be a shame if Leah lost that innocence.

"Well, me and Betty Jo had a swell time. I'm gonna marry her."

"What?" Clay studied his friend's beet-red face. "You've only known her a few months."

"As you said, we're leaving soon. Think about it. If we get married, she'll get my allotment. She'll be able to afford a real place, won't have to live in that converted chicken coop anymore."

The housing shortage in town was bad indeed, and Clay grimaced.

"And, you know . . ." Gene gazed away with a smile. "I sure wouldn't mind some time together as husband and wife before we ship out."

Clay chuckled and rolled his eyes. "Yeah, that's a foundation for a strong marriage."

"It's worked since the dawn of time. Don't knock it."

Clay would never find out, and he no longer minded.

His company gathered around the pit, about eighteen feet on each side, waist deep, lined with logs on the sides and sawdust on the ground.

"First platoon, shirts off. Second platoon, shirts on. Everyone in."

Clay unknotted his shirt from around his waist, and Gene unbuttoned his. Poor man fought a losing battle against sunburn. But the shirtless platoon had an advantage.

Rudder and Taylor and Lombardi stood nearby.

Clay had to do his best. He'd decided on his new approach—

fast, fierce, and fair. Wrestling and football had taught him to be fierce and fair. He only needed to add speed. By now he knew the strengths and weaknesses of the men in his company. When replacements arrived, he could size them up during drills so he could act quickly when it was time to fight.

Abandoning good sportsmanship didn't seem fitting, even in time of war.

Clay jumped into the pit and plotted his strategy. His platoon had to toss out all the members of the other platoon—without getting tossed out themselves. There were no rules, and injuries were common.

Manfred Brady stood by the wall, cracking his knuckles. About four inches taller than Clay and built like an ox, he'd expect to be the last man attacked.

Lombardi blew the whistle.

Clay charged at Brady from the side, low and fast, and barreled into the man's torso. Using the judo moves they'd been taught, Clay kept his momentum going, swung one shoulder down behind the man's hips, and used Brady's own height and weight to heave him out of the pit.

Brady swore at him.

Clay kept moving. Frank Lyons shoved wiry little Ernie Mc-Killop out of the pit. McKillop's high-pitched scream said Lyons was fighting dirtier than dirty.

From behind, Clay clamped his left arm around Lyons's chest and grasped his head with his right arm.

A sharp pain in his forearm. Lyons had bitten him. So the man was used to biting—was that how he'd lost that chunk out of his ear?

Clay didn't lose his grip. He boxed the man's ear so he'd stop chewing him, and he buckled his knees. Lyons sagged in his grip. Now to hoist him out.

Someone yanked Clay's hair and swept one leg out from under

him. Lyons turned, jammed his fingers into Clay's windpipe, and the two men flung Clay out of the pit.

Coughing, he stared up at the blue sky, then pushed himself up to his knees. He'd done pretty well. Only a third of the men remained in the pit, and it had taken two men to remove Clay.

But would a middle-of-the-road performance be enough to stay in the Rangers?

6

"Good night, gentlemen. We'll open tomorrow morning at eight."
Leah let out the last three soldiers and flipped the sign on the
library door to read "closed."

Leaning back against the closed door, she grinned at her domain.
Darlene said she was crazy to enjoy being alone in a library late
at night, but it was heavenly.

After she turned off unneeded lights, she retrieved her purse from
behind the circulation desk and headed to the stacks. Tonight she
was up to the 280s in the Dewey decimal system, and she pulled
out a volume about the Orthodox Church.

At a table she pulled a composition book and pen from her
purse. Perhaps this book would yield a picture of the ornately
decorated church in her memory or of a Greek surname.

No pictures graced the pages, but Leah transcribed a few names.
None sounded right.

The ink flowed so smoothly from her new pen. She'd purchased
a celluloid pen with a swirl of greens that reminded her of a moun-
tain brook, but it wasn't the gold pen of her dreams, the sort of pen
her classmates had received from family for high school graduation.

44

What would it be like to have family to love her and give her a personal gift? Since she and her sisters had been sent to an orphanage when their parents died, their other family members must have been dead or in Greece.

Leah had spoken Greek well enough to assume her parents were immigrants, but she'd spoken English well enough to conclude the immigration wasn't recent. She'd clung to the Greek language, but Mr. and Mrs. Jones had beaten her every time she used "that foreign heathen talk."

With a shudder, Leah riffled through another chapter. It was for the best that she'd fallen ill and they'd abandoned her in Des Moines.

If only they'd given the orphanage more information about her background. Leah had been allowed to read her report before she left Iowa, which had been both painful and futile.

Mr. and Mrs. Jones claimed to have lost her birth certificate and adoption papers. They said her name was Leah Jones and not to let her say otherwise—she was a lying, storytelling kind, always making up silly names for herself. Like "Thalia."

They'd only adopted her to help in their store one day, but when they lost the store in the Depression, they had no more need for Leah.

"Can't afford her. Too sickly. Never stops crying," the report had read. They hadn't said where they'd adopted her from and had marched out without looking back.

"Thank you, Lord," Leah whispered. "Thank you for leading them to a good orphanage."

She simply had to find the blessings, even in the bleakest conditions.

A clicking sound, and Leah looked toward the circulation desk. Nothing. But the service club next door was open until ten thirty, so soldiers would be milling around outside. That must have been what she heard.

Leah perused the final chapters, but the book hadn't helped. None had. Was finding her sisters a hopeless quest?

Callie. Polly. She remembered their sweet baby faces.

In third grade, Leah had read a book about Greek mythology in the school library and had seen her own name among the muses. If her parents had named her Thalia, after the muse of idyllic poetry and comedy, was it possible they'd named the twins Calliope and Polyhymnia, after the muses of epic and sacred poetry?

Even if it weren't true, the idea captured Leah's imagination.

She turned in her composition book to the poem she was writing. It needed one more stanza, but the words evaded her.

> Three muses dance, their hands entwined
> A circle of love, as one.
> Thalia laughs, an idyllic song
> Of earth and fields and home.
> Calliope calls, an epic ballad
> Of valor and heroes and might.
> Polyhymnia chants, a sacred hymn
> Of praise and truth and faith.

Still no final stanza. Leah leaned back in her chair and stretched.

Odd. The door to the storage room behind the circulation desk stood open, and the light was on. They always kept the door closed, since Miss Mayhew said it gave the library a neater appearance. And Leah had a lifelong habit of turning off lights upon leaving a room.

This time she must have forgotten. Perhaps she was more tired than she realized.

After she shelved the book, she crossed the library to the circulation desk. She swung open the half door in the desk, stepped inside the storage room, and switched off the light.

A hand slapped over her mouth. She cried out, muffled by rough, digging fingers.

Someone yanked her left arm behind her back. Pain exploded in her shoulder, and she tried to scream.

"One sound and you die."

Her eyes burned with tears. The man stank of musk and onions and beer. The scent of a wolf.

Gene Mayer sang "The Girl I Love to Leave Behind" as he and Clay left the service club, where they'd watched the movie *Stage Door Canteen*.

"The Army was a good choice for you, G. M. You're killing that song."

"Ha. You're just jealous 'cause I've got a girl to leave behind." In the pale moonlight, Gene grinned. "Saturday I'm asking Betty Jo to marry me."

Clay strolled beside the long club building toward their barracks in Block 19. "Unless Rudder gives us another night exercise."

Gene groaned.

Two days earlier, the Rangers had run the assault course until two in the morning with live ammunition firing overhead. Then reveille at 0545.

They passed the library. Lights shone inside, but dimly. Was Leah still there? The library closed at nine thirty, but it was almost ten thirty. And an awful lot of men roamed in the dark.

Clay frowned. "Say, go on without me. I'm going to see if Leah needs an escort to the bus stop."

"An escort?" Gene mimed dipping a girl low and smooching her.

"An escort only. A lady shouldn't walk around alone at night."

"Whatever you say, Pax." Gene strolled away, singing "Here comes the bride . . ."

Clay rolled his eyes and trotted up the stairs. This would be hard to live down.

The sign on the door read "closed," but Clay tested the doorknob and it opened. The library was dark except the central reading area—which was empty. "Leah?"

A muffled thump and a shuffling sound came to his right, from behind the circulation desk, inside a darkened room.

Every sense went into high alert. Someone was in there. If it were Leah, she would have said something.

Clay had nothing to use as a weapon. He wiggled loose his necktie, which could be used against him, and he stuffed it in his pocket.

His heart rate rising, Clay padded around the circulation desk, low and swift. Was it a thief? But what was there to steal in a library? Or had a soldier sneaked in with a girl for a tryst? Clay would feel real stupid if it turned out to be a raccoon.

The half door in the desk stood open, and Clay darted through and crouched in the attack position outside the back room.

A tryst, all right. In the dimness, a man knelt buttoning up his pants beside a woman on the floor, more undressed than dressed.

Disbelief and rage billowed up. Two years before it had been Adler and Ellen in a tangled mass of bare limbs and discarded clothing on the garage floor. His girlfriend. His brother.

But this was Leah! A gag slashed white across her face, and her eyes met his—frantic and terrified. And there was blood.

Clay's rage snapped to the man, a soldier in khakis. A knit cap with two holes cut in it concealed his face.

No time to analyze. Clay leapt over Leah and tackled her assailant.

They grappled, and the attacker flipped Clay onto his back. The man reached for something on the ground, and light flashed on steel.

A knife! Clay parried the thrust, then jabbed straight fingers into the man's windpipe, the same move Lyons had used so effectively on him.

The assailant coughed and jerked back. Enough for Clay to kick free.

Silhouetted against the light from the doorway, the man sat on his knees, knife in hand.

Clay scrabbled up and chose his next move.

The attacker's cheeks jutted out as if he were smiling. Then he swung around and plunged the knife into Leah's chest.

"No! Leah!"

The man dashed away with his knife. If Clay chased him, he couldn't help Leah.

Clay scrambled to her. "Leah! Leah!"

She was conscious, her eyes squeezed shut in pain.

He ripped off the gag and assessed the knife wound. "Leah, talk to me."

"He—he—" She swept her hand down over her clothing, trying to cover herself.

Clay only looked at the wound, at the blood spilling out. Right upper chest below the clavicle. Arteries and veins ran through the region. "Leah, we're going to stop the bleeding and get you to the hospital, all right?"

She looked up at him, breathing hard and ragged, not a tear in her eyes.

"That's a brave girl. Stay nice and calm." He ripped off his shirt, buttons pinging onto the floor. "This is for a bandage. No need to worry."

He yanked off his undershirt, rolled it into a ball, and pressed it firmly into the wound.

Leah moaned but barely stirred.

Clay held one shirtsleeve in each hand and whipped his shirt in a circle, rolling it into a bandage. He laid it across the wound, tossed one end over her left shoulder, and tucked the other under her right arm.

"I'm going to lift you to tie this." He worked his arm behind her shoulders.

She cried out.

Her left arm lay at a crooked angle. That vermin had dislocated her shoulder, and Clay's gut burned.

"I'll be gentle, but I need to tie this so I can transport you." He carefully draped her left arm across her stomach, and she groaned.

"That's a good girl. You can do this." He lifted her shoulders just enough to pass the bandage behind her, and he knotted it beside her neck on the left. "Bear with me. This may hurt, but we need to get you to the hospital."

"I under . . . stand." Her voice was faint.

He pulled her skirt down and arranged the remnants of her blouse to cover her somewhat, but her life was more important than her modesty.

Clay scooped her into his arms. "How are you doing?"

She nodded, her eyes unfocused.

No! He couldn't let her bleed to death. "Stay with me, Leah."

He strode through the library and kicked open the door. A jeep, a jeep. Why wasn't there a jeep on the road when he needed one?

The hospital at Camp Forrest was about a mile away, and Clay took off running. The few soldiers on the sidewalk looked at him in alarm.

"Out of the way! Medical emergency!" Clay had never run so fast, and he'd never been so thankful for log drills and daily runs and marches with full combat gear. Thank goodness Leah didn't weigh any more than that gear.

He turned down the road to the hospital, breathing hard but evenly. Leah never cried out, but occasional moans meant she was still conscious. *Lord, help me. Don't let her die.*

The hospital at last, a complex of long, low buildings, and Clay ran to the admissions building and kicked hard on the door. "Help! Medical emergency!"

A nurse opened the door and gasped.

Clay strode in, panting. "Get a stretcher."

"My stars." The nurse darted to a hallway. "Doctor Reeves! Emergency!"

A physician in his thirties ran out and stared at Clay and Leah. "What happened?"

"Her name's Leah Jones. Eighteen-year-old female, assaulted, knife wound to the upper right chest below the clavicle, dislocated left shoulder, probably raped."

"Prep the OR," the physician said to the nurse, then addressed another nurse behind him. "Call the military police."

Medics arrived with a stretcher, and Clay laid Leah on it.

Her head lolled to the side, her eyes shut and her mouth open.

Clay collapsed to his knees. Two years ago, he hadn't been able to save Adler's fiancée, Oralee. *Please, Lord. Let Leah live.*

7

"'Four hands were immediately laid upon me, and I was borne upstairs.'" Mrs. Bellamy laid the book in her lap and frowned at Leah. "Are you sure *Jane Eyre* is the best book for you?"

"It is." From her bed in the Camp Forrest Hospital women's ward, Leah smiled at the Red Cross volunteer in her gray uniform dress. The muscles in Leah's face didn't hurt, but her voice came out weak. "As dreary as it can be, *Jane Eyre* is a story of hope and fortitude."

"All right." Mrs. Bellamy was so pleasant to look at, a plump woman in her thirties with light brown hair in smooth rolls about her sweet face. "That's enough for today, Miss Jones. I don't want to tire you."

"Thank you for reading to me. I miss books."

Mrs. Bellamy tilted her head with a curious look that transformed into a smile.

Leah had only been in the hospital for five days, but if it weren't for the volunteer, she wouldn't be able to read at all. Her left arm was bound in a sling, and the knife wound and surgery had affected muscles she needed to move her right arm.

Mrs. Bellamy stood. "I'll come back tomorrow if you'd like."

"Please. It's a comfort."

The volunteer's face buckled, and she laid a warm hand on Leah's. "I'm so sorry this happened to you, but every day you're going to feel better. I won't lie and say your life will return to normal. Everything has changed, but you can come out stronger for it."

"With the Lord's help, I will." Leah forced the words out, words she knew to be true, words she clung to when brutal memories darkened her mind.

Mrs. Bellamy blinked rapidly, squeezed Leah's hand, and wheeled her cart of books and magazines to the next patient's bed.

The Lord would indeed help Leah through this as he'd helped her all along. Hadn't he sent Clay Paxton to save her life?

The instant the wolf had laid the knife on the floor beside her head, she knew he'd planned to kill her when he was done. Since he hadn't used the knife in his initial attack or to threaten her to keep silent, the knife could only serve one purpose.

Leah's thoughts careened. Her breath came fast and hard. She stared at the bare wooden ceiling and willed her breathing and her mind to calm. The Lord had been with her. The Lord would continue to be with her.

"Excuse me, Miss Jones?" Lieutenant Glassman, the ward nurse, stood at the foot of Leah's bed. "Are you up for a visitor?"

Leah tried to sit up. Pain shot through her chest, and she winced and lay back down.

She'd only had three visitors. Darlene had made two short, cheery visits on her way to work. Miss Mayhew had visited the day after surgery, when Leah had been groggy. The librarian had voiced concern and shock and had asked Dr. Reeves how long until Leah could return to work. A month, and Miss Mayhew had not looked pleased.

That day, the military police had questioned Leah, but she'd had so little to tell them. Khaki uniform with no insignia. Dark hair below the cap. He'd only spoken one sentence, with a Midwestern accent. The MPs kept questioning the man's accent and skin color. Was she absolutely certain the man was white and not Negro? Yes, she was. Any hint of a foreign accent or smell or manner, as if a German prisoner of war had slipped out of the enclosure and slipped back in? No, none.

"I'll tell him to come back later," the nurse said.

"I'm sorry. Who is it?"

"The man who brought you in the other day." A conspiratorial look flashed in her brown eyes. "Honestly, we all thought *he'd* attacked you—you know his kind—but the MPs cleared him."

Light and air filled her chest. "He saved my life. Yes, I want to see him very much."

"All right." The nurse shrugged and walked away.

Leah checked to make sure her pajama top and blanket were in place, but Clay had already seen her in all her shame.

She shuddered. However, Clay had acted like a physician with her. A gentleman.

He approached, the shoulders of his khaki uniform shirt darkened by raindrops. "Hello, Leah."

"Clay! I'm so glad you came."

His smile relaxed, and he set a box on her bedside table. "I brought you chocolate from the PX."

Only the sling could keep her from reaching for it. "A whole box? For me?"

He chuckled and sat in the chair by Leah's bed. "Just a little box, and don't you dare indulge without asking your doctor, you hear?"

"I won't. I'm so glad you came." Why was she repeating herself?

"I'm sorry I took so long. I came the next morning. They told me you'd come through surgery fine, but they wouldn't let me see you. Then my commanding officer sent us on a three-day march and field exercise. This was my first chance to visit." Clay pulled off his garrison cap and assessed her from head to toe, one corner of his mouth crimped. "How are you feeling?"

"Much better, thank you. I'm very tired, of course."

"Are you in any pain?"

"Only when I move."

"All the more reason to rest so you can heal." He really did have a physician's manner, even kinder than Dr. Reeves.

"I'm glad you came, because I need to thank you for saving my life."

Clay lifted half a smile. "Reckon I ought to thank you too, for clearing my name with the MPs."

"I can't believe they thought—"

"Nah." He waved one hand as if erasing her words. "When a man brings a battered woman to a hospital, they'd better ask questions and a lot of them."

Leah couldn't remember much about the trip other than a bumpy run and Clay's strong arms. How could anyone have thought he had harmed her after he'd fought off an armed assailant and performed lifesaving first aid? "You were so brave."

Clay shrugged. "I didn't do anything special."

"You fought him. You attacked him. You weren't even scared."

"I knew I wasn't going to die."

Leah's mouth hung open. "But he had a knife."

"That's not how I'm going to die—" He sliced the word in half, his eyes wide and shocked.

What a curious thing to say. "What do you mean?"

Clay mashed his lips together and shook his head.

"Do you know?" Leah said. "No one knows how he'll die. Right?"

"It's not something . . ." He rubbed the back of his neck and glanced around. "I don't tell people. They'd think I'm crazy."

Leah held her breath watching his discomfort. "I would never think that."

His gaze returned to her, questioning and unsure and somehow vulnerable, as if he needed the faith of just one soul.

"I believe you," she said.

He leaned his elbows on his knees. "You ever have a dream that you're about to die? And you wake in a cold sweat?"

"Like when you're falling. Yes."

"Well, I have a dream like that about once a week, every time the same." He spoke quietly but firmly. "Only in this dream, I do die. When I wake up, I feel complete peace."

"Oh my." She'd never heard of such a thing.

"I'm in battle, in a foxhole, and I have to throw a grenade into a pillbox." Clay made a small throwing motion. "There's a machine gun inside, and I can see the bullets coming nearer. I feel one hit, and I go down. My buddies storm the pillbox, then all goes black and quiet. And I know—I know without a doubt that's how I'll die. That's why I joined the Rangers."

"Aren't you . . . shouldn't you be trying to avoid it?"

He smiled as if amused. "You'd think so. It's hard to explain, but I know the dream came from the Lord. I want it to come true."

For his sake, she wanted to understand, but how could she?

"I was in a pit." Clay studied the cap he held between his knees. "My brothers stole my future. I told you that. Wyatt stole my college money, and Adler stole the girl I'd planned to marry."

"Oh dear." He hadn't mentioned the girlfriend before.

"That was only the start of it. My life was a pit. I was miserable. Then God gave me this dream and showed me the way out. Never once has it bothered me. It always brings peace, even joy."

And peace radiated from his face.

"I know I'll die for a good cause." His eyes shone with . . . anticipation? "Then I'll be with Jesus, so what's to fear? 'To die is gain.'"

"Philippians," Leah whispered, but she didn't quote the first part of the verse, the part Clay seemed to have forgotten—"To live is Christ."

Clay gave her a sheepish smile. "Thanks for trying to understand. My parents don't. They think I'm fatalistic because I've lost so much. But that isn't it. Not at all."

"No. I can see that." She saw a man embracing a purpose. What a shame that the purpose was to die.

"I haven't told any of the fellows." He fiddled with his cap and glanced around the ward. "The Army might deem me mentally unfit and boot me out."

"I won't tell a soul."

"I'd appreciate that." Then he laughed. "Say, I promise I didn't come to talk about death and dying. I came to cheer you up."

She laughed a little, but pain zinged through her wounds.

"Maybe I shouldn't cheer you up after all." He made a comical face.

"Just having company cheers me up. The pain isn't as bothersome as the boredom. I can't hold a book, but the Red Cross lady read to me today, which was lovely."

Clay's brow creased. "Your arms."

Leah wiggled the fingers in both hands, determined to regain strength. "Yes, but she promised to read to me tomorrow. Stories are the best medicine, don't you think?"

"Distraction does help control pain."

"It's more than that. Stories lift you." Leah closed her eyes to savor the memory. "When Mr. and Mrs. Jones left me in Des Moines, I was very sick and very sad. But a volunteer—we called her Granny Norris—she read to us in the sick ward. She read *Heidi* and *Pollyanna* and *The Secret Garden*, tales of orphans and invalids who learned to be cheerful, to seek good, and to prevail. I learned to do the same."

"Even now." Only the hint of a question colored his deep voice.

"Even now. I don't have to look hard to find the good. You

stopped that man and brought me here, and the doctors were able to operate and stop the bleeding. And Mrs. Bellamy from the Red Cross attends my church, and I think we could become friends. And now . . . why, I have my very first box of chocolates."

Black eyebrows sprang high. "Your first?"

"Mm-hmm. There are even more blessings I can't yet see. But I will. I only have to watch."

Clay had a most unusual expression, his mouth bent in a slight smile, but his eyes were dark and sad. "I reckon you will."

8

In the mock Nazi village built for Ranger training, Clay and the other five men in his squad crouched beside "Butch's Biergarten."

Another squad hunkered behind an enormous oak tree in front of the fake town hall, the company's objective. Sniper fire from the Biergarten pinned that squad in place.

Sergeant Lombardi leaned forward, sweat dribbling from underneath his helmet down his lean face. "Mayer, Paxton—count to twenty, then through this window to distract the sniper. Rest of you, follow me through the front door." He led the squad around the corner to the left.

Counting in his head, Clay eyed the window about five feet above the dirt. "My turn."

Gene nodded and got onto hands and knees.

At the count of twenty, Clay readied his M1 Garand rifle, used Gene's back as a stool, climbed through the open window, and jumped to the floor.

Only six feet away to his right, a soldier leveled a rifle through a window facing the street. He spotted Clay.

Clay's mission wasn't to take out the sniper, only to distract him while Lombardi's force stormed the building. But at the door, a sandbag "soldier" had swung down, and McKillop was struggling to bayonet the thing out of the way.

The sniper turned his rifle in Clay's direction.

No time. Clay swung his rifle butt up under the sniper's rifle, making the man fling up his arms.

Clay slammed his rifle across the man's chest, then grabbed the man's upraised arm and twisted it down around the rifle.

The man cried out and folded down to the ground to release the pain in his shoulder.

Gene hopped through the window. "Well done, Pax."

Holman, Rubenstein, and Lombardi burst into the room, while McKillop shook his bayonet free from the sandbag.

"Dirty fighting." Lombardi broke into a grin. "Nice work."

"Thanks, Sergeant." Clay released the sniper's arm and helped him to standing.

The soldier rubbed his shoulder and glared at Clay. "Yeah. Real nice."

"Next objective." Lombardi motioned them out of the Biergarten.

"Sorry." Clay gave the sniper an apologetic look and followed his sergeant. He was sorry the man was in pain, but not sorry he'd used the move.

Ever since he'd fought off Leah's attacker, his philosophy had shifted.

When Leah's life was at stake, the rules of sportsmanship hadn't applied, and they wouldn't apply on the battlefield either. In combat, all that mattered would be his unit's objective and his buddies' lives.

If he wanted to fight well in combat, in training he needed to practice every technique at his disposal.

Clay ran with his squad, low and fast, hugging the buildings. When they passed the giant oak, the second squad fell in behind Clay's.

After he'd helped Leah, Lieutenant Taylor and Sergeant Lombardi had stopped making noise about transferring him. But he had to continue to prove himself. The praise lavished on him for that rescue had an expiration date.

The town hall stood at the end of the street. To its right, a trio of Rangers tossed charges into a shed meant to be an enemy outpost.

The building exploded, and a man screamed and fell to the ground.

Lombardi passed the man by.

Clay dropped to his knees beside the wounded man. "What happened?"

He could only scream. His hand was blackened and bloodied, and he might have lost a finger. He must have held on to the charge too long.

"Hold still." Clay opened the pouch on his cartridge belt that held his first aid kit. "Let's get this ban—"

"Paxton!" Lombardi dropped back and glowered at Clay. "Leave him. Get your tail in motion."

"Rangers don't leave men behind."

"The Rangers won't, but you will. Leave him for the medics." A sarcastic smile split his dirtied face. "Unless you'd rather be a medic."

"No, Sergeant." He'd reached the expiration date. Clay ran after Lombardi and shouted "sorry" to the wounded man.

Holman kicked open the front door of the town hall, Ruby threw in a smoke grenade, and the rest of the men stormed inside. Within five minutes, the hall was secured.

Afterward, Clay headed back outside. Two medics were loading the injured man onto a stretcher.

Clay fastened the pouch for his first aid kit. The urge to heal was strong, but he had to suppress it for the greater good.

The company fell into formation and marched back to camp

double time for lunch. In the afternoon they'd have lectures and demonstrations on demolitions and booby traps.

G. M. marched beside Clay on the dirt road while cicadas hummed in the grass and scrub oak. "Going to the hospital again tonight?"

"If I can."

"Sounds like a date." Gene's grin spread wide and goofy. "Mark my words. You're going to join the ranks of us married men."

Clay whistled. He still couldn't believe Gene was getting married on Saturday. His friend had never been happier, but how many of these rushed wartime marriages would last?

"So . . . ?" Gene turned the full goofiness to Clay.

"So what? She's like a little sister." Clay swatted away a cloud of red dust.

Gene swatted too. "I've got a little sister, and I don't treat her that nice."

"You're a bad brother."

Now Gene swatted Clay. "I'm a great brother, but I don't play violin for her."

Clay had borrowed a violin from the service club, and when the nurse allowed it, he played classical music and American folk songs for the ladies on the ward.

He avoided mariachi tunes to keep the memories of playing with his brothers at bay. The Gringo Mariachis—stupid name for a group. Clay was only half gringo.

"You're over there almost every evening."

Clay shrugged. "She doesn't have any family, and she hasn't been in Tennessee long enough to make friends. She's lonely and bored."

"I bet she *loves* your visits." Gene stretched out the word *love* so long no one could miss his meaning.

But Clay pretended to. "I reckon she enjoys them."

At the front of the formation, someone began singing "Don't Sit under the Apple Tree," and Clay joined in to shut down conversation.

Leah always brightened when Clay visited, but not in an infatuated sort of way. Clay felt bad for her. He played for her and read to her. Now that she could sit up and use her arms, he brought magazines and books.

Her improving health did his heart good. She'd looked so pale and weak on his first visit, determined to be cheerful but obviously shaken.

Over time she was regaining color, and her cheer seemed less forced.

For such a young and tiny thing, she had strength at her core. She was going to be all right.

9

Rita Sue Bellamy set her hands on her well-padded hips and gave Leah a mock glare. "You don't even need me anymore, sugar."

From her bedside chair, Leah smiled up at the Red Cross volunteer and closed *The Valley of Decision*. "Books are wonderful, but you're even better company."

Rita Sue chuckled and sat on the bed. "You've stolen my chair as well."

"I have, and I'm going on walks around the hospital grounds." Leah set the book on the nightstand beside another box of candy from Clay. "How are the children?"

"Enjoying their summer vacation. Luella and Sally make about a dozen mud pies a day—and throw them at Joey."

Leah laughed. "They sound delightful."

"Would you like to meet them?"

"Oh yes." The only thing Leah missed about the orphanage was the little children.

Rita Sue smoothed the skirt of her button-front Red Cross dress. "Mercer and I would love to have you over for dinner after church when you're discharged."

"I'd love that." With Rita Sue, Leah didn't feel odd, despite the age difference.

Darlene was a good friend and had visited Leah in the hospital several times, but Darlene didn't truly understand Leah. And Leah didn't truly understand Darlene.

"Excuse me?" Myra Mayhew stood at the foot of the bed.

"Oh! Good afternoon, Miss Mayhew." Leah pushed to standing.

"No, no." The librarian waved her hand. "Please sit."

Leah eased back down.

Rita Sue stood. "I'll come back later, sugar."

"Thank you." Leah smiled at her, then at Miss Mayhew. The librarian wore a smart silver-gray suit and a matching little hat, and Leah stroked her blue pajama trousers as if she could transform them into her sage green suit.

"I'm glad to see you looking so well," Miss Mayhew said.

"I feel much better, thank you. I can't wait to return to work. I'm sure you must be busy."

"I am." She sighed. "The Army sent two soldiers to help, but they're—well, one is practically illiterate."

"Oh my."

"Do you know . . ." Her brow wrinkled. "Do you know when you can return to work?"

The librarian seemed more concerned with staffing than with Leah's welfare, but then she'd only known Leah for a short time. Still, it pricked her heart.

Leah worked up a smile. "Dr. Reeves expects to discharge me from the hospital next week, and I should be able to return to work the following week. But he won't make any promises until he's sure I'm strong enough."

"Oh yes." A smile lit up Miss Mayhew's pretty face. "You must regain your strength."

"Thank you."

After the librarian departed, Leah reached for the latest box of candy from Clay. Her muscles strained in a good way, stretching and rebuilding the weak tissue.

She opened the box and smiled at the licorice allsorts inside. So many jolly colors and stripes and sprinkles, and the anise scent felt clean and invigorating.

Leah popped one into her mouth and chewed it slowly. The taste of coconut wasn't one she favored, but she imagined a Hawaiian beach at sunset and ukulele music, and the taste fit.

Would Clay visit tonight? Not only was he fine company, but the visits seemed to cheer him too, especially when the nurse let him play the violin. Then he'd stroll the ward and take requests. His music was so lively, so heartfelt, so touching, and it lifted everyone's spirits.

A dozen beds lined the long building, filled with women who worked at Camp Forrest or whose husbands served or worked there. Some had undergone surgery to remove appendices or tonsils or gallbladders, and some had been injured on the job or in car accidents.

All were weak and all were bored, and Leah was glad her friend could bring some joy.

Despite the teasing of some of the patients, Leah never thought of Clay as anything but a friend.

His manner to her was kind and generous, but he never looked at her like the other patients' husbands and boyfriends looked at them.

Leah chewed on a licorice button, pale pink with sprinkles and a delicate flavor.

The heroines in her favorite novels would have moped if such a splendid man saw them only as friends, but Leah didn't. The thought of any man touching her where the wolf had touched her—well, it made her sweat and hyperventilate.

Maybe it would be different if she were in love. It would. It had to. But she didn't want to find out for a very long time.

"Good day, Miss Jones." Dr. Reeves came to the foot of the bed with a clipboard.

"Hello, Dr. Reeves." Leah gave him a curious look. It wasn't time for rounds.

He wore a solemn face.

Leah's breathing stalled.

Dr. Reeves cleared his throat and looked at his clipboard. "I need to discuss a test result with you."

A test result?

Her stomach constricted around the tiny bits of licorice. Such a grave expression could only mean bad news. What if it kept her away from the library much longer? Would she lose her job?

What then? What would she do?

Oh Lord. She clutched the box of candy. *Please help me.*

10

"I'm glad you're here, Private." The ward nurse met Clay at the door. "Miss Jones requested no visitors, but she couldn't have meant you. She needs cheering up tonight."

What had happened? Clay glanced down the ward. Part of him wanted to rush to Leah's bedside, and the other part wanted to honor her wishes and leave.

Dr. Hill had taught him to respect patients' privacy in order to maintain trust, but right now gnawing concern drove his feet down the aisle.

Leah wasn't reading in the chair as usual. She lay curled up in bed, clutching the blanket under her chin, staring at the empty bed beside her.

Clay made his voice as soft as possible. "Leah?"

She startled, glanced up at him, and closed her eyes. "I—I'm sorry. Would you mind? I don't feel like talking." Her face was as pale as on the night she'd almost bled to death.

Clay lowered himself into the chair and set the violin case on the floor. "You don't have to talk. I could read to you."

She shook her head and rolled over, away from him.

Clay licked his lips. "I have the violin. I could play for you."

"No, thank you."

What was wrong? She hadn't withdrawn after she'd been attacked, after she'd almost died. However, his curiosity gave way to compassion. "All right. I'll sit here and pray for you, but I'm not leaving. You shouldn't be alone tonight."

Leah gasped and glanced back over her shoulder, brushing black curls off her face. "They told you?"

"No one told me anything. The nurse just said you needed cheering up."

Leah's head flopped down to the pillow. "It's useless."

"Hey, now. Where's the young lady who can find good in any situation?"

"There is no good in this."

Clay sighed. "Give it time."

"This can never be good. Never." Her voice choked.

Everything in Clay wanted to force her to tell him what was wrong so he could heal it, but something deep inside restrained him, lowering his head and his eyelids. "Father in heaven, I don't know what happened, but you do and you're the only one who needs to know. Your child Leah is hurting. Please hold her tight and comfort her. Please—"

Leah hauled in a loud breath, almost a sob. "I'm pregnant."

Clay's eyes flew open. "Pardon?"

"I—I'm going to have a baby." She curled up even tighter.

Clay's mind whirled between shock at the news, fury at the man who did this to her, and aching concern for Leah.

The last time he'd heard those words, he'd only felt fury and humiliation. Ellen Hill standing on his parents' doorstep, her belly swollen with Adler's child, begging to be taken in after her parents moved out of town and left her behind.

But Leah . . . she was an innocent. She was only eighteen and had no family to care for her.

"Oh, Leah. I'm so sorry. What are you . . . do you know what you're going to do?"

"I have to give her up." She drew in a deep, rattling sigh. "Dr. Reeves and Mrs. Bellamy talked to me. If I kept the baby, I'd have to work to support her, but I don't have anyone to watch her while I work. And I might not be able to find a job. People would question my—my virtue."

"That's not fair." Clay's fists clenched. "He forced himself on you."

Leah rolled onto her back, staring at the ceiling. "No one would ask how."

Clay pounded his fists on top of each other. It wasn't fair. It wasn't true. But she was right. All people would see would be an unwed mother.

She rubbed her forehead. "We'd have to live on charity, in poverty. I can't—I won't do that to her. Giving her up for adoption is her best chance."

He had to start thinking like a physician, not a friend. "It is. It's for the best."

"I know. I know it is. But all I've ever wanted is a family, and now I have someone and I have to give her away." She clapped her hand over her mouth and slammed her eyes shut.

Clay's gut seized. Not fair. Not right. "I'm so sorry."

Leah cupped her free hand over her belly and pulled in a long breath. "It's for the best. Dr. Reeves told me of a home for unwed mothers. I'll go there when I start to show and I—I lose my job."

That too? Clay winced. She'd lose her job on top of everything else?

"After the baby is born, they'll find a home for her." Leah's face twisted. "But what if they're like the Joneses and beat her, or what if they can't find a home and they—they put her in an orphanage?"

He ached for her distress. "I'm sure they'll find a good home."

"I'll never see her again, just like my sisters. They said I wouldn't want to see her, that she'd only remind me of that man, but I know she wouldn't. I know I'll love her. I'll always love her."

Clay's chest collapsed. Leah already loved that child. The way she shielded her belly with her hand. The way she'd already decided it was a girl. Whether or not she ever saw her baby, she would always love her and she would always mourn.

Half a dozen platitudes flitted in his head, and he shot them all down. Time would never fully heal this wound. God would work some good out of this, but not the good Leah wanted.

She had to choose between giving up her baby and raising that baby in poverty and disgrace. No matter what she did, she'd lose her job and she'd probably lose her chance to attend library school.

The rapist had stolen her future as surely as Wyatt and Adler had stolen Clay's, and his hands and jaw set like stone.

"You can leave now." Leah rolled her head on the pillow and lifted a faint smile to him. "There's nothing to say, and that's all right. I understand."

If only he could fix this, but his medical kit lay empty. "I wish . . ."

"It's all right. Just pray. Please pray."

"I will." He picked up the violin and stood. "I'll visit tomorrow if I can."

"Thank you." She smiled, almost as serene as the day he'd met her.

That smile made his gut twist harder than if she'd burst into tears.

He strode out of the ward and into the hot humid night. Prayer was powerful. It was. But what about that verse in the book of James? If someone was naked and hungry, it was worthless to tell her to depart in peace and be warm and filled.

Sometimes a man needed to offer a blanket, a hot meal, or a bandage.

"Lord!" Clay stopped on the concrete path between the long narrow hospital buildings, and he raised his face and his voice to the starry sky. "I only have a hundred bucks or so. I have nothing to give her, nothing but my name."

And the stars brightened, and light poured through them into his eyes and his mind.

His name.

The pinpoints of light coalesced into a beam, illuminating his path with utter clarity, every step marked and sure to the very end.

No, he needed to think about this. He pressed his hand over his eyes to block the light, to think clearly, but the light chased down every objection and turned every dark spot bright. In any other circumstances, the idea would be crazy. But in his circumstance—in hers—nothing could be more logical.

Clay spun back to the women's surgical ward, and he marched, then jogged, then ran. Up the stairs, through the door, past startled nurses, to the foot of Leah's bed, breathing hard.

She frowned up at him.

The light couldn't contain itself, and he opened his mouth. "Marry me."

Leah shook her head a bit. "What?"

"Hear me out." He set the violin on the chair and paced beside her bed, each step of his feet imprinting the steps of his life. "It's all so clear. I was telling God I had nothing to offer you but my name—and that's the best thing I could give you. Marry me, and you take my name with all the rights and privileges attached to it."

She stared at him, slack jawed, and she scooted up to sitting. "Clay? That—that's crazy."

He held out both hands as if he held his name in a gift box. "No, it's perfect. Marry me, and you can keep your baby."

"Keep . . . ? No. I already decided to give her up. I know it's the right thing to do."

"This is better. Think about it. I told you about my dream, how I know I'm going to die soon."

"Clay—"

"Hear me out. Please." He couldn't stop pacing. "That dream frees us to marry. Frees us."

"You shouldn't talk like that."

Clay had to make her see. "While I'm alive, you'll receive an allotment as my wife. It isn't much, but it's enough to support you and the baby. You won't have to work. You won't have to find someone to watch the baby."

Leah pressed both hands to her cheeks and lowered her chin, shaking her head. But she didn't cover her ears.

Clay took a step closer. "When I die, you'll receive my GI life insurance. Ten thousand dollars. That's—"

"No!" She jerked her head up. "Ten thou—Clay, that should go to your family."

He grinned. "Don't you see? Marry me, and you'll be my family, you and the baby. That much money will keep you going five, six years. By then she'll be in school and you can work. Or you can marry again, of course. You're set for life."

She clutched the blanket in a tight roll across her lap, her lips pressed together. "What if you live?"

"I won't."

"What if you do?" She raised stricken eyes to him. "I believe you about the dream, but what if you *are* wrong? What if you live—and I hope you do, I really do. What then? You'd be burdened with a wife you didn't love."

And she'd be burdened with a husband she didn't love.

Clay groaned and clamped one hand around the back of his neck. He wasn't going to survive, but he had to pacify her. "All right then. If I survive—but I know I won't—then we'll get divorced. I—I'll say I met someone else and cheated on you, so you can divorce me. I'll still provide for you."

"How can you say that?" Sparks flashed in those brown eyes. "How can you treat marriage so lightly? Marriage is a sacred bond, a promise before God and man."

This was going horribly wrong. He stared at the ceiling and sighed. "I'm not. I promise I'm not. But I know that isn't going to happen. I know beyond a doubt that I'm going to die."

"I don't like it at all. It's an awful reason to get married."

"Is it?" He lowered his gaze to her. "One of the reasons God created marriage was to care for mothers and children. That's what I want to do. I want to care for you and your baby. I want you to raise that baby yourself as you should."

Leah wrapped her arms around her middle and lowered her chin.

At last he was getting through to her. "Your baby will have a name and a father. I'll be her father. I'll gladly call her my own. She'll never have to know who her real father is. She'll never have to be ashamed. You'll always be able to show her my picture and say, 'There's your daddy, the war hero.'"

Her shoulders hunched up.

The baby's real father . . . another thought seized him. "Listen, we won't live together, so you don't have to worry about any of . . . of that. I have to live on base, and we're shipping out soon. I won't—I'll never touch you. Not like . . ."

She shook her head. "I don't like the idea."

"I do. Can't you see this is the best way?" He squatted beside her. "You said you couldn't see any good in this, but I do. I see great good. You can raise that little baby and have a family. No disgrace. No poverty."

Leah pressed her hand over her eyes. "No poverty? Only because of charity. I won't take your charity. I promised myself I'd never accept charity again. I won't."

"No, no, no." Clay dropped to his knees and took her free hand in his. "It isn't charity. You'd be doing me a favor."

She peeked over the top of her hand. "A favor?"

"Yes, ma'am. Right now, my only purpose in life is to die."

She winced.

"It is." He squeezed her narrow hand. "I'm training hard so I can go into battle and die saving my buddies. But this—marrying you would give my life an even better purpose. Knowing that I helped you and your little one, that I provided for you . . . well, that would make me the happiest man in the world."

The fight left her shoulders and her cheeks, and she slid her hand from her eyes to her mouth. Her brown eyes teemed with questions, with a desire to believe.

Clay pressed his hand to his chest and smiled. "Come on, Miss Jones, have a heart. Here I am, down on my knees, begging you to make me happy and marry me. Would you, please? Would you do me the honor of becoming Mrs. Clay Paxton?"

Leah fell silent for far too long, but then she slowly nodded. "Yes. Please."

"Thank you." He planted a kiss on the back of her hand. He hadn't felt so good in over two years.

11

Darlene Bishop adjusted the short veil over Leah's face and frowned. "I don't understand you. A month ago, you didn't even want a date, and now you're marrying a man you hardly know."

Seated in the chaplain's office in Camp Forrest's main chapel, Leah fingered the smooth fabric of the cream-colored suit the girls in the boardinghouse had given her as a wedding present. "I've never known a finer man."

"You've never known *any* man."

"Now, now." Rita Sue Bellamy handed Leah a bouquet of creamy roses. "I think it's romantic. Clay saved her life and visited her almost every day in the hospital. It's no surprise to me or to anyone on the ward."

"Thank you." Leah inhaled the heady floral fragrance. Only Clay, Rita Sue, and her doctors and nurses knew she'd been violated during the attack, and only they knew about her pregnancy. That was how it needed to stay so that everyone would believe Clay was the father.

A soldier peeked into the office. "Excuse me. Are you ready, Miss Jones?"

"I am." Today she'd lose the name of Jones, which always reminded her she was unwanted and unloved. Clay didn't love her, but he cared for her and he did want to marry her.

Leah stood slowly, still a bit weak and lightheaded.

"I'll go sit with my family." Rita Sue pressed a kiss to Leah's veiled cheek. "You look ravishing."

Leah didn't know what to do with the compliment or the affection. "Thank you."

After Rita Sue left, Darlene stepped close, her brow furrowed beneath her flower-strewn hat. "Are you sure, sugar? It isn't too late to back out."

"I'm sure."

"You know Latins can be hot tempered, don't you?"

"Oh, not Clay."

Then Darlene giggled. "Of course, you're also getting a Latin lover. That might make it all worthwhile."

Leah felt ill, and not from the tiny life growing inside. Why did people assume things about Clay just because his skin was brown? More than one of the nurses had thought Clay was the rapist for that reason.

"It's time," the chaplain's assistant said.

It was indeed. Leah and Darlene followed him into the foyer.

In a second, Mendelssohn's "Wedding March" resounded from the organ on the balcony overhead. Leah tightened her grip on her bouquet. This was happening to her. To her?

The chaplain's assistant beckoned, and Darlene sashayed down the aisle.

Behind her bouquet, Leah pressed her hand to her belly. By marrying Clay, Leah could give her baby a home with her own mother and the name of a good father. *For you, little girl.*

Somehow she knew the baby was a girl. If a boy was born, she'd love him as dearly, but she was a girl and her name was Helen. The name meant *light*, because this child was light shining from Leah's darkest days.

The chaplain's assistant nodded to her.

Leah drew a deep breath. If only her father were there, offering his arm with his brown eyes twinkling. If only her mother were waiting in the sanctuary, dabbing at tears. If only Callie and Polly were her bridesmaids instead of Darlene, her twin sisters in matching floral dresses.

"Miss Jones?"

Leah blinked at the chaplain's assistant and stepped into the doorway alone.

She peered through the filmy veil. The sanctuary was so large, with dozens of wooden benches under the peaked roof. Everyone stood and looked at her.

To her right stood a dozen Rangers in olive drab dress uniform, a few with girlfriends or wives. To her left stood the Bellamy family and the four other girls from the boardinghouse.

And Clay stood at the altar, grinning at her.

The chaplain's assistant cleared his throat.

Oh yes, she was supposed to walk down the aisle.

She did so, past rows and rows of empty pews. The attention unnerved her, so she focused on Clay, beside the chaplain and Gene Mayer.

Clay stood straight and solid in his olive drab jacket, trousers, and service cap, with his khaki tie knotted at the collar of his olive drab shirt. He was such a nice-looking man. He was handsome too, but she preferred nice looking to handsome.

Anyone would think Clay smiled out of love, but he smiled from the joy of giving.

Despite what he said, this was charity, but Leah would accept it with gratitude as she'd accepted it all her life. At the orphanage, they said God provided for every need.

If only God didn't always choose to provide for her through charity.

At the altar, she took Clay's offered arm and faced the chaplain. Leah hadn't held a lot of arms, but Clay's was thick and hard with strength she wanted to bend toward. Those arms had fought off the wolf, bandaged her wounds, and carried her to the hospital.

The chaplain greeted Clay and Leah and the congregation. He also had a nice face, long and narrow with gray-blue eyes that curved when he smiled, which was often.

He spoke from 1 Corinthians 13 about charity. In the King James Version, *charity* meant *love*, and the Lord's sense of humor warmed Leah inside.

In this chapel, everyone but Clay, Leah, and Rita Sue thought this marriage was based on romantic love. Instead it was based on biblical charitable love.

Since her parents died, she hadn't had anyone to love. She loved her sisters, but in a nebulous way, only remembering them as babies. She'd been fond of Miss Tilletson at the school library and of her friends. But true love? She hadn't given it or received it.

Now she had a baby to love. She glanced up out of the corner of her eye at Clay's strong profile. She had Clay to love too.

Not romantic love, but the kind of love in 1 Corinthians—long-suffering, kind, not seeking her own way, not easily provoked, not thinking evil of the other—"Beareth all things, believeth all things, hopeth all things, endureth all things. Charity never faileth."

"Please face each other and repeat your vows."

Leah handed Darlene her bouquet.

Clay wrapped his hands around Leah's. His eyes were so warm, and he smelled good this close, of coffee and aftershave.

He spoke his vows with assurance, even though many of the words didn't apply to them. They'd never have and hold each other as married couples did, but he would provide for her and give her a name and a future.

"Till death do us part." Clay's mouth twitched, as if that part of the vow amused him.

It didn't amuse her. He'd only married her because he believed he wasn't long for this earth. For his sake, she wanted to believe him. But also for his sake, she hoped he was very wrong.

Leah repeated her vows after the chaplain, her voice thready.

They exchanged rings. Hers was more delicate, but the rings matched, marking them as belonging to each other.

Her heart seized. She hadn't belonged to anyone since she was four.

"I now pronounce you man and wife. You may kiss the bride."

The kiss. Why hadn't the chaplain skipped that part? Clay shouldn't have to kiss a woman he didn't love. On the other hand, a kiss would support the charade that they did love each other.

Clay lifted her veil over her hat. He wore a flat smile, his eyebrows drew together, and he leaned close, so all she smelled was coffee. "I want to do this right," he whispered. "But I don't want to hurt you."

Because of the wolf. But the wolf had never kissed her. "You won't hurt me."

A slight lift of his eyebrows, as if asking her permission, and she nodded, just a tick of a nod, not breathing, not blinking, not believing.

Clay tilted his head. Was she supposed to do the same? She didn't know what to do.

Then Clay's lips settled on hers, and her lips knew what to do, molding to his as warmth and light bloomed inside. Oh, this was what the poets wrote about! The novelists and the composers and the lyricists writing for generations upon generations. Now Leah knew too.

Clay pulled away, breaking the connection. He gave her a jerky little smile and faced their beaming friends.

Leah turned too, clutching Clay's arm. She hadn't anticipated the joy and she hadn't anticipated the danger—the danger of falling for a man destined to die.

12

Clay scraped the last bit of fluffy white frosting off his plate. "Thank you for organizing this reception."

"You know our motto—the Red Cross is at your side. In this case, it was pure joy." Mrs. Bellamy sipped a cup of coffee. "President Roosevelt was most obliging, putting an end to coffee rationing last week."

A little blonde girl hid behind Mrs. Bellamy, peeking at Clay with a mischievous smile.

Clay returned it full force. He missed Mama's big Ramirez clan and all the little cousins. "The cake is delicious."

"Thank you." Mrs. Bellamy giggled. "You should have heard the ladies at church grumble when I asked them to give up their sugar rations for yet another wedding here at Camp Forrest. Then I told them Leah was an orphan and didn't have a mama to bake for her. Well, you should have seen those sugar crocks fly open."

"Thank them from me. Leah hasn't had a lot of nice things in life." He glanced behind him. The Rangers flirted with the boardinghouse girls, especially with Darlene, who worked at the PX nearest the Rangers' barracks.

Leah sat at a table chatting with Gene and his girlfriend—no, his wife, Betty Jo.

Good to see that Leah was sitting down and had cleaned her plate. She looked pretty in that creamy suit and hat, with her hair pinned up in rolls and curls and things. Real grown up.

"She's a sweet girl," Mrs. Bellamy said.

"She sure is." He felt tiny arms around his knees. The little girl sat on his foot and grinned up at him, a yellow bow around her ringlets.

"Sally Bellamy!" her mother said.

"I don't mind." Clay lifted his leg with the giggling child attached. "I need my daily calisthenics."

Mrs. Bellamy sipped her coffee and smiled at her daughter and then at Clay. "You take good care of Miss Leah, you hear?"

"Yes, ma'am. That's why I married her."

"Mm-hmm. It's time for you to spirit your bride away."

His bride? Yes, Leah. She was laughing at something Betty Jo said, color in her cheeks again, thank goodness.

Mrs. Bellamy whisked Sally onto her hip. "Private Paxton has to leave now, sugar pie."

"Bye, Pwivate Paxton." Sally pressed a hand to her forehead in a salute.

Clay snapped up his best salute for her. "Good day, Miss Bellamy. And Mrs. Bellamy, thank you again for everything you've done."

"My pleasure."

The Red Cross had even secured dinner and room reservations at the swanky King Hotel in Tullahoma. Clay would sleep on the floor, but he wanted to give folks every reason to believe that he was the father of Leah's child.

Clay crossed the room and offered Leah his hand. "Ready to leave, Mrs. Paxton?"

She looked pleasantly surprised, and she laid her hand in his. "I am."

G. M. stood and cupped his hand around his mouth. "All right, everyone. Time to send off the newlyweds."

Darlene handed Leah a suitcase and winked at her. "Don't come home too soon, you hear?"

Leah dipped her head as if studying the suitcase handle.

Clay had better get her out before double entendres started flying. He led Leah to the door, picked up his haversack, and faced the guests. "Thanks for everything, y'all."

G. M. clinked his fork on his coffee cup and whooped. The clinking and whooping spread around the room.

Oh no.

"That means you've got to kiss her, Pax," Gene called.

Not a good idea. But he looped his arm around Leah's waist. She stiffened, then relaxed.

Clay aimed a grin at his buddies. "I'm fixing to do a lot of that, but not in front of y'all." Then he swung Leah right out the door.

"Sorry about that. Here, let me take your suitcase." He released her and led her from the reception room out through the chapel.

Thank goodness he'd dodged that bullet. The kiss during the wedding ceremony had about done him in. She'd looked paralyzed when he lifted her veil, and he'd thought he'd kiss wooden lips.

Boy, was he wrong. She'd kissed him back, and the sweetness of it . . .

Granted, he hadn't kissed a girl for over two years, but he couldn't remember any kiss so sweet. He couldn't let it happen again. The last thing he needed was to fall for Leah. When he went into battle, he didn't want anything to hold him back.

"We have plenty of time to call my folks before we head into town for our portraits and dinner." Clay opened the chapel door. "Would you like me to hail a cab? The telephone center is about three blocks away."

"I can walk." Leah frowned at her suitcase. "But you shouldn't have to carry my things as well as yours."

He laughed and headed down the street. She certainly wasn't a princess. "Nonsense. I'm used to twenty-five-mile marches with full combat gear. This is nothing."

"Still—"

"I mean this is *nothing*." He held up her suitcase between thumb and forefinger. "I thought girls packed heavy."

"I don't know why." Leah shrugged. "What do you need? A change of clothes, a comb, a toothbrush, and toothpaste. Darlene told me the hotel will provide towels and soap. Isn't that nice of them?"

"You've never stayed in a hotel, have you?"

"No. I'm so excited." Her face shone. "I've never eaten dinner in a restaurant either. Darlene and I had sandwiches in a café after I received my first paycheck, but a real dinner? I can't wait."

She really did need someone to take care of her.

Leah twisted her wedding ring as she walked.

"The ring—does it fit all right?"

"It fits perfectly." She stretched her hand before her. "I've always wanted a piece of jewelry, and look how pretty it is."

Her first piece of jewelry, and he'd only bought her a plain gold band? "I should have gotten you something nicer."

"Nicer? What could be nicer?" She twisted her hand in the sun. "The simplicity allows you to admire the beauty of the gold."

Some of the Rangers had ribbed him about getting married. "Kiss your paycheck good-bye," they'd said.

They didn't know Leah Jones.

Leah Paxton.

Clay climbed the steps to the telephone center, identical to every other building at Camp Forrest. "I like calling home on Saturday evenings when the fellows are out on the town—no lines. This is early for me. Hope my folks are home."

"Yes." Her voice sounded as small as when she'd said her vows, probably nervous.

He couldn't blame her when his stomach was turning this way and that.

The lady at the front desk directed them to an open booth. Clay motioned for Leah to take the seat. Then he set down the luggage, removed his stifling wool jacket, and had the operator put him through to Kerrville, Texas.

As the connections went through, Clay leaned back against the doorjamb. Daddy and Mama would be shocked, since he'd never mentioned dating anyone. At least he'd told them about rescuing Leah.

"Hello?" Daddy's voice, deep and gruff.

"Hiya, Daddy. Hope you don't mind me calling early."

"Never. Lupe, it's Clay."

Clay heard his mama in the background, saying, "So early?" He could picture his parents scooting two chairs under the phone on the kitchen wall, holding the receiver between them.

"*Hola, mijo.* How are you?"

"Fine. Listen, we only have five minutes, and I have big news for y'all."

"Oh?" Mama said.

Clay sank his hand into his trouser pocket. "Remember me telling you about Leah Jones?"

"That poor girl," Mama said. "Everyone from church is praying for her. How is she?"

"She's out of the hospital. But she isn't Leah Jones anymore. She's Leah Paxton."

In the silence, Clay held his breath, staring at the opposite doorjamb, avoiding Leah's gaze.

"Did we hear right?" Daddy said. "Leah Paxton?"

"You may be getting older, Daddy, but your hearing's just fine. Leah and I got married about two hours ago. She's sitting here with me."

"Married?" he said. "How well do you know this girl?"

"Well enough to know she's the one." Clay clenched his hand in his pocket so the strain wouldn't show in his voice.

"You had a wedding? Without us?" Mama sounded hurt. "Oh, Clay, we would have come."

No time for that in these circumstances. "Sorry, Mama, but my battalion is leaving soon. I didn't want to wait."

"Wyatt and Adler are gone." Mama's voice quivered. "Every day we pray they come home, but right now you're the only son we have, and this may be the only wedding . . ."

Clay grimaced and rested his head back. He hadn't meant to hurt them.

"Never mind that, Lupe. Water under the bridge," Daddy said. "Congratulations, son. We're happy for you."

"Oh yes. We are . . . so happy. We've always wanted a daughter. What's she like?"

That was better. Clay winked at his bride, who looked like a rabbit facing a stewpot. "She's about the cutest little thing you've ever seen. No taller than you, Mama. Curly black hair and pretty brown eyes. She's real smart too. She's a librarian. I'll send you our wedding portrait."

"Was her family able to be there?" Mama asked. "I hope so."

"She's an orphan, so no. She was raised in an orphanage."

Mama gasped. "Oh, the poor child. Put her on. Please let me talk to her."

Clay held out the receiver. "They want to talk to you."

Leah pressed back against the wall as if she wanted to bust a hole through and escape.

He chuckled. "They already love you."

Her expression melted into wonder, and she took the phone. "Hello? Mr. and Mrs. Paxton?"

Clay could hear Mama's excited jabbering.

"All—all right," Leah said. "I'm from Iowa, from Des Moines . . . Since June. I started working at the Camp Forrest Library a few days after I graduated from high school . . . I'm eighteen . . . Yes, it's been—a big change."

Clay heard the operator's warning. Only one minute remaining.

"Before I hang up, I want to thank you for raising Clay." Leah lowered her face. "He—he's the kindest, most generous man. Thank you . . . Good-bye."

She handed Clay the phone, but she didn't look at him. "They want to talk to you."

Clay held the phone to his ear. "I'm back."

"She seems like a very nice young lady," Daddy said.

"She's wonderful." Mama's voice choked. "*Mijo*, you've made me so happy. You believe you have a future again. I'm so glad—so glad you'll go off to war with a reason to live."

Was that what they thought? He stifled a groan. This hadn't changed a thing, but if it made his parents happier for the remaining few months of his life, so be it. "I ought to say good-bye before we get cut off."

"Yes. Good-bye and congratulations," Daddy said. "Give that wife of yours a big kiss from us."

"I'll do that." Clay hung up.

Now he had to keep that promise. He kissed Leah on the forehead, much safer than what Daddy had in mind. "From my parents."

Big brown eyes turned up to him. "What does 'mee-ha' mean? Your mother kept saying it."

Mija meant he had the best mother in the world. "*Mija* means *daughter*."

Leah's mouth dropped open.

"I'll tell you what else it means." Clay rested his forearm on the wall over her head and leaned closer so he could keep his voice low. "It means our baby will have doting grandparents to spoil her rotten."

Her eyes shimmered, and she clapped her hand over her mouth.

Clay perched on the edge of the little bench beside her and offered his handkerchief.

"Thank you, but I don't—I don't cry." Her voice broke, and she took the handkerchief.

He rested back against the wall while contentment filled every compartment of his soul. Not only was he giving Leah and the baby a comfortable life together, but he'd given them a big family that would keep loving and supporting them long after he was gone. He hadn't even thought of that before the phone call.

He'd given his parents a gift too. Clay would die, and Wyatt and Adler might never come home again. But now Daddy and Mama had a daughter to cherish and a grandchild on the way.

Leah sniffed. "I suppose all brides say this, but this is the happiest day of my life."

Clay couldn't contain his grin. "Mine too."

13

Leah held the tiny soap to her nose and inhaled cleanliness and luxury. She had a bathroom to herself, with no girls pounding on the door or crowding at the sink.

Clay's canvas toiletry kit lay unrolled on a cabinet. Pouches held razor and blades, toothbrush and paste, shaving cream, soap, comb, and mirror. What a clever thing.

No sounds emanated from the bedroom. When she had awakened, Clay had been asleep on a blanket on the floor. How odd to sleep in the same room as a man. Yet the rhythm of his breathing had a comforting effect.

After Leah buttoned her yellow floral dress, she arranged curls and bobby pins the best she could.

Leah eased the bathroom door open. Daylight brightened the room through the drawn curtains. Holding her breath, she padded past Clay to the chair by the window.

Perhaps she could write a poem. Since the attack, her emotions had been too jumbled to put into words. She took her composition book from her purse, but the blank page mocked her.

Leah's gaze drifted to Clay. Watching him sleep felt too private and intimate.

He lay on his stomach, one arm crooked above his head, a white T-shirt taut across his back. One bare leg protruded from under the sheet, as sturdy and muscular as the rest of him.

For the first time, words alone felt inadequate to describe the sight before her. If only she were an artist, so she could sculpt him in bronze.

His breathing became jerky, and his eyelids twitched. Was he dreaming? Now his cheek twitched, his fingers, his foot. Suddenly he exhaled, long and low, and his eyes opened.

Before she could look away, his gaze met hers. Dark eyebrows hiked up, and his face fell.

So did Leah's heart. Was this how her biblical namesake felt on her bridal morning when Jacob discovered he'd married a woman he didn't love? *"Behold, it was Leah."*

Clay snuffled and pushed up to sitting, dragging the sheet across his lap. "G'morning."

"Good morning." She kept her voice cheery.

He leaned his head back against the wall. "Had that dream again."

"Just now?"

"So real. Honestly thought when I opened my eyes, I'd see Jesus's face."

Instead he'd seen hers. No wonder he'd been disappointed.

He rubbed his eyes with the heels of his hands, then turned to her. "Say, you look as fresh as a daisy. How long have you been up?"

"About half an hour. When the sun rose."

"Huh. I'm usually a light sleeper." He stroked his jaw. "Reckon I should make myself presentable before church."

It seemed a shame. He looked cute with his hair sticking up and dark stubble accentuating his jawline.

Clay wrapped the sheet around his waist, grabbed his trousers from the clothes rack, and entered the bathroom.

Leah turned pages in her composition book. So many unfinished poems, all in want of a lyrical word or a phrase with the right cadence or a final stanza to complete the thought—including her poem about three dancing muses.

Prickling pain dug in below her collarbone, and she pressed her fingers over the scar and crossed her legs hard. That poem was supposed to remind her of her little sisters—not of the wolf and his bite.

Clay emerged from the bathroom, his hair slicked back, his jaw shaven, and his T-shirt tucked into khaki trousers. He looked nice like that too, but so serious.

He plopped onto the foot of the bed. "Reckon I ought to brief you on my family, seeing as how you and my parents will be writing and calling."

They would? How little Leah knew about families and marriage.

Clay leaned his elbows on his knees. "I warn you, it's ugly."

"All right." He didn't realize how many ugly stories she'd heard in the orphanage.

"How much did I tell you about my brother Adler?"

Leah sorted the details. "He's the one who lost his fiancée, right? Then he blamed your brother Wyatt and tried to kill him. You stopped him, and he ran away. You said something about him . . . stealing your girlfriend."

Clay snorted. "I was being polite. It was the night Oralee died. After Dr. Hill and the sheriff took care of matters, we all returned to the house. Adler went outside to cool down, and I went upstairs to change. That's when I discovered Wyatt had stolen my college savings."

"Oh dear. The same day? How horrible."

He strode to the clothes rack and picked up his khaki shirt.

"Then it was my turn to go outside and cool down. I heard noises from the garage, and I found Adler and Ellen together. She was comforting him." He spat out the word *comforting*.

"Oh no." Did he mean what she thought?

Clay shoved one arm into a sleeve. "I've never been so angry. My parents heard us fighting and pulled us apart. Daddy was so disgusted, he told Adler to get out of his sight."

That explained why Adler ran away. "And she—your girlfriend—ran away with him?"

He wrestled on the other sleeve. "If only she had. Would've saved everyone a heaping load of heartache."

"What do you mean?"

Clay leaned back against the wall and stared at the ceiling, his shirt hanging unbuttoned. "He got her pregnant."

"Oh my goodness." Leah clapped her hand over her mouth.

"Her daddy's a physician—Dr. Hill. He was my mentor. He figured it out when she was four months along. They kicked her out and left town. She showed up at my parents' front door, begging them to take her in. And they did."

How kind of them. Leah rested her hand on her belly, understanding Ellen's dismay.

Clay buttoned his shirt. "Everyone in town thought the baby was mine. Rumors were flying."

"That must have been dreadful for you."

He whipped his tie around his neck and entered the bathroom. "I couldn't go to college, couldn't become a physician, had to stay at a job I hated, my girlfriend had betrayed me and was bearing my brother's baby, and everyone thought *I* was the villain."

The poor man. "No wonder you called it the pit."

Clay stopped knotting his tie and met her gaze. "Yes, the pit. I couldn't live under the same roof as her. I couldn't. So I moved in with Uncle Emilio and Aunt Celia. My parents wanted me to marry Ellen for the baby's sake, but we both refused. She said she loved Adler and insisted he'd come back and do right by her. He didn't, of course."

Sympathy for Ellen welled up, but she didn't voice it.

Clay jerked the knot into place. "The second that baby was born, everyone knew he wasn't mine—white skin, blond hair. No one demonized me anymore. Instead they pitied me."

Leah's sympathy flowed back to Clay where it belonged. "Is that when you were drafted?"

He stepped behind the door for privacy. "I wish. My job protected me from the draft. Boy, was I glad when they ended deferments for men under twenty-three and my number came up."

Now she understood his eagerness to leave home. "Is Ellen still living with your parents?" What had she thought when Clay called after the wedding?

He leaned against the doorjamb, his shirt tucked in, his face softer and sad. "She died a few months after the baby was born. Driving too fast in the rain, went over the embankment into the Guadalupe River."

Leah gasped. "Oh no. The baby?"

"Timmy was home with my parents. Still is. They're raising him."

They were indeed kind. "I can't imagine how difficult that must have been. Thank you for telling me."

"Thanks again for marrying me." He flipped up a sad smile and sat on the end of the bed. "I can't help wondering what might have happened if I'd talked Ellen into marrying me."

If Leah had been his wife in more than name, she would have embraced him. "You wonder if she might have lived?"

He shrugged. "No way of knowing. But you gave me a second chance, a chance to do it right this time. So, thanks."

She smiled into his warm eyes. Kindness ran in a thick vein in the Paxton family. What an honor to be a recipient.

※

In the early afternoon heat, Clay squeezed Leah's arm. "Are you sure you want to do this?"

Leah studied the library façade, once her dream, now her dread. "Yes."

"You don't have to. You'll receive my allotment."

They'd spent all morning on the business side of marriage, changing her name, combining bank accounts, and making her his beneficiary and next of kin.

She set her jaw. "I want to do my part, both for you and for the war effort."

"All right." One corner of his mouth puckered. "If I can, I'll be here at nine thirty to walk you to the bus stop. If not—"

"I know. Leave when the library closes and only with an MP escort." While she had still been in the hospital, Clay had talked to Miss Mayhew about having a night guard. Since the wolf hadn't been snared, Leah didn't argue. She fought off a shudder.

"Are you—"

"Absolutely sure." She injected her voice with conviction. "You'd better report for duty."

"Yes, ma'am." Clay gave her a sharp salute. "I'll see you later."

She waved good-bye and headed toward the library.

While Clay remained in Tennessee, they needed to act like newly-weds. The lack of a good-bye kiss was appropriate on base, and his training schedule and her evening shifts would justify the lack of time together. Clay planned to put in frequent requests for leave, as a new husband would, and they might need to spend another weekend or two at the King Hotel for appearance's sake.

Leah wouldn't mind. After the initial awkwardness, their time together had been enjoyable and comfortable.

The door flew open, and Leah startled. How long had she paused on the threshold?

"Pardon me, miss." A straw-haired soldier grinned at her and trotted down the stairs.

Not the wolf. Leah straightened her sage green suit jacket, entered the library, and inhaled.

Musk and onions and beer.

Her heart raced, and she slammed her eyes shut. No. She was safe. Safe. She breathed deeply until all she could smell was ink and ideas and imagination.

Bright lights banished the shadows, and she turned to the circulation desk. She angled her body so she couldn't see the storage room, but her peripheral vision revealed the door was shut.

Thank goodness. Would she ever be able to enter that room again?

Her upper lip tingled, but she smiled for the librarian at the typewriter behind the desk. "Good afternoon, Miss Mayhew."

The pretty brunette beamed at her. "I'm glad you're back, Miss Jones. Are you feeling well?"

"I am." Her fingers coiled around her purse strap. "Only my name isn't Miss Jones anymore, but Mrs. Paxton."

Miss Mayhew's wrists drooped on the typewriter keys. "Mrs. . . . ?"

"Paxton. Mrs. Clay Paxton." Her smile rose from the pleasure of bearing such a fine name. "The man who rescued me."

"You . . . got married?"

"Yes, on Saturday."

The librarian swiveled her chair, leaned her elbows on the desk, and massaged her temples. "You've been here less than two months, more than half that time in the hospital, and now you're married."

Leah winced. "Yes, ma'am."

"I thought you wanted to go to library school."

Grief swamped her, but she had to pretend she didn't know she was pregnant and that her dream remained. "I do."

Round and round went graceful fingers beside high cheekbones. "I never knew one married girl who graduated from library school. They had husbands to care for, then babies. They all dropped out. You should have thought this through more carefully."

Leah had thought this through with exceptional care. She lifted a flimsy smile. "It all happened so fast."

Miss Mayhew slipped cards inside pockets of new books, and she stacked the books with noise unsuited for a library.

Leah's shoulders clenched. If she reacted like this to marriage, how would she react to pregnancy? Would she fire her on the spot? Leah had so little time to earn money, so little time to search the library for clues about her past.

"You might as well get to work. These have been cataloged and are ready to be shelved." Miss Mayhew stood and passed the stack of books to Leah.

Pain wrenched through her shoulder and chest. She cried out, and the books tumbled. Loud thumps fired through the library. Chairs scraped over wood, and dozens of soldiers stood and stared.

Leah pressed her hands over the fire in her chest where she'd been stabbed. In this building. Only a month ago.

"Oh my stars. Miss Jones!" Miss Mayhew rushed from behind the desk. "I mean, Mrs. Paxton. Are you all right?"

Leah fought to catch her breath. "I guess I can't carry that much weight yet."

"Here. Have a seat." Miss Mayhew guided her to a chair. "I'm so sorry. What was I thinking?"

"I'm fine." Leah did her best to smile. "You were thinking I meant what I said, that I was ready to work."

"Thoughtless of me." She bustled behind the desk and pushed out the cart. "Use this and only when you're ready. Please sit as long as you need."

"Thank you." She kept pressure on the wound as Clay had done that night.

Miss Mayhew knelt and picked up the books, straightening pages and closing covers. "I was rude and thoughtless. I didn't stop to think what you'd been through."

"It's all right."

"No, it's not. Why, I didn't even congratulate you. How rude. And I'm very happy for you. You married a good man."

The pain dulled, and Leah lowered her hands. "I did."

14

CAMP FORREST
FRIDAY, SEPTEMBER 3, 1943

Clay stood at attention at the foot of his cot, his gaze fixed on the bare wooden barracks wall above Manfred Brady's head. With all the turnover, Brady and Frank Lyons had been transferred into Clay's platoon, to the other squad in his section. Even if Clay didn't like those two, he had to admit they were good Rangers.

The men's uniforms and gear lay in order on their cots for their final inspection at Camp Forrest. Tomorrow evening, the 2nd Ranger Battalion would board a train for the Scouts and Raiders School in Fort Pierce, Florida, to train in amphibious assault. Clay's fingers curled in anticipation.

Lieutenant Taylor strode down the aisle. "Listen up, men. Major Rudder has issued twenty-four-hour passes."

Someone whooped, but Clay didn't even stir.

"Those can be revoked. Understood?"

"Yes, sir!" Clay shouted with the rest of his platoon.

"Report back at 0800 tomorrow. Everyone is dismissed except Paxton. Paxton, come here."

What? He hadn't whooped. Clay marched down the aisle, past

G. M.'s sympathetic gaze, past his buddies packing and making plans involving liquor and women.

He stood at attention before the lieutenant, but his gut squirmed. Lately he'd fought hard. What had gone wrong?

"At ease."

Clay clasped his hands at the small of his back.

Cool gray eyes assessed him. "This is your last chance to change your mind about becoming a medic. You have a wife to think about. Being a medic would be safer."

Would it? Medics went into combat with the infantry. He'd even heard of enemy snipers aiming for the red crosses on medics' helmets. "Sir, my wife supports my decision. Besides, Major Rudder has a wife, and children to boot. He's not a medic."

"We could really use you."

They could assign him to that duty, and yet they hadn't. "Sir, if I haven't failed in my training, please don't ask me again."

Taylor sighed. "A waste of a fine mind."

Clay tapped his wristwatch and lifted half a smile. "If it's fine with you, sir, I'd like to say good-bye to my wife."

Lieutenant Taylor chuckled. "Dismissed."

Clay hustled back to his cot to pack. Finally, he'd silenced that threat to his dream.

TULLAHOMA
SATURDAY, SEPTEMBER 4, 1943

Rain pelted the umbrella Clay held over Leah's head. Dawn lightened the sidewalk as he hurried her from the King Hotel to her boardinghouse. "We're set. Our paperwork is complete, and you have my parents' address and my APO address. The Army Post Office can find me anywhere."

"All set." Leah's voice sounded small, or was it merely lost in the rain?

Over the past month of marriage, she'd become like a sister. "I know you don't want to show too soon, but eat a nutritious diet. And I know you want to help with the finances, but listen when your doctor tells you to quit your job, you hear?"

She gave him a teasing smile. "Yes, Dr. Paxton."

He chuckled. With her, he was free to talk about medical matters. With her, he was free to talk about anything. He'd miss that.

Since his letters would be censored by Lieutenant Taylor and hers might not be private, they wouldn't discuss her pregnancy until she made her announcement when she was four months along—three months along if Clay had been the actual father.

Clay turned up the walkway to her boardinghouse. A golden glow came from a few windows in the two-story white home. Under the eaves, he shook out the umbrella and set it to dry on the porch.

Leah smiled at him in her khaki raincoat and the hat she'd worn at the wedding. "Well, you're off to have adventures in exciting new places."

"I am." He glanced pointedly at her flat abdomen. "You'll have some adventures too."

She lowered her chin. "My adventures will be much quieter than yours."

What should he say? A simple good-bye didn't seem adequate, but a drawn-out departure didn't seem fitting.

Leah turned up her face to him with the barest smile.

Something shifted inside him. He'd never see her again.

He'd never see that smile again or those eyes. In the book of Genesis, Leah was described as "tender eyed." The phrase conveyed weakness, but the Leah standing before him wasn't weak. Vulnerable, but not weak. And tender. Very tender.

He was staring. Clay cleared his throat. "Reckon I ought to get back to camp before Sergeant Lombardi turns me into pumpkin pie."

Her smile deepened. "Good-bye, Clay. I'll write often, and I'll pray even more often."

"Thank you. I will too. Good-bye."

All he could think about was the wedding kiss, the awkwardness and sweetness. If he kissed her now, it wouldn't be awkward. It would be an appropriate farewell. It would be sweet.

And it wouldn't be wise. Neither one of them could afford a stronger attachment.

Instead he held out his arms and gave her a sheepish smile. A husband would embrace a wife, and a brother would embrace a sister.

She took a half step, and he closed the gap and wrapped his arms around her. My, she was tiny, only up to his chin and not much to her.

Her arms inched around his back. "Be careful, Clay. I know you have an important job, but please be careful."

"You be careful too. Don't go anywhere alone, night or day, especially on base."

A shaky laugh fluttered against his raincoat. "I don't think that's entirely possible."

His fingers curled around the belt of her coat. If only he could stay and keep her safe forever.

A sigh escaped. He'd done what he could. He'd leave her in the Lord's capable hands.

Clay planted a quick kiss on her cheek. Not quick enough. He still noticed the softness, the smoothness, and the scent of hotel soap.

He stepped back. "It was an honor knowing you, Leah Paxton."

She ducked her chin and turned for the door. "And . . . and you too."

Clay turned up the collar of his raincoat, pulled the bill of his service cap lower, and headed into the rain. He had a dream to fulfill, and he had to do that alone.

SUNDAY, SEPTEMBER 5, 1943

Leah let excess batter drip off the chicken drumsticks.

Rita Sue Bellamy nudged her. "Slather it on nice and thick. You're in the South now."

Leah dunked the drumsticks. "So many eggs."

"They aren't rationed, and we have chickens out back."

Would she ever become accustomed to plenty? Leah plopped the heavy-laden drumsticks into the sizzling oil in Rita Sue's cast-iron pan.

The Bellamy children bustled around the kitchen, lit by an electric lamp to counteract the gloom of the rainy day. Nine-year-old Joey cut out biscuits, seven-year-old Luella shucked peas, and six-year-old Sally set silverware on the dining room table.

Rita Sue adjusted the ties on her apron. "You did fine work cutting up that chicken."

"Everyone helped in the orphanage, and I help Mrs. Perry in the boardinghouse."

"When Clay comes home, he'll be pleased to find a good cook waiting for him."

Leah dipped chicken wings in the batter. "I hope so." But he'd never come home, and she'd never cook for him. Clay's premonition of his own death strained within her, but she'd promised not to tell anyone.

Where was he now? Had he arrived in Florida? That was so far away.

She could still feel his arms around her, engulfing her in security.

"I think those wings are ready."

Leah almost dropped them. "Oh."

Rita Sue patted her shoulder. "Don't give in to fear, sugar."

"I won't." She didn't have to look far to find the good. "I'm proud of him. He told me how well the Rangers did in North Africa and Sicily, and now he'll do his part."

"Excuse me, Mama." Joey held the biscuit pan.

Rita Sue opened the oven door. "Here you go, baby boy."

"Mama . . ." Joey slid the pan into the oven.

"I won't be able to call you that much longer." She tousled his curly blond hair.

"You shouldn't call me that *now*." Joey laughed and wiggled free.

Rita Sue frowned toward the dining room. "Girls!"

Leah followed her gaze to where the two little girls bickered by the table.

"She's bossing me!" Sally called.

Luella stamped her foot. "She isn't doing it right."

"Luella, let her be and bring me those peas."

The girl stuck her tongue out at her sister and stomped into the kitchen. "She always gets her way 'cause she's the baby."

Rita Sue turned to Leah, rolled her eyes, and stuck out her tongue.

Leah smothered a laugh. She wanted to soak in every detail of family life. In only seven months, she'd create a home for baby Helen. How could she be a good mother when she barely remembered her own?

After Rita Sue put the peas on to boil, she pushed aside the white ruffled curtains over the sink. "Oh, that sweet husband of mine. I thought he was reading."

Leah peeked through the window and the pouring rain. In the backyard, Mercer hammered in the doorway of a little house with tar paper on the walls.

Rita Sue opened the back door. Rain angled through, and she shut it a bit. "Mercer, put down that hammer and get out of the rain, you hear? It's the Sabbath day."

"Ah, it's not work if I enjoy it," he shouted back.

"Come wash up. Dinner will be ready in five minutes." Rita Sue shut the door, wiped her hands on her apron, and grinned at Leah. "Fifteen minutes, but he doesn't have to know that."

Leah smiled and turned over the drumsticks. "What's he fixing?"

"He's building a rental house." Rita Sue pulled platters and bowls from the cupboard. "Mercer works in the bank all week, so he likes to work with his hands when he can. We have plenty of space out back, and there's a serious housing shortage in town."

"That's nice of you."

"The house is turning out cute—one bedroom, a kitchen and bath, perfect for . . ." A smile spread across her face, and she planted a hand on her hip. "Perfect for you."

"Me?"

"You can't stay in the boardinghouse much longer."

Leah gave her a warning look. Rita Sue had promised not to tell even her family about the pregnancy. "In a few months I'll ask Mrs. Perry for a private room."

"Trust me." Rita Sue lowered her voice. "You'll want space and privacy."

Leah carried the pan of peas to the sink, tipped the lid just inside the rim, and drained pale green water. She'd never had privacy in her life.

"It's perfect. It'll be ready in a month or two, and we'll only ask seven dollars a week."

Seven. Leah poured the peas into a serving bowl. After the baby was born, Clay's allotment would rise, but she'd lose her library earnings. "I . . . I'll ask Clay."

Rita Sue piled fried chicken on a platter. "Wouldn't it be fun to be neighbors?"

"It would." But Leah wanted to find a cheaper option.

Mercer walked into the kitchen. "Where's this fine chicken dinner you promised?"

Rita Sue passed him with the platter and smacked a kiss on his lips. "Coming right up. Children! Dinner's ready!"

Leah took off her apron, brought out the peas, and sat across from Rita Sue.

At the head of the table, Mercer said grace, then loaded plates. "So, you kids go back to school on Tuesday."

"Hurray!" Joey said. "Mrs. Carruthers lets the kids act out the Battle of Chattanooga."

Luella made a face. "I don't want to go back."

Sally pulled on Leah's sleeve. "I get to start first gwade."

"How exciting," Leah said.

"What are you going to do with all your free time, darlin'?" Mercer winked at his wife.

She laughed. "Finally clean the last of the mud pie off my kitchen floor."

The girls giggled.

"And may I have the truck on Tuesday, Mercer?" Rita Sue passed a plate to Luella.

"Sure. Picking up more books?"

"Books?" Leah asked.

"For the Victory Book Campaign." Rita Sue laid her napkin in her lap. "The Red Cross collects the books in bins around town and brings them to the library. They sort them and send them to Nashville. Then the VBC sends the books to our servicemen in training camps and overseas."

It was such an important program. "May I help? I'm free in the morning."

Rita Sue's face brightened. "I'd love that. Why, we'll make a volunteer of you yet."

Wouldn't that be wonderful? Oh, to be on the giving side of charity for once.

15

"Go! Go! Go!" Sgt. Tommy Lombardi yelled.

Clay ran into the surf pushing a black rubber raft with six other Rangers.

"Faster!" Gene shouted in front of Clay, on the left side of the raft. "Gotta beat that breaker."

On the right side, Ernie McKillop stumbled.

Frank Lyons shoved McKillop aside, sending him face first into the water.

Bob Holman cussed at Lyons, and both men lost hold.

"Watch out!" Clay fought the raft.

The wave raced toward them, and Clay braced himself, thigh deep in the ocean. The wave broke against his head and shoulders, and he hopped along to keep his footing.

The raft broached, and Clay and the others washed like flotsam onto the white sand.

Their Navy instructor sneered at them, hands on hips. "Bunch of landlubbers."

Clay dragged the raft onto the beach, then collapsed onto his backside.

Holman marched up to Lyons. "That was cold, even for you."

Not even a spark in Lyons's dark eyes. "He was in the way."

Lombardi held up both hands. "You have to work together. This isn't the assault phase of the exercise. If a man goes down, wait and try again."

Clay shook his head at Lyons and snugged his billed fatigue cap lower to keep the hot sun out of his eyes. Even if a man went down in combat, you didn't shove him out of the way.

The blue Atlantic spread before him, tinged pink from a jellyfish invasion.

The day before, the 2nd Ranger Battalion had arrived at the Scouts and Raiders School and had set up camp at the joint Army and Navy facility. Today they'd started training. They were supposed to complete the thirteen-day course in eight days, but not at their current rate.

No one knew where the Rangers would be sent, but they had to be versatile, whether for commando raids or as the spearhead of an invasion force. That meant they had to know how to make amphibious assaults.

Clay swatted away nibbling sandflies and got to his feet. "Come on, y'all. This time we'll get it."

The Rangers assembled around the raft, shaped like a fat bullet.

Sergeant Lombardi held on to the stern. "Go on G. M.'s orders."

Clay helped maneuver the raft. "That's right, y'all. Listen to G. M. He grew up playing on the Hollywood beaches."

"Santa Monica." Gene's blue eyes almost disappeared in his sunburnt face. "Hollywood doesn't have a beach, numbskull."

"Same thing." Clay grinned at his buddy.

Gene studied the Atlantic. "Now! Go!"

Clay plunged into the foamy edge of the ocean. The raft rode up a swell then down the far side.

"Get in," Gene shouted.

Gene and McKillop hopped in from opposite sides, then Clay and Lyons, then Ruby and Holman, with Lombardi climbing in at the rear.

Clay straddled the tubular rim, grabbed the paddle, and dug into the warm water. The raft climbed another swell, tipped with white, and down they slid on the other side.

Gene whooped. "We made it. Head for the buoy."

"That's it, fellows," Lombardi said. "You've got to be as close as brothers."

Clay gritted his teeth and sliced the water with his paddle. Nothing close about the Paxton brothers. Wyatt and Adler still found ways to hurt him, even in their absence.

A letter from Daddy and Mama had arrived the day he left Camp Forrest. They'd received Clay and Leah's wedding portrait and were enthralled with their daughter-in-law. And they longed for the older sons' return so the family could be whole again.

They would welcome Wyatt and Adler just like that? They'd ignore theft and fornication and betrayal and how the men had ruined Clay's life?

Wyatt and Adler had never even apologized. Not one word in over two years, and they were forgiven, no questions asked. That felt like yet another betrayal.

Rubenstein yelped and rubbed at his leg.

McKillop cussed. "Stupid jellyfish."

Sure enough, stinging rose on Clay's left leg, and his muscles jerked in response. The tiny pink jellyfish worked their way up trouser legs and stung like crazy. "When we get back to shore, rub your legs with sand to get the nettles out."

"Yes, doc," the men said in unison.

Clay winced. Why couldn't he keep his mouth shut? He didn't

want the boys to know he'd almost gone to college. He just wanted to fit in. And he didn't want the questions.

The Rangers navigated around the buoy and aimed for shore. The stinging increased, dozens of tiny pinging, burning pains all over his lower leg.

Stung as much as his parents' words. They forgave so lightly, so easily.

Clay squinted into the sun and frowned at the flat green Florida shore. He thought he'd forgiven his brothers, but what did it really mean to forgive?

Was he supposed to forget everything they'd done? Was he supposed to say it didn't matter that they'd stolen his future? To say he didn't mind?

But it did matter and he did mind.

Clay dug the paddle into the water, over and over. *How? How am I supposed to forgive, Lord? What do you want me to do?*

Couldn't talk to the fellows about it. Last thing he wanted was pity.

Leah.

His paddling paused, and he reminded himself to keep pace.

He had to write her anyway so everyone would think they were madly in love. He'd planned to write short letters about his activities and the scenery. Nothing personal.

But Leah knew his history, she understood, and she had the baffling ability to forgive the unforgivable—abandonment, rape, attempted murder. She'd suffered more than he had, but she didn't live in bitterness and resentment.

I do.

Clay groaned and attacked the waves. Resentment was a sign that his forgiveness stopped at the surface. Somehow he had to let it penetrate his soul.

TULLAHOMA, TENNESSEE
TUESDAY, SEPTEMBER 7, 1943

Carrying only four books, Leah held open the door to the Tullahoma Public Library for Rita Sue and her box of books. "I wish I could carry more."

Rita Sue leaned close, her hazel eyes sharp. "You're in your first trimester. No heavy loads."

"Yes, ma'am." Leah followed Rita Sue inside.

She'd visited before on several occasions. The library was the smallest Leah had ever seen, but its rich perfume offered Leah some hope in her search for her sisters.

A tall, large-boned woman approached wearing a tan suit. Hair like polished pewter wreathed her angular face, and a warm smile bestowed the beauty denied her by nature. "Good morning, Mrs. Bellamy. And . . . we haven't met, young lady, but I've seen you in the stacks."

Rita Sue headed toward a side room. "Mrs. Sheridan, may I introduce Mrs. Clay Paxton. She's a librarian at Camp Forrest. Mrs. Paxton, Mrs. Sheridan is our town librarian."

"Oh, you're Myra's new girl. She was so excited. I haven't talked to her since you arrived."

Leah's smile wavered. Mrs. Sheridan had missed the gossip. "I'm thankful for my job."

Rita Sue set down her box among stacks of books and boxes. "As a librarian, Mrs. Paxton might be able to help with your biggest problem."

Mrs. Sheridan clapped her hands together. "The Victory Book Campaign."

"So many books." Leah set hers down on a long table.

"They've been piling up since May." Mrs. Sheridan swept her hand around the crowded room. "That's when the Army and Navy announced they'd no longer accept VBC books."

Leah frowned. "Why don't they want them?"

"A third of the books are unsuitable. Folks donate books like this." Mrs. Sheridan held up a battered book with only one cover.

"Or this encyclopedia set." Rita Sue set her hand on a stack.

"Some sweet lady thought our servicemen would want to read the Bobbsey Twins, bless her heart." Mrs. Sheridan cocked one eyebrow. "Also, hardbacks are heavy—expensive to ship and burdensome for our boys to carry in battle."

Leah remembered an article she'd read in the newspaper. "That's why they're publishing the Armed Services Editions."

"Yes. Titles our servicemen want to read, in thin paperbacks designed to fit in a back pocket."

Leah brushed her hand over *The Bobbsey Twins at the Seashore.* "What will you do with these?"

"We're awaiting word from VBC headquarters. Our poor little library is already packed to the rafters, so we don't have room. Most likely we'll donate them to the scrap paper drive."

"Scrap!" Leah clutched the sweet story. "Can't we find them a home?"

Mrs. Sheridan and Rita Sue exchanged a knowing smile, which they turned to Leah. "How would you like a project?" Mrs. Sheridan said.

"Oh yes." Ideas raced through her head. "Miss Mayhew is always complaining about her acquisitions budget."

"While we're waiting for word from New York, why don't you sort the books and ask Miss Mayhew? If the VBC grants permission, we'll enrich the camp's library."

"I'll ask her today, and I can start sorting right now. I don't have to go home for lunch for another hour." Leah bent to pick up a box.

"Let me," Rita Sue said in a dark tone.

"Yes, ma'am." Lifting only four books at a time made her feel like an invalid again, but she wouldn't do anything to endanger her baby.

Rita Sue set the box on the table, then wiggled her fingers at Leah. "See you later, sugar."

"I'll leave you to your work," Mrs. Sheridan said. "Holler if you need me."

"I will, ma'am." Leah unloaded the first box and sorted it. Questions arose to ask Miss Mayhew, and Leah pulled her composition book and pen out of her purse.

So many titles she'd never seen before. Could any of them hold clues to her past?

A book about Mexico, and Leah flipped through. Clay's heritage—so colorful and festive. For a wedding gift, Mr. and Mrs. Paxton had sent Leah a generous check and a length of intricate lace that had belonged to Mrs. Paxton's grandmother.

The most beautiful thing Leah had ever owned.

Except Clay's heritage didn't belong to her. If he died, Leah would return the lace. Or if he divorced her.

She shuddered and picked up four books from a box on the floor. On top lay *Heidi*.

"My dear friend." The dust jacket was tattered around the edges, but inside—oh, Johanna Spyri's enchanting story and Jessie Willcox Smith's wondrous colored illustrations of Heidi's Alpine home.

No children frequented the camp library, so the novel belonged in the discard pile.

Leah hugged the book. How could she abandon a friend so dear? A friend who'd offered solace and inspiration when she was sick and alone and abandoned?

She peeked into the reading room. The clock read 11:44—how time had flown. She caught the librarian's eye. "Mrs. Sheridan? I'm going home now. I'll come by next Monday morning, maybe before."

"Thank you for your help."

Leah grabbed her purse and the book and darted out of the

library. Since the book was slated for destruction, no one could call it stealing.

At the end of the block, Leah admired her new old friend in the warm sunshine. Other than her Bible, this was the first book she could call her own.

16

Clay paddled toward shore over waves sparkling with moonlight. The rubber raft rose and fell, but after a week, most of the Rangers had overcome their seasickness.

At the stern of the raft, Lt. Bill Taylor peered through field glasses. "The blinking yellow light is straight ahead."

Along the shore of lengthy Hutchinson Island, which paralleled the eastern Florida coast, colored lights flashed, some steady and some blinking, each signaling to one of the Rangers' six assault companies or the headquarters company.

Tonight was the 2nd Battalion's final examination at the Scouts and Raiders School.

Clay shot a grin behind him at Gene, his friend's face barely recognizable behind green and black camouflage paint. Tonight was going to be fun. Despite the jellyfish, sandflies, and mosquitos, his time in Florida had been great—full of adventure and learning useful skills.

In "Plan Surfboard," they were to assault the town of Fort Pierce and take it. The shore was guarded by Coast Guard patrolmen with dogs, Navy sentries, and Civil Defense wardens—who had been alerted for the exercise.

This would make a great story to tell Leah.

Clay had just received his first letter from her, written in fancy cursive. She'd included a poem she'd written. He didn't know she wrote poetry, but then he hadn't known her long.

In third grade, she'd read a book about Greek mythology and learned her namesake, Thalia, was the muse of idyllic poetry. So she tried her hand at poetry and loved it. In her letter she'd said, "Words make delightful playthings. They cost nothing, they never wear out, and no one can ever take them away from you."

She certainly had a refreshing way of looking at things.

"I'm glad you're going in first, Pax," Sid Rubenstein said from the back of the boat. "You've got a death wish."

"Nah." But he joined in the chuckling. A few days ago, his squad had been ordered to land their raft on a rock jetty in rough seas. While the other men waffled, Clay had just leaped onto the nearest rock.

It wasn't that he wanted to die, but since he knew how he *was* going to die, he also knew how he *wasn't*. And it wouldn't be in a training accident. That washed away fear.

"Yeah, Pax," McKillop said. "You go first and take the bullets for the rest of us."

Someday, but not today. "Don't worry, McKillop. I'll fend off those little old ladies with rolling pins for you."

"Watch out, Fort Pierce," Holman said. "Paxton's Latin blood is boiling tonight."

"Silence, boys," Lieutenant Taylor said. "We're getting close."

Clay aimed for that yellow light. Holman didn't know what he was talking about. Sure, Clay had gotten in a few scrapes when he was little. But by second grade, he'd realized that in fights with white boys, Clay was always to blame. In fights with Mexican boys, Clay was never to blame. That's when he'd decided to back out of scrapes.

The only time he'd fought as an adult had been against Leah's attacker, and that was to protect, not in hot blood.

The sound of the breakers increased, and palm trees whished in the cool breeze.

Another scene blinked in his head, as persistent as the yellow light on shore. Adler and Ellen in a knot of pale flesh, the stink of booze heavy in the air.

Clay's blood had boiled that night. He'd kicked and pummeled his brother, over and over, while Ellen scrambled under the truck, screaming her lungs out.

Thank goodness she'd screamed.

At some point, Clay had lost his balance and caught himself on Daddy's workbench. His hand had landed on a tire iron, and he'd hoisted it overhead.

In that moment, he'd wanted Adler to hurt. In that moment, he hadn't been innocent Joseph cast into a pit. No, in that moment, he'd been Joseph's brothers, thirsting for vengeance.

Sweat tingled on Clay's upper lip and his breath came hard, and not from the exertion of paddling.

Two sharp vibrations in the raft—Lieutenant Taylor's signal to catch the next swell.

Clay shook off the memory and paddled with all he had. When the wave washed toward shore, he dropped his paddle into the boat and took his M1 Garand rifle off his back.

Rubber scraped on sand, and Clay scrambled out of the raft, swinging his rifle in an arc. No sign of patrolmen.

The other men hopped out, picked up the raft by the handles, and ran inland. At the tree line, the lieutenant joined Clay in the lead.

Clay scouted the best path through the palms and pines, avoiding the sharp palmettos that could rip a hole in the boat—and would infuriate the Navy men at the school.

On the far side of the narrow island, Clay pressed up to a palm tree. Only the sounds of the lapping waves and the distant town greeted him.

He poked his rifle and his head to the right of the tree. All clear on the beach, so he stepped out onto the sand and peered back at the trees to check for hidden patrols. Looked good.

Clay motioned the squad forward.

The men quietly carried the raft to the water's edge and launched it.

The squad paddled across the Indian River, the long sound that separated Hutchinson Island from the mainland. The blacked-out town of Fort Pierce lay ahead. Tonight the town was meant to be a German submarine base, and each company had different objectives to take.

If only Clay could engage in conversation to distract him. But his mind latched on to that night in the garage. Usually his memories stopped at his discovery of the traitorous pair.

Not the fight. Not the tire iron.

If Ellen's screams hadn't brought out Daddy and Mama, Clay would have used that tire iron. What if he'd hit Adler on the head? What if he'd died? Clay would have committed murder.

He tried to calm his breath as he scooped saltwater over and over.

Daddy had wrestled Clay back. Clay would have overpowered his father and resumed his attack on his brother if not for Mama.

Sweet Mama shoving a shotgun into Clay's chest, tears streaming down her face. *"If you kill him, you'll go to the electric chair. I'd rather shoot my own son than see that happen. I won't lose both of you."*

Clay squirmed in his damp fatigues, and his heart wrenched. He'd been gravely wronged that day, but he'd also committed a grave wrong.

"Dear Lord," he whispered, then silenced himself. *Lord, I'm guilty too. Forgive me for hurting my brother, for wanting him to die.*

His chest folded in on itself. Did Adler feel the same swamping guilt when he contemplated his sins? Did Wyatt? Because it felt awful.

Several pats on his side of the raft. He was paddling too hard, and he slowed down. He had to set aside his turmoil and focus on the mission.

A pier came into view, and they paddled the raft up onto land to the left of the pier.

Clay checked for patrols while the squad stashed the raft among bushes.

Everything looked as it did on the map in briefing. City Hall lay about five blocks away by a zigzag path.

Taylor knifed his hand west, and the Rangers ran. As scout, Clay led, with the lieutenant behind him. He paused at the corner and peeked around, but the street was deserted, and he only heard a radio playing "Begin the Beguine." The residents probably knew to stay inside when the Scouts and Raiders came to town.

Clay led the men one block north. Motion ahead, and he signaled for the squad to take cover. They pressed into doorways and behind palm trees.

Six dark figures with the unmistakable silhouette of the M1 helmet. "Ours," he whispered.

A few blocks north, another block west, across the railroad tracks, and City Hall rose before them, a two-story Mediterranean-style stucco building with arched windows and a tile roof.

Taylor motioned for a halt. Two men stood at either end of the building with rifles and tin-pan helmets from World War I—Civil Defense.

Taylor tapped his watch and held up two fingers—two minutes.

Then he gestured to Holman, McKillop, and Ruby, and pointed toward the back of the building.

Holman checked his watch and led McKillop and Ruby behind City Hall. After two minutes, they'd attack the sentry at the west end, while Taylor, Clay, and Gene attacked from the east.

They edged closer, low and ready. Clay couldn't help grinning. Those poor wardens were in for a surprise.

Taylor signaled the assault.

Clay burst into running, his rifle raised. The sentry spotted them, startled, and reached for the whistle around his neck.

"Drop it!" Taylor pointed his Thompson submachine gun at the sentry, right up to his chest. "Drop the rifle too."

Shoulders slumped, the middle-aged watchman obeyed and lifted his hands in surrender. Voices and a scuffling sound—the other watchman was disarmed too.

Taylor pointed to the roof.

Gene and Ruby shimmied up palm trees. At the top, they swayed back and forth and jumped to the roof. Then they pointed their rifles out over the street.

McKillop and Holman escorted their prisoner to Taylor.

The lieutenant pulled his handie-talkie radio from the case on his back and pulled out the antenna. "Taylor to Rudder. City Hall secure."

"What have you done with my daughter?" The first sentry's voice warbled.

"Your daughter?" Lieutenant Taylor asked.

The man's face agitated. "She's only seventeen, and one of your men made off with her."

Clay frowned. The Rangers hadn't had an hour free since they arrived.

"Sir, our men haven't set foot in town until tonight," Lieutenant Taylor said. "Can you tell me what happened?"

"Peggy went to the movies with her girlfriends on Saturday night, and she went home alone. Only she never came home."

"Have you reported this to the police?" Taylor slung his Tommy gun over his shoulder.

The man pressed a trembling hand to his forehead, dislodging his helmet. "They think she ran away, but not my Peggy. She'd never do that."

"I'm sorry this happened, sir." Taylor had a soothing voice when he wanted to. "All our men are accounted for, but I'll report the situation to our commanding officer and the commander of the school."

"Thank you." He sagged back against the stucco wall.

Holman and McKillop sauntered away, and Clay followed. Time to form a perimeter.

Shouts rang out around town, and radios squawked. Sounded like the Rangers were taking their military objectives.

"Bet I know what happened to that girl," Holman muttered to McKillop. "One of those sailor boys knocked her up, and she went to 'visit an aunt' for nine months."

Clay stopped in his tracks. How could he talk about a girl in such a callous way? A girl like Leah. Had this Peggy found herself in a predicament like Leah's, with disgrace or exile as her only choices?

Clay breathed out a prayer for Peggy and her family, and another prayer of thanks that God had let him help Leah.

17

Rita Sue drove her pickup truck down Forrest Boulevard into camp. "Any news from Clay?"

"Just yesterday." Leah ran a finger under the waistband of her skirt. Tonight she'd let it out another inch. Thank goodness she wasn't showing yet. "His battalion left Florida. The school said they were the best unit they'd ever had. In the final exercise they took Fort Pierce by storm."

Leah didn't mention how the Rangers had taken Fort Pierce by storm the following evening on leave—a night of drunkenness and brawling. The entire battalion had been confined to quarters for the rest of their stay, even those who had behaved, like Clay and G. M.

"Where's he going next?" Rita Sue waved a jeep through at the intersection.

"Fort Dix in New Jersey for advanced tactical training." She spoke slowly to get the term correct. "He's excited about it."

"I'm glad he's doing well." Rita Sue pulled the truck in front of the library, stepped out, and flagged down a trio of soldiers. "Excuse me, gentlemen. Could y'all lend us a hand, please? We could use a few pairs of strong arms."

The soldiers brightened. "Sure, ma'am."

"Thank you. Please carry these boxes inside for Mrs. Paxton."

Leah gave them an awkward smile, feeling inappropriately empty-handed. Even though she was three months along in her pregnancy, the time most ladies made their announcements, Leah had to wait another month.

She waved good-bye to Rita Sue and held the door open for the men. "Thank you, gentlemen. Please set them on the circulation desk."

Miss Mayhew approached from the card catalog. "Oh my! Isn't this wonderful?"

Leah thanked the soldiers and opened the first box. "I'm only partway through the Victory Book Campaign collection. More will be coming."

"I'll take anything I can. The Army prefers the Armed Services Editions, but those only go to the troops overseas. Here in the States, we've depended on the VBC to supplement our purchases. But the Army cut that off."

Leah stacked books on the desk. "Such a shame."

Miss Mayhew inspected a copy of William L. Shirer's *Berlin Diary*. "Has the library in town decided what to do with the books we don't want? It's criminal to scrap them."

"We received permission to do with them as we please. I'm determined to find good homes for them."

Miss Mayhew rested one hand on the desk and the other on her hip, her blue eyes narrowed at the unfinished ceiling. "You said there are quite a few children's books. How about the school libraries?"

"I talked to them last week. They already carry most of the books we have. Except the Davidson Academy said they never have enough."

"That's the school for colored children, isn't it?" Miss Mayhew shuddered. "I can't stand the segregation here in the South."

"Me neither. I'm glad we can supplement their library. However, there are still lots of books they don't want either." Leah nibbled on her bottom lip. "Do you know if there's an orphanage in the area?"

"I don't know. I've only been in Tullahoma for a year." She frowned at a copy of John Steinbeck's *The Grapes of Wrath*. "Do orphanages have libraries?"

"Mine didn't, but a true home, a good home, should have books. Mine will." Somehow it would. The Bellamy home had a pair of bookshelves flanking the fireplace, with the bottom two shelves bright with children's books. "Where there are books, children read."

"It applies to adults too." Miss Mayhew swept a smile around the bustling library. "Many of these boys only have an eighth-grade education. Even the high school graduates didn't read much after they left school. But here they do. They're bored. They're too tired from training to do sports. So they read."

"And they read a lot." Leah enjoyed her conversations as the men discovered the joy of a good book.

"Your orphanage idea has merit." Miss Mayhew opened a drawer and handed Leah the phone book for Coffee County.

Leah thumbed through, and her heart warmed. Right in Tullahoma, in an area Leah hadn't explored. "Coffee Children's Home, how would you like some books?"

FORT DIX, NEW JERSEY
WEDNESDAY, SEPTEMBER 29, 1943

"Battalion dismissed!" Major Rudder called.

Five hundred Rangers broke formation on the parade grounds at Fort Dix.

Gene peered down the left sleeve of his khaki shirt. "Swell patch."

"Sure is." On his left shoulder, Clay stroked the brand-new patch. Yellow letters on a blue diamond declared "Rangers." Too bad it didn't read "2nd Rangers," since five battalions had now been established. The 1st, 3rd, and 4th Battalions were fighting in Italy, and the 5th Battalion was training back at Camp Forrest.

"Look at us—privates first class." Gene inspected the new silver-on-black chevron on Clay's sleeve. All the privates in the Rangers had been promoted, and Clay wouldn't turn down the extra six dollars a month.

"Say, let's use your swanky new camera." Gene posed, pointing at his sleeve. "Won't our wives be proud?"

"Yeah, let's." When they'd arrived at Fort Dix, Rudder had issued weekend passes. Clay and Gene had visited New York City, and Clay had purchased a Brownie camera.

Leah had his service portrait and the wedding portrait, but he wanted the baby to have more pictures of her daddy.

Clay and Gene joined the stream of men heading to the mess for dinner.

"You heard 'Big Jim,'" Clay said. "We're getting five-day passes. Want to visit Washington, D.C.?"

"Let me guess. A library."

Clay gave his buddy a light punch on that chevron. "Only the Library of Congress itself."

"The foolish things a man does for love."

Clay shrugged. Love had nothing to do with it. "The price of being a married man."

"But oh, the benefits." Gene whistled.

Clay punched him harder in the chevron.

"Hey." Gene rubbed his arm. "I wasn't thinking of *that*. I mean, it's nice to know someone cares about you, supports you, depends on you. Makes you feel good inside."

"Yeah, it does." Marrying Leah had complicated his life—but enriched it.

"Excuse me. Are you Private Paxton?"

Clay faced an officer about his height, Capt. Walter Block. He saluted. Swell. He'd avoided the new battalion surgeon since the man's arrival at Fort Dix. "Yes, sir."

Dr. Block returned his salute, a smile crinkling his friendly face. "Major Rudder wanted me to meet you."

This again? Clay stifled a groan. "Sir, I don't want to be a medic."

The physician laughed. "He also told me you'd say that."

Clay motioned for Gene to go on without him. "Sir—"

"I'm not trying to recruit you. Major Rudder said you have an interest in medicine, and I enjoy meeting people who share my interests."

Rangers passed Clay and Doc Block with quizzical looks. If the fellows learned about his interest in medicine, they'd ask too many questions and bring up too many memories.

"I'm headed to the mess myself." Doc Block gestured down the path. "Must keep up my energy for those marches."

Clay fell in alongside the officer. He had to admire him. He'd been a pediatrician in Chicago before the war and had volunteered for the Rangers. Even though he was forty and medical officers weren't required to participate in the long marches, he did.

"Major Rudder said you'd been accepted into a premed program."

Major Rudder talked too much. "I went into the family business instead. The past is past."

"I understand." The captain strolled between the white clapboard buildings. "I heard you did an exemplary job performing first aid on a woman who was assaulted at Camp Forrest."

Clay's breath caught at the memory of Leah's terrified eyes and gagged mouth. And the monster who hurt her still roamed free. "I—I did my best."

"You saved her life. Do you mind if I ask what you did? Rudder is a football coach. He was no use at all."

Clay hesitated, but clinical interest lit the doctor's eyes, reminding him of his conversations with Dr. Hill in Kerrville. And the crowd had passed by.

126

Using medical terminology, Clay listed Leah's injuries and the procedures he'd performed. Doc Block asked questions and contemplated what had been done during surgery, while Clay shared what he'd read in the text in the library.

It felt like going home to the man he'd once been. How many afternoons had he spent in Dr. Hill's office, observing his mentor in the examination room, discussing patient care, and reading texts? Those had been good days, filled with promise and purpose.

A bittersweet ache formed in his chest over what should have been and would never be.

They reached the enlisted men's mess, and Dr. Block offered his hand—not exactly military protocol. "A pleasure talking to you."

Clay shook his hand. "Thank you, sir. I enjoyed it too."

Dr. Block headed toward the officers' mess. "If you ever want to chat, you know where to find me."

"Thank you, sir." But he didn't plan to.

18

In the town library after closing time, Leah tried not to crumple her sheet of paper. A dozen well-dressed ladies chatted, waiting for the board meeting. Despite Leah's pinned-up curls and her camel-colored suit, she didn't belong.

"You'll do fine." Rita Sue wore a bottle green suit that complemented her light brown hair and hazel eyes. "It's a wonderful idea."

"Good evening, ladies." A woman in her seventies entered the library. Although she was only an inch or two taller than Leah, she carried herself as if she were taller than Mrs. Sheridan. Her gaze landed on Leah, and silver eyebrows rose. "Who have we here?"

Rita Sue gestured to Leah. "Mrs. Channing, I'd like you to meet Mrs. Clay Paxton. She's a librarian at Camp Forrest and a new volunteer."

Leah shook the offered hand. "How do you do, Mrs. Channing."

Eyes of indeterminate color bore into Leah's. "Your name's on the agenda. My, such confidence in one so young. Bless your heart."

Leah had been in town long enough to know "bless your heart" didn't always mean what it said. But she smiled. "Thank you, ma'am."

Mrs. Channing swept past her to the head of the table. "Take your seats, ladies."

Leah leaned close to Rita Sue. "Why is she running the meeting instead of Mrs. Sheridan?"

"She's Mrs. *Channing*," Rita Sue whispered, as if the name alone was the answer.

Channing . . . Come to think of it, Leah had seen the name on several businesses in town.

Over the next half hour, the ladies discussed the budget and maintenance and programs.

Mrs. Channing adjusted her reading glasses. "Next on the agenda, a proposal from Mrs. Paxton."

"Thank you, Mrs. Channing." Leah laid the typewritten sheet before her and read out loud. "As you know, the library has been collecting for the Victory Book Campaign and has accumulated a large quantity of books since May when the Army and Navy stopped accepting donations. Thank you for agreeing to donate books to the Camp Forrest Library. Miss Myra Mayhew sends her heartfelt gratitude, as do our men in uniform."

Murmurs of appreciation circled the room.

Leah took a deep breath to smooth the wrinkles in her voice. "On the first of this month, the American Library Association voted to close the campaign at the end of the year. The first item in my proposal is for the Tullahoma Library to continue to collect books, with appropriate donations to be sent to the Camp Forrest Library."

"The floor is open for discussion," Mrs. Channing said.

"I love the idea," Rita Sue said. "The Red Cross collection bins are already in place. I'm willing to continue collecting the books, and Mrs. Paxton is willing to sort them and bring them to Camp Forrest. We'd only need new signs on the bins."

The proposal passed unanimously.

Leah's heart raced with joy. "The second part of the proposal concerns the books that Camp Forrest does not accept. One-third of the donations are worn out or are not suitable for soldiers. The Victory Book Campaign allows us to scrap such books, but I propose that we find homes for those in good condition. The school librarians are interested in some of the titles. I propose that we donate those titles to the schools, with the remainder to be donated to the Coffee Children's Home."

Mrs. Channing wrinkled her nose. "I'm on the orphanage board. They don't have a library."

Leah smiled at her. "All the more reason to start one."

Mrs. Channing sighed and removed her glasses. "They're orphans, Mrs. Paxton. They come from the basest of backgrounds. Dirty, illiterate hooligans."

Leah pressed back in her seat, the barbs stinging no less for their familiarity. Dirty orphans didn't deserve books, and they didn't belong at meetings with ladies from good homes.

"If there's no further discussion . . ."

"There's further discussion." Rita Sue nudged Leah.

How could she speak up? But if Leah didn't speak up for the orphans, who would? "My parents died when I was four years old. I was raised in an orphanage."

A few gasps.

Something kindled inside Leah. "As a child, I found my home in stories. Good literature teaches children to be resourceful and brave and cheerful and compassionate. Don't we want orphans to learn those lessons so they can become good citizens?"

Ladies nodded around the table.

Not Mrs. Channing. "You are the exception. The orphans here are a filthy, unruly lot. Far better to donate the books to the scrap drive. With such a serious paper shortage, that would be most patriotic."

Some murmurs and more nodding.

Leah couldn't afford to lose this battle. That kindling built in heat. "Hitler burns books."

Every eye turned to her. Mrs. Channing's gaze sliced but didn't penetrate.

Leah's shoulders had never felt straighter. "The slogan of the Victory Book Campaign is 'Books are weapons in the war of ideas.' To destroy a book that would benefit someone else seems most unpatriotic. We must train the next generation, even children who are unwanted—especially children who are unwanted. Arm them in this war of ideas. Give them books."

"Brava, Mrs. Paxton." Mrs. Sheridan clapped her hands together.

"I move that we table this proposal." Twin red dots flamed on Mrs. Channing's pale cheeks. "Next month I expect to see a report on all options for disposal of those books. On to the next item on the agenda."

Rita Sue clasped Leah's hand under the table. "Good job," she whispered.

Was it? The starch dissolved in Leah's spine. Was it right for her, a stranger in town and so young, to speak that way to her elder?

She'd just made an enemy of one of the most influential women in town.

US Army Military Intelligence Training Center
Camp Ritchie, Maryland
Friday, October 22, 1943

On the drill field, the instructor pointed the German machine gun toward hills painted in green and gold and red. "The *Maschinengewehr 42* fires over 1500 rounds per minute."

Clay let out a whistle, as did others in his platoon. The 2nd Ranger Battalion had come to Camp Ritchie in Maryland for two days of instruction at the Military Intelligence Training Center. After an all-night field exercise taking Hill X from German-speaking defenders wearing Nazi uniforms, the Rangers were receiving a speed course in German weaponry.

The instructor spoke with a German accent. Many of the "Ritchie Boys" were Jewish refugees from Germany who wanted to use their knowledge of German language and culture to fight the Nazis.

"This is the first time you will hear this sound, but it will not be the last." The instructor fired the machine gun.

A sound like fabric ripping rent the air and Clay's soul.

Everything blurred around him. It was *not* the first time he'd heard that sound. And it would be the last sound he would ever hear.

At least once a week, he heard it in his recurring dream. He didn't know whether to be impressed at the accurate detail in his dream—or to be stunned with the fresh knowledge that it would come true.

He stared at the hills in the distance until the colors became distinct again and his lungs filled with the crisp, cool air. This would be his last autumn, and he would never experience summer again. Neither would many of the men around him, but only Clay knew it for a fact.

The Rangers lined up to try their hand at the *Maschinengewehr 42*. In combat they might need to use German weapons.

Clay stood at the end of the line so he could compose himself as the ripping sound tore him apart again and again.

Since the dream first appeared, he'd only experienced a peaceful, driven sense of anticipation. Why the sudden melancholy?

Clay crossed his arms in his green herringbone twill fatigues. Was it because he'd soon leave the United States, never to return?

His wedding ring rubbed against his other fingers, and he sighed. No, it was Leah. Before he married her, his only joy had come from pursuing the dream. Now he found joy in giving to her and through their friendly correspondence.

In the process, he'd lost his focus.

But he wouldn't change a thing. The thought of Leah at a mother's home preparing to give away the only person she loved—well, it broke his heart.

Still, he had to be careful. God had sent the dream to assure Clay that his earthly misery was coming to an end, but also so he wouldn't waver when life didn't seem so miserable, so he wouldn't falter when that ripping sound came his way.

Besides, he'd promised Leah he was going to die, and he was a man of his word.

That made him chuckle.

Gene faced him. "What's so funny?"

Clay fished around for something. "Can you imagine me infiltrating behind enemy lines and passing for German?" He lifted his brown hands.

Gene cracked up, then gave a comical Nazi salute. *"Jawohl, Herr Kamerad!"*

The instructor sent Gene a sharp, dark-eyed look. "Do it right, or even your Aryan looks won't save your hide."

He then demonstrated the salute and made the platoon do it until they did it right.

Clay had to be prepared for whatever mission he received.

FORT DIX, NEW JERSEY
MONDAY, OCTOBER 25, 1943

On his cot, Clay set aside his olive drab service jacket, freshly marked with his name. Yet another requirement in the Rangers' "Preparation for Overseas Movement."

"I swear." Bob Holman marked a pair of underwear. "If we have to watch another Army film, I'll shoot the projectionist."

Clay laughed. They'd completed their stateside training. Now they waited. While they waited, Rudder kept them in shape with physical conditioning, marches, and weapons drills.

"Mail call!"

Clay dashed outside with everyone else.

In the street between the wooden-walled eight-man tents, a private stood beside a jeep loaded with bags of mail.

As the man read names, Clay shivered in his fatigues. The tent was warmed by a potbellied stove, but he needed a sweater under his uniform in the New Jersey fall. A lot colder than Texas.

"Paxton!"

Clay grabbed a thick and squishy letter from Leah. "Please," he muttered. They'd agreed she'd officially announce her pregnancy to him about this time, and then she'd announce it in Tullahoma. She was four months along, and soon the pregnancy would announce itself.

He opened the envelope and pulled out two yellow baby booties, and he whooped. "I'm going to be a daddy!"

His buddies gathered around. "Congratulations," . . . "Now you're shackled for good," . . . "Sure you're the dad?"

Clay glared at Frank Lyons and his smirking dark eyes. "Sure, I'm sure."

"Can't believe you beat me." Gene grinned at him. "When is she due?"

Clay skimmed the letter as if he didn't know the agreed-upon due date. "Early May."

"May, April, March . . ." Lyons ticked off the months on his fingers.

"It's nine months, you numbskull," Clay said. "We were married in August."

The congratulations resumed, and the men turned to their letters.

Clay fingered a tiny yellow bootie. For the second time, a woman in his life was bearing a child he hadn't fathered. With Ellen, he'd prayed everyone would realize he wasn't the daddy. With Leah, he prayed everyone would believe he *was* the daddy.

He could still see Ellen in Mama's rocking chair, knitting tiny garments for Timmy. Had she been scared and remorseful behind her phony cheer and her insistence that Adler would return for her?

She'd paid a steep price for her sin. Too steep.

True compassion for the woman he'd once loved filled his soul. *Lord, I forgive her.*

Thank goodness the Lord had let him redeem himself with Leah. She was a true innocent. She deserved nothing but happiness and security from now on.

19

Leah scraped scrambled eggs into Mrs. Perry's serving bowl. "These smell so good."

Mrs. Perry grunted and slid pancakes onto a platter. "You certainly eat your fair share."

Leah winced at her sharp tone. "I guess I'm gaining back my strength."

"That's not all you're gaining." She glanced at Leah's stomach.

That stomach turned. Leah couldn't delay her announcement any longer. Every day for the past week she'd tried to speak but had failed.

She brought the eggs out to the dining room and took her seat between Darlene and Thelma, across from Adelle, Faye, and Verena, all of whom worked at Camp Forrest—from the laundry to the bakery to the mess.

Leah scooped a portion of pancakes and eggs and courage. "I have an announcement."

When everyone looked her way, she forced a smile. "I'm expecting a baby."

Darlene gasped and grabbed Leah's arm. "You are? My heavens! I'm so happy for you."

Leah's smile relaxed. Darlene had been distant lately, and Leah didn't know why.

"I thought so," Mrs. Perry said. "Skinny thing like you mushrooming like that."

"When are you due?" Thelma's sweet smile more than made up for the homely face the other girls mocked.

"The first of May."

Mrs. Perry spread oleo on her pancakes. "Give me two weeks' notice before you move out."

Leah's fingers tightened around her fork. "Is it possible to have a room—"

"No children. That's my rule. I don't want no squalling babies in here."

A long sigh, but Leah concealed it. "Yes, ma'am." She'd look for a new place around the first of the year.

Darlene tossed her napkin onto the table. "Any of y'all have fifty cents I can borrow? I can't find my pay from last week, and I want to see if the beauty shop can squeeze me in this morning."

"I do." Leah pushed back her chair. It felt so good to give rather than receive.

"Stay put, Mama. I saw your purse on your bureau." Darlene trotted upstairs.

As she ate, Leah fielded questions. If only Miss Mayhew would receive Leah's news as enthusiastically this afternoon.

Footsteps thumped downstairs. "Why, you little thief."

Leah whipped around in her chair, and her blood ran cold.

Darlene marched to the dining room, brandishing dollar bills. "My pay! You stole it."

"What? No. I didn't steal—"

"Four five-dollar bills—exactly what I was paid on Friday."

Red-hot anger warped Darlene's features, and she waved the bills in Leah's face.

Leah's breath raced. Just like in the orphanage. Stealing. Accusations. Falsehoods. "I was paid on Friday too. I promise, it's mine. I would never steal from you—from anyone."

"Liar!" Darlene kicked Leah's chair. "You told me yourself—you used to steal from your friends."

Leah ducked her head, her face tingling with coldness. It was all over. "Just little things—things they'd lost. I stopped years ago."

"My mama said never to trust an orphan. I should have listened to her." Darlene stomped her foot. "Mrs. Perry, I will not put up with this."

Mrs. Perry stood, crossed her arms over her ample chest, and glared at Leah. "Two things I don't abide—girls entertaining menfolk upstairs and thieving. Get out."

Leah's chest collapsed. "But I didn't take her money. We all know she always loses things."

"Convenient for you, eh?" Mrs. Perry barked out a laugh. "Should never have rented to a raggedy little good-for-nothing. Get out of my house."

Leah stared. But only Thelma looked sympathetic. The hard expression on her landlady's face and the appalled looks of the other girls said the sentence would never be revoked. "When do you want me to leave?"

"Right this minute. We'll watch you pack, make sure you don't snitch anything else."

Nothing to do but obey. Leah trudged upstairs and pulled the dress shop box from under her bed.

"I'll help." Darlene flung open bureau drawers and dumped the contents on the floor.

Leah winced but kept packing. When girls ganged up in the orphanage, she'd learned to keep her head down, her mouth shut, and to escape quickly. And to never, ever cry.

Thelma knelt in front of her, holding her compact. "Where do you want this?"

The unexpected kindness made Leah's eyes water more than the familiar cruelty. She grabbed her old canvas schoolbag. "In here. Thank you."

Thelma gathered Leah's toiletries into the schoolbag while Leah filled the box with clothes.

Then Leah pinned on her hat, slipped on her raincoat, slung her purse and schoolbag over her shoulder, and picked up her box.

Mrs. Perry stood back from the doorway. "I'll follow you out to watch those sticky fingers of yours."

Somehow Leah's feet made their way downstairs and out onto the porch.

The door slammed behind her.

Rain pelted the sidewalk and made the leaves shiver.

Leah pulled her hood over her hat and arranged her coat around the cardboard box the best she could. With her hands full, she couldn't raise her umbrella.

At the end of the block, she stopped. Where to? She didn't belong anywhere.

Tiny puffs of her breath turned white and floated away. She had nowhere to go. Nowhere.

No matter how bad her life had been, she'd always had a place to sleep. Even when her parents died.

She could still see the terror in her mother's eyes. "Thalia! The babies!"

Leah had fallen, rolled to the curb, pebbles scratching her cheek and hands, the carriage with her twin sisters clattering beside her. A double thump, and a black car screeched to a stop where her parents had stood only a moment earlier. In their last moments, flinging their daughters to safety.

Death had torn her parents from her, but she'd had a roof.

Always a roof. She'd been unwanted and abandoned, but never without a home.

Her chest heaved, and rain splattered her face. She was a good-for-nothing orphan, a godless heathen.

Leah would always hear the word *heathen* in Mrs. Jones's outraged voice, feel the slap across her mouth, see Mr. Jones grabbing the switch. *"I'll teach you not to use that foreign talk in my house."*

"Leah? Leah Paxton?"

She blinked, her eyelashes heavy from the rain.

A pickup truck parked across the street, and Mercer Bellamy peeked out the window. "What are you doing out in the rain?"

She could only shake her head.

"Let me give you a lift. Rita Sue would have my head if I left you in this downpour." He jogged around the truck and opened the passenger door.

Only a lifelong habit of obedience carried her into that truck.

Mercer climbed back in. "Where to?"

Leah stared at the dashboard and shook her head.

"Are you all right?"

No. No, she wasn't.

"I'll take you to Rita Sue." He turned the truck around, drove a few blocks, and parked in front of his house. Then he opened the door for Leah and reached for her box.

"No." Leah clutched it tight and walked to the house.

Mercer passed her and opened the door. "Rita Sue! Leah's here. Something's wrong."

"Leah?" Rita Sue stepped out of the kitchen in a housedress. "What's wrong, sugar?"

"Found her out in the rain." Mercer smacked a kiss on his wife's cheek. "I need to get to the bank."

Rita Sue guided Leah to the kitchen. "What's wrong? Is it the baby? Clay?"

Thank goodness, no. The concern in Rita Sue's hazel eyes loosened her vocal cords. "My landlady kicked me out."

"Because you're pregnant? No." Rita Sue pried the box from Leah and set it on the table. "You didn't tell her Clay isn't the father, did you?"

"No." Leah removed her coat, draped it over one chair, and sat in another.

Rita Sue perched on the edge of the kitchen table beside her. "Couldn't pay your rent?"

Leah grasped the edges of the chair seat. She had to be honest and tell the whole story. "Darlene said I stole her pay—twenty dollars. I didn't, but Mrs. Perry believed her."

Rita Sue frowned. "Why would she believe Darlene over you?"

Leah squeezed her eyes shut until red spots appeared in the blackness behind her eyelids. "I used to steal. I told Darlene about it, and   and she told Mrs. Perry."

"You did?" Rita Sue's voice went tight. "What did you steal?"

Oh no. She'd lose Rita Sue's friendship as well. "In the orphanage we all took extra food whenever we saw it. And—and I stole other things—things children left out in the rain or abandoned or lost. But I haven't stolen anything for years, ma'am. I promise."

Rita Sue let out a long sigh. "That wasn't right."

"I know." Leah pinned her gaze on her former friend. "I know it wasn't right. I stopped and I returned what I could and the Lord forgave me and—"

"No." Rita Sue waved her hand before her face, her glistening eyes. "I meant it wasn't right for them to hold your past against you. I'm so sorry this happened, sugar."

A thickness built in Leah's throat and behind her eyes. Rita Sue believed her? Just like that?

"The rental house won't be ready for another week or two. It's yours and no arguing." Rita Sue sniffled and picked up Leah's box. "We'll put you in the spare room for now."

Leah's head spun at the mercy, and she gripped the seat edge even harder. "I—I won't be able to pay until Friday. Darlene took my money."

Rita Sue snorted and marched to the stairs. "And who's she calling a thief? Come with me, sugar. This week's free. You're our guest."

Leah stood on shaky legs and gathered her coat and schoolbag. "Are you sure?"

"Sure as sure can be." Rita Sue leaned over the banister and beckoned with her chin. "You write that husband of yours and tell him you have a new address, with people who care for you."

Leah followed her friend upstairs, but a swirl of nausea filled her belly. She'd have to tell Clay why she'd moved. She'd have to tell him about Darlene's accusations and Mrs. Perry's verdict and her own past. Never once had she told Clay she used to steal.

She clamped one hand on the banister for balance. Clay had been the victim of theft. What would he think to learn his wife was a thief?

"Lord, no," she whispered. She was preparing to lose him in battle, but to lose his respect and regard as well?

How could she bear it?

20

Clay whistled at the sight of the massive gray ship rising before him. "Y'all can't say the Army isn't good to us. We're taking a cruise on Britain's finest ocean liner."

Behind him in line, Bob Holman snorted. "Something tells me we ain't getting staterooms."

Nope, they'd cram some fifteen thousand troops onto the HMT *Queen Elizabeth*.

Clay stepped forward in line, his M1 steel helmet heavy on his head, his field pack on his back, his rifle on his shoulder, and his duffel bag in hand.

A Red Cross lady stood beside a stack of boxes. "Everyone take a book. There are thirty titles, so you can share on board."

"Thank you, ma'am." Clay took Walter Lippmann's *U.S. Foreign Policy*—one of the new paperback Armed Services Editions.

"I got *The Adventures of Tom Sawyer*," Bob Holman said. "How about you, Ruby?"

"*Hopalong Cassidy Serves a Writ.*"

Something for every taste, and Clay grinned. Wouldn't Leah like to see?

143

An officer stood at the foot of the gangplank with a roster. "Paxton!"

"Clay!" He took a blue card from the officer and headed up the gangplank. The card read "Keep this card. Sleeping quarters: Room M 21." M had to be for the main deck, and the card's color designated their shift for eating at the mess.

The steep gangplank clanged below Clay's feet. They'd spent the past week and a half at Camp Shanks, outside New York City. Since the crack of dawn, they'd been marching and riding in trucks.

Higher and higher, until a sailor admitted them inside and motioned toward the stern of the ship. They jostled down passageways designed for genteel passengers, not grungy Rangers.

Clay opened door M 21. A nicer sign below read "Second-class lounge."

A large room filled floor to ceiling with four-tiered canvas bunks. No room for lounging, that was for sure.

McKillop pointed. "Hey, look! A bar."

"Yeah, like they'd leave us any booze," Holman grumbled.

Clay set his gear on a bunk and slipped on his garrison cap. "Let's explore, y'all."

His squad followed. Soon they'd be restricted to the blue section of the ship at the stern, with other enlisted men in the red section at the bow and officers in the white section amidships.

For some reason, the Rangers had been allowed to board early and had the run of the ship.

Clay climbed a staircase with brass banisters. The ship hadn't been fitted out in her ocean liner finery before the war broke out, but he could imagine how swanky she could have been.

He headed out onto the sundeck, but there was nothing sunny about Manhattan in November.

Under lifeboats suspended from davits, Clay stood at the railing and looked down the river, packed with warships, freighters, and tugboats. Skyscrapers poked toward the clouds, but he couldn't spot the Statue of Liberty.

Gene leaned his elbows on the railing. "Say good-bye to the USA, boys. Next time we see her, the war will be over."

Sid Rubenstein lit a cigarette. "Won't be long, now that the Rangers are coming."

"Reckon the invasion won't come till spring though," Clay said.

McKillop leaned toward Ruby's Zippo lighter and lit his own cigarette. "Hope they send us on raids first, so we can shake up the Jerries and get some licks in."

Raids. Chilly air stilled in Clay's lungs. He'd always pictured dying in a big battle, but what if he died in a raid? That could come long before spring.

If only it could wait until after the baby was born. *Not yet, Lord. Please.*

HMT *Queen Elizabeth*
NORTH ATLANTIC
THURSDAY, NOVEMBER 25, 1943

Clay stood with his rifle at "right shoulder arms" inside a door amidships, guarding the sundeck from any enlisted men foolish enough to venture into officers' country.

The 2nd Ranger Battalion had been allowed aboard first because they had military police duty, which they hated.

Clay's stomach rumbled. The passing officers kept grumbling about the ship's British crew serving pork for Thanksgiving, but Clay was too hungry to care.

The door opened, admitting a blast of freezing North Atlantic air and two naval officers. Clay snapped his rifle vertically in front of him, presenting arms. They saluted but barely met his gaze.

Private First Class Nobody.

An Army officer dashed upstairs, green in the face. No time for protocol. Clay shoved open the door, and the man ran to the rails. They'd been at sea for three days, but seasickness still prevailed.

Not for Clay.

One summer his family had taken a vacation on the Gulf of Mexico. When they went sailing, not one Paxton had gotten seasick. Mama insisted her spicy cooking had toughened their stomachs.

An Army Air Forces officer climbed the stairs wearing an olive drab overcoat and a crushed service cap. The flyboys' military courtesy tended to be as sloppy as their caps, but Clay presented arms smartly.

The officer didn't look him in the eye as required, but he flapped his hand toward his forehead.

Tall, blond, broad shouldered, a familiar set to his chin.

Clay's mouth fell open. It couldn't be.

The man opened the door and stopped short. "Hoo-ey!"

Icy air snaked around Clay and into his soul.

Adler.

No. It couldn't be.

But that voice. The way he pulled on his gloves and turned up his collar. Then he strolled aft, and his profile eliminated all doubt.

Clay's hands coiled around his rifle, and everything inside him burned and ached. That night in the garage, Clay had told Adler if he ever saw him again, he'd kill him.

Now Clay was the one holding a firearm, not Mama.

As soon as the urge rose, it receded, and he shouldered his rifle. He didn't want to kill Adler. He never had. That night he'd just wanted to banish him from home.

Now he just wanted to banish his brother's image from his mind.

"Hiya, Pax. I'm relieving you."

Clay startled.

"Are you all right?" Gene asked. "Thought you never got seasick."

"Just hungry." Clay looped his rifle strap over his shoulder and headed downstairs. Only the black-and-white MP brassard on his arm allowed him to tread sacred officers' country. He rapped a fist on the brass banister.

On the promenade deck, one level down, Clay passed Frank Lyons standing sentinel, and he marched into the blue section and out onto the small area of open deck allotted to enlisted men. Only half a dozen GIs braved the cold.

He grasped the rail and heaved in lungfuls of frigid air. Gray waves spread out below the gray sky, meeting on the horizon in a dark haze.

Adler was alive and thriving. The draft had snared him, but his two years of college bought him an officer's commission. Clay hadn't had that opportunity.

The Army Air Forces, the glamour boys. Probably a fighter pilot if he knew his brother. Swooping around in a fancy plane, making girls swoon, not even caring about the girl whose life he'd ruined, not even knowing about the little boy he'd fathered.

He pounded his gloved fists on the railing.

Adler had sinned that day, trying to kill Wyatt, getting drunk, stealing Clay's girl, and having his way with her. Who had been punished? Not Adler. No, never Adler.

Clay had been punished, and he was still being punished.

Adler was an officer. Clay a private.

Adler soared high and free. Clay was trapped low in a pit.

"Lord, how can I forgive?" he muttered.

Daddy and Mama had already forgiven Adler. They would be thrilled that their golden boy was alive. They'd be proud. They'd lavish him with love.

But they'd worry about him flying. Considering how many dents Adler had put in Daddy's truck, their fears would be grounded.

Better they didn't know Clay had seen him. Why get their hopes up for naught?

Clay squeezed his eyes shut. *Lord, I know I'm supposed to forgive him, but I don't know how.*

He'd asked Leah how she'd forgiven the couple who'd adopted her only to abandon her. She'd replied that she concentrated on the good. The Joneses had taken her to an orphanage where the people were kind. She'd always had food and clothing and shelter. And she'd found beauty in leaves and clouds and words.

He wanted the serenity she had. Even after she'd been raped and almost murdered, she still found good.

Clay opened his eyes and concentrated. Fresh air filled his lungs. His uniform protected him from the cold. A meal awaited him. He was healthy and stronger than he'd ever been.

He had loving parents. He had good friends in Gene and Leah. Good leaders served over him, and he belonged to the best outfit in the US Army.

It wasn't the life he'd wanted, but wasn't that the case for almost every man on board?

They were farmers and shopkeepers and insurance salesmen. But now they were soldiers and sailors and airmen, and they had a job to do.

As for Adler, didn't the Lord cause the sun to shine on the wicked as well as the good? God had chosen to shine that sun brightly on Adler and let the rain fall on Clay.

A chuckle huffed out. "All my fussing won't change your mind, will it, Lord?"

"Paxton! D'you hear me?"

Clay's head jerked up.

Sergeant Lombardi stood in the doorway, his face twisted in annoyance.

Something told Clay that wasn't the first time Lombardi had called him. "Yes, Sergeant. Sorry, Sergeant."

"Get your tail in here."

That's right. It wasn't the Rangers' hour on the open deck. Now he'd get KP duty, but it had been worth it to put cold air in his hot head. He headed back inside. "Yes, Sergeant."

Tonight—after he finished cleaning the galley—he'd write a long letter to Leah.

21

How was it possible for Clay to be even handsomer than in her memories?

Leah admired the snapshot as she walked down Jackson Street. Every day she picked a different photograph to carry. Today she'd chosen the picture of him pointing to the stripe and patch on his sleeve. Such a wonderful grin.

She was also partial to the pictures of him reading a book on the steps of the New York Public Library and of him and Gene at the Library of Congress, arms around each other's shoulders.

Leah passed the grand brick tower of the United Methodist Church.

Clay had mailed the camera and photographs on November 20, and she hadn't heard from him since. He said it would be a while, which implied he was heading overseas.

Leah pressed his picture to her chest. *Lord, this might be selfish, but please keep him safe.*

She crossed Warren Street and tucked Clay's photo in her purse.

The chipper tone of his letter told her he didn't yet know she'd been kicked out of the boardinghouse—or why. But then she had taken over a week to summon the words to write him. What would he think to know she had once been a thief and that everyone still saw her that way?

How would Clay react? Would he react like Darlene and Mrs. Perry, wondering why he'd believed a raggedy good-for-nothing? What if he thought Leah had tricked him and manipulated his sympathy, and he annulled the marriage?

Part of her wanted to reject the idea as contradictory to Clay's character, to insist he would never be cruel.

Except something about her had attracted cruelty her whole life. Orphanage staff who wrenched her from her baby sisters. Adoptive parents who abandoned her. A stranger who decided she deserved rape and attempted murder. A friend who falsely accused her of theft and had her kicked out of her home.

Leah's jaw stiffened, and her breath and her step quickened. Why? Why did people think she deserved such treatment just because her parents had died?

A middle-aged gentleman bustled past, his shoulders hunched against the cold.

It was well below freezing, although clear and bright. A lady from church had loaned her a maternity coat in a toasty shade of brown. Leah had resisted all the secondhand clothing until Rita Sue assured her even well-to-do ladies shared maternity clothes.

Leah forced her jaw to relax, and she shoved her thoughts toward the blessings. Yes, she'd been treated cruelly, but she'd also been blessed beyond measure.

She still couldn't fathom the luxury of her new home—a bedroom, bathroom, kitchen, and living room all to herself. Why, the house was even furnished with a bed, a bureau, a table, and two chairs.

The Lord had been with her. The Lord would continue to be with her.

A sign by the sidewalk read "Coffee Children's Home." The

two-story Victorian had a friendly feel, despite the faded whitewash and the loose flagstones clinking under her feet.

Leah rang the doorbell.

A slender woman opened the door. Her gigantic eyes and frizzy gray hair gave her a flustered look.

"Good morning. I'm Mrs. Clay Paxton from the library."

"Please come in. I'm Miss King, the director. Let me take your coat. May I pour you some coffee? Tea?"

"No, thank you." Leah took off her coat and let Miss King hang it on the coatrack. Only six months earlier she'd been drinking milk in an orphanage and hanging up her own coat.

The smell of Lysol filled her nostrils, and the sound of small children playing filled her ears. The older children would be at school.

Miss King led Leah into a room filled with long tables and benches. "This is the dining room, where the children do their homework. We'll put the books in here."

Scuffed floorboards and scratched-up tables, but all was clean. "This is nice."

"We do what we can." Miss King fussed with a wiry strand of hair above her ear. "I'm pleased to say we can officially accept the book donation."

"Officially?" When she'd talked to Miss King on the phone the day before, she'd heard nothing but enthusiasm.

She tucked the strand into her bun, but it sprang free. "I'm afraid I spoke out of turn. At last night's board meeting I was in a bit of trouble for accepting the donation without asking. The chairwoman was not pleased."

Mrs. Channing again. "I'm sorry. Are you sure—"

"Yes, yes." She pushed a bench into line. "The board voted her down. I practically begged. We're packed to the rafters with children, and we need to keep them occupied."

A baby's cry pierced, and Miss King aimed a sigh upstairs. "With an Army camp in town, you can imagine how many unwanted babies come our way."

"I—I can imagine." She stroked her rounded belly and was rewarded by a fluttery greeting from her much-wanted baby.

Miss King cocked her head and picked up a handkerchief under a table. "We still have so many older children who were abandoned during the Depression."

"But the economy is strong now. Haven't people begun to adopt?"

"Not with the men overseas and the wives working at Camp Forrest."

"I—I hadn't thought about that."

"And donations have fallen." She rubbed her foot over a stain on the floor. "The war effort takes priority, so other charities struggle. If it weren't for Tullahoma's best families, I don't know what we'd do. We're barely staying afloat."

If only Leah could contribute, but it didn't feel right to give out of Clay's allotment. "Do you need volunteers?"

Miss King's gaze darted to her. "Sure do. It's hard to hire staff since we pay less than Camp Forrest. And with all the ladies working, it's hard to find volunteers."

"I'm interested. I have to quit my job in January, and I won't return after my baby is born. Would it be possible to bring my baby along?"

Miss King fiddled with that strand of hair. "A woman of your standing? You wouldn't want your child here. I love these children dearly, but some are a bit rough and uncouth."

Leah's chest ached. That was how everyone had seen her. "All the more reason to help."

The director's shoulders relaxed. "Well then, I'll see you in January."

She managed a smile. "You'll see me in a few days with a load of books."

22

"Those artillery boys will be hopping mad." Clay chuckled and ran with his squad back to the rendezvous point.

"Happy Christmas to you, old chaps," G. M. called in an affected English accent.

Thank goodness the foliage kept them concealed from their opponents in the field exercise. And thank goodness Lieutenant Colonel Rudder had assigned the exercise to help the men forget they were spending Christmas far from home.

Not such a happy Christmas for the boys of the US field artillery battalion stationed in Bude. The Rangers had tracked the artillerymen's position, infiltrated past their security, removed the breechblocks from the 155-mm howitzers, and let air out of the tires. Mission accomplished.

Clay's squad ran along a narrow path lined with tall hedges and arching tree branches. A cool wind blustered up from the Celtic Sea onto the Cornish downs.

For the past three weeks, the Rangers had traipsed the downs in speed marches and runs. They'd trained with combat-seasoned British Commandos. And almost every day they'd scaled the hundred-foot-tall Upton Cliffs, first with a safety line and then without.

Clay hopped over a low rail fence into the clearing where his platoon gathered. He found Lieutenant Taylor and reported his squad's success. With Bob Holman injured, Clay had led the squad on this exercise.

Holman sat propped against a tree, surrounded by Gene, Ruby, and McKillop.

Clay joined them. "We've scaled how many cliffs, and you sprain your ankle on level ground."

"If I hadn't, I wouldn't have heard the scuttlebutt." Holman's blink was slow and uncoordinated. Just how much whiskey had he nipped before the exercise? "Overheard Big Jim talking to Tay-Tay. D'you 'member in Florida when that girl went missing?"

"Yeah." Clay could still hear her father's anguished voice.

McKillop tapped a cigarette out of a pack. "Betcha they found her holed up in a beach shack with some sailor boy."

"Nope. Found her dead."

Clay sucked in a breath. "Dead?"

"Yep. The school commander wrote to Rudder and the COs of the other units at Fort Pierce at the time. They found the girl raped, stabbed, and dumped in a swamp."

Raped? Stabbed? Like Leah. Clammy air clogged his lungs, and he got to his feet. Where was Rudder? He needed to talk to him.

"Pax?" Gene frowned.

Clay motioned for his buddy to come with him, and he marched back to the rail fence.

"What's the matter?" Gene sat on the fence.

"Wonder if it's the same guy who attacked Leah. She was— she was stabbed." He'd never told anyone she'd also been raped.

Gene's face scrunched up in thought. "I'm sure it's a coincidence. There were fifty thousand soldiers at Camp Forrest."

"Yeah. True." Clay pulled off his helmet and ran his hand through his damp hair.

Telling Rudder wouldn't serve much of a point. Only five hundred men had gone to Florida.

But what if Leah's assailant and the Florida murderer were the same man? What if he was in Cornwall? Clay hadn't seen the attacker's face, but the attacker had seen Clay.

His chest squeezed with fear, but he puffed it away. If it were true, the rapist had already had plenty of opportunity to attack Clay. Besides, Clay was going to die in battle, not at the hand of a Ranger.

"That poor girl," Gene said. "Only seventeen."

"I know." Leah was only eighteen. Was she keeping safe?

Half a dozen letters waited at the home in Bude where he and Gene were billeted. When the mail finally caught up to the Rangers, he and Gene had decided to save it for a Christmas treat.

Now it would be bittersweet. In Florida, a family's worst fears had come true.

SATURDAY, DECEMBER 25, 1943

Clay pulled the five-button olive drab sweater over his head and tugged it into place. Pretty snug. Mama didn't know how much muscle the Rangers had put on him.

But those muscles, chilled in the under-heated Cornish home, softened at the warmth of the sweater and the thought of Mama knitting and praying for him.

Sitting in Mrs. Trevithick's chintz armchair, Gene held up a red-and-blue striped necktie. "What was Betty Jo thinking?"

Clay laughed. "Unless that's bulletproof, that ain't gonna help you."

"No fooling." Gene knotted it around his neck. "Maybe I'll

wear it under my uniform on D-day to remind me what I'm fight-ing for—going home."

"That's what I like about you, G. M.—your patriotism." Clay unfolded the note from Mama. She hoped he didn't mind receiv-ing only a sweater. They'd sent a nice check to Leah for the layette and the nursery.

Layette? Nursery? Babies needed lots of stuff, didn't they? At least Leah would have more money from him now.

Rudder and Taylor had been pleased with Clay's leadership the day before—and had been appalled at Holman's drunkenness on duty. Holman had been busted down to private, and Clay was promoted to corporal and leader of the rifle squad.

"Grandma's ribbon candy." Gene held up a box and wrinkled his nose. "Wish we'd opened gifts last night. I could have brought it to the children's party this morning."

"Reckon you won't have trouble getting rid of candy." The kids had enjoyed the party the Rangers had thrown, with Santa Claus, cartoons, and gobs of candy mailed from the States. Since sweets were heavily rationed in Britain, the children were thrilled.

Clay picked up a brown-paper parcel from Leah, postmarked November 1 and labeled "Don't open until Christmas." He'd obeyed and hauled it over on the *Queen Elizabeth*.

Inside lay an olive drab scarf. He looped it around his neck and tossed one end over his shoulder. In her note Leah stressed that she'd purchased the yarn from her library earnings. When would she feel comfortable spending his money—*their* money?

She'd also written him a Christmas poem, decorated around the edges with crayon bells and candles and angels and mangers, compliments of the Bellamy girls.

Light on the snow, through a Child, in our hearts,
On the hearth, in his words, in ours.

Song in the bells, by the Host, on our lips,
> Ringing bright, winging high, bringing hope.
Life in a tree, through the Cross, in our souls,
> Ever green, evermore, ever His.

My, how he preferred that to a necktie. In the hands of his dreamy wife, words were more than just playthings.

He found the next letter, dated November 15. It wasn't like her to leave long gaps between letters. Why hadn't he noticed that before?

Clay ripped open the envelope. Was something wrong?

Dear Clay,

This is a difficult letter to write. You have given me your good name, your money, and your family. You've also given me your kindness, trust, and respect. With this letter I am prepared to lose many, if not all, of these.

Clay's eyes hazed over. Had she cheated on him? Had she found someone else and cheated on him? They might not be in love, but their vows meant something, didn't they?

He bolted to standing. "I'm going for a walk."

"Sounds good."

"By myself. See you later." He marched out, tossed a wave to elderly Mrs. Trevithick in the kitchen, and jogged downstairs from the flat above the fish-and-chips shop.

He ran alongside the Bude Canal, past holiday cottages and tourist shops. The locals were used to seeing Rangers running. Even if it was Christmas Day.

Clay ran faster, hating himself for getting fooled by another woman—and hating himself for thinking the worst of Leah before he had the facts.

He crossed the footbridge over the lock at the end of the canal and jogged onto the beach. The tide was way out, and Clay sank to his knees on the sand under the overcast sky. Waves crashed before him, and low green bluffs curled around the beach.

"Lord, please let me be wrong." He opened Leah's letter again.

On November 2, Darlene accused me of stealing twenty dollars from her. The money was my own pay from the library, but Mrs. Perry believed Darlene and evicted me from the boardinghouse. It's taken me all this time to work up the courage to tell you.

You see, Clay, Mrs. Perry had a reason to believe Darlene. When I was younger, I often stole. I stole food. I stole lovely things that other children misplaced. I stole lonely things that other children mistreated. A few months ago, I mentioned this to Darlene, and she told Mrs. Perry when she accused me of stealing her pay.

I haven't stolen anything in years, and the Lord has forgiven me and has wiped my slate clean. However, Darlene and Mrs. Perry will never see me as anything but a thieving orphan. I'll understand if you see me the same way. When you proposed, I should have told you about my past. I knew you'd been gravely injured by theft, and telling you would have been kind and fair. I'm sure you never would have married me if you'd known I used to steal. Since I didn't tell you at that time, I'll understand if you should annul the marriage.

For future correspondence, see the address below. Mr. and Mrs. Bellamy are letting me rent a little house on their property.

Please know I'm sorry for all I've done.

> *With deep regret,*
> *Leah*

The scarf itched and choked, and Clay tugged it off and dropped it to the sand.

Leah had a history of stealing?

Who was she? Was she an "Allotment Annie," one of those women who tricked soldiers into marrying them so they could collect the allotment, maybe even the life insurance?

Clay rested his hands on his knees, stared at the golden sand, and groaned. No, of course not. She hadn't tricked him. He was the one who'd pushed for marriage.

He sighed, smoothed the letter, and tucked it inside his sweater.

Growing up, he'd always had everything he needed. What if he hadn't? What if he'd spent his childhood in an orphanage? Or on the streets? Would he have turned to theft? "I don't know, Lord. I don't know what I would have done in her place."

The scarf lay rejected in a heap beside him. Clay drew it across his lap and brushed away grains of sand.

He couldn't blame her for not telling him earlier. First, it was all in her past, in her youth, forgiven and overcome. Second, if everyone thought like Darlene and Mrs. Perry, she was wise to keep quiet.

He dug his fingers into the knit where Leah's fingers had worked. Telling him had taken courage, especially since she thought he'd annul the marriage. Why would she think that? Why would she think he'd abandon her and make her give up that little baby?

Realization slammed into his chest. Abandonment was all she knew. Why would she expect anything else from him?

He had to reassure her. Clay pushed to his feet and draped the scarf around his neck.

A chill wind slapped him in the face.

November 15? She'd written that letter a month and a half ago. By saving her letter for a Christmas treat, he'd left her in the lurch.

She wouldn't receive his reply for another week or two, maybe four.

That wouldn't do. He marched back across the sand. He'd send a cablegram today.

No, it was Christmas. First thing tomorrow morning. He'd make the message vague enough for all the eyes that would see it, yet clear enough for her.

"I won't abandon you, Leah." He crossed the footbridge and broke into a run, desperate to write his reply. "I won't."

23

Leah brushed a finger along the book spines in the 720 section of the library. Architecture. How she'd hoped to peruse that section.

She'd never sift through Camp Forrest's collection again. Dr. Adams wanted her to quit now that she was in her third trimester, and today was her last day. Since everyone thought she was only five months pregnant, Leah stated that her recent surgery had made the doctor cautious.

Her fingers halted on a book on early American architecture. What if it contained a photo of one of the buildings in her memory? She would never see it.

Leah sighed and shelved two volumes from her cart. Hoping to find clues about her hometown and surname in library books had been naïve. Her childhood memories were foggy and sparse and distorted by time.

Although she would never stop yearning to know her name and to find her sisters, bearing the Paxton name and feeling her daughter's tiny kicks eased the ache.

"Leah Paxton," she whispered, and she wheeled her cart to the next aisle.

Thank goodness she could keep that name. The arrival of Clay's cablegram had nearly torn her heart out. She was preparing herself for a telegram come spring, not right after Christmas.

But the message soothed her qualms: "NO NEED TO WORRY STOP NOTHING WILL CHANGE STOP LETTER COMING STOP YOURS CLAY."

Leah shelved books in the 800s. She hadn't received that letter, but she no longer feared annulment. And he'd never signed his letters "yours" before. How could one word fill her with such warmth and joy?

Her cart empty, she pushed it toward the circulation desk. At the card catalog, Miss Mayhew chatted quietly with Miss Elliott, who had started the first of the year.

Miss Elliott had graduated from the library school at Emory University and could catalog, research, and make acquisitions, as well as work the circulation desk, a more qualified librarian than Leah and a suitable replacement.

The two graduate librarians laughed softly about something. Already they were colleagues. Leah had never been more than an assistant.

Grief pooled in Leah's lungs. Miss Elliott was living the life Leah had wanted. It would never be hers, because she'd been orphaned and abandoned and assaulted.

Why did people like Miss Mayhew and Miss Elliott receive all the good things in life? Why did Leah receive all the bad things? Why did everyone mistreat her?

A flutter of kicks in her belly, and Leah drew a deep breath to calm down.

Clay didn't mistreat her. And her original dream might have died, but a new one had formed—raising this sweet child and giving her a happy home.

Leah walked at a fast clip down Moore Street under a moonless sky. At eleven o'clock, few lights shone from windows. An icy breeze wafted around her legs, and a bush beside her rustled.

Leah scooted away, her heart hammering. Every shadow, every noise made the scar on her chest throb.

An MP escorted her every night from the library to the bus stop at Camp Forrest. But no one escorted her the three long blocks from the bus stop to her home.

Was the wolf still out there? He'd wanted her dead, and he'd failed. Was he stationed at the base? Or had he shipped out with one of the many units that had trained at Camp Forrest?

The Bellamy house stood on the corner of Washington and Moore. In daytime, a cheery brick home. At night, dark and brooding. Leah inched into the backyard, watching for unfamiliar shapes in the victory garden and by the chicken coop.

Praying, she dashed to the little house. She thrust her key in the lock, flung open the door, turned on a lamp, and threw the deadbolt. She might be the only person in Tullahoma who kept her doors locked, day and night.

Leah sighed and leaned back against the door.

Everyone assumed Leah loved the privacy of her new little home, but she wasn't used to sleeping in a room alone. In a house alone. With straw-thin doors and windows and walls that would succumb to one puff of the wolf's foul breath.

She could still feel his darkness crushing her, pounding, ripping, humiliating.

"No. No." Leah pressed her fists to her chest. "I'm home. I'm safe. The Lord is with me. The Lord is with me."

When her heart rate finally settled down, she hung her hat and brown swing coat on the hook.

A flash of white on the linoleum—a letter! Rita Sue always slipped Leah's mail under the door. Oh, how she needed a distraction. The airmail envelope edged by diagonal red and blue stripes signaled a letter from Clay.

"It's from your daddy, baby girl." Leah lowered herself to squatting and picked up the letter. The postmark read December 26, the same date as the cablegram.

"Please, Lord. Please let this be his reply." She settled into the rocking chair Mrs. Whipple from church had loaned her.

Leah devoured the first line: "My dear wife"—with *wife* underlined.

Relieved laughter welled up. He'd never addressed her that way. Always simply "Dear Leah."

The next line read "I want to make one thing clear—I will never abandon you. I made vows to you and to our child, and I will never break them."

"Thank you, Lord. Thank you." With that security, she could bear any censure.

I admit your confession struck me, since my life has been altered by theft.

However, please don't feel bad that you didn't tell me you used to steal. You were young, it was long ago, and you've changed—so it was never any of my business. Seeing how Darlene and Mrs. Perry reacted, I don't blame you for not telling me.

As for your past theft, there's nothing for me to forgive. First, you did me no harm. Second, I understand why you stole things. Yes, it was wrong, but it stemmed from your compassionate heart that hates to see anyone or anything abandoned. That sweet empathy is one of your greatest strengths.

Third, it's all in your past. In your youth! You've confessed and changed, and that isn't who you are anymore. You told me when you could have easily kept silent. I admire your courage and integrity.

Thinking through this illuminated a dark area in my soul. When I first told you about my brothers, you said you could understand why I hadn't forgiven them. I was taken aback, because I thought I had forgiven them.

You saw through my polite words. Although I've forgiven them on the surface, deep inside I still resent them.

It was easy to forgive you because there was no personal injury, I understood your motives, and you repented long ago.

Both Wyatt and Adler did cause me injury, and neither has repented. I understand Wyatt's motives—he feared for his life and needed to get out of town. But I'll never understand Adler's motives. Sure, he was grieving Oralee, he was angry that I'd spoiled his revenge on Wyatt, and he was drunk, but to do what he did? I'll never understand.

So Wyatt only meets one of my criteria, and Adler meets none.

However, my criteria don't matter. Only God's do.

Jesus didn't say to forgive people only if you understand why they sinned. He didn't say to forgive only if people are remorseful and they change.

He said to forgive, and he said not forgiving is a sin. So guess what, Leah? I'm a rotten sinner.

I have a whole lot of pondering and praying to do. I need to figure out what it means to forgive, to go past saying the words to meaning them. How do I stop resenting them? I don't know, but I'm fixing to find out.

I tell you what, little wife of mine—because that's what you are and that's what you'll remain till death do us part. Pray that I'll be able to forgive my brothers before it's too

*late, and I'll pray that you can see yourself as the fine young
woman you are and not as a thieving orphan. Sound fair?*
  Take care of yourself and our baby.

        Yours,
        Clay

Leah pressed the letter to her chest. "I will. I'll pray for you."

She hurt for him—for the pain his brothers had caused and
any additional pain she'd inflicted. Yet she basked in his security.
He wouldn't annul the marriage. He called her his little wife. He
signed it "Yours" again.

He wasn't perfect, but he was a man of his word, honest, open,
and determined to forgive those who had set his life on a course
he hadn't wanted.

Why had the Lord brought such a man to befriend her, to save
her life, and to give her a family?

She held the letter before her face, longing to inhale his essence.
"Lord, help me, but I love him."

24

"That's the way. Y'all can do it." Clay shielded his eyes from the sunshine glancing off the white chalk cliffs. In the chilly afternoon, dozens of Rangers climbed ropes up the two-hundred-foot slopes on the Isle of Wight.

Whatever mission Gen. Dwight Eisenhower had in mind for Rudder's Rangers, it had to involve cliffs.

Clay's boots slipped on the large pebbles on the beach, and he dug in his toes. The tall lace-up Corcoran jump boots worn by the 2nd Rangers had led to multiple scuffles with paratroopers, who claimed only they had the right to the footwear. But scaling cliffs without a safety line was no less dangerous than jumping from a plane with a parachute.

A loud cuss, and a man tumbled fifteen feet to the beach— Manfred Brady.

Clay scrambled over to give aid, but Brady stood, shaking his meaty fist and blaming his squad members for his fall.

"Hothead." Clay returned to the foot of the rope he'd soon ascend.

Since Christmas, he'd scrutinized the men who'd been in the

battalion since Camp Forrest. Could any of them be Leah's assailant or the murderer?

He had little to go by. Medium height and build. Leah had noticed dark hair under the cap, but in low light even medium shades looked dark.

At first Clay had concentrated on hotheads. But Leah's assailant had obviously tracked her routines, lain in wait, and lured her by turning on the light in the storage room. That spoke of a cold and calculating man.

If the Florida murderer was a Ranger, he must have sneaked out at night and rowed into town, since they'd never had leave before the girl's disappearance.

"Paxton, you're up." Lombardi held out the rope.

"Yes, Sergeant." He made sure his bayonet was loose in its scabbard in case he needed it, then grabbed the rope.

Up he went, hand over callused hand. In gym he'd always been good at rope-climbing, but he'd always feared falling and breaking his neck.

Not now, and he grinned. He wouldn't die in a fall. Even if he fell, he wouldn't be injured badly enough to keep him out of the invasion. His dream freed him to climb just as it had freed him to marry Leah.

Chalk and sandstone scraped his hands and fell away from beneath his feet. His breath was hard but steady, and his muscles announced their presence without pain.

To either side, Rangers in fatigues ascended, calm and steady. They knew they were strong, they knew they were good, and they knew this was for a purpose.

About ten feet to the top, and Clay savored the cool air and the sounds of surf, seagulls, and soldiers.

The rope went slack.

Clay cried out and grabbed at the cliff with hands and feet, scrabbling for a grip.

Chalk gave way under his fingers, and he slid, the slight outward slope slowing his fall. "Help me, Lord!"

The bayonet! Clay whipped it from the scabbard and stabbed it into the cliff.

It held.

"Thank you." He groped around with his feet and his free hand until he had a solid hold.

"Paxton!" Lombardi yelled up to him. "You all right?"

"Could use a rope, y'all." He pressed his whole body to the cliff, and his breath brought up puffs of white dust.

His heart pounded like crazy. That had been close. Thank goodness he'd been the last man to climb so no one else had been endangered.

He peered down the slope. The rope lay in a tangled coil on the pebbles. That could have been him, dream or no dream.

"Pax!" Gene's voice came from above, almost frantic. "Grab hold."

Something whapped the back of his steel helmet.

A rope, and Clay took it. He wiggled his bayonet free, clenched it between his teeth, and climbed to the top.

Holman and McKillop yanked on the rope. Gene and Ruby grabbed Clay's arms and hoisted him up onto horizontal ground.

Clay dropped the bayonet and lay flat, his fingers working into cool blessed grass. "What happened?"

"Lyons tripped over the line." Contempt warped Sid Rubenstein's voice.

"What?" Clay pushed up to his knees and pulled in a ragged breath. Why on earth had Lyons been near the lines? They all knew better than that.

"Yeah, Lyons." Ernie McKillop glared at him. "What were you thinking?"

"It was an accident." Lyons shrugged. "Sorry."

"Glad to hear it." Clay couldn't keep sarcasm out of his tone.

If any other man in the battalion had caused such an accident, he'd have fallen all over himself apologizing and thanking heaven no one had been hurt.

Not cool and calculating Frank Lyons.

Not that dark-haired man of medium build, and Clay's blood chilled.

Was it on accident? Or on purpose?

Or was Clay imagining things after looking too hard for the attacker? As G. M. had said, it was probably a coincidence, two unrelated crimes, neither by a Ranger.

"You all right?" Gene held out a hand.

Clay took it and got to his feet, shakier than he cared to admit. "Yeah."

Lieutenant Taylor strode over, concern all over his face. "Paxton, I heard what happened."

"I'm fine, sir." Clay brushed chalk from his Parsons field jacket.

"Quick thinking saved your life."

"And good training." He managed a smile.

"I'll talk to Lyons." Taylor set a hand on Clay's shoulder. "Skip the next climb and take a rest. Glad we didn't lose you."

"Thank you, sir." Clay wandered away alone, praying thanks for his survival. He wanted to die doing something good, not in an accident.

The prayer and the scenery calmed him down. The Isle of Wight tucked neatly into the triangle of a bay at Southampton and Portsmouth, and gray ships passed below, warships and freighters and troop transports. Blue skies and wispy white clouds arced over bright green downs, white cliffs, and frothy blue sea.

Even prettier than the Texas Hill Country. If Leah were here, she'd write a poem.

Far from the Rangers' exercise, Clay sat down, stretched his legs before him, and leaned back on his elbows. Since Christmas, the tone of Leah's letters had shifted. Darlene's betrayal was causing her to question in a way the assault hadn't. Maybe it was the pro-verbial final straw.

She'd raised a flurry of questions. Why did people feel it was all right to mistreat her because her parents had died? Why did people exclude other people from stores and restrooms and train cars because their skin was black? Why did people persecute and murder other people because they had different religious beliefs?

Clay puffed out a hard breath. He had no answers. That's what had started the whole war—people declaring other people had no worth and no right to land or life.

His fingers dug into the grass. He'd assigned similar motives to his brothers. When they stole from him, he'd felt worthless. He, as the half-breed half brother, didn't deserve to go to college and become a physician and marry the pretty blonde. Maybe Wyatt and Adler thought that way, and maybe they didn't, but that's how it felt.

Worthless.

Clay got back up to his feet. Leah wasn't worthless, and neither was he. And hadn't his brothers always treated him fairly before that day? Hadn't they always defended him and stood up for him? Maybe their actions on that day stemmed from pure fear and grief and anger. Didn't make it right. But it also didn't mean they considered him worthless.

And was Clay really any better than they were? Both he and Adler had lost the women they loved that day. Both he and Adler had lashed out in rage.

Clay's head sagged back. He wasn't any better. Not one whit.

Leah's letters overflowed with hope that he would forgive his brothers and be reconciled with them.

Forgiveness, yes. But reconciliation?

Clay strolled to the edge of the cliff. Little waves washed the pebbly beach below, inching toward the bluff.

Spring and the invasion approached as relentlessly as the tide.

He wanted to forgive his brothers fully before he died. Maybe he'd send letters to them in Kerrville in case they ever came home.

Reconciliation required seeing them in person, and he had no interest in that. Even his brief sighting of Adler on the *Queen Elizabeth* had been too much.

At least the war made reconciliation impossible. While Clay scaled cliffs on the southern coast, Adler would be stationed at an airfield north of London. And who knew where Wyatt was?

Something Leah had written poked at him. She'd given up hope of finding clues about her family.

Leah had two sisters, and she'd do anything to see them again.

Clay had two brothers, and he'd do anything *not* to see them again.

"Lord, could you—" He groaned and kicked a pebble down the slope. For the sake of the war effort, he didn't dare pray to postpone D-day. "Help me out. I've got a long way to go."

25

Leah admired *Heidi* on the bookshelf at the Coffee Children's Home. Keeping the book for herself didn't seem right when her dear friend belonged with the orphans.

Two fifth-grade boys knelt before the eight volumes of the 1921 *World Book Encyclopedia*.

"All right, Mikey." Leah massaged her aching lower back. "Your report is on James Polk. Which volume will you choose?"

He mouthed the alphabet. "This one—it has *J*."

"Dumbbell," his twin brother Marty said. "It's by last name—*P*."

"No name-calling." Leah sat at a table, careful to keep her knees together despite the baby's weight pushing them apart. "Marty, your report is on Woodrow Wilson."

"I already have it—*W*." He thumped into his chair, almost tipping it over. "I'll find mine before you do, Mikey."

Unruly brown hair flopped as the boys raced each other, and Leah smiled at their competition.

Did her sisters compete or work together? Were they inseparable or torn asunder like the Paxton brothers? Were they even in the same location?

"Found it!" Mikey jammed a bony finger at the page, then groaned. "It's so short. How can I write a three-page report?"

"You'll check out books from the school library," Leah said. "This will help you know what to look for. Also, watch for asterisks—those mean there's an entry in the encyclopedia."

"Like 'Mexican-American War'?" Mikey's narrow face contracted over each syllable.

"Yes."

Mikey darted from his chair and closed the encyclopedia.

Leah stuck a finger in place just in time. "Use a bookmark."

"Mine already has a bookmark." Marty slung a color postcard onto the table. "But listen. This here says Woodrow Wilson's still president."

"Yes, it's old but . . ." Leah slid the postcard closer, and her heart stilled.

A glorious library. Tall stained glass windows sent a rainbow of light over tables and bookshelves, and a Gothic ceiling soared above, studded with electric lights like a starry sky.

She could almost smell the leather and lemon oil.

All disappeared around her, all sight, all sound, all but the memory. Somehow Leah's numb fingers turned over the postcard—University of Chicago, Harper Memorial Library.

Chicago. She came from Chicago. The picture and her memory fused and expanded and came to life, and she laughed for joy.

"What's so funny, Mrs. P.?"

All this time she'd been looking for the answer in books, and now she'd found the answer *inside* a book. "I'm from Chicago. Chicago."

"Mrs. P.?" Two sets of brown eyes stared at her, bewildered.

She gathered her senses. "Read your articles and take good notes."

"Yes, ma'am," they said in unison.

Leah stroked the postcard. She could almost feel her parents' hands in hers, one on each side, as she gazed at the magnificent ceiling. The University of Chicago. Had her parents been students, faculty, staff, or simply visitors?

If only she could hop on a train and visit, but travel was discouraged late in pregnancy and would be extremely difficult with a baby.

Besides, where would she go? The Chicago area had to hold dozens of orphanages, and could they help with so little information?

The only details she had were the year of 1929 and the sisters' first names—Thalia, Callie, and Polly. She believed Callie and Polly were short for Calliope and Polyhymnia, so that all three girls would have been named after Greek muses of poetry.

Searching dozens of orphanages would take days, and staying in a hotel would be expensive and impractical with a wee one.

Still—she pressed the card over her heart—she knew where she came from. Tonight she'd tell Rita Sue and write a gushing letter to Clay. They would be delighted.

"Mrs. Paxton?" Miss King leaned inside the dining room. "Time for the board meeting."

"Thank you." Leah tucked the postcard inside her purse. "Goodbye, boys. Check out books, and we'll work on the reports over the weekend."

She pushed herself to standing. If she was this large at eight months, how much larger could she get? She smoothed the cranberry gabardine over her belly, thankful the coat-like cut of the dress gave her a more professional look for when she presented her proposal. She couldn't wait to surprise Miss King.

Leah followed the orphanage director to a room with a square table. Five ladies stood chatting, including Mrs. Channing, but sweet Mrs. Whipple from church was also present.

"Good afternoon, ladies." Miss King scarcely looked like herself in a smart navy suit, but her hair still defied bobby pins. "Please meet Mrs. Clay Paxton, our newest volunteer."

"Well, Mrs. Paxton." Mrs. Channing raised her chin. "You're certainly trying to insert yourself into Tullahoma society."

That didn't sound like a compliment, but Leah smiled. "Tullahoma has been kind to me, and I enjoy returning the favor."

"You sweet girl." Mrs. Whipple took both Leah's hands, and pretty wrinkles fanned around her gray-blue eyes. "We're so pleased to have you."

After the ladies fussed over Leah's belly, they took their seats and started the meeting.

Leah could barely pay attention between her excitement over Chicago and her eagerness for her proposal. What a lovely day.

Baby Helen rolled, as if dancing for her mother's double joy.

"Any new business?" Mrs. Channing said.

"I'd like to make a proposal." Leah smoothed her notes and restrained her smile so she wouldn't look childish.

"I shouldn't be surprised." Mrs. Channing took off her reading glasses. "Go ahead."

Leah dove in. "Since the Coffee Children's Home is having financial woes, I'd like to propose a fund-raiser. We could hold a pancake breakfast in early summer. We could set up tables on the lawn, and the children could serve. The only rationed ingredients are a bit of oil and sugar, so we should have no trouble making the purchase. With a tasty breakfast and darling children in attendance, the people of Tullahoma will be eager to support this worthy cause."

She looked up with a smile. However, Mrs. Channing's eyes blazed, Mrs. Whipple frowned down into her lap, and the two other ladies wore stern expressions.

"Mrs. Paxton?" Miss King looked almost frantic. "You should have consulted me first."

Leah's stomach fell as far as the baby allowed. What was wrong?

"Financial woes?" Mrs. Channing's thin red lips agitated. "I beg your pardon. The Channing family donates generously, as do all the families on this board."

"Yes, Mrs. Channing." Miss King's voice warbled. "All our needs are met. We lack for nothing."

Leah gaped. That wasn't what Miss King had told her, what Leah saw with her own eyes.

"Yankee carpetbagger," the lady next to Mrs. Channing muttered. "Prancing into town, thinking she knows what's best for us."

"Oh dear. That isn't what I meant."

"Be kind, Mrs. Ross." Mrs. Whipple frowned at the woman. "She may be misinformed, but her heart's in the right place."

"Even if we did need money, your proposal would fail." Mrs. Channing closed her notebook. "In case you're unaware, there's a war on. The needs of our boys in the service prevail. The orphans are a drain on society, especially now. Folks would resent being asked to pay for luxuries for the children of immoral mothers and ne'er-do-well fathers."

Leah sucked in a burning breath. How could someone who felt that way sit on an orphanage board?

"With all the war bond drives, folks are tired of giving." Mrs. Whipple's brow furrowed, and she wouldn't meet Leah's gaze. "I'm afraid very few people would attend."

"Especially if the children served the food." Mrs. Ross grimaced.

Leah's back stiffened. "The children are clean, and the house is sanitary."

"We—we do our best, but I know what folks think." Miss King worked a strand of hair between her fingers.

Why wasn't the director defending her home, her hard work, and her children?

Mrs. Channing stood. "Motion dismissed and meeting adjourned."

Miss King leaned forward. "Before y'all leave, please know I appreciate your generosity in supporting our little home. I'm most grateful, and so are the children. We want for nothing."

"I'm glad someone sees that." Mrs. Channing swept out of the room.

The other ladies departed without giving Leah a glance.

Standing up required even more work than usual. Her whole body felt like lead.

"Mrs. Paxton, I appreciate your help with the children." Miss King twiddled her hair at a frenetic pace. "I do. But please don't make plans without consulting me."

"I won't. I—I'm so sorry." Leah trudged to the door.

She hadn't meant to insult the donors, but she had. She thought she'd understood the needs of the home and the heart of the community, but she hadn't.

Who did she think she was? A dirty orphan had no right to sit on boards with society ladies and make proposals.

Leah stepped outside and opened her umbrella. The rain tapped accusations on the fabric above her.

She didn't belong in Tullahoma or Des Moines or even in Chicago.

She trudged back to her borrowed home in her borrowed clothes with her borrowed name.

Leah would never belong anywhere.

26

"Thanks for the ride." Clay leaned inside the truck window and handed the driver two ration packs of cigarettes.

The older gentleman's face lit up. "If I had the petrol, I'd take you blokes all the way to London."

Clay laughed and joined G. M. at the roadside as the truck chugged on its way. Cigarettes were better than cash, which was good since the men had no cash.

Gene studied the map. "About a mile to Barnstaple Junction."

The men headed up a narrow lane through high hedgerows, fragrant with spring.

"Time for us to show *initiative*." Clay used one of Lt. Col. Jim Rudder's favorite words.

After breakfast, Clay's company had been ordered to divide into pairs and meet at the Marble Arch in London at 0900 the following morning. No money allowed. No questions would be asked about how they'd arrived.

Many of the men "requisitioned" bikes or cars. Clay understood the purpose. One day the Rangers might be behind enemy lines and need to steal vehicles. But in friendly England, it didn't seem right. Gene agreed, so they'd decided to sneak onto a train and pay for their tickets after their return.

They passed through a village of white homes with slate roofs. Training hadn't let up since they'd returned to Bude from the Isle of Wight. Rudder and the top brass in the Rangers had visited London recently and returned ashen faced. Speculation was, they knew the invasion plan and it was a bear.

All the more reason to train hard.

Hedgerows crowded the lane, and Gene ducked under an overhanging branch. "How's the missus? Another month or two to go, huh?"

Less than that, but Clay nodded. "Her doc thinks she may deliver early. How's Betty Jo?"

"Great. They work her hard at the laundry at Camp Forrest, but she likes it."

"Good. Leah misses working at the library, but she enjoys her volunteer work."

But what he wouldn't give to have a word with that Mrs. Channing for talking to Leah in such an overbearing way. Leah was only guilty of innocence and zeal and standing up for the downtrodden, all of which were virtues in Clay's eyes.

Soon the town of Barnstaple came into view, and they found the depot, built of mismatched brownstone with cream trim and a slate roof, full of rustic English charm.

Clay straightened his waist-length olive drab "Ike jacket" and made sure his drab trousers were still tucked into his Corcoran boots. They needed to look wholesome.

Inside the depot, they instigated their plan and stood in the ticket line. When the man in front of them went to the window, Clay glanced at his watch and motioned Gene to the timetable on the wall.

Barnstaple had a direct line to London's Paddington Station, so they wouldn't have to transfer trains.

After a few minutes, they went out to the platform. They might not have tickets, but at least they'd been seen in line.

"What do you want to see in London?" Clay asked.

Without money, they couldn't see much, but the conversation made them look like fellows on a furlough. Too bad Clay couldn't visit the British Library for Leah. Of course, he'd sent her the camera, so he couldn't take pictures anyway.

She'd sent him a dozen photos—standing outside her house, sewing tiny nightgowns on Rita Sue's sewing machine, sitting in a rocking chair in a sparsely furnished living room, and more. He couldn't believe how big she was, or how cute she looked so big.

The train huffed into the station, and Clay and G. M. stepped into an empty compartment. They planned to fake sleep to ward off the conductor. If caught, they'd get off at the next station and repeat the ruse on the next train.

A man in his fifties joined them, a gray mustache breaking up his square face.

The British were reserved, but Clay didn't want to be rude. "Good morning, sir."

He peered at Clay, not smiling, but not frowning. "Going on a bit of leave, are you, chaps?"

"Yes, sir."

"Make the most of the time you have." He gazed out the window as the train pulled away from the station. "I was at the Somme in the trenches."

In the First World War. Clay pulled in a long breath. "I reckon that was tough."

"A Hun bayonetted me in the side, but I muddled through." He kept looking out the window.

"I'm sorry, sir."

Gene yawned loudly. "Pardon my manners."

His buddy had a point. They couldn't be seen as awake when

182

the conductor arrived. "Pardon us, sir. We were on maneuvers all night. Reckon we'll be mighty poor company."

"Rest while you can."

"Thank you, sir." Clay settled down with his pack for a lumpy pillow.

Soon Gene was snoring, nothing fake about it. The man could sleep anywhere.

Clay affected slow, even breathing, with startles and snuffles when the train jostled.

After about half an hour, the door to the passageway opened. "Tickets?"

"Please don't disturb these chaps," the veteran said. "They don't have long."

"Very good, sir."

No, Clay didn't have long. A few weeks? A few months at most. Not long ago, that would have filled him with relief. But not anymore.

He wanted to live long enough to know Leah and the baby had come through childbirth. He wanted to see a picture of the child who would bear his name after he was gone. *Just a while longer, Lord. Please.*

Clay marched under Paddington Station's great arched ceiling. "We made it."

"That veteran helped. I think he was on to us."

"I'm sure of it."

About ten feet to their left, the gentleman looked their way.

Clay stopped and saluted. Gene did too.

The former Tommy clicked his heels and saluted them back, his expression sad and distant.

He knew what the GIs were about to face, and Clay's chest

constricted. He didn't feel bad for himself—he'd go to glory. But his buddies who survived would carry memories for life.

A new thought struck him hard. *Lord, please don't let Gene see me die.*

Out in the ticket area, Clay pulled out his map. "We won't be able to see much, but there's a lot in walking distance."

"We'll see more if we do things my way." Gene set his pack on a bench, pulled out a K ration box, and removed the box that held four cigarettes. Then he tapped out the contents—rolled-up pound notes—and he kissed them. "This, my friend, is Underground fare and dinner and little gifts for our wives."

Clay laughed. "That, my friend, is *initiative.*"

Close to midnight, Clay and G. M. trudged back through Paddington Station. They'd seen the major London sights and eaten at a real British pub.

Clay's feet had a familiar ache. "In Bude all we do is moan about twenty-five-mile marches. So what do we do in London?"

"March twenty-five miles."

"Sure do." And he'd loved it.

Only a few people milled about the station, and some soldiers and sailors dozed on benches. Clay found two empty benches. "This here spot's as fine as any."

"Yep." G. M. stretched out with his pack for a pillow. "Nighty-night, Paxy."

"Nighty-night, Gee-Mee." Clay arranged his pack, but he couldn't sleep with London swirling in his memory—Buckingham Palace and Westminster Abbey and Big Ben, the Tower of London and St. Paul's and the Tower Bridge.

He'd always wanted to see London, but he never thought he would. Leah would love the book he'd bought with pictures of the city, including the British Library.

But Wyatt filled his thoughts. His oldest brother had loved Charles Dickens and Sherlock Holmes and had talked about visiting someday.

Clay hadn't seen him for going on three years, and he . . . he missed him. Missed him with a gaping cavern in his belly. Wyatt was the quiet one, responsible and thoughtful, while Adler was the fun brother, mischievous and adventurous.

Did they regret what they'd done? Had they changed?

Clay would never see them again, which hurt. But honestly, what would he say to them? He didn't trust himself not to punch them in the face.

On the other hand, a good pop in the nose might make it easier to forgive them.

He chuckled. Probably not what the Lord had in mind.

A keening sound climbed high, dove low, and rose high again. Clay blinked his heavy eyes. Was that an air raid siren?

Recently, the German Luftwaffe had been sending bombers back to London. This Little Blitz had followed a three-year lull in major air raids since the Blitz.

Gene's snoring competed with the siren, and Clay shook his friend's shoulders. "Wake up. It's an air raid."

"Huh?" G. M. sat up. Wrinkles from the canvas pack crisscrossed one cheek.

"Air raid." Clay grabbed his pack. "Big planes, big bombs, big booms. Let's find a shelter."

"You fellas must be new in town." Three American airmen sat on the next bench in leather flight jackets and crush caps.

Clay's breath caught, but Adler wasn't among them. "Yes, sir."

"Rookies," the second airman said.

The first puffed out a plume of cigarette smoke. "Listen, pal. The Krauts do this 'most every night. Nothing to fuss about."

Gene closed one eye, switched eyes, and his head slumped forward.

Clay could carry him in a pinch, but this wasn't a pinch. He sat beside his buddy.

Curved girders arched high above him, with windows in a band along the top. Searchlight beams swung into view and out, brightening the cloudless sky.

Above the siren's wail came a new sound, steady and insistent. Airplane engines.

The flyboys sat up straighter.

A whistling sound high above.

"Wake up, Gene. We've got to get down to the Tube." He'd seen the stairs not far off. Rookie or no, it was time to move.

"I'm coming."

More whistles, and the Rangers ran toward the stairs with the flyboys right behind them.

A sound like shattering glass, screeching metal, ripping earth. A force slammed into Clay's back and knocked him to his hands and knees.

He cried out but couldn't hear himself.

The sound receded. Glass tinkled in the distance.

Clay drew in a deep breath and assessed himself. Not even a scratch on his palms, thanks to his rope-climbing calluses.

Gene and the three airmen sat back on their heels, dazed but unharmed.

His ears ringing, Clay stood and turned around. Far down the tracks, smoke and dust rose and a gaping hole in the roof framed twisted girders. Thank goodness there were no trains or benches down that way. But what a lot of damage.

One bomb among thousands. One night among hundreds.

"This—this is why we're here."

27

Leah caught her breath and looked at her watch. That contraction had arrived twelve minutes after the last one. Thank goodness Clay had sent her a wristwatch in February for her nineteenth birthday.

She pushed herself out of the rocking chair and surveyed her home. All was ready. Her morning chores were complete. Her suitcase had been packed for weeks, and every morning she added her toiletries and nightgown.

Mercer had put up a wall to divide the bedroom in two. In the new little nursery stood a bassinct with cheery lemony bedding. The bureau was a good height for changing diapers, and the drawers were filled with snowy diapers and the tiny shirts and kimonos and drawstring nightgowns she had sewn.

Leah smoothed her hands over her gigantic belly. Dr. Adams had told her to call when the contractions were ten minutes apart, but twelve was close to ten. What if ten minutes came at noon and the nurse was on her lunch hour? What if Leah had to give birth all alone at home?

She couldn't risk her daughter's life.

Leah crossed the backyard and knocked on the Bellamys' back

door. No one answered, as expected. Mercer would be at the bank, Rita Sue volunteering at the Camp Forrest hospital, and the children in school.

Leah opened the door. Rita Sue had told Leah to use their phone at any time, but the kitchen felt oddly unfamiliar without the Bellamy family, and the whir of the phone dial under Leah's finger sounded loud enough to summon every police officer in Coffee County.

"Good morning. Dr. Adams's office." Nurse Hutton's high-pitched voice greeted her.

"This is Mrs. Paxton. I'm in labor. My contractions are twelve minutes apart."

"I'll let Dr. Adams know. Go to the hospital when they're ten minutes apart."

"Yes—" Leah's belly went rigid, not painful but very uncomfortable. She glanced at her watch. "That's . . . now."

"All right, hon. Go on in. Dr. Adams will meet you at the hospital later."

In a few minutes, Leah headed down Washington Street with the suitcase Rita Sue had loaned her, feeling small and alone. Another contraction hit, and she braced herself on the trunk of an elm tree.

She knew the Lord was her provider and true Father, but right then, all she wanted was someone to hold her hand and tell her everything would be all right.

If only Clay could be that someone. He was so strong and calm and knowledgeable in that physician-like way of his.

The contraction subsided, and she turned onto Grundy Street and inhaled spring-scented air. With Easter only a few days past, flowers blooming around front porches, and a baby about to be born, everything sang of life.

If only spring didn't mean death for Clay.

She shuddered and stroked her belly. She wouldn't think of that today.

Thank goodness she only had one more contraction before she reached the Queen City Hospital. Since Leah was no longer employed at Camp Forrest, she couldn't go to the familiar hospital on base.

The building was small and simple in the modern streamlined fashion.

A middle-aged nurse in crisp white greeted Leah. "I'm Nurse Simmons. Please follow me." She came out from behind the desk and gestured to a row of chairs. "When your husband arrives, he can wait out here."

"My husband—he's in England, in the Army."

"Well, never you mind." She led the way down the hall. "Will your parents be coming?"

"No, ma'am. I'm an orphan."

"Oh." Nurse Simmons snapped her gaze over her shoulder to Leah. "I'm sorry."

Time to focus on the good, and Leah smiled. "My friend Mrs. Bellamy will visit. And I'll telegraph my husband's parents in Texas. My baby will never be alone."

Neither would Leah. Never again.

Pain ripped through Leah's body, searing all the places the wolf had hurt. But this was a good pain, a productive pain, a life-giving pain. Leah pushed into it and embraced it.

Wet, warm, tumbling release.

"Here we are," Dr. Adams said.

Panting, Leah strained to see between her knees. Where was she? Where was her baby?

A tiny cry rose, as old as time and as new as spring.

"Helen." Leah laughed and flopped flat on her back, sweat tickling her hairline. "Thank you, Lord. Thank you."

"Congratulations, Mrs. Paxton," Dr. Adams said. "It's a girl."

"I know." Leah grinned and laughed.

The nurses and doctor moved in choreographed motion. So much activity for such a wee person.

"I want to see her." Leah glimpsed a tiny red foot, toes splayed wide. "I want to see my baby."

"All in due time," Nurse Simmons said, her back to Leah.

A young redheaded nurse came over and massaged Leah's belly. "She's a good size for being two weeks early."

Dr. Adams's gray-eyed gaze darted to Leah. In this room, only he knew Leah's story and knew she was actually two weeks late. "I'm not surprised. Mrs. Paxton followed my instructions and took good care of herself."

Why wouldn't they turn around so she could see Helen? The baby's cries spoke to a part of Leah's soul she didn't know existed, now awakened and alert and attuned to this young person. "Please. I want to see her."

"Do you have a name picked out?" The redhead kneaded Leah's belly like bread dough. Freckles dotted her round cheeks.

"Her name is Helen Margarita Paxton." Leah smiled at the lovely, appropriate name. Helen, a Greek name that meant *light*. Margarita, after Clay's grandmother on the Ramirez side, and it also honored Rita Sue. And Paxton, a precious gift from Clay.

"We'll help you send telegrams to your husband and in-laws." Nurse Simmons flapped open a little blanket.

"Thank you." But they were trying to distract her from her dearest and only desire. Helen's cries were gentling but still called to her. "How much longer?"

"You'll see your baby in the morning," the redhead said. "We need to take her to the nursery, and you need to rest."

Dr. Adams held up one hand to the nurse and gave Leah a solemn and momentous look. "Are you sure you're ready to see her?"

Leah swallowed hard. What if something about Helen reminded her of the wolf? Although Leah hadn't seen his face, what if she'd met him and recognized some feature in her daughter? But would that change her love? Never. "I want to see my baby."

Dr. Adams nodded to Nurse Simmons.

"Here she is, Mrs. Paxton. Please stay flat on your back. It's very important." Nurse Simmons laid a blanketed bundle beside Leah on the mattress.

Helen's face peeked out, set like a jewel in the folds of white flannel, red and wrinkled and capped with black hair.

"Hello, baby." Leah laughed and stroked that sweet face, seeing her daughter for the first time, yet knowing her better than she'd ever known another human being. "My Helen. My daughter."

The baby's face softened, and her eyes opened, dark and bright and soulful.

"Hello, baby. Hello, sweet girl." Leah stretched to kiss her baby's warm, firm cheek. Her love swelled and strengthened and deepened until it filled every corner of her being.

"She's beautiful," the redhead said. "She has your mouth."

Did she? Leah studied her, touched her, and memorized every detail.

"Do you see your husband in her?" Nurse Simmons asked.

She shouldn't . . . and yet. "Her eyes. They're Clay's eyes."

It couldn't be, yet it was. How sweet of the Lord, and how fitting. Every time Leah looked at her daughter, she'd see the man she loved, the man who'd allowed them both to live.

28

"Mail call!"

Silence fell over the mess hall. As hungry as Clay was after a day of training, he craved letters more than food.

Names rang out, and Rangers got up from benches. A week earlier, three of the six assault companies had transferred to Swanage on the south coast between Weymouth and Southampton. The other three companies remained at the British Assault Training School in Braunton, not far from Bude. Clay had enjoyed his week at Braunton, which had focused on taking out fortified positions. Like the pillbox in his recurring dream.

"Paxton!"

Clay forked the last bite of mutton into his mouth and retrieved an envelope addressed in Daddy's strong script. He worked his finger under the lip and headed back to his seat.

"Paxton!"

Two in one day. He grinned and reversed course. A smaller envelope this time—a cablegram. From Tennessee!

Clay ripped it open. "HELEN MARGARITA PAXTON BORN

APRIL 12 STOP 7 POUNDS STOP MOTHER AND BABY WELL STOP YOURS LEAH."

He whooped. "It's a girl! I'm a daddy!"

Clay laughed and read each word again. Of course it was a girl. Hadn't Leah known from the start? His funny mystical bride.

His pals crowded around, congratulating him.

"Too bad our rations don't come with cigars," Ruby said.

McKillop waved him off. "Pax doesn't smoke anyway."

Gene slapped him on the back. "Good job, old man."

"Helen Margarita Paxton," Clay murmured. Leah's Greek heritage, Clay's Mexican heritage, and Clay's white heritage, all wrapped up in one fine name.

His friends occupied themselves with mail and meals.

Clay leaned back against the stone wall in the mess hall of the school where the Rangers were billeted, and he studied Leah's message. He'd met his goal and lived long enough to hear the news.

Why did it feel insufficient?

He wanted a picture. He wanted to see that baby. He wanted to drop everything and fly across the Atlantic to the two of them. Forget D-day. Forget the dream.

Clay sighed. He'd feared this would happen. His resolve was weakening, his desire lessening. The dream still came at least once a week, increasing in intensity. The end was coming, but now the thought filled him with sadness rather than joy.

His dinner finished, Clay turned in his tray and headed outside to read Daddy's letter.

It was still light out, thanks to Britain's wartime double summertime. The school perched on a cliff overlooking the bay, and silvery clouds stretched in ribbons over the water.

Clay sat cross-legged on the sparse grass and opened the letter, written well before the baby's birth.

Dear Clay,

I have good news. Wyatt wrote home! Finally, we've heard from one of our prodigals, and your mother and I couldn't be happier. He's alive and well and serving as a naval officer on the same island you are.

He wants you to know he's sorry he stole your money. He meant to pay you back that summer, but he made a bad investment and lost it all. That's why he joined the Navy—so he could earn money to pay you back. He'll send the check soon and write you at that time. He feels awful for what he's done.

We've written back, telling him you're in the Army and that Adler ran away, but we didn't tell him what happened between you and Adler. That's not our tale to tell.

Wyatt asked us not to give you his address right now, and we'll honor that. We did send him your address so he can send his apology. We pray you'll accept it, and we pray you two can meet overseas.

If only we could hear from Adler too. Nothing would make us happier than to see our family whole again. When that day comes, you three boys will see Mama and me running to you down the road, and you'll smell the fatted calf on the barbecue.

"Great news," Clay said from between gritted teeth. "Just great."

He stuffed the letter inside his Parsons field jacket and shoved himself to standing.

Like Adler, Wyatt hadn't suffered one whit, and Clay marched along the cliff. A naval officer, was he? Walking around in a smart navy blue uniform, probably in some swanky headquarters, far from cliffs and foxholes and machine-gun bullets.

"Swell." Clay kicked at a tuft of grass. Wyatt felt bad? Good. He ought to.

He planned to pay Clay back? Sure, he did. Even if he did, fat lot of good it'd do Clay with only weeks to live.

And Daddy and Mama wanted to throw a party for Wyatt and Adler, just like for the Prodigal Son who wasted his inheritance on "riotous living."

Except Wyatt had wasted Clay's money, not his own. And Adler did his "riotous living" with Clay's girlfriend.

Did Daddy expect Clay to leap for joy?

He grabbed a rock and hurled it off the cliff like a hand grenade.

What had Daddy meant about running to the *three* of them? Clay hadn't run away. He'd served at Paxton Trucking while Wyatt and Adler shirked their responsibilities and left Clay to do their work. He'd hated that job, but never once had he failed his father.

Another rock, and Clay sent it flying. "Daddy never threw a barbecue for me."

His own words smacked him in the chest and buckled his legs.

He fell to his knees, the cool wind drying his widened eyes, the truth wringing out his soul. "Oh no. I'm the elder brother."

Clay might be the youngest Paxton boy, but in his heart he was the Prodigal's elder brother.

He reached into his breast pocket and whisked out the tiny soldier's Bible with its leather cover and the brass plate on the front that read "May the Lord be with you."

Where was that parable again? The gospel of Luke, chapter 15.

He knew the story backward, forward, and upside down, and he already knew Jesus was talking to him. Most people thought the parable was spoken to lost sinners, letting them know the Father wanted to welcome them home. And sure, the parable did say that.

The first three verses stung, but he read them out loud, needing to hear them. "'Then drew near unto him all the publicans and sinners for to hear him. And the Pharisees and scribes murmured, saying, This man receiveth sinners, and eateth with them. And he spake this parable unto them.'"

Unto the Pharisees. Not unto the sinners, and Clay's head sagged back.

The Pharisees grumbled about Jesus welcoming sinners. The elder brother grumbled about the father welcoming the Prodigal. And Clay grumbled about Daddy and Mama welcoming Wyatt and Adler.

"I'm the elder brother." The wind riffled the tiny pages, and Clay read the whole story—the last four verses twice, his voice as rough as the ground beneath his knees.

"'And he answering said to his father, Lo, these many years do I serve thee, neither transgressed I at any time thy commandment: and yet thou never gavest me a kid, that I might make merry with my friends: But as soon as this thy son was come, which hath devoured thy living with harlots, thou hast killed for him the fatted calf. And he said unto him, Son, thou art ever with me, and all that I have is thine. It was meet that we should make merry, and be glad: for this thy brother was dead, and is alive again; and was lost, and is found.'"

Clay's hands coiled around leather and brass and wafer-thin paper, and shame bowed his head low. "Son, thou art ever with me, and all that I have is thine."

As miserable as those last years in Kerrville had been, he'd always had his parents' company and wisdom. He'd enjoyed Mama's chili and Daddy's jokes.

Wyatt and Adler might have flourished out in the world, but they'd done so alone.

Daddy and Mama were right to rejoice that their son had returned, repentant and grieving.

For so many years, Clay had seen himself as wronged. Now he was just plain wrong.

"Lord, forgive me." He returned to the Scripture. The parable

SARAH SUNDIN

ended there. Did the elder brother continue to grumble? Did the Pharisees? Or did they see the wonder of the Father's mercy and join in the celebration?

He gripped the Bible hard, willing the truth to transform his brittle heart. "I want to, Lord. I want to forgive. I need to forgive."

29

Rita Sue fingered the bouquet of pink carnations on Leah's hospital bedside table. "That baby gets prettier every day. Boy, do I see your husband in her." She gave Leah a wink.

"Me too." Sitting up in bed, Leah glanced at the clock. Two long hours until the nurse would bring the baby for her next feeding.

"I need to go home and make dinner." Rita Sue tucked her purse under her arm. "You're coming home tomorrow, aren't you, sugar?"

"Yes, ma'am."

"I'll bring the truck. The kids can't wait to meet the baby. But, sugar? She needs a nickname. Helen's too grown-up for that little dumpling."

Leah smiled. Helen was the perfect name. As small as she was, Helen exuded light and dignity.

After Rita Sue left, Leah slid her feet into her slippers. It felt good to walk around the maternity ward after five days lying in bed and another five sitting in bed.

Leah picked up Clay's V-mail—tiny but so quickly delivered.

She padded to the window, her white cotton nightgown brushing her ankles. Only one other mother was in the ward, fast asleep.

The V-mail had arrived that afternoon, and Leah had read it twice. Mr. and Mrs. Paxton had told her about Wyatt when the hospital let her make a long-distance call to Texas. Now Clay knew too, and he'd poured out his heart to her about acting like the Prodigal's elder brother.

In the afternoon sunlight, Leah squinted at Clay's handwriting. His letter had been written on a special V-mail form and photographed in England, then the microfilm had been shipped overseas and the letter reprinted in miniature in the US.

> For the past three years, I've sat on a seesaw in the up position. I've taken satisfaction in my perch, high in the knowledge of my righteousness and looking down on my brothers' wickedness.
>
> Full forgiveness would level that beam, and I admit, that's why I've resisted.
>
> Now I see how wrong I've been.
>
> My lack of forgiveness only heaps sin onto my side of the beam, leveling the balance whether I like it or not. Now Wyatt and Adler have something to forgive me for.
>
> One way or the other, that beam will be leveled. I can do it my way, adding the weight of my sin to the beam. Or I can do it God's way, releasing the weight of their sin in my life and letting them rise.
>
> Only one way leads to peace. Only one way leads to restoration. I am choosing that way.

Leah kissed the page. "How I love you, you wonderful man."

Now to write her reply. The Lord would have to help her select the right words and speed her letter to Clay. Spring was deepening, and time was running short.

With her pen and her new box of V-mail stationery in hand, Leah sat in the bedside chair.

A man and woman entered the ward. The man was tall with graying blond hair, and he wore a gray suit. Small but sturdy, the woman wore a lavender floral shirtwaist dress, silver streaked her black hair, and dark eyes shone in the deep bronze of her face.

Could it be? "Mr. and Mrs. Paxton?"

"Leah! *Mija*!" The woman rushed over, kissed Leah's forehead, and grasped her shoulders. "Let me look at you. Why, you're even prettier than your picture. Isn't she, Will?"

"She certainly is." His Texas twang sounded so much like Clay's it hurt.

"I—I didn't know you were coming."

Mr. Paxton removed his fedora. "We wanted to surprise you. We're here to meet that baby girl and get the two of you settled in at your house."

Leah set aside her stationery. "You came all the way from Texas. My goodness."

Mr. Paxton handed Leah a heavy package wrapped in pink paper. "For the baby."

"Oh my." Leah eased off the tape and folded back the paper to reveal a red wooden truck with "Paxton Trucking" painted on the side in white.

"I made it thinking she'd be a boy." Mr. Paxton shrugged and grinned.

"She's the first Paxton girl in ages." Mrs. Paxton's shoulders and smile lifted as one. "What a breath of fresh air the two of you are."

Leah spun little wooden wheels. "It's wonderful, and it's all hers. Thank you so much."

Already her daughter had a Raggedy Ann doll from the Bellamy family and a fuzzy white bunny rabbit from sweet Mrs. Whipple, who seemed to have forgiven Leah for her blunder at the orphanage board meeting.

"Would you like to see Helen?" Leah asked.

Mrs. Paxton gazed to the door. "I thought you'd never ask."

Leah led them to the nursery with its large window facing the hall. "There she is." She pointed to the baby on the right, fast asleep and covered with a pink blanket.

A nurse spotted Leah, scooped up Helen, and brought her to the window, tilting her so her grandparents could see her face.

Mrs. Paxton pressed close. "*Abuelita*'s here, little one. Oh, look at her, Will. Isn't she the prettiest little thing?"

"Sure is." He grinned. "My, she's tiny. Can't believe our boys were that small."

"You and I get a whole month together, peanut," Mrs. Paxton cooed.

Leah blinked a few times. "A month?"

Mrs. Paxton made kissing noises toward the baby. "A new mama needs help with the baby and the household chores. You have a six-week lying-in period, and you need to rest. Clay said you'd turn me down, so I wrote your friend Mrs. Bellamy. She's letting me stay in her spare room, since you don't have space in your house."

Leah kept blinking as all her needs and concerns evaporated. "What about Timmy?"

"My sister will watch him when Will is at work."

"I . . . I don't know what to say."

Mr. Paxton chuckled. "Don't say nothin'. When Lupe makes up her mind—"

"Oh, you're no better." She wrinkled her nose at her husband. "I'll stay for a month, but your father-in-law will go home this weekend."

"The business, you know." He gestured over his shoulder with his thumb. "By the way, we brought a trunk of Clay's things."

"Clay wanted them here with you," Mrs. Paxton said.

"Oh my goodness." Leah's breath hitched on her swollen throat. Was there no end to this family's generosity?

Mrs. Paxton gasped and pressed her hand to her chest. "Oh! She's waking up."

"Would you look at that? She's got your eyes, Lupe—and Clay's. Sure as shooting."

Leah studied her mother-in-law and saw the resemblance. "I hope her disposition is as sweet as Clay's."

Mrs. Paxton flashed a smile. "Clay was the sunniest child you ever did see."

Sunny? Clay was thoughtful and kind, but Leah wouldn't describe him as sunny.

Helen's face reddened and scrunched up, and the nurse walked away with her. Despite the muting effect of the glass, the baby's cries made Leah ache.

Her hands stretched out. She wanted to be the one to comfort her daughter. Thank goodness they'd be going home tomorrow.

Mrs. Paxton looped her arm through Leah's and led her back to her room. Leah returned to her bedside chair, and Mr. Paxton pulled up chairs for him and his wife.

Mrs. Paxton set her purse on her lap. "I wish you'd known Clay before '41. We're praying our sunny boy will return to us."

Leah was just praying that he'd return at all. "I pray so too."

"Remember, Lupe," Mr. Paxton said. "War changes a man."

"Yes, but if he and his brothers . . ." She turned bright eyes to Leah. "We haven't told you yet. We heard from Adler."

"Adler? I thought you'd heard from Wyatt."

"Only a few days later." Mr. Paxton flipped his hat in his hands. "Both in one week."

"We've missed them . . . so much." Mrs. Paxton's voice shook. "Three years. It's such a relief to know they're both alive and well."

Leah bit her lip, afraid she'd reveal that Clay had seen Adler on the ship. "How is he?"

Mr. Paxton stretched out long legs and grinned. "He's a P-51 fighter pilot, wouldn't you know? That boy was always a daredevil."

"He's in England," Mrs. Paxton said. "That is no coincidence. God is orchestrating their reunion."

"Do you think they can meet?" Leah fiddled with the hem of her bed jacket. "I doubt they're in the same area, and Clay rarely gets leave."

"It'll happen." Mrs. Paxton gave a strong nod.

Her husband shrugged. "If Clay can forgive them."

"Of course he will. Right, Leah?"

How much could she reveal without betraying Clay's confidence? "I'm afraid it won't be easy."

"She's right." Mr. Paxton leaned his elbows on his knees. "What his brothers did to him? They didn't just steal his money and his girl. They struck at who he was as a man. That's a lot to forgive."

"He will," Clay's mother said. "He has to."

He did have to forgive, not just for his own peace of mind, not just for Wyatt and Adler's sake, but for the whole family. "Clay's the key, isn't he?"

Mrs. Paxton frowned at her. "The key?"

"Clay is the key." Leah stroked the warm gold of her wedding ring. "His forgiveness is the key to restoring your family."

"*Our* family." Mrs. Paxton squeezed Leah's hand.

Mr. Paxton chuckled. "You're in this mess too, young lady."

Leah smiled, even though she was only in the family temporarily. But for whatever time she had, she'd fight for them and with them. "I am indeed."

30

Clay stood at the bow ramp in the British Landing Craft Assault as the little LCA chugged across Lyme Bay.

Eager anticipation rippled among the twenty-one men—two of the three sections in Clay's platoon. Exercise Fabius was a full-scale dress rehearsal for D-day, so realistic that when his company had boarded their British transport, the *Ben-my-Chree*, in Weymouth, half the men were convinced it was the real deal.

Live naval shells flew overhead, shredding the gray morning sky and leaving concussion trails along the water.

Lyme Bay teemed with vessels—the landing craft speeding to shore, the hulking transports farther out to sea, and the destroyers and cruisers belching fire and smoke and shells.

Was Wyatt on one of those ships? Clay shook his head and focused on the mission, on the green land before him, the golden crescent of Blackpool Beach, and the cliff beyond, the objective of D, E, and F Companies.

Two miles south at Slapton Sands, the other three companies of 2nd Battalion and the entire 5th Ranger Battalion were landing with the 29th and 1st Infantry Divisions. "Twenty-five thousand men," he murmured, his voice lost in the noise of shelling and boat engines.

The largest amphibious training exercise ever, the brass said.

Four fighter planes zoomed overhead, P-47 Thunderbolts of the US Ninth Air Force.

Not Adler's planes.

Clay squirmed in his field jacket. Daddy's letter about Adler had arrived a few days earlier, and Clay was digesting it.

Adler felt deep remorse, Daddy said, not just for his sins, but for how he hurt everyone. All torn up inside, and he wanted to write Clay an apology. Well, good.

Daddy hadn't given Adler's address to Clay because he wanted his own letter to arrive first. He and Mama were figuring out how and what to tell their middle son. Adler didn't know he was a father, and he didn't know Ellen was dead. It'd be hard on him.

Fine. Clay had dealt with the consequences of Adler's sins for three years. About time Adler dealt with them too.

He hated feeling vindictive again, just when he was making progress, but Daddy's letter had ripped the scab right off the wound.

Only forgiveness could slap a bandage on that wound so it could heal. Clay had to take that hard step and write his brothers. Since he didn't have their addresses, he'd send the letters home for his parents to forward.

The shore drew near. A naval shell slammed into the cliff, spewing out a geyser of dust and rock.

"All right, sailor boys," Clay muttered. "Time to let up."

They must have heard him, because the noise fell away.

Beside Clay, Lt. Bill Taylor leaned his elbow over the left front corner of the LCA. "Let's hope the Rangers' bad luck doesn't follow us today."

"Bad luck?" Clay frowned at the platoon commander.

"Didn't you hear?" Ernie McKillop nudged Clay from behind.

"Fellow in the 5th Rangers told me. Right after we left Braunton, they found another dead girl."

"What?" Clay stared into McKillop's wide-set eyes.

"Stabbed and naked and dumped at sea."

Stabbed. Most likely raped. A weight crushed Clay's chest, like when he'd wrestled Leah's attacker.

His gaze swept the Rangers, found Frank Lyons behind McKillop, and locked on him.

Lyons stared back, then his face went flat and still. He blinked and glanced away.

Clay's breath rushed out. He turned to Gene on his right, who looked as alarmed as he felt, then to Taylor. "Is Colonel Rudder looking into this, sir?" he asked in a low voice.

"Why?" Taylor's square chin drew back. "It wasn't a Ranger. The girl's boyfriend was the town drunk, always fighting with her and everyone else. Sure enough, he skipped town when she disappeared. Last I heard, they were still looking for him."

"All right." Clay drummed his fingers on the bow ramp in time to his racing heartbeat. It wasn't a Ranger, wasn't Frank Lyons. But the man still made the hairs on his arms stand at attention under his field jacket.

A scraping sound on the bottom of the LCA.

"Here we go, men!" Taylor yelled.

The ramp of the LCA creaked open and thumped onto the beach, splashing Clay with cold water.

Clay roared and charged forward, pounding down the steel ramp and across the beach, pebbles giving way beneath him.

Nothing to shoot, but he held his M1 Garand rifle ready. Teams of men set up equipment and fired rockets. With sharp booms, grapnels shot into the air, trailing rope.

Clay eyed the grapnels as he ran. They disappeared over the edge of the cliff, and the ropes flopped against the cliff face. Some were plain rope and some had toggles.

He slung his rifle over his shoulder, grabbed a plain rope, and shimmied up, bracing his feet against the cliff as he went.

"This is nothing," Gene said from a toggled rope beside him.

"No fooling." Maybe fifty feet tall and not too steep, a cliff the Rangers could scale with bare hands.

To his left, Sid Rubenstein set up a tubular steel ladder and climbed it. Bob Holman passed Ruby another section to add to the top.

The Rangers had learned every possible way to climb a cliff. No matter what obstacles they found on D-day, they would conquer them.

Near the top Clay readied his rifle, and he scrambled over the edge.

One hundred feet ahead lay two concrete pillboxes, smoke streaming out of the gun slits. An earlier platoon had already secured the primary objective, so Clay gathered the other four men in his rifle squad and jogged to the road, the next objective. They were to proceed to Combe Point at the mouth of the Dart River, and then to Dartmouth.

On the road the squads formed into sections, the sections into platoons, and they marched.

"Hope D-day is this easy," Gene said with a grin.

"Wouldn't that be nice?" Clay eyed the trees and stone walls, but no Germans would pop out today. Not even an Englishman. All the civilians had been evacuated from the region so the GIs could practice.

South Devon had been chosen for its resemblance to their objective on the far shore, wherever it might be. Whenever it might be.

Clay figured he had a week or two left on earth. A week or two to write those letters and fully forgive.

Leah's words scrolled through his head, and he pulled her letter from his pocket, the letter that had arrived before they boarded the transport. It felt strange knowing his parents were in Tullahoma with her and the baby, two disconnected parts of his life joining—as he'd hoped they would. Obviously, they'd been talking about him.

Clay darted his gaze between the road, the Rangers, and the stationery.

I pray constantly that you'll completely forgive your brothers. This is for your own good, so you'll be at peace knowing you've done right by them. This is for Wyatt and Adler, so they can rest in the knowledge of your forgiveness and love. Despite all that's happened, I know you love them dearly.

This is for your parents, who love all three of you and long for you to forgive each other. Please remember your parents' love for Wyatt and Adler doesn't diminish their love for you. It never has, and it never will.

This is also for the sake of your family as a whole. Clay, you alone hold the key to restoration and peace. Your parents have forgiven your brothers, and they say Wyatt and Adler have forgiven each other. That leaves you, my sweet husband.

My sweet wife. What wisdom, written with assurance. What compassion—for Clay, for his parents, and for the brothers-in-law she'd never met and had heard nothing good about.

Clay pulled the snapshot from the envelope, the picture of Leah holding baby Helen to face the camera. Over and over he'd studied Helen's face—so tiny it only intensified the desire to see her, to watch her expressions and hear her cries and coos.

And Leah. Something in his chest stirred and rolled. She'd changed. Nothing girlish or naïve remained. She was a woman. A beautiful woman.

The way those dark eyes looked to the camera, still dreamy but with a new poise. And the way her lips tipped up at the corners, serene but strong.

Clay had married a lost waif who needed his protection and

his giving. Along the way, something had changed. She'd begun giving to him. He craved her words, soft but true. He needed her.

He loved her.

Clay stifled a groan and tucked the photo and letter back in his pocket. He was afraid this might happen. He was afraid he'd fall in love. Now he couldn't deny it any longer.

Through an opening in the shrubbery, the cliff fell away beside him. So like their objective on the far shore.

Where he'd die.

Clay kept his feet moving, although the stirring in his chest transformed to churning. For three years, he'd wanted to die to escape the pit of his life. But now the pit wasn't miserable. It was downright cozy. He belonged to the best unit in the US Army, and he had the sweetest wife and baby girl in the world.

If his brothers hadn't . . .

Clay's eyes stretched wide, taking in gravelly path and trees and clouds and insight.

If his brothers hadn't cast him in the pit, he never would have been drafted. He never would have joined the Rangers. He wouldn't have been at Camp Forrest—

His blood ran cold.

He wouldn't have passed the library that July night. Leah would have bled to death. Even if she'd lived, Clay wouldn't have been there to marry her. She would have given Helen up for adoption.

"Oh, Lord. Thank you," he murmured. *Thank you for the pit. Thank you—thank you for letting my brothers take away my future so Leah and Helen could have a future.*

His chest convulsed. He gasped long and hard—quickly faked a cough to divert his friends' attention.

Clay could barely breathe, barely walk, barely think, everything upside down and backward and topsy-turvy.

And everything turned right side up for the first time in three years.

31

On the church lawn, Miss King from the orphanage peeked into the carriage—not easy with Luella and Sally Bellamy guarding "their" baby. "My, she's good. I hope this means you can volunteer again soon. The children keep asking about you."

Leah rolled her hands around the handle of the baby carriage. "Thank you."

"Happy Mother's Day." Miss King wiggled her fingers at Leah and Rita Sue.

In front of the stately brick church, Mrs. Paxton chatted with Mrs. Sheridan from the library, Mercer chatted with three men Leah didn't know, and Joey Bellamy played tag with some older boys.

Leah frowned at Rita Sue. "Why would Miss King want me back?"

Rita Sue tilted her head, making the pink flowers on her hat sway. "Why wouldn't she?"

"I insulted the donors."

"Pff." Rita Sue leaned close and lowered her voice. "Mrs. Channing is insulted if the weather doesn't do her bidding. Never you mind her."

Leah turned the carriage to keep the sun out of Helen's eyes. "But I'm not . . . well, I'm not like the other ladies who sit on boards and volunteer. I don't belong."

"Don't belong?" Rita Sue set one hand on an ample hip. "Sugar, if you want to belong, you have to join."

Leah's mouth drifted open. She'd never thought of it that way.

Rita Sue retied the pale green ribbon at the end of one of Sally's braids. "Some groups you're born into, some you're invited into, and some you have to worm your way in. You just received an invitation."

"I—I did."

"Yes, you did. I don't want to hear any more talk about not belonging, you hear?"

"I hear." Leah smiled at her daughter, asleep on her back in her ruffled white bonnet, her arms stretched out as if fencing. "I do enjoy reading to the little children and helping the older ones with homework. And Helen's so good, I could bring her. Maybe in a few weeks. Yes, definitely."

"That's the way."

"I wish I could do more. They really are having financial woes, but Miss King can't ask for more donations without insulting the current donors. They think no one will help because the children are"—Leah swallowed a hot, hard lump—"a drain on society."

One of Rita Sue's eyebrows rose to the rim of her hat, challenging Leah. "Do you agree?"

Memories dragged on her heart . . . "Scram, you hooligans" . . . "dirty orphans" . . . "unwanted."

But Mikey and Marty and the other children at the home were sweet and silly, same as Jocy and Luella and Sally and Helen. They had great worth, and something hardened in Leah's neck. "No child is a drain on society. Orphans can't help it if they don't belong . . . Rita Sue, you're brilliant!"

"Hear that, girls?" Rita Sue tugged on Sally's braid. "I'm brilliant."

Luella and Sally giggled.

Rita Sue laughed. "Don't you sass me, young ladies. Round up your father and brother and Mrs. Paxton."

The girls scampered off.

The idea took shape in Leah's mind. "You are—you're brilliant. 'If you want to belong, you have to join.' The orphans don't belong in town. They're someone else's unwanted children. So they have to join the community—by contributing. If they can be seen as assets . . ."

Rita Sue's hazel eyes glimmered in the spring sunshine. "No, you're the brilliant one. Keep going. What are you thinking?"

"Something for the war effort. Maybe they could collect scrap, plant victory gardens, sell war bonds."

"I like it. Let's talk tomorrow morning."

Luella and Sally finished herding, and the Bellamy and Paxton clans walked up Washington.

Mrs. Paxton fell in beside Leah. "I like that Mrs. Sheridan. She hopes you can volunteer at the library again."

Leah's heart strained in that direction. But even good babies couldn't spend an entire morning in a library, and Rita Sue was busy with her own home and volunteer duties. "Maybe I could find another mother to trade babysitting with."

"That's the spirit." Mrs. Paxton stroked her corsage. "I've always loved Mother's Day."

"This is the first one I've enjoyed." And she'd enjoyed it two-fold—for being a mother and for having one. Mrs. Paxton had become dear to her over the past three weeks.

"Ah, *mija*." Mrs. Paxton squeezed Leah's arm. "Do you remember your mother?"

"A bit. I was four when my parents died. I remember they read to me and sang to me, and we spoke English and Greek. And I remember they loved the three of us girls so much."

"You have sisters? I didn't know that. Where do they live?"

"I don't know. They were babies. Twins. The Jones family

adopted me, but not them. Then they left me in Des Moines. All my life I've wanted to find my sisters. I just found out we came from Chicago, but I can't do anything with that information."

"Why not?"

Helen moved her arms, dragging the blanket up over her face. She fussed, and Leah tucked the blanket down. "You sound like Clay. He keeps telling me to go to Chicago."

"Then go."

Leah laughed. "Diapers to wash, nursing, baby baths—I can't imagine traveling with a baby, staying at a hotel. Not to mention the expense. Besides, there must be dozens of orphanages in the Chicago area. I wouldn't know where to begin."

"That would be difficult." Mrs. Paxton squinted one eye in the way she did when she was thinking.

Did Clay do that too? Leah couldn't remember. It'd been so long since she'd seen him, and her heart folded in

Back at the Bellamy property, Leah returned to her little house with her mother-in-law.

Mrs. Paxton pulled on the apron Leah had made from her "good" gray dress from the orphanage. "Go take care of the baby, and I'll get the *frijoles refritos* cooking. The beans soaked all night."

"Thank you—Mama." The word was difficult but came easier each day.

Leah settled down with Helen in the nursery chair. Rita Sue said bottle feeding was the modern and civilized way to feed a baby, but Dr. Adams and the mother's book from the Department of Public Health insisted nursing was healthier for the baby—and far less expensive. Leah enjoyed how her daughter molded to her body and heart and soul when she nursed.

After Helen was satiated, Leah changed the wet diaper and dropped it in the pail. Tomorrow morning she'd wash diapers again. Thank goodness Rita Sue let Leah use her washing machine and wringer.

"Here she is, all fresh and happy," Leah said.

"There's my girl." Mrs. Paxton made faces at Helen. "She's always so bright-eyed in the late morning. See how she watches us?"

"I know." Leah kissed a tiny hand and passed the baby into her grandmother's eager arms. "What can I do for dinner?"

"Nothing for now." Mrs. Paxton sat in the rocking chair, and Leah pulled up a kitchen chair.

The living room looked much homier. The Paxtons had brought Clay's little tabletop radio, his violin, and a couple dozen books, which Leah was devouring. They'd also brought some of Clay's boyhood toys and books for Helen.

"We made the tortillas yesterday, and we'll start the carnitas and sauce in an hour." Mrs. Paxton waved a rattle in front of Helen. "This is Clay's favorite enchilada recipe. Mind you, don't tell him you're learning my secrets. Just surprise him when he comes home."

Leah tried to smile, but it wobbled.

Mrs. Paxton lowered her eyebrows. "Don't worry. He'll come home."

"Yes, Mama." He'd taken to writing daily, and so had she. Each morning could bring the invasion, and after that, how long would he have?

"Has he . . . has he ever mentioned a strange dream?" Mrs. Paxton's brow furrowed.

With the truth unlocked, relief flowed out. "Yes. He says it comes weekly."

"Even now? But everything's changed." She rocked harder. "For so long, he didn't want to live. But now he has you. Now he has his daughter, his own blood."

Leah's heart ripped. Mrs. Paxton thought Helen was Clay's blood—hers too—the only child of her only child. It was a lie.

Leah clutched her arms across her belly. "Oh, Mrs. Paxton, I have to tell you the truth."

"Not Mrs. Paxton. Mama."

"No. Mrs. Paxton. I'm not really your daughter."

"You're married to my son, aren't you?"

"Yes, but he only married me because of the baby."

Mrs. Paxton's mouth rounded, then she dropped her chin. "I see. I—at least you did the right thing and—"

"Oh! Not like that." Leah's fingers dug into the too-soft flesh around her waist. "Please don't think less of Clay. Think more of him."

"I won't tell anyone. Not even your father-in-law."

"No, it's not like that." Leah stood and walked to the wedding portrait on the wall. Clay looked so handsome in his service uniform, his smile white in his strong face. "He—he told you I was attacked and stabbed, and that he saved my life. But he didn't tell you I was also—I was—that man—violated me."

"Oh my goodness. Oh no. You poor child."

Her breath strained in her tightened chest, and she stroked the rim of the wood frame, forcing herself to concentrate on Clay rather than the wolf. "When I found out I was pregnant, Clay offered to marry me so I wouldn't have to put my baby up for adoption. So she could have a good name. So I could have his allotment to raise her."

Mrs. Paxton murmured.

Leah faced her, and her heart wrenched at the turmoil on her face. "Helen—she isn't really Clay's daughter. And she isn't really your granddaughter. I'm so sorry."

Mrs. Paxton pressed the baby to her chest and lowered her face over the downy black hair on Helen's sweet head.

The only sound in the room was the creak of the rocking chair.

Leah hugged herself. Now she'd driven away someone she was growing to love, someone who loved her little girl like a real grandma. But she had to tell the truth.

Mrs. Paxton drew a deep breath, her head still bowed over Helen's. "You know I didn't give birth to Wyatt or Adler, don't you?"

"Yes, ma'am."

She raised dark eyes just like Clay's. "They look nothing like me and don't carry a drop of my blood, but they're my *sons*. I love them the same as I love Clay, and I always will."

"I—I understand, but this—"

"Helen is my grandchild, and I love her the same as I love my Timmy. Both babies—" She bit back a sob and shook her head. "I don't care how they came into the world. I love them, and they're mine."

Leah's gut churned. How she wanted to accept the acceptance, but it didn't seem right. "But Mrs. Pax—"

"Mama, and don't argue with me." Her voice wavered. "Don't you argue. You married my Clay, and you love him. I can see it in your eyes."

"I—I do." But why did love have to hurt, squeezing and twisting everything inside her?

"I know he loves you too."

Leah lowered her face. She refused to shatter that illusion as well.

"So you're my daughter and always will be, and Helen will always be my granddaughter. Understood, *mija*?"

Leah raised her gaze to this woman she had no right to claim as family. But something stretched between them, a mutual love for Clay and for Helen.

That was the right. That was the claim. That was family.

Leah breathed it in deeply. "Yes, Mama."

32

The only sound in Clay's ears was the scratching of pens on paper. Occasionally, Rangers murmured to each other, but overall a hushed reverence filled the quarters in the old school.

After Exercise Fabius, Clay's company had returned to Swanage on the southern coast, along with the rest of the 2nd Ranger Battalion. More cliff climbing, with extra training on using the rocket-propelled grapnels, now mounted on the LCA landing craft. They were also experimenting with extension ladders from the London Fire Department mounted on DUKW amphibious vehicles.

Dozens of Rangers lounged on cots writing letters. They were strong, smart, well trained, unified, and confident bordering on arrogant. They were ready.

Down the length of the room, Frank Lyons met Clay's gaze without smiling, and a chill ran through Clay. Something about that man. Nothing definitive to report to Rudder, just a needling suspicion.

Clay returned his attention to his stationery boxes. Enough dillydallying. All around England, vehicles transported troops to marshaling areas close to the southern ports. Rudder had told the

217

men to write any letters they wanted mailed before the invasion. After the men were briefed on their mission, the mail would be impounded so no classified details could be leaked.

Clay's time was running out. He'd continue to write, but today's letters were the last he could guarantee to be mailed before he died. They'd be the most difficult five letters of his life.

The first would be easiest, and the only one short enough for a V-mail. He filled the one-page form responding to Leah's latest letter, which reported on Helen's cuteness and how Leah enjoyed the time with his mother. Clay kept the letter light, praised the baby, thanked Leah for her advice, and told her he was writing his brothers.

Now for the long and difficult letters. They would all go in one thick envelope to Kerrville.

Dear Daddy and Mama,

Things are getting busy over here, and I wanted to tie up all loose ends. I've enclosed letters to Wyatt and Adler—please forward the letters immediately, as I don't have their addresses. There's also a letter for Leah—please mail it to her only in case of my death.

You'll be happy to know the letters to my brothers are ones of forgiveness. This hasn't been easy, but it's necessary. As my wise wife says, my forgiveness is the key. As the youngest and as the half brother, I feel odd being in charge, but so it is. The half is the key to the whole.

After I'm gone, I want the Paxton family to be reunited and restored, with my Leah and Helen included, of course.

Please don't think I'm fatalistic. I'm not. I just know my work on earth is done. My brothers are forgiven, the road to family peace is open, and I've provided for my wife and daughter. Thank you for taking my girls under your wings. I hope you can persuade Leah to move to Kerrville.

*Please forgive me for taking so long to forgive my broth-
ers. I wore my grudges as my badge of honor as a wronged
man. But that was as grave a sin as any they committed. I
made myself their judge, and that's not my role.*

*Daddy and Mama, thank you for a lifetime of loving me.
You raised me well and taught me the importance of faith,
compassion, integrity, and hard work. You provided a home
full of wisdom, humor, common sense, and heaping piles of
love. I love you with all my heart.*

Your son,
Clay

Now for his brothers. He'd hoped they'd receive their letters
before D-day. It was ridiculous to mail the letters to Texas first,
but what could he do without their addresses?

Dear Wyatt,

*I pray this letter will reach you before everything heats
up over here.*

*I need you to know I've fully forgiven you. On that day
three years ago, you acted out of a legitimate fear for your
life. Although I was upset not to go to college and medical
school, I've found my place in the Rangers. It's a good fit,
and I'm glad to be here. I've enjoyed my training, and I know
we'll accomplish great things. Please don't beat yourself up
about the changed course of my life. Much good has come
out of it, and I see the Lord's hand in it all.*

*I appreciate that you want to pay me back. Part of me
wants to forgive your financial debt, but I reckon you
wouldn't rest until it was repaid anyway. And as a husband
and father, I'd be foolish to turn the money down. So I thank
you in advance.*

It's my deepest desire that our family would be restored. Don't ever doubt our parents' forgiveness. At times I've resented their easy and generous forgiveness, but it only reflects the forgiveness of our Savior.

Please forgive me for taking so long to forgive you. My resentment was an offense against the Lord's forgiveness of my own sins.

I'm glad to hear you've found such an honorable way to serve. On that day, I'll feel better knowing my big brother may be at sea, protecting my back.

You always protected me, you know. No one dared pick on me for being half Mexican, because you and Adler wouldn't stand for it.

I always looked up to you as the voice of reason and restraint, of compassion and good cheer. Your quiet strength showed me a vision of manhood different from what Daddy and Adler showed me—and more in keeping with my personality. You have influenced me for great good, and I thank you. I love you, and I miss you.

Please rest in the knowledge of my total forgiveness and love.

Your brother,
Clay

Clay stretched and scooted back on the cot. He slipped the letter in an envelope and marked it "Wyatt Paxton," with room for his parents to add the address. Then he pulled out a sheet of stationery for the brother he'd been closest to—and was now furthest from.

Dear Adler,
You're probably reading this with trepidation, and I don't blame you. The last time you saw me, I told you I'd kill you if I ever saw you again.

Please forgive me. Forgive me for beating you up, for threatening you, for driving you away from home, and for taking so long to forgive you.

I'm glad you've turned to the Lord for forgiveness. Please know I've fully forgiven you as well.

If anything, your actions have altered your life far more than mine. Ellen's lack of love for me would have surfaced at some point, and I'm glad I didn't marry a woman who loved someone else. This freed me to marry my Leah, who has been a blessing.

I've been pondering how difficult it must be for you to hear about what happened in your absence. Rest assured that Ellen's death had nothing to do with you, only with her reckless driving. And Timmy is Daddy and Mama's pride and joy. He's your spitting image. Sometimes God brings great light out of our darkest moments. Timmy is that light.

Three years ago, Daddy ordered you to leave and I ordered you never to return. Both orders have been rescinded. Our parents long to welcome you home, and I want you to return as well. Nothing would make me happier than for our family to be restored.

Just so you know I'm sincere, I saw you on the Queen Elizabeth. Daddy said you saw me too, but it must have been at a different time. I was standing guard, and I had a rifle. And Adler, I didn't use it. Trust me, you're safe.

I'm glad to hear you're a fighter pilot, and I'm sure you're a good one. Every time I hear airplanes overhead, I look for you, not that I'd recognize your plane. It makes me feel good that when I go into action, you'll be overhead protecting us boys on the ground. Once again, Adler Paxton will beat up any bullies who pick on his little brother. And if I see any enemy planes chasing you fellows, I'll pop a few rounds their way.

I miss you, Adler. You made my life fun and adventurous. Without your example, I don't know if I'd have been Ranger material. You showed me how to balance excellence in school, sports, and friendship. Your humor and high spirits always lifted me. I've probably never told you, but I love you very much.

Please know my forgiveness is genuine and deep.

Your brother forever,
Clay

Clay inserted the letter in the envelope and wrote "Adler Paxton" on it.

A strange thing happened as he wrote the letters. The more he wrote, the more he wanted to be kind, to reassure his brothers, to grant them peace after he was gone, with no regrets. The more he wrote the words of forgiveness, the more he felt them, the more he meant them, and the more he knew them to be right and true.

One last letter. The most difficult of all.

My darling wife,

If you're reading this letter, it means you've already received a telegram. I pray this letter won't cause any additional distress. You're a strong woman, and I know you'll bear the loss of our friendship with grace.

Take comfort in knowing I'm with Jesus, as I take comfort in knowing you and Helen are set for life. The GI life insurance will easily last six years, and the check from Wyatt will cover another few years. Perhaps you could use it to pay for library school when Helen starts school.

To make the money stretch further, I urge you to accept my parents' invitation to move to Kerrville. This would place you in the midst of family. Our daughter would have more aunts, uncles, and cousins than she could shake her pudgy fist at.

I also think you're just what the Paxtons need. Daddy and Mama have forgiven Wyatt and Adler, but things could be tense. Your sweet spirit would be a tonic for my ailing family.

As for your own family, once again I urge you to visit Chicago. I pray the Lord will lead you to your sisters.

Thank you for your example. Your devotion to your family showed me the importance of my own. Your wise words and mercy toward all who have harmed you helped me to forgive my brothers and to let them know of that forgiveness.

You may be wondering the purpose of this letter. Everything I've written summarizes what I've told you before. Maybe I wrote it so you'd have it in one place. More likely, I did it to procrastinate.

Leah, for the past week, I've been debating whether or not to tell you something. I don't debate the truth of what I have to say—from the moment I realized it, I've had no doubts. I debated because I didn't know if it would bring you comfort or discomfort. I've decided it'll do more good than harm.

When I married you, I'd hoped we wouldn't become too attached to each other, since we both knew how this would end. I felt affection for you, like a brother giving to a little sister. Somewhere along the line, things changed. The little sister became a lovely woman. The giving brother became the recipient of your wisdom, grace, and compassion.

My love for you has shifted and grown and deepened. Leah, I've fallen in love with you.

You can see why I waited to confess this until after I was gone. If you had returned my feelings, it would have only led to more anguish when I died. If you hadn't, it could have caused an awkward rift between us. Selfishly, I didn't want to lose you so close to the end.

I'm confessing this as my last gift to you. My sweet Leah, I want you to know how lovable you are. Since you were four, you've had no one to love you, no one to tell you how wonderful you are. Although our daughter adores you, she won't be able to voice it for years.

So I'll voice it. I love how you can't bear for a book to be scrapped. I love how you knew Helen was a girl before she was born. I love how you write poetry, how you cling to your sisters, how you search for the good even in the dark. And I love how you gently but forcibly urged me to do the right thing and forgive my brothers.

You are beautiful and modest and kind and faithful and merciful. And the memory of our too-short kiss at the wedding has undone me more times than I care to admit.

I don't write this to make you squirm or so you'll mourn me more. I say this only to build your confidence in the lovely woman you are.

Go live your life to the fullest of God's purpose. Love our daughter and raise her well. Give your best to libraries as a librarian or a volunteer. Marry again with my heartfelt blessing. Most of all, continue to grow in faith and love.

I love you, my darling, my muse, my Thalia.

I was blessed to be your husband.

> *Yours,*
> *Clay*

His breath caught. His throat felt rough, his nose stuffy, and his eyes burned.

He didn't want to leave her, but he had no choice.

Clay bent his head over the letter, his heart splayed out on paper. *Lord, I've lost my desire to die. So please strengthen my resolve.*

33

Wheels rattled on the pavement as Leah pushed Helen in the baby carriage, Mrs. Paxton pulled the Bellamy children's wagon, and Rita Sue pushed a wheelbarrow.

Leah paused and adjusted her new summer hat to keep the morning sun out of her eyes. "Thank you again for helping the children's home with the scrap drive."

"It's a pleasure," Rita Sue said. "I know y'all need adults to help with the little ones—as well as wagons and wheelbarrows."

Mama steered the wagon around a pothole. "Besides, I can't wait for everyone to see these kids as assets, as giving, not taking."

"Today they *are* taking," Leah said. "Taking scrap."

The ladies laughed.

"Lupe, have you told her yet?" Rita Sue asked.

"Told me what?"

Mama changed hands on the wagon handle. "Now I can tell you about yesterday's errand—I spent the day at the library."

"The library? I thought you were shopping."

"I didn't want to raise false hope." Mama turned onto Jackson

Street. "Mrs. Sheridan is quite the research librarian. We now have a list of addresses of all the orphanages in the Chicago area."

Leah stopped, and her mouth hung open.

Rita Sue smiled and motioned her forward with her chin. "Move along."

Mama wore a smug expression. "I was planning on returning to Kerrville at the end of May, but I'll stay an extra week. You and I are taking the train to Chicago—the *Dixie Flagler*."

Leah's head whirled. "But that's—I couldn't—how?—the baby."

"It's all set. We're staying with my cousin's daughter in Chicago. She has two little ones, so we'll have supplies and can wash diapers. And I can watch Helen while you search."

"But that's so expensive."

Mama flapped her hand. "Will insisted, and Clay's been nagging me to make you go. These Paxton men are generous to a fault. That's mighty handy sometimes." She winked at Leah.

All the pictures she'd seen of the city scrolled through her mind, but the picture she couldn't see was the one she longed for most dearly—Callie and Polly.

Mama puckered one corner of her mouth. "You aren't used to receiving gifts, are you?"

"Yes, I am." Leah frowned into the borrowed baby carriage. "I've received charity all my life."

"Ah, *mija*. It's not the same. This is a gift of love."

Leah blinked over grainy eyes. Biblical love from Clay. Familial love from Mama Paxton. "So when do we leave?"

Mama grinned. "Sunday, June 4. Helen will be seven weeks old."

Leah smiled at her sleeping daughter, dressed in a light kimono for the warm day. "I'm sure she'll be a good traveler."

On the lawn at the Coffee Children's Home, Miss King passed out red, white, and blue sashes to the children. Wagons and carts bore hand-lettered signs reading "Coffee Children's Home for Victory!"

"Mrs. Paxton!" Miss King looked even more flustered than usual, but in a happy way. "The children are so excited about this scrap drive."

"I'm excited too." Leah braced herself as two of the girls hugged her, one on each side, and Leah hugged them back.

Miss King leaned closer. "They can't join the Scouts or the Junior Red Cross, because we can't pay their dues. They're itching to do something for the war effort."

"Of course, they are," Mama said. "I'm glad my Leah thought of a way for them to help."

Miss King divided the children into pairs, with an adult or older child minding each group, including Mama and Rita Sue.

Leah was assigned to ten-year-old Mikey and six-year-old Hattie. The little girl had arrived at the orphanage recently when her foster father was drafted and her foster mother took a factory job. Since the child was one-quarter black, Miss King said it would be difficult to place her in a home, which broke Leah's heart.

Hattie climbed into the wagon, but her large dark eyes followed Mama Paxton. "That lady has dark skin."

"Yes, she does." Leah nodded for Mikey to start pulling the wagon down Dechard Street. "Her family comes from Mexico, where it's sunny and warm."

Hattie pulled one of her little black braids and squinted at Leah. "Your skin's kinda dark too."

Leah inspected her bare arm in the sunshine. At last she'd lost enough weight to wear her yellow floral dress again. "My family came from Greece, where it's also sunny and warm."

"I'm dark."

"Oh, I think that's because some of your family came from Africa, where it's sunny and warm. Now, Mikey has lovely pink skin—"

"Pink! That's a girly color." Mikey glowered at her.

"A manly shade of peach." She gave him a reassuring smile.

"But when he spends too much time in the sun, he turns redder than the stripe on your sash. You and I don't, Hattie."

"Here's our street." Mikey turned onto Franklin and up to a white bungalow.

"All right, children. You know what to say." Leah motioned them up the walkway, while she stayed behind with the baby.

Mikey rang the doorbell, and a young woman in a green floral housedress and a blue gingham apron answered the door. Two small children peeked out from behind her.

"Good morning, ma'am." Mikey tipped his cap to her. "We're from the Coffee Children's Home. We're collecting scrap. Got any tin or paper we can turn in for you?"

"Oh my! Aren't y'all sweet? I have a heap of paper and metal scrap out back, and I haven't had time to haul it in."

"We'd be happy to do that for you, ma'am."

"Meet me out back." She shut the door.

Mikey and Hattie ran around the house, the wagon clattering behind them. In a few minutes, they returned, the wagon half full.

"Good job," Leah said. "At this rate, we'll be the first back."

Mikey's grin stretched the width of his narrow face. "Told Marty I'd beat him. Come on, Hattie."

Hattie didn't move. She lifted a foot capped with a white bobby sock and a sturdy brown shoe. "Teacher and Principal were fighting over me."

Fighting? "How's that?"

"Teacher says I'm not white, and she shouldn't have to have me in her class."

Leah's gut contracted and burned.

"Principal says I'm not black enough for the colored school, so they have to keep me." Hattie twisted her dusky arm in the warm air. "I'm not white. I'm not black. I'm nothing."

"Oh! Darling girl!" Leah stopped the baby carriage and scooped Hattie up onto her hip. "You are not nothing. You are something."

The girl lowered her chin.

Leah fingered one of her braids. "This isn't nothing. I can feel it. It's something." She tapped her nose. "This isn't nothing. It's something."

One slight shoulder shrugged.

Leah poked her lightly in the side, prompting a giggle. "See? Nothing can't laugh. Only something can laugh. You are something. In fact, you're something special."

Mikey faced them, his hands coiled into fists. "Who's your teacher, Hattie? I've a mind to pop her in the nose."

"Hush," Leah said. "No one's going to pop anyone in the nose, you hear?"

Mikey groaned. "I hear. But I oughta. Miss King says we're all created in God's image—you, me, Hattie, the Negro boys and girls at the Davidson Academy. All of us."

Leah smiled and hugged Hattie. "That's right. Listen to Miss King. She's a wise woman. Every person is special to God. *You* are special to him. Don't you ever forget that."

Don't you either. The voice flitted into Leah's ear, so faint, she thought Hattie had spoken, but the child was squirming out of Leah's arms.

Made in God's image. Special. Beloved. Belonging.

Leah glanced into the carriage to her darling sleeping daughter, then back toward the children's home, where she was welcome, and where she'd come with her mother-in-law and her dear friend, who had enveloped her with friendship and love.

Yes, she did belong.

34

The thirty-two men in Clay's platoon gathered around a large table in a tent. Clay's lungs filled with the heavy smell of damp canvas, but his veins filled with anticipation.

Lt. Bill Taylor leaned big hands on the blanket-draped table. "This is it, boys."

Ernie McKillop whooped, and the men laughed.

Clay grinned. As soon as they'd arrived at the camp outside Dorchester, the MPs had strung barbed wire around their enclosure. Confined to the marshaling area, the Rangers knew what was happening.

Now they'd finally learn the plan Rudder and the other officers had sweated over.

"You are some of the few troops in this invasion who will know the full scope of the plan before we board our transports. That's because you need to know not only your individual objective, but that of your squad, your section, your platoon, your company, and both Ranger battalions."

That's why Clay liked the Rangers. The combination of individual and group responsibility resonated with him.

Taylor flopped over part of the blanket, revealing a map. "This is where the Allies will be invading—in the Normandy region of France."

Clay edged closer with his buddies.

Taylor pointed to the end of the map. "From the left flank to the right, the British will land here on Sword Beach, the Canadians on Juno Beach, and more British on Gold. US V Corps will land on Omaha, and US VII Corps on Utah. In V Corps, the 1st Infantry Division will land to the left, the 29th to the right. The 2nd and 5th Rangers are attached to 29th Division."

Clay crossed his arms. A broad enough front to handle the large number of troops but narrow enough to support each other. Wise.

"This is the Rangers' objective, Pointe du Hoc." Taylor pointed to a triangle of land between Omaha and Utah. "The Germans have six French-made 155-mm guns on this point. These guns have a range of 25,000 yards. That's over ten miles, boys. Far enough to reach Utah, Omaha, and the fleet offshore."

Clay let out a low whistle at the semicircle around the point showing the range.

Lieutenant Taylor flung the blanket off the rest of the table, revealing a contoured rubber map. "This shows the assault area for the 29th Division. Here's the plan. Ranger Force A will consist of Companies D, E, and F of the 2nd Rangers—you boys. We'll land directly at Pointe du Hoc."

Gene nudged Clay and grinned. Yep, they'd received the best assignment.

"Force B is Company C of the 2nd Rangers. They'll land on Charlie Beach at the far right of Omaha, to the right of the D-1 draw at Vierville-sur-Mer. They'll climb the cliff, proceed to Pointe de la Percée, take out the guns and radar station there, then meet us at Pointe du Hoc."

A climb and a five-mile hike. Those fellows would be busy.

"Force C consists of our Companies A and B, plus all six companies of the 5th Battalion. They'll wait offshore. If our mission is successful, they'll land at Pointe du Hoc to reinforce us. If we fail—"

"Fat chance," Manfred Brady said.

Taylor lowered his eyebrows. "If we fail, they'll land at Dog Green Beach to the left of the D-1 draw, and they'll make their way to Pointe du Hoc. No matter what, the Rangers are taking out those guns."

"Yes, sir."

"Come with me." Taylor marched to another table and slid the blanket off another rubber map. "This is Pointe du Hoc."

Clay murmured in appreciation, along with the other men.

A thin dagger of land stabbed the sea, surrounded by steep cliffs and a narrow strip of beach. At least their cliff-climbing skills wouldn't go to waste.

"Here are the six guns." Taylor touched six positions in a V, then the tip of the point. "And an observation post. The point is heavily defended with minefields, barbed wire, machine guns, antiaircraft guns, and a network of trenches and bunkers. But the defenses are set up against an attack from the land, not the sea. After all, these cliffs are one hundred feet tall."

Laughter whipped around the tent.

"Come on, Lieutenant." Gene elbowed Clay. "Can't you get us a better challenge than that?"

Taylor sobered. "This time you'll have Germans shooting down at you."

The laughter dribbled away.

The platoon leader straightened up and crossed his arms. "Pointe du Hoc will get a thorough working over by Allied aircraft and ships. They'll bomb the stuffing out of this place. But we must be prepared."

"Yes, sir."

"Before we embark and while we're on board, you boys will be busy." He gestured around the tent. "We'll have more briefings. You'll study maps, aerial photos, and sand tables. You'll memorize the terrain, the tides, and the location of every gun and defensive position. You will each receive an individual objective and will know it well."

Clay nodded. The triangle of land was marked up with indications for bunkers and gun emplacements. Which one was the structure from his recurring dream? Where would he die?

Something stretched and tugged in his chest, pulling him away from that dream—the longing to see Leah and Helen, Wyatt and Adler, Daddy and Mama.

Clay forced himself to look around the tent at Gene and Ruby and Holman and McKillop. At Taylor and Lombardi and all the others.

Every man in the platoon had loved ones back home. Every man had reasons to live. And every man was willing to sacrifice his life for the greater good. To take out those guns and protect the soldiers on Omaha and Utah and the sailors at sea. To assure the success of D-day and the Allied cause, to free the enslaved peoples of Europe and protect the folks back home.

Clay stifled a chuckle. It wasn't as if he were solely responsible.

But if every man worked together and put others above self, the Allies would succeed.

Clay ran his finger along the rubbery rim of the cliff. *Lord, don't let me falter.*

WEYMOUTH, ENGLAND
THURSDAY, JUNE 1, 1944

"Lovely day for a seaside stroll, old chap, what what?" Gene said in his affected English accent.

"Estás loco, viejo." Clay shook his head at his crazy old man friend.

But Gene had a point. The Rangers marched in columns of two down the Esplanade in Weymouth. Filmy clouds and big silver barrage balloons floated in the bright blue sky. To Clay's right, three- and four-story buildings lined the Esplanade, including the stately gray Victoria Hotel and a quaint building striped with alternating red and white bricks.

The blue bay stretched away to his left. Sandbags and rolls of barbed wire served as a reminder of when Britain feared an invasion. Now they were launching one.

Sergeant Lombardi sang "I've Been Working on the Railroad," and Clay joined in.

They were all dressed for combat, in Parsons field jackets, trousers tucked into Corcoran boots, and net-covered steel helmets emblazoned on the back with an orange diamond with a blue "2" in the middle for the 2nd Ranger Battalion.

Clay wore his pack on his back, his gas mask in a black neoprene case on his chest, and his cartridge belt around his waist, loaded to the brim. He carried an M1 Garand rifle, while others carried BAR Browning Automatic Rifles, Tommy guns, mortars, carbines, and pistols.

In front of him, Pete Voinescu paused to rearrange his hefty medical pack, and Clay halted his step so he wouldn't run into the medic. Pete had better not waste too many supplies on Clay in his final moments.

A twinge in his chest. He'd tied up his loose ends, but Daddy had unraveled one.

With Mama still in Tullahoma, only Daddy had read the letter in the pack Clay had mailed. Daddy—always quick and impulsive—hadn't read it carefully. He assured Clay that if the worst should happen, he'd mail Clay's letters to Wyatt, Adler, and Leah.

Except Clay had only asked him to hold Leah's letter until after his death. He'd wanted his brothers' letters mailed immediately. Now they wouldn't receive his forgiveness before the invasion.

Nothing Clay could do about it now.

Lieutenant Taylor led the platoon into a tent along the Esplanade. A sign read "From the folks back home through the American Red Cross."

The smell of coffee and donuts filled his nostrils, and he pulled out his tin canteen cup and lined up.

American women in gray-blue uniforms ladled coffee from a giant vat into the Rangers' cups and passed them donuts.

"Thank you kindly, miss." Clay nodded to the young lady, small and dark haired like his Leah, and he took a swig of nice hot coffee.

"Thank *you*," she said in a soft voice, also like his Leah.

Clay's throat contracted, and he almost choked. Was that the last time he'd hear a woman's voice? See a female face?

Outside, on the far side of the tent, Clay passed photographers and a movie camera, and he faked a grin and lifted his cup to those folks back home who'd sent young ladies to serve him his last donut. To his parents. To Leah.

Clay chewed his donut as the Rangers fell back into formation and resumed their march. A seagull swooped down for a bite. Clay shooed him away, and the bird squawked in protest.

He didn't want to die anymore, but he was ready. He'd been praying constantly. The joy hadn't returned, but the peace had, and resolve had taken root and held.

At the end of the Esplanade, a spit of land thrust into the harbor, topped with the massive white Weymouth Pavilion, covered with domes and balconies and other turn-of-the-century ornamentation.

Clay crossed the spit of land to a canal, where a dozen gray-blue landing craft were docked. His squad and three others lined up by their vessel. They'd used the same LCA in numerous amphibious exercises, and today it'd take them out into the harbor to their LSI transport, *Ben-my-Chree*.

"We're ready for you chaps." A Royal Navy officer checked off their names on his manifest.

Clay gave his name, then led his squad down concrete steps cut into the pier and out onto a floating wooden dock. The British crew gave him a hand, and he stepped down into the belly of the LCA. The men took their seats on two benches along each side and one down the center.

Clay straddled the center bench and arranged his pack and rifle to make room for the other men.

"Smoke?" McKillop held up a pack of Lucky Strikes, and Clay passed it on by.

When all the men were crammed in, Lieutenant Taylor signaled to the coxswain. The motor revved, and the boat putted down the canal.

The side of the landing craft was above Clay's head, and he couldn't see where he'd come from or where he was going.

Low in a pit once again.

The pit had turned out to be the right place for him, and he was thankful for all that had happened there, but it was time to leave.

Clay stood and braced himself against the armor-plated plywood of the hull, and other Rangers stood too. Brisk air flowed over his face and into his soul.

The boat trotted over the blue waves with its herd, each LCA with a wake like a plumy white tail.

Farther out in the harbor sat giant gray warships and transports, as the huge invasion fleet received the horde of soldiers and prepared to sail.

The Rangers were scheduled for another briefing tonight on board the *Ben-my-Chree*. At last they'd hear the date for D-day.

How many days, how many hours until he left the pit for good?

Behind him, Lombardi sang "Over There" in his rough bass.

Clay laughed at the song from the previous war and then joined in the appropriate lyrics. The Yanks were indeed coming, and someday soon it would be over, over there.

Clay grinned at Gene and Ruby and Holman and McKillop. He wouldn't see that day, but he'd do his bit to make it happen.

Resolve and peace and purpose wove together into a rope, strong and true. It would hold.

35

Leah clutched sleeping Helen to her chest as she fought to keep up with Mama Paxton's brisk pace down the train platform.

The station lights illuminated the *Dixie Flagler*'s sleek aluminum sides. What a sumptuous journey, with reclining seats and an elegant dinner. The ladies' lounge and restroom had even been roomy enough for her to nurse and change the baby.

Since the train left Nashville at one thirty, Leah had spent her time playing with the baby and watching the Midwest roll by.

A year had passed since she'd taken the train south from Des Moines. The year before, she'd worn that dumpy gray dress with a long braid down her back, wide-eyed and innocent.

Now she was a mother in a chic grassy green suit with her hair rolled up under her sweet summer hat. She was no longer innocent, but she felt stronger and wiser.

At the baggage car, Mama gave the porter their claim ticket, and the man stacked their bags onto a trolley.

Three stylishly dressed black women stepped out of the baggage

238

car, and Leah's heart lurched. How unjust that segregation in the South required them to ride back there just because of the color of their skin. No reclining seats. No elegant meals.

Leah gave them a nod and a small smile as they passed. She would acknowledge their worth, even if no one else did.

The porter wheeled the trolley into the station, and Leah followed with Mama.

Although it was ten o'clock at night, hundreds of people filled Dearborn Station. So many sailors in bright white tunics and bell-bottom trousers, their "Dixie cup" caps at rakish angles.

Three soldiers passed in olive drab service uniforms, like Clay had worn at their wedding. She'd received a letter from him yesterday, each letter a treasure. The invasion hadn't occurred, but the nation crackled with tension as summer rose on the horizon.

By the ticket windows, a poster showed a crowd of soldiers boarding a train. The caption read "Is your trip necessary?"

Leah winced and did a double step to catch up to Mama. Should she have taken a seat in wartime for a personal errand?

"Daddy!" Three school-age children darted through the crowd and slammed into a sailor. He lifted the youngest high, laughing and grinning.

Leah's shoulders relaxed. Yes, her trip was necessary. If she had even the slightest possibility of reuniting her fractured little family, she had to take it.

The porter led them outside and hailed a taxi.

Behind Leah, a tall square clock tower soared above the red brick station building.

The scent of the city was gently familiar, reaching into her mind and whispering to sleeping memories, urging them to awaken and step into the light.

A yellow taxi pulled up. The porter loaded the luggage into the trunk, the driver held open the back door, and Mama motioned Leah inside and tipped the porter.

Leah settled in. Helen made a face and turned toward Leah's chest. "A little longer, sweetheart," Leah cooed.

Mama sat and gave the address to the driver, and the cab pulled away from the curb.

"I'm so excited." Mama folded gloved hands over her purse. "Tomorrow morning we'll sit down with Juanita and a map and the list of orphanages, and we'll plan your trip."

"Tomorrow morning." Leah gazed out at the darkened city and smiled. Somewhere out there were the answers she longed for. Somewhere out there her sisters might even be sleeping.

They'd be fifteen years old now. What did they look like? Sound like? Did they love school as she had? Books? Poetry? Or did they love jitterbugging and movie stars and baseball? She couldn't wait to find out.

Please, Lord, let me have the chance.

CHICAGO
MONDAY, JUNE 5, 1944

The massive gray stone building didn't look familiar from the outside, nor when Leah stepped inside.

But how long had she been in an orphanage before the Joneses adopted her? All she remembered was struggling as Mr. Jones carried her over his shoulder—crying for her sisters.

Leah shuddered. A horrible day, but today she had a chance to reverse it.

"May I help you, ma'am?" the nun behind the desk asked, her young face round and smiley under her habit.

"Yes, ma'am—sister." Since Leah didn't see any Greek Orthodox orphanages on the list, she'd try all the homes—Catholic, Protestant, and Jewish. "I'm looking for my little sisters. My parents died when I was four, and my sisters and I were placed in an orphanage, but I don't know which one. I was adopted, but without my sisters."

The nun folded her hands on the desk. "Your adoption papers should list the orphanage."

"I don't have them. The family who adopted me—they abandoned me at an orphanage in Des Moines without my birth certificate or adoption records."

"Oh dear." The nun clapped her hand over her mouth. "What an awful thing to do."

"It was, but I've forgiven them." Leah wound her fingers around her purse strap. "I know you must be busy, but could you search your records for my sisters and me?"

The nun pulled out a sheet of paper. "Your names, please?"

"My name is Thalia, and my sisters are Callie and Polly—possibly short for Calliope and Polyhymnia. I think we were all named after Greek muses."

"Oh my." Thin dark eyebrows rose. "Last name?"

"I don't know. I was only four, and I couldn't pronounce it."

"Oh dear." The nun nodded toward an office in the back. "Our records are filed alphabetically by last name."

Leah's chest contracted around her shrinking heart. "It sounded like Ka-wa-los."

"I'm so sorry, ma'am." Her light brown eyes went round. "Our records go back to the 1890s, and we had up to eight hundred children at a time during the Depression. You can imagine how many files we have."

Tall cabinets lined the wall in the office. If only Leah could search them, but of course, they wouldn't let her.

"Thank you anyway." It wasn't the nun's fault, so Leah worked up a smile. On the paper she wrote down all the information she had and her contact information in Chicago and Tullahoma. "If you should happen to find something . . . but I understand. I do."

"Thank you, ma'am." The nun's smile looked thin but sympathetic.

Leah headed outside into the balmy afternoon, and she leaned back against the rough stone façade.

What now? She was supposed to visit two more homes before she returned to Juanita's house to nurse Helen, but she'd have the same problem at every orphanage.

Was it even worth it? Had she come all this way for nothing?

Leah pressed her fingers to her temples. The familiar ache of longing for her family deepened, here in this city where she'd lost them.

36

The LCA cranked into a right turn away from the *Ben-my-Chree*, and Clay banged into Lt. Bill Taylor. "Sorry, sir."

"It's all right." Taylor looked over his shoulder. "It's 0430, boys. Here we go."

Clay followed the lieutenant's gaze. Somewhere above the overcast, the moon shone dim gray light on the other twenty Rangers and the British boat crew.

The landing craft chugged forward at six knots over bumpy waves. It would take two hours to travel the twelve miles from the transport area to Pointe du Hoc, where the Rangers were due to land at 0630.

He stood up so he could see over the side. Although he'd never be able to tell the story of what he'd done on D-day, he didn't want to miss a single one of his last moments.

Clay gripped the bow ramp, and cold saltwater misted over his face. He squinted at the two columns of boats—a British motor launch that would guide Force A to shore, four DUKWs, and twelve LCAs—ten carrying the Rangers and two carrying supplies.

Lt. Col. Jim Rudder rode in the leading LCA. He was supposed to have stayed on the command ship USS *Ancon* to direct both the 2nd and 5th Battalions. But when the Force A commander had gotten rip-roaring drunk the night before and had punched Doc Block, the commander had been escorted off the transport. Rudder had taken his place.

Clay didn't mind having the football coach leading his team.

What a team. Clay stood in the bow with Lieutenant Taylor on his left and Gene on his right. Holman, McKillop, and Ruby sat behind them. Clay's rifle squad would be first off the boat. Behind them sat Sgt. Tommy Lombardi with the Browning Automatic Rifle squad, including Manfred Brady and Frank Lyons. In the rear sat the two squads from the other section.

A wave hit the side of the LCA, and cold water slipped over the side of the boat. Clay fought off a shudder. If Lyons wanted to kill Clay, today would be the day to do it.

Then he chuckled. He wouldn't die at the hand of Frank Lyons.

A low rumble built overhead, approaching from the north, a deep and persistent drone. Had to be the Lancaster heavy bombers of the Royal Air Force, which were scheduled to dump bombs on the point starting at 0450.

A retching sound behind him. Bob Holman leaned over with a paper bag to his mouth. Then he tossed the bag overboard, wiped his mouth on his sleeve, and groaned.

Come to think of it, the ride was pretty rough for any stomach that hadn't been toughened by Mama's chili peppers. Clay pulled his bag from inside his field jacket and handed it to Holman.

One less thing for Clay to carry. The Rangers were traveling light. Two bandoliers of ammo crisscrossed Clay's chest, and his cartridge belt was loaded with ammo, grenades, and one chocolate D ration bar. All the men's packs and extra ammunition and rations and demolitions would land with the two supply LCAs. As for luxury items, Gene wore Betty Jo's red-and-blue necktie under his uniform, and Clay carried his serviceman's Bible with Leah and Helen's picture tucked inside.

Gene leaned in front of Clay. "Say, Lieutenant? Should we bail?"

An inch or two of water sloshed around Clay's boots. With the extra layer of armor, the British LCAs rode lower in the water than the American LCVPs.

"We're fine." Taylor peered into the darkness and nodded behind him. "But I don't like the looks of that boat—D Company, I think."

Sure enough, one landing craft rode even lower in the water. Motion flickered above the top line of the boat—the Rangers bailing, most likely.

"Just to be safe." Gene took off his helmet, scooped some water, and flung it over the side. The wind caught it and flung half of it back in. He scrunched up his face at Clay. "The wind is fighting for the Germans."

Clay chuckled and scooped a helmet-full himself. Bailing didn't hurt, and it might help. But he emptied it on the other side.

Taylor cursed. "Forget what I said. Everyone, bail."

What had changed? With his next scoop, Clay glanced back toward the low-riding LCA—only the bow was showing, and small white splashes appeared in the inky water. It was going down.

Clay wanted to order the coxswain to swing around and pick up the men in the water, but the coxswain wouldn't listen. And rightly so. Not only did they have to stick to their timetable, but the extra weight would endanger their own craft.

"Lord, send someone to rescue them." Clay's helmet scraped along the plywood bottom of the hull.

For the next half hour, the LCA plodded through the waves, and the men bailed off and on and vomited off and on.

Clay's years working in Dr. Hill's office had also steadied his stomach. For the first time in years, he smiled at the thought of his former mentor. A good man who had given so much to a boy he'd believed in and supported, despite the color of his skin.

The gray light rose, and faint colors emerged—the dark khaki of the men's field jackets, the brownish-green of their trousers, the orange diamonds on the backs of their helmets and the blue diamonds on their sleeves. Gene's red hair and Holman's green face.

Clay peered across the water. A dark band appeared between gray sea and gray sky, and orange fires glowed from the aerial bombardment. Normandy.

A sound like a train approached, loud and furious, and Clay ducked with all the other men. A naval shell and a big one.

The boat shuddered, and the concussion wave pressed Clay even lower. Had to be the battleship USS *Texas*, which was supposed to bombard Pointe du Hoc starting at 0550.

He sat up. More shells crossed in streams of colored light, too many to count. Whopping 14-inch shells, bigger than basketballs. The thunder of the impact, the fires that rose—how could any man stand it?

But . . . the shells should have been landing straight ahead. They weren't. They were landing about forty-five degrees to their right. "Say, Lieutenant, are we off course or is the *Texas*?"

Lieutenant Taylor frowned. "Don't think it's either. Must be another ship and another battery. Look—there's a destroyer ahead shelling the point. Must be the *Satterlee*."

"Must be." But the *Texas* was the only battleship in their sector. The others were shelling gun batteries around Omaha and Utah Beaches.

Another half hour of chugging and bailing. The sun rose behind the clouds, the last sunrise Clay would ever see.

His gut squeezed, but he kept pitching water over the side. He'd done everything he needed to do. Today he had to focus on the mission and the mission alone.

With both elbows on the bow ramp, Taylor lowered his field glasses and wiped sea spray off his face. But he didn't wipe off the frown. "You might be right, Paxton."

"Right?" Clay shook out water from his helmet and put it on his head. The land features grew clearer and clearer.

Taylor pointed straight ahead. "That's not Pointe du Hoc. I'm pretty sure it's Pointe de la Percée."

The point ahead was soft and round. To their right, where the shells were exploding, the point was sharp. Through the smoke and fire, a familiar notch in the tip took shape.

Taylor cussed and faced the stern. "MacNab! We're off course."

The coxswain waved him off, but then he shaded his eyes, frowned, and called out orders to the other three crewmen.

The LCA made a sharp right turn, and Clay thumped down to the center bench. He grabbed the ramp and got back to his feet.

All the LCAs turned right, with Rudder's craft leading the way.

"Man alive." They were indeed off course, and Clay's jaw fell open, collecting a mouthful of seawater. He spat it out.

The relentless noise of naval shells suddenly stopped, and Clay yanked up his left sleeve. It was 0630—H-hour, when they were supposed to land. When the naval bombardment was scheduled to lift. And their objective lay about three miles away.

"Good Lord, help us."

CHICAGO

"That's my sweet girl." Leah tied a bow to the side of Helen's kimono, pressing tiny kicking legs out of her way with her forearm.

A smile curved into her baby's plump cheeks, and she kicked harder.

Leah kissed those cheeks, one after the other. "Who has the prettiest smile? Helen does."

Helen grabbed a lock of Leah's hair.

She eased herself free and lifted the baby to her shoulder. "Ready for another fun day with *Abuelita*?"

Out in the living room, Mama and her cousin's daughter, Juanita Romero, sat by the radio. They both looked at her, faces stark.

It was today, and Leah sank onto the couch and tuned her ears to the announcer's cultured voice: "Under the command of General Eisenhower, Allied naval forces, supported by strong air forces, began landing Allied armies this morning on the coast of France."

"That's all the news they have." Mama's voice wavered, and she turned off the radio dial. "Naval forces—my Wyatt. Air forces—my Adler. Allied armies—my Clay. Our Clay."

Helen wiggled in Leah's lap, and Leah tightened her grip on her daughter. The child didn't know that at that moment her daddy was fighting for his life. Might even be dead.

Leah sucked in a breath, and it snagged all the way in.

"Let's pray." Mama moved to the couch and clamped her hand on Leah's forearm. "Almighty God, we pray for our boys. Please keep them safe and hold them in your hand."

Leah prayed along, but something about the prayer felt askew. What if Clay was correct and it was God's will for him to die today? Was it right to pray only for his safety?

She sprang to her feet. "I think—today I'll go to that Greek Orthodox church I wanted to visit."

Sympathy flooded Mama's brown eyes. "Maybe you should take a day off from your search."

"I can pray there just as easily as I can pray here. And I need—I need to be busy." She returned to the guest room, laid Helen in the bassinet, and packed baby supplies in her bag. "I'll take Helen. I'll come back at noon to feed her."

"Are you sure?" Mama leaned against the doorjamb.

Leah tied on the baby's bonnet. "I need to have her with me."

Before long, Leah stepped off the bus on LaSalle Drive with the baby in her arms. The Annunciation Cathedral stood grand and golden brown with twin square towers framing the entrance.

Something tugged at Leah's memory, but in a flimsy way.

She joined the stream of people flowing through the door to pray for the boys in France.

In the cross-shaped sanctuary, a riot of color met her eyes. Stained glass flung light in all directions. Paintings, overlaid with gold, sparkled in every hue. A screen blocked one branch of the cross, covered with more paintings of saints and the Holy Family.

"I've been here," she whispered, and she sank into a pew.

All around, people chanted prayers. Leah had hoped to speak to a priest, to see if anyone remembered a family with three little girls with poetic names. There were only a few Greek Orthodox churches in Chicago, and this was closest to the university.

Now her search felt trivial with the man she loved fighting on Nazi-occupied shores.

Leah settled the baby on her lap and bowed her head. With everyone chanting around her, she felt no need to pray silently.

"Oh, Lord. You love Clay even more than I do. You know how much I want him to live. But more than that, I want him to do your will."

Her breath clogged her throat, but she swallowed her fears and breathed in conviction. "Grant him courage, Lord. Grant him strength to do all he has to do. No matter the cost. No matter . . . the cost."

It hurt. It hurt so much to say, but it needed to be said. She needed to release Clay. She needed to grasp the only hand that would always be there for her.

"Thank you. Thank you for giving him to me, for all he's done for me and the baby, for all he's meant to me. But he's yours, Lord. He's yours."

Leah gathered her baby closer. "She's yours too. And so am I. You're my Father, my only true Father, now and forever. I know—I know you'll never leave me. Even if you take Clay from me, Helen from me, Mama Paxton from me, you'll never leave me."

Helen cooed.

Leah kissed her bonneted head. "Please hold me together, come what may. Comfort me. Help me be strong for Helen, for Mama. You are my rock and my tower and my Father."

All around her, frantic and desperate prayers sounded.

Leah lifted her face to a dome soaring above, to the image of the Father with his arms outstretched, surrounded by the soft blue of peace and the glittering gold of heaven, the promise of joy, of eternal belonging.

And she smiled.

37

A bullet pinged off the steel-plated hull of the LCA, and Clay hunkered low, his uniform drenched in frigid water. To reach Pointe du Hoc, the Rangers had to race parallel to the coast, only a few hundred yards offshore.

Except LCAs didn't race. The Germans were taking plenty of potshots.

"What about Force C?" Gene clamped his helmet on his head.

Clay groaned. "Doesn't look good."

The 5th Ranger Battalion and two companies from the 2nd waited offshore. If they didn't receive the signal from Force A by 0700, they would land on Omaha Beach instead of at Pointe du Hoc.

Clay's watch read 0644. How could they possibly reach the point and climb those cliffs in only sixteen minutes? "Guess we're on our own."

"Good thing we only need the two of us to clear that point." Gene winked at him.

A roar overhead. Naval shells!

Clay rose just enough to see over the side. Not far offshore a small warship belched smoke and fire. "A destroyer. They must have seen us in trouble."

"Trouble?" Sid Rubenstein snorted in a sarcastic way. "We're not in trouble."

"You tell that destroyer then." McKillop punched Ruby in the arm. "I'll take the help."

Taylor removed his helmet. "Now that we have cover, let's bail."

Clay obeyed. The extra weight of water slowed the plodding LCA even more.

Each time he stood, he surveyed the scene. Naval shells flew overhead and slammed into the bluffs to their left. Ahead, Pointe du Hoc drew nearer and higher, its light brown cliffs jutting out to sea.

Taylor made hand signals to the LCA ahead of them. "All right, boys. Rudder just signaled us. All three companies will land on the east side of the point rather than dividing up. Makes sense. It'd take too long for D Company to round the point and land on the west."

Clay nodded. The narrow beach would be more crowded, but they'd make do.

"I saw a DUKW go down," Brady said. "Took a Jerry shell."

Several men swore. Somewhere along the way, they'd lost one of the supply LCAs too. Now Force A had only nine assault craft, one supply boat, and three DUKWs. That left about two hundred men, with no reinforcements coming.

Clay blew out a sharp breath. *Lord, please don't let me die until after we meet our objectives. We need every man.*

The remaining water wasn't worth scooping, so Clay strapped on the assuring weight of his helmet. Chilly rivulets tickled down his scalp, but he couldn't get any wetter or colder.

If the cliff facing him were in England, Clay wouldn't have

thought anything of it. Sure it was steep, but at one hundred feet it wouldn't challenge the Rangers.

However, it was in Nazi-occupied France, and the USS *Texas* had lifted her fire a half hour before. Any Germans who had survived the bombardment would have had time to recover and man their positions.

Motion at the top of the cliff caught his eye.

"They've seen us," Taylor called. "Prepare to return fire."

Clay shrugged his rifle strap off his shoulder and hefted the familiar twenty pounds of dark wood and steel. After he flipped off the safety, he poked the rifle barrel over the bow ramp. He didn't want to kill. He didn't. But he had to climb that cliff, disable a 155-mm gun, and set up a roadblock to protect the troops on Omaha and Utah.

That sound—the ripping sound of the German *Maschinengewehr 42* that Clay had heard at Camp Ritchie and in his recurring dream. Yellow flashes lit up the far left of the cliff, and Clay fired eight rounds in that direction, slow and steady, the recoil of his M1 rifle thumping into his right shoulder. The clip pinged out, empty, and Clay slipped a new clip out of his bandolier and snapped it down into place in his rifle.

To the left, Rudder's LCA dropped its bow ramp, and men poured out. The rockets fired, and six grapnels shot into the air, trailing ropes and white smoke behind them. The grapnels arced midair— and fell to the beach.

Taylor whipped around and cupped his hand to his mouth. "MacNab! Wait until—"

Two rockets fired at the rear of the craft, deafening Clay.

Taylor waved his arms frantically. "Wait until we're closer!"

"This is as close as we get, mate," the coxswain said.

The bow ramp slammed down into the water, a good twenty-five feet from shore.

Taylor swept his arm in a circle overhead. "Let's go, men!"

Clay charged down the bow ramp and into frigid water up to his waist. He plowed forward, pointing his rifle to the cliff. A man in German field gray stood at the edge of the cliff and hurtled something over—a grenade.

Clay fired a shot, and the German scampered backward.

The last four rockets fired from their LCA, the rising grapnels passing two falling grapnels midair. "Please let them hold."

Bullets zinged past, burrowing into the water.

Clay's heart raced, and he plunged forward, his shins slicing the water, his boots fighting for traction.

Up onto the beach, maybe thirty yards deep. Pebbles scattered underneath his boots, hit his calves.

Clay scrabbled ahead, rifle and gaze high. Three grapnels disappeared over the cliff, and the ropes flopped against the earthen face. "Come on, boys!"

The fourth grapnel descended, and Gene dodged behind Clay, out of the way.

Clay grabbed the first rope, a plain line, and he tugged it hard. It gave way, and Clay jumped back. "Watch out!"

"This one's good." McKillop grabbed a toggle line and started climbing.

"So's this one." Ruby worked his way up a plain line.

Clay stood with his back to the cliff, waiting his turn, catching his breath.

Nine gray-blue LCAs sat just offshore, and Rangers flowed out, over the beach, skirting giant craters. Ropes dangled over the cliff, and men worked their way up.

That machine gun kept up its racket far to his right, and bullets skittered over the beach.

"Medic!"

Clay's breath caught. Several men lay on the beach, and his feet edged their direction.

No. Not today. "There's 'a time to every purpose under the heaven.' This isn't my healing time."

In front of his LCA, a man lay at water's edge, clutching his leg and crying out.

Sergeant Lombardi!

Clay looped his rifle strap over his shoulder and ran to him.

Lombardi's left knee was stained bright red, and his lower leg sat at an awkward angle. He spotted Clay and grimaced. "Get up that cliff, Pax!"

Clay hooked his hands under the man's armpits. "In a minute."

"What've I always told you? Leave the wounded for the medics."

Clay dragged him across the beach, his heels digging into the loose stones. "If I leave you here, there won't be anything left for the medics."

A thumping sound, and Lombardi screamed. Red bloomed on his right ankle—hit again!

"Medic! Medic!" Clay pulled harder, right up to the cliff face, and he shoved Lombardi into a depression.

"Should've—made you —a medic," Lombardi said through gritted teeth.

"Can't hear you, Sarge. Got a cliff to climb, a gun to disable, and a road to block." He wrapped his hands around the plain rope.

"And a—a section to lead."

Clay stared down at his section leader. Lombardi wouldn't be climbing any cliffs today, so Clay nodded. Granted, each man knew his objective, so they didn't need much leading.

Above him the men of his squad were making their way up, with Holman following McKillop on the toggle line, and Gene following Ruby on the plain line. On the beach, the four men of the BAR squad strafed the cliff edge with their automatic rifles.

A bright orange flash out to sea. A destroyer fired at Pointe du Hoc, but a different ship than earlier.

That might not be Wyatt, but Clay sure appreciated the Navy.

Time to climb. The rope was wet, but Clay started up, familiar muscles tightening and working.

When his feet slipped on the muddy cliff face, his hands held. And when his hands slipped, his feet held.

McKillop scrambled over the top, and shots rang out.

"Come on, y'all. Faster!" Clay pumped his arms and legs, determined to catch up with his buddies.

Ruby went over the top too.

"I can't do it." Holman clutched the rope about ten feet from the top and lay flat on a hump on the cliff. He'd suffered from seasickness for over two hours, and he still looked green.

Clay kept climbing. "You have to. Ruby and McKillop need you."

Holman moaned and resumed his climb. "I can't."

"You don't have a choice. You can't stay there. And you can't hold up the line."

"Move it, Holman!" Brady shouted from below, with Lyons right behind him.

Holman cussed, climbed another foot, then sagged. "I just can't."

At the top of the cliff, Gene crawled over the edge.

"G. M.! Wait up. Cover me." Clay jammed his toes into the mud and hauled himself over the top.

Gene knelt before him, rifle raised. "You're covered."

Clay swung around to the other rope, went down on one knee, and leaned over the side. "Come on, Holman! One more step, then I can help you."

Holman's hand shook, but he wrapped it around the rope and pulled himself up.

"That's it." Clay grabbed both his friend's forearms, dug in his heel, and pulled. "You're almost there."

Another foot higher, and Clay latched onto his collar and heaved the man up onto the cliff top like a dead fish.

Then Clay slung off his rifle and swept his gaze around.

"This way!" Gene jumped into a crater.

Clay scrabbled down inside. He'd never seen a crater so big—it had to be twenty feet across. So that was what a 14-inch shell did.

He flopped on his stomach against the side of the crater and peeked over the edge.

All those rubber maps. All those sand tables. Worthless.

The land before him bore no resemblance to any map, to any land he'd ever seen. Pocked by giant craters, swirling with wispy smoke, all landmarks obliterated.

"What now?" Holman slithered into the crater, with Brady and Lyons behind him.

Clay knifed his hand westward. "Let's find that gun."

CHICAGO

Today might turn out to be the saddest in Leah's life, and yet sweet, joyful peace swirled inside. "Thank you, Lord. Thank you for showing me the good."

In Leah's lap, Helen sucked on her fist.

Leah kissed her tiny nose, then prayed for comfort and strength for everyone in the church. How many of them had husbands or brothers or sons or fathers fighting today? Even those who didn't have a loved one overseas needed comfort. All those servicemen were America's boys.

Across the aisle, a woman in her sixties stared at Leah.

Oh dear. She didn't know the rituals of this church, and she'd probably violated some protocol. Leah gave the lady a little smile and nod, and she stood to leave. She had time to visit another orphanage or two before lunchtime.

In the foyer, dim light from the overcast day filtered through the windows of the door.

"Excuse me?"

Leah turned.

The lady who had been watching her raised a nervous smile. "Please pardon me for staring. You must think me terribly rude. I—well, you remind me so much of a dear friend. I—oh my." She pulled a handkerchief from the breast pocket of her beige suit.

"That's all right, ma'am."

The woman dabbed at her eyes, and her smile flickered. "Please pardon me. You do remind me of her. Something about you. Why, even the way you were praying and the way you walk and the way you're holding your baby. Except the last time I saw my friend, she was holding two babies. Oh dear. Look at me. I promise, I don't usually act this way."

Two babies . . . ? Leah could barely breathe. "Your friend—she's gone?"

"I'm afraid so. A long time ago." She drew in a deep breath and gave her head a little shake. "Well, thank you. I've missed her, and it was—it was nice to remember her."

Leah moistened her drying lips. "When did she die? In the '20s—1929?"

The woman blinked large brown eyes. "Why, yes. I believe that was the year."

"What was her name?" Leah stepped closer. "Your friend? What was her name?"

"Althea. Althea Karahalios."

All the air rushed from Leah's chest. "Karahalios. Ka-wa-los."

"Are you—are you all right, ma'am?"

Leah laughed, high and staccato. "Karahalios. Althea Karahalios. She had children, you said. Tell me. Did she have three girls? Please tell me."

The woman's wide mouth drifted open. "Are you . . . ?"

"My name is Thalia. Did she have a daughter named Thalia?"

The woman clamped her handkerchief over her mouth, and tears shimmered in her eyes. "Little Thalia. Oh my. Look at you. All grown up with a baby of your own."

A manic, joyful laugh burst out. "You knew me? You knew my mother? My sisters?"

"Why, yes." She stretched out tentative, shaky fingers.

Leah grabbed her hand. "Tell me. Tell me everything you can."

"Oh my. Oh my. I can't believe this." Her hand trembled in Leah's. "Your parents—they came from Greece not long before you were born. Yes, Althea was expecting. Your father—Georgios was on faculty with my husband at the University of Chicago. Georgi was an expert in Greek poetry."

Laughter tumbled out, idyllic and epic and sacred. "Of course. Of course he was. And my sisters? My sisters? Do you know what became of them?"

Her face crumpled. "We never heard what became of you girls. Your parents had no family in America, so you were taken to an orphanage. Everyone at the church wanted to help, but times were hard. By the time a family offered to take you in, you'd all been adopted."

Leah nodded, over and over. "They were adopted. Good. Adopted."

"You weren't together? Oh dear. I'm so sorry."

"I'm going to find them. Today. Today I'll find them." Leah shifted Helen on her shoulder, opened her bag, and pulled out one of the slips of paper she'd written out for the orphanages. "This is my information, where I'm staying in Chicago this week, my home address. Please, if you think of anything that might help me. Oh! Your name?"

That wide mouth turned up in a smile. "I'm Irena Demetrios."

"Mrs. Demetrios. Thank you. You're an answer to almost fifteen years of prayer." Leah clutched Mrs. Demetrios's shoulder and pressed a kiss to her wet cheek, shocked at her own impulsivity.

"Such a pleasure to see you again, Thalia."

Leah raced out the door. "Thalia Karahalios, daughter of Georgios and Althea."

For the first time in fifteen years, she knew who she was.

38

Clay made a chopping motion to signal his squad forward.

He and Gene threw themselves against the wall of the crater and fired a few rounds, while Holman, Brady, and Lyons ran to the next crater. Then they laid down fire so Clay and Gene could join them.

"Don't see any Krauts," Holman said.

"Not yet." With so many bunkers and trenches and craters, the Germans could pop up anywhere. Even behind them.

Clay peered over the edge of the crater. There it was! Their target 155-mm gun lay in a circular open gun pit rather than a closed casemate. Camouflage netting was draped over the barrel.

No sign of activity, but Germans could be hiding in the underground shelter behind the gun.

They'd have to approach from that direction. Clay signaled for Brady and Lyons to cover, and he motioned ahead.

Low and fast, Clay darted toward the unmanned gun.

Sensing Gene and Holman behind him, Clay yanked a grenade from his belt. He hurdled the concrete rim, found the dark opening to the shelter behind him, pulled the pin, and tossed the grenade inside.

The concussion made his legs wobble. Gene and Holman jumped inside the shelter to clear it while Clay covered Brady and Lyons's approach.

"No one in here." Gene climbed back out with Holman behind him.

Brady yanked off the shredded camouflage net and swore. "This ain't a gun."

Clay stared. "That—that's a telephone pole."

"Where's the gun?" Gene asked.

Clay scanned the landscape, marred by days of aerial bombing and today's naval bombardment. "The Germans must have moved the gun after the bomber boys did their work." The telephone pole would have fooled the aerial photographers.

Brady spread his arms wide and snorted. "All this—for nothing?"

"Not for nothing." Maybe the other five guns remained in place. Regardless, they had a second objective. "To the assembly point."

In leapfrog fashion, Clay led his makeshift squad to a crater, then followed them toward the next. On the way, something caught his eye—parallel tracks. Partly obscured by chunks of earth, the tracks led inland from the gun pit. Maybe they could find that gun after all.

The crack of a gunshot. Clay squatted and saw a depression to his right. He jumped in.

A trench. He slammed back against the wall and whipped his rifle in a semicircle.

The trench ran about twenty-five feet south, then bent to the right.

Clay huffed out a breath. Not a safe place, but also not where he was going to die. At least the trench ran in the correct direction.

He edged toward the bend. With his finger on the trigger, he said a quick prayer, then popped around the corner, leading with his rifle.

No one, and his breath tumbled out.

He crept forward to the next zig in the trench.

A scuffling sound behind him. Friend or foe?

Clay spun around to his left, rifle at his hip.

Someone barreled into him, butted his rifle up and away. It fired into the air.

Lyons!

Clay's foot swept out beneath him. Lyons threw him to the ground, his forearm across Clay's throat, his knee grinding into Clay's rifle arm above the elbow.

Clay grunted in pain. "I knew it was you."

"You're the only one who ever will." Lyons tossed aside his BAR and unsheathed his knife. "And not for long."

Clay gripped the wrist of the man's knife hand, his heart pounding. This wasn't how he was supposed to die. It wasn't. But how could he defeat Lyons when he was losing air and stars flickered in his vision?

Lyons breathed vomit-scented breath in Clay's face and brought the knife closer to his neck. "I'm looking forward to watching you die."

"Like the girl . . . in Florida." Clay ran through all the dirty fighting tactics in his head. None fit. "The girl . . . in Braunton."

Lyons chuckled, confirming both suspicions. "Your turn."

Clay's vision turned gray, and his arm shook with the effort of keeping the knife away. He bumped his hips under Lyons, anything to slow him down.

Lyons readjusted his position, sliding one leg down next to Clay's.

And he lost.

Clay's favorite wrestling move. He twined both his legs around Lyons's knee. Then he jerked Lyons's leg hard to the side and heaved his hips.

Lyons cried out and tumbled to the side.

Clay scrambled away and gasped for air. Where was his rifle? With a string of curses, Lyons rose with knife in hand.

There! The rifle lay on the ground, pointing at Clay. He grabbed it by the barrel.

Lyons lunged forward.

Clay spun his rifle around and groped for the trigger.

Then Lyons grunted and halted, his eyes wide in surprise. His body jerked, he grabbed his neck, and he crumpled to the ground.

But Clay hadn't fired! His finger slipped into the trigger.

Behind Lyons. A man in gray. A machine pistol.

Clay squeezed the trigger.

He hit the man square in the left upper quadrant of the chest, and the man flew backward.

Clay sagged to his knees. He didn't want to kill the German, but he had no choice.

Before him, Frank Lyons moaned and squirmed.

Clay tossed Lyons's knife over the side of the trench, then yanked open the pouch for his first aid kit. "Let me see."

"What?" Lyons grimaced. Blood pulsed between his fingers. An artery had been hit. He'd bleed out in minutes.

Clay tore open a field dressing, applied it to the wound, and clamped Lyons's hand over it. "Press on this hard. It'll buy you a minute to pray. Pray God will forgive you, 'cause you're going to meet him mighty soon."

Lyons's lip curled. "You're not going to try to save my life?"

"Not even Doc Block could do that. And I've got a road to block." Clay unbuckled Lyons's cartridge belt. The Rangers could use the extra BAR ammo, and he didn't want to leave grenades with Lyons.

A bloody hand clamped around Clay's forearm. "That dame in the library—her kid's mine."

Clay found himself smiling. "Nope. She's all mine. Your name dies with you today."

He broke free, slung Lyons's BAR over his shoulder, and held his rifle in position. He gave the dying Ranger one last look. "By the way, she forgave you. And so do I."

Clay edged around the corner and stepped around the dead German. He prayed for forgiveness and thanked God for saving him to finish the job he'd been given.

A strange lightness filled his chest. Frank Lyons would never hurt another woman again.

CHICAGO

Leah stepped off the bus, her arms empty without Helen. When she'd told Mama her good news, Mama had insisted she watch the baby so Leah could visit more orphanages. If only Leah had thought to ask Mrs. Demetrios which orphanage the girls had been taken to.

This was the third home. The brick building didn't look familiar, but that meant nothing.

Leah opened the door. No one sat at the desk. To the left an office door stood ajar, and a radio announcer's voice floated out, solemn and strident.

Perhaps she should be glued to the radio too, but Clay would want her busy and searching for her sisters.

"Hello?" she called.

The radio turned off.

"Yes?" A woman in her fifties peeked out with a face strangely plump for her trim figure and far too stern to be working with children.

Leah put on her warmest smile, held out a sheet of paper with her information, and gave her standard speech about her search.

"Very well." The woman puffed out a sigh. "Come into my office."

"Thank you, Mrs.—"

"Miss Stratford." Her heels clunked on the hardwood. "Hmm. Kay-ray-hay-lee-us. One of those foreign names."

"It's Karahalios, ma'am, and it's Greek. But I'm an American citizen." Leah took a seat in front of the desk. "Besides, the Greeks are on our side."

Miss Stratford raised a thick eyebrow and opened a file cabinet. "Kay . . . ray . . . Here we are."

Leah blinked over and over, but yes, Miss Stratford was carrying a manila folder. "We—we were here?"

The woman sat behind her desk and opened the folder. "November 10, 1929. A George—oh, I can't pronounce these foreign names—husband and wife killed, struck by a car. Three daughters, a four-year-old and eight-month-old twins. Oh, these crazy names."

"I'm Thalia, the oldest." Leah strained to read the faded handwriting upside down.

Miss Stratford lifted the folder. "You were adopted on November 20."

"I was separated from my sisters."

"Often necessary. Says here the Jones family wanted a girl to help in their store someday. They didn't want babies. Something— hard to read—didn't want crying and diapers. And look at that date—a month after the stock market crashed. We couldn't take any chances."

"My sisters? They were adopted? Did they stay together?"

"Yes, they were adopted together."

Leah leaned forward, her heart beating wildly. "Where are they? Who adopted them?"

Miss Stratford drew back. "I can't tell you. All adoptions are closed."

Leah gasped. "But they're my sisters."

"I'm sorry, Mrs. Paxton. It isn't possible."

She collapsed back in the chair. She'd come so far . . . so close . . . and now nothing?

Miss Stratford's face softened. "However, I can show you the information pertaining to you. Would you like to see it?"

What did it matter if she couldn't find her sisters? Yet how could she not? "Yes, please. I know so little about my past."

She pulled out a paper. "This is fine. So's this. Some have carbon copies. You may have the copies."

"Thank you." A photograph was attached to one of the papers with a paper clip. A sad-faced curly-haired girl sat on a bench with her tiny arms around two dark-haired babies. "Oh my."

She'd never seen a picture of them. "May I? Is it too much to ask?"

"Very well. You may have it."

Leah held the picture before blurry eyes. This might be the only glimpse she'd ever have of her sisters.

"Miss Stratford?" A young woman in a white apron leaned into the office, hair askew. "It's that Yardley boy again. He's throwing dishes in the dining room."

"That barbarian. Belongs in a mental asylum." Miss Stratford bolted from her desk. "Pardon me, Mrs. Paxton."

What a horrible woman to have in charge of an orphanage. Leah stared after her, then at the empty doorway, then at the manila folder.

Her hand stretched out.

A voice screeched in her head. *Thief! Thief! Rotten little thief!*

The voice lied. These were *her* sisters. Taking what belonged to her wasn't stealing.

She slid the folder close.

On the first page: "Three girls: Thalia Karahalios, Calliope Karahalios, Polyhymnia Karahalios."

She almost laughed. She'd been right about their names!

At the bottom of the page . . . "Thalia Karahalios adopted by Mr. and Mrs. Norman Jones, November 20, 1929."

On the next line . . . "Calliope and Polyhymnia Karahalios adopted by Mr. and Mrs. Hobart Scholz, November 26, 1929." With an address!

Leah memorized it and glanced to the door. A ruckus toward the back of the building assured her Miss Stratford wouldn't return for a while.

She pulled her pen from her purse and wrote her sisters' information on the paper she was allowed to take. Then she reassembled the folder.

A notepad sat on the desk, and Leah wrote a note, thanking Miss Stratford for the papers, the photograph, and the pieces to her past.

Leah tucked her papers into her purse. She had so much more than pieces.

39

Clay ran down the exit road with two Rangers from another company, the only men he'd found at the assembly point. Either Gene and his friends had already proceeded, or they were—no, he wouldn't think of that.

Booms of artillery fell behind him, closer and closer. Might be German artillery or it might be the US Navy, unaware that the Rangers were already so far inland. Didn't matter where it came from. It only mattered that he needed to run.

His breath came in hard puffs, and Lyons's Browning Automatic Rifle bumped against his back.

Ruins of a farmhouse appeared, and Clay dropped to a squat. Jagged stone walls with broken windows, a collapsed roof, and shrubbery that could conceal the enemy.

American voices called in the distance. Three Rangers ran past the farmhouse unmolested. They must have already cleared the buildings.

"Come on, men." Clay ran in a zigzag path, his gaze sweeping the bushes and walls and windows.

On the far side of the house, he jumped into a trench, but it ended soon. Open field stretched ahead. Half a dozen Rangers ran across alone or in pairs, taking different paths, as they'd been trained.

Miller from the other company tilted his head to the left, and Clay nodded. He'd go to the right and he'd go first.

Up out of the trench, and his feet pounded over the grass. Fewer craters this far south to slow him down—or to hide in.

A machine gun rattled to his right—but far away. Small arms fire cracked to the left, and closer.

Someone lay splayed on the ground. Clay didn't dare stop to help, but one glance told him it was too late. It was Ernie Mc-Killop. And he was dead.

"Oh, Lord." Clay groaned and ran harder. He was supposed to die today, so McKillop and Gene and Holman and Ruby could live.

He slid into the trench on the far side. According to his mental map, it would lead to the second objective, the coastal highway between Grandcamp-les-Bains and Vierville-sur-Mer

American voices soothed his ears as he drew closer. He climbed out of the trench about twenty feet from the highway and yelled out the call sign so he wouldn't get shot by his buddies.

"Paxton." Lieutenant Taylor gave him a nod. "What's the word?"

Clay scanned the group—Holman, Ruby, Brady, the other two men from the BAR squad, about a dozen others. Where was Gene? He fought off a sick feeling. "Holman and Brady probably told you. No gun in our emplacement, only a telephone pole."

"Same at the other five positions." Taylor gestured with his Tommy gun across the road. "Patrols are searching for them. Len Lomell saw tracks down there."

"Good. I saw tracks heading south from our emplacement."

"The highway's secure. We're expecting the 116th Infantry Regiment and the Rangers from Omaha around noon." Taylor gestured east, toward Vierville, and then to the west. "We expect German reinforcements from the south and the west, so that's where we'll set up defenses. We need one more patrol down this lane."

269

"I'll do that, sir. Holman, Ruby, you're with me." Clay led them across the paved highway and down the dirt lane, flanked by tall hedgerows. Twenty feet down the lane, Clay found a gap in the hedgerow—an empty field lay on the other side.

"Anyone seen G. M.?" The question caught on his throat.

"Nah." Ruby checked the other side. "We lost contact with him on the way to the assembly point, same as you and Lyons."

Clay's shoulders tensed. "Lyons is gone."

Ruby groaned. "Oh, man."

"I saw McKillop go down a few minutes ago." Holman pointed his rifle down the lane. "I'm sure he's fine."

This wasn't the time to tell Holman his best friend was dead. "I'm sure Gene's fine too." If Gene was gone, Clay would find out soon enough, either here or in heaven.

Right now he had to find those six guns. Even if the guns were placed several miles inland, the Germans could do serious damage with 155-mm shells.

Leapfrogging and checking through the hedgerows, the three men proceeded about three hundred yards. At the end of the lane, another ran east to west.

Clay crouched at the corner and poked his rifle and his head around to the right, while Ruby checked to the left. All clear.

Holman darted across and peered through the hedgerow on the far side. "An orchard."

Clay joined him. Apple trees filled the field, heavy with moss and tiny green apples. If he wanted to hide artillery, an orchard would be a good place to do so.

To the right, the lane ended in about a hundred yards. Clay headed that direction. Every twenty feet or so, he surveyed the orchard while Ruby and Holman covered him.

About thirty yards from the end of the lane, he heard something. He motioned for Ruby and Holman to get down. They dropped, pointing their rifles in opposite directions.

Clay flattened himself to the hedgerow. Sticks and leaves poked him, and he edged up to see through the thinning brush near the top.

To his right, shapes broke up the neat pattern of trees—angled shapes. Five of them.

The guns! Each pointed west, straight toward Utah Beach.

Motion beside the closest gun. Clay ducked a bit, then poked the tip of his rifle through.

A man with the rounded silhouette of an M1 helmet.

Clay sighed in relief. A Ranger.

A soft pop. A fizzing sound.

A thermite grenade—good. The grenades created massive amounts of molten heat and could weld shut the breech or the traversing mechanism of a gun, quietly disabling it.

Clay tapped Ruby's and Holman's feet. "One of ours. He found the guns. Let's cover him."

Then two Rangers ran north up the lane—including the man with the thermite grenades.

"That's Sergeant Lomell," Ruby said. "And Jack Kuhn."

"Great." With that branch of the lane clear, Clay motioned in the other direction.

Fifteen minutes later they returned to the highway. No sign of enemy activity, thank goodness, and Clay reported to Lieutenant Taylor.

Taylor grinned. "D Company found and disabled five guns, E Company blew up the ammunition dump, F Company cleared Au Guay, the roadblock is set, and we've sent runners to Rudder at his headquarters on the point. All before 0900."

"Great news, sir." Now they just had to hold off any German counterattacks and wait a few hours for the force from Omaha Beach.

Taylor gathered the men. "All right, boys. We have about fifty men here at the highway. We'll set up defensive positions down this north-south lane and at the east-west lane bordering the orchard."

Clay's squad received an assignment toward the middle of the orchard lane, and they headed east down the highway.

Ahead lay the village of Au Guay. Ancient stone houses and mossy stone walls stood silent and wary.

Clay turned right down a dirt lane. If it weren't for the rifle in his hand and the sound of gunfire in the distance, it would make a pleasant stroll in the country.

But everything felt crooked. Down these lanes lay no craters to serve as his pit, no pillboxes to storm.

Had he misinterpreted his dream? Had his imagination played tricks on him?

Clay tripped on a root. He hadn't felt so unbalanced in years.

CHICAGO

Leah burst through Juanita's front door. "I found them! I found my sisters!"

"You did?" Mama Paxton rose from the chair by the radio. "Are they here in town?"

"I hope so. I have the name and address of the couple who adopted them. Well, at least their address fifteen years ago. I need a phone book."

Juanita emerged from the nursery, bouncing Helen on her shoulder. "First, you need to take care of this sweet thing. She doesn't like formula."

"Of course she doesn't." Leah took her daughter, who fussed and squirmed. "Come on, sweetheart. Mama's here."

"While you're nursing, I'll look in the phone book," Mama called from the kitchen.

"Thank you." Leah settled in the rocking chair, unbuttoned her blouse, and called out Hobart Scholz's address. "I hope they're still in Chicago. I'm so thankful it's an unusual name."

Helen latched on and calmed.

Leah rocked, her foot tapping restlessly. "Anything yet?"

Mama came to the door with the phone book and a smile. "There's a Hobart Scholz in Chicago. Not the same address, but he's in this very neighborhood."

"Oh!" Everything in her wanted to bolt out the door, but she settled back. "My sisters have lived without me for fifteen years. I suppose they can wait another thirty minutes."

"Remember," Mama said, "the girls will be in school."

Yes, they would. "I should call first anyway, to make sure it's the correct Hobart Scholz."

Mama closed the phone book, one finger marking the page. "And give them time to prepare. This could be a shock."

But what a pleasant shock to find a long-lost sister.

Above the contented sounds of Helen's swallowing rose the radio's static, and Leah's heart shifted. She didn't mean to forget about Clay—only to keep busy. "Any news from France?"

"Only that it's going well. It's too early for details." Worry creased Mama's forehead.

Leah cradled her tiny child. Her love for Helen was far bigger than her heart, and she knew she'd never stop loving her or worrying about her. What must it be like for Mama Paxton, knowing all three sons were in mortal danger?

How long would they have to wait? The radio wouldn't deliver news on the Paxton boys. If Clay had survived, his letter to Leah wouldn't arrive for weeks. If he hadn't, the telegram could arrive in days.

She shuddered and pulled her baby closer.

After Helen finished, Leah burped her, changed her diaper, and laid her down for a nap, right on schedule.

Out in the kitchen, Mama grinned and pointed to the telephone on the wall. "Ready?"

"Yes." She memorized the phone number and dialed, her finger and heart trembling.

Mama pulled a chair over, and Leah sat down.

One ring. Two rings. Three. Leah bit her lip. What if they weren't home?

"Good day. Scholz residence."

"Hello." Leah's voice tumbled out. "I'm Leah—Mrs. Clay Paxton. Are you Mrs. Hobart Scholz?"

"Yes . . ." Expectation warmed the woman's voice.

Leah's shoulders relaxed. "Do you have daughters named Callie and Polly?"

"Yes. Are you one of their friends?" She sounded so sweet and friendly.

"I'm quite fond of them." Leah ran her damp hand along her skirt and glanced to Mama Paxton for courage. "Although I haven't seen them for almost fifteen years. I'm their sister."

"Their . . . sister? They don't have a sister." Mrs. Scholz's voice sharpened.

Leah worked her finger into the coil of the phone cord. "My maiden name is Thalia Karahalios."

A gasp on the other end. "I've never—I've never heard that name."

"My parents were Georgios and Althea Karahalios. They were killed in 1929. I was four, and Callie and Polly were eight months old. But I remember them well."

"That isn't—that isn't possible." Her voice shook and lowered. "They never mentioned another—another child."

"At the orphanage?" Sadness seeped into Leah's chest. How could they not have mentioned her to her sisters' adoptive parents? "Another family adopted me first. I didn't want to leave my sisters, but I didn't have a choice. I've been looking for them ever since. Would it be possible for me to come over and see them?"

"Oh! Heavens, no." Mrs. Scholz's voice quivered. "Absolutely not. They—they don't know they're adopted." She whispered the last word.

"Why—why not? Shouldn't they know?"

"No, of course not. The social worker told us not to. She said it was best, so the girls would never be ashamed of where they came from." Tears heaved through her words. "They're our daughters. They've always been our daughters."

Leah's breath came fast and shallow. "Yes, but—"

"Telling them—oh, I couldn't. I couldn't hurt them like that. They're such happy, well-adjusted girls, so active and well liked. I can't let you upset their world. I won't." Conviction solidified in Mrs. Scholz's tone.

Leah's head shook back and forth. "But they're my sisters, the only people left from my family. I—I love them."

"I beg you. If you do love them, let them be. Please let them be."

"But—"

"Please, Mrs.—Mrs.—Please don't contact me again. Good day." She hung up.

Leah gaped at the dead phone.

Mama Paxton laid a hand on her shoulder. "Oh, *mija*. I'm so sorry."

"But they're my sisters. My family. *My* family." Something burned in her belly, and she thumped the phone into the receiver.

She usually took hold of anger and molded it into the safe shape of sadness, but now she let it pulse hot in her veins.

Mrs. Scholz had no right. Callie and Polly were Leah's family by birth, by blood.

How dare this woman tell Leah she didn't belong with her own family?

Leah couldn't accept that. She wouldn't.

If she wanted to belong, she had to join.

40

For the second time that night, the gunfire stopped as abruptly as it had started.

Straining to see in the dark, Clay pointed his rifle through the top of the hedgerow. He hadn't seen a single enemy soldier or fired a shot since sunset. Both night counterattacks had come far to Clay's right in the orchard, rather than in the wheat field he faced.

He sank lower in the foxhole he shared with Ruby. How many more times would the Germans attack? How much longer could the Rangers hold out?

Close to midnight, Colonel Rudder had ordered the detachment to hold the position by the highway while the main force held the point by Rudder's headquarters. A lot of distance and a whole lot of Germans separated them.

South of the highway, eighty-five Rangers formed an L-shaped defensive line, with the angle of the L pointing southwest. Clay guarded the middle of the lower leg near the command post.

What a ragtag group—members of the three companies that had climbed the cliffs, plus twenty-three men from the 5th Ranger Battalion, the lone contingent to arrive from Omaha Beach. Boy, were they welcome.

"Lieutenant!" Footsteps thumped up the dirt lane, and a man jumped into the command post foxhole. "The Krauts took the angle, then retreated. No word from D Company. I think they're wiped out."

Clay puffed out a breath, and Ruby shook his head. Things weren't going well.

The commanders talked in voices low enough to conceal their words, but not their anxiety.

Everything about the night felt sideways. Clay wasn't supposed to be here. Since he hadn't died on D-day, when would he? The war in Europe could last weeks, months, even years. When would he see that pillbox from his dreams? Would he ever?

What if he . . . survived? What then? He hadn't even considered having a future since the recurring dream had begun.

Something strange and energizing filled his chest. Hope. It was hope. Hope of reconciliation and love and family.

For the past few months, he'd occasionally desired a future. Now, on the far side of D-day, that longing had grown into hope. And hope was even more dangerous than desire.

Clay groaned and checked his rifle ammo. BAR ammunition was scarce, and few grenades remained. Some of the men were using German guns and grenades.

Thanks to Frank Lyons, Clay still had two American grenades. He'd given Lyons's BAR and ammo to a Ranger who'd lost his rifle.

Clay rested against the cold dirt wall of his foxhole and peeked through the hedgerow. Peeking back at him from behind thin clouds, an almost-full moon cast silvery light on the long narrow wheat field, bound by hedgerows.

His eyelids dragged low, and he shook himself. He'd been awake for almost twenty-four hours, and in that time he'd eaten two pancakes aboard the *Ben-my-Chree* and part of a chocolate D ration bar.

Clay pulled out the D ration and gnawed off a bite. Bitterness warped his mouth, but it'd keep him awake. The Army had designed the bars to taste bad so soldiers would save them for emergencies. It certainly worked.

Ruby's head slumped forward. Clay extended his elbow to nudge him, then retracted it. Let the man sleep while he could.

Shuffling in the dirt behind him. Sergeant Markowitz from another section squatted by Clay's foxhole. "Lieutenant Taylor says if the Krauts attack again, retreat to the point. And no wild firing. Save your ammo."

Clay sighed. "Yes, Sarge." He didn't want to retreat, but if they'd lost D Company, they'd lost their right flank. The Germans could infiltrate behind them and cut them off.

Markowitz proceeded down the lane to Brady and Holman's foxhole.

"All I know is I'm not surrendering," Ruby muttered. "They're not taking me alive."

"Yeah. I understand." If the Germans murdered their Jewish neighbors, how would they treat Jewish soldiers fighting for the enemy?

No matter what, Clay would protect Ruby. Maybe Clay was meant to die in the hedgerows. Maybe it wasn't the location of his death that mattered, but the fact of his death.

Whistles sounded in the field to the south, and the wheat rustled.

Clay sprang up and shoved his rifle through the brush.

"Klaus!"

"Friedrich!"

"Hans!"

Why were the Germans shouting roll call? Locating each other? Trying to scare the Rangers?

Clay licked his dry lips and opened his eyes wide to the darkness.

Gunfire broke out in front of him, yellow muzzle flashes, bright tracer fire.

He fired at a muzzle flash, another, another.

Machine-gun fire shredded the hedgerow above him, and he ducked. Branches and leaves pelted his helmet and back.

Up to his feet, another few shots. His ammunition clip pinged out, and Clay rammed another into place.

An explosion behind him shook the ground—a mortar shell in the open field behind his hedgerow.

"Lieutenant!" A Ranger thundered down the lane toward the command post. "The Germans have broken through. We couldn't hold 'em. There's guys getting killed everywhere."

"To the highway!" Taylor yelled.

"Get going, Ruby. I'll tell the others." Clay scrambled out of the foxhole and to Holman and Brady's position. "To the highway! Taylor's orders."

Holman cussed out the orders. "I can hold 'em."

Gunfire rang out to the northwest, behind the lines of the next platoon, the steady burps of a German machine pistol. Was that gun in Nazi or Ranger hands?

"Don't be a fool. Get moving." Hunched over, Clay darted back the way he'd come. Good. Ruby had left.

Next to the command post ran a north-to-south lane. To the south, flashes and stuttering gunfire filled the lane. The men in the outpost had to be putting up a fighting retreat.

Clay pointed his rifle that way. But in the darkness he didn't dare add his own bullets, in case he hit a Ranger.

Instead, he ran north, following other hunched-over Americans, keeping his feet high to avoid roots and rocks and branches.

A scream from close to his former position. "I surrender! *Kamerad!* Don't shoot!"

Clay stumbled and caught himself on the hedgerow. That was Bob Holman. Why hadn't he obeyed the order?

He ran up the lane, pausing to check the fields through gaps in the hedgerows. The gunfire sounded farther and farther away.

Finally his boots thudded on blacktop.

To his left Rangers gathered on the highway, calling off names and companies. Clay called out his.

"Back to the point," cried a lieutenant Clay didn't recognize in the dark. "We'll split up, take different paths."

Made sense. That way all of them wouldn't get captured or killed, and maybe some would make it through.

"Hey, Pax." Ruby sidled up to him. "Where's Holman? Brady?"

"I heard Holman surrender. Don't know about Brady. Told them to get out."

Ruby grunted. "Holman never could listen to no one."

"Glad you listened." Clay's throat suddenly constricted. He and Ruby were the only ones left from their squad. Although he refused to give up on Gene. Not yet.

"Let's go!" That was Lieutenant Taylor.

Clay and Ruby followed. About a dozen men jogged up the exit road in twos and threes, back the way they'd come in the morning.

Clay kept his rifle ready and his ears tuned. But he only heard Ranger footfalls and his own huffing breath. For some reason, the Germans hadn't pursued them.

He didn't take any chances. He checked behind walls, inside trenches, and around shattered tree trunks.

The Rangers turned off the exit road and headed toward the cliff they'd climbed. Clay and Ruby leapfrogged between craters, but only distant gunfire sounded, deep and booming.

At the edge of the cliff, Taylor slipped down into a crater and Clay and Ruby followed.

Headquarters, with a dozen or so Rangers, including Colonel Rudder, thank goodness.

Taylor reported the situation to Rudder, the officers' voices low and grim.

"Clay? Ruby?"

He spun around at the familiar voice. "G. M.!"

His buddy sat leaning back against the crater wall, his lower right leg swathed in white.

Clay grabbed his outstretched hand and shook it hard. "What happened?"

"Sniper shot me through the calf." Gene gestured to the dark shape of a bunker close by. "Doc Block patched me up and sent me back out to fight. That's the aid station."

The old longing pulled Clay toward the bunker. Maybe the physician could use some help. But if he'd sent Gene out to fight, he'd surely send Clay skedaddling.

"I've been guarding HQ." Gene chuckled. "You should've seen Lieutenant Eikner. The radios have been giving us trouble, but remember how the lieutenant brought that old signal lamp from the last war? He used it to call in fire from the *Satterlee*. The destroyer took out those machine guns to the east. When the *Satterlee* ran out of ammo, the *Thompson* took over."

"Wow."

"Paxton, Ruby." Taylor set a hand on Clay's shoulder. "We're setting up a perimeter. Let's go."

"Me too." Gene pushed up onto his good leg. "I can hobble just fine."

Arguments filled Clay's mouth, but he swallowed them. In the same position, Clay would have done the same thing.

"Come on, buddy." Clay drew Gene's arm up over his shoulder so he could support him. "Let's find a nice spot to watch the sunrise."

His breath caught. He would indeed watch another sunrise.

CHICAGO
WEDNESDAY, JUNE 7, 1944

Leah pushed Juanita's baby carriage across the street and two houses down from her sisters' address. Helen dozed under her pink blanket.

Leah had told Mama and Juanita that she planned to visit the University of Chicago and then city hall so she could obtain her birth certificate. That was true.

But first, Callie and Polly. This morning she'd watch to see which direction the girls went to school, then in the afternoon she'd return and introduce herself. If she did so now, the girls would be late to school and would have a hard time concentrating in class.

Something inside her writhed. Was she wrong to defy their adoptive mother's wishes? Mama and Juanita were saddened by Mrs. Scholz's decision but said it was her right.

Leah disagreed. The girls belonged to her as surely as Helen did.

Certainly Clay would agree. Hadn't he urged her to visit Chicago so she would be reunited with them?

Clay . . .

The news in the papers and on the radio was vague—the landings had been successful but costly. How costly? Had they cost her the man she loved?

Leah pulled out the clipping of President Franklin D. Roosevelt's prayer from yesterday's afternoon newspaper. With her own thoughts scrambled by worry and anger and distress, it helped to focus on the printed prayer.

The president's words spoke to her soul: "Almighty God: Our sons, pride of our Nation, this day have set upon a mighty endeavor, a struggle to preserve our Republic, our religion, and our civilization, and to set free a suffering humanity. Lead them straight and true; give strength to their arms, stoutness to their hearts, steadfastness in their faith."

Leah glanced to the Scholz residence, still and quiet, then back to the clipping: "Some will never return. Embrace these, Father, and receive them, Thy heroic servants, into Thy kingdom."

Her throat tightened, and she added a prayer that Clay would do the Lord's will. She read on: "And for us at home—fathers, mothers, children, wives, sisters, and brothers of brave men overseas—

whose thoughts and prayers are ever with them—help us, Almighty God, to rededicate ourselves in renewed faith in Thee in this hour of great sacrifice."

A breeze ruffled Helen's blanket, and Leah tucked it into place. Whatever she faced in the coming days, she had to find the good and lean on the Lord.

A door opened—the Scholz home.

Leah tightened her grip on the baby carriage.

Two dark-haired girls trotted down the steps, crossed the street, and headed in Leah's direction, books in arms.

"Callie!" A middle-aged woman stood in the doorway, waving a paper. "Your essay!"

The taller of the girls gasped, whirled around, and ran across the street. "Oh, Mother! You're divine! Simply divine." Callie kissed her on the cheek.

She laughed. "And you're full of baloney. Off you go. I love you."

Leah's feet rooted in place. Something about her sister's voice sounded familiar, like this city, the church, and the postcard of the library. Was that her mother's voice?

Callie ran across the street to her twin. "I can't believe I forgot it."

"I know," Polly said. "You worked so hard on it."

The sisters she'd once known and loved approached. They didn't look like Leah, but they shared her curls, her coloring, and her build. What else did they share?

"I can't wait to read it out loud." Callie grinned at her paper. "I quote a particularly romantic Shakespearean sonnet, and I plan to look straight into Bobby Horton's dreamy eyes as I recite it."

"You wouldn't."

"I would. Watch me."

Her sister loved poetry too, and Leah couldn't breathe, couldn't breathe at all.

Callie flung up one arm dramatically. "'Let me not to the marriage of true minds admit impediments. Love is not love which alters when it alteration finds, or bends with the remover to remove: Oh, no! it is an ever-fixèd mark.'"

Polly giggled. "That wonderful bard. Poor Bobby doesn't stand a chance."

The girls came closer, taller than Leah by several inches, nourished by better food and attention than Leah had received. Thank goodness they'd found a loving home.

The girls spotted her.

"Good morning, ma'am." Callie pressed a hand to her chest. "Lovely morning for a sonnet, is it not?"

That gratitude raised a smile. "It is."

Polly shook her head at Leah as they passed on the sidewalk. "Pardon my sister, ma'am. She's loopy."

Her eyes—it was like looking in a mirror.

Callie grabbed Polly's arm and hugged it. "But I'm your loop-de-loop."

"You are." Polly laughed.

And the two little muses walked away. Away from Leah.

Certainty crushed her chest, her breath, her hope, her dreams.

They were complete apart from her, happy and healthy and together.

Leah had to let them go.

41

Clay opened his eyes. Or was he still dreaming?

Pale morning light filled the giant bowl of the crater. Clay rested with his head about two feet below the rim on the southern side. The dirt, the pebbles, the tuft of burnt grass—everything was just like in his recurring dream.

Clay swallowed hard, his mouth dry. He took his canteen off his belt and took a swig, just like in his dream. Only this time he tasted the metallic water and felt it drop into the emptiness of his stomach.

This was no dream. This was his dream coming to life.

Dizziness swept through him, but he shook it away. *Lord, give me strength.*

Gene dozed beside him. So much for staying awake while Clay slept. On the far side of the crater Ruby watched over the northern rim, and Taylor stirred awake at Ruby's feet.

Clay inched higher. Light gray powder dusted the edge of the crater. He found a notch in the rim and peered through.

A pillbox stood about one hundred feet away, where Clay knew it would be, one of the giant reinforced concrete casemates the

Germans had been building to house the 155-mm guns. The guns had never been installed.

Murmuring voices came from that direction—and not in English.

Clay sank back into the pit. *Help me do this, Lord.*

He nudged Gene awake, then crawled to Lieutenant Taylor. "Sir, there's a casemate over yonder. Germans inside."

Taylor rubbed bleary eyes. Had anyone—other than Gene—gotten any good sleep? "It was clear last night. Of course, the Krauts have tunnels and trenches connecting everything."

"Yes, sir."

Taylor crawled over and looked over the top for a minute, then slipped back inside. "Ruby, go get the fellows in the crater next door." He tilted his head toward the saddle of ground where two craters intersected.

"We've got to take it," Clay said. That casemate had a line of fire to Rudder's headquarters and to the observation post on the tip of the point, still occupied by Germans. The Rangers would be trapped at headquarters and wouldn't be able to take the observation post, and Clay's detachment would be cut off from HQ.

Worse, the Germans could use that position to cover a counterattack against the weakened American force. Only about ninety Rangers still bore arms, some of them wounded like Gene.

Taylor squatted and drew in the dirt—a C shape for the casemate and circles for the two craters, like an elongated version of a child's drawing of a face.

Half a dozen Rangers crawled over the saddle into Clay's crater.

"Here's the deal." Taylor drew a line like a cigarette in the face's mouth. "They have at least one machine gun in there, small arms too, I'm sure. I don't know how many men—at least two. We can't make a frontal assault. We'd get slaughtered."

Yet Clay would indeed make a frontal assault.

"We need to take it from behind." He nodded to John Perkovich from the other platoon. "You and Ellis still have a satchel charge, right?"

"Yes, sir."

"The machine gun is trained to our right, our best line of approach to the rear. To our left, there's a bunch of rubble that would slow us down. We wouldn't stand a chance going that way."

Clay set a finger near the pebbles Taylor was placing to indicate the rubble. "We need a distraction on our left flank to draw fire, so Perkovich and Ellis can circle round and blow the back door."

Taylor sat on his haunches and sighed. "I'm open to ideas, boys."

"I can run up here." Clay drew a line beside the rubble. "I've got two grenades. I'll toss one in, two if needed."

"No." Taylor frowned at him. "It's suicidal."

Clay shrugged. That was beside the point, but he had to convince the lieutenant. "Not if we do it right. I'll sneak up as close as I can. Soon as they spot me, have a couple fellows lay down covering fire. We'll make a racket over here, make them think we're attacking from the left. That'll draw their fire."

"Not for long."

"It'll make them duck, slow them down. Soon as they start moving that machine gun, Perkovich and Ellis make a run for it."

Taylor rubbed his stubbled chin. "I don't like it."

"It's the only way."

Taylor's gray eyes fixed hard on Clay. "You once told me it wasn't your healing time. You'd better pray it's your killing time."

"Yes, sir." It was also his dying time. But he was ready. He had to be.

Taylor assigned some to the demolitions squad and others to cover Clay with a BAR, rifles, and a whole lot of noise.

The men went to their positions, and Clay rested against the side of the crater.

Furrows cracked the dirt on Gene's forehead. "Are you sure, Clay? I don't like it."

He'd never been so sure of anything in his life, and he smiled. "Just cover me, buddy."

Clay turned his gaze to the gray clouds, the fragments of blue. How many more breaths did he have? How many heartbeats?

He reached inside his field jacket, pulled his Bible from the breast pocket of his shirt, and opened it to see the picture of Leah and Helen. *Good-bye, my loves.* A kiss, and he tucked the Bible back in place.

God had given him the dream so he'd have courage and peace at the end. He did, but it was a dark and sad peace.

At the saddle, Taylor exchanged hand signals with the demolitions team, then signaled Clay. Whenever Clay was ready.

He was ready. He was. But his muscles and brain felt like mush. *Lord, get me through this. Get me home to you.*

This was for a purpose, to take that casemate and protect the Rangers' position. If the Germans wiped out the 2nd Battalion, they could move more artillery to the point, artillery that would endanger the fleet and the landing beaches.

For his buddies. For his brothers.

One long deep breath, and Clay crawled up to the rim of the crater. The German machine gun was still trained to the Rangers' right flank. Soft German voices bounced over the battered landscape, light laughter.

Clay pulled out a hand grenade, the ridged cast iron heavy and cold, and it settled into his palm like a baseball.

It was time. Clay climbed over the side, Joseph rising from his pit, rising to what he'd been called to do, created to do.

With his gaze and ears fixed on the casemate, he crept closer, hunched over, his muscles taut and ready to sprint, his heart and lungs pumping in tandem.

A sharp cry from the German side.

Clay yanked out the pin and broke into a full run.

Shouts and gunfire blasted behind him, good old American rifles.

The *Maschinengewehr 42* opened fire, ripping into his memories, the sound he'd heard in his dream, on the training field, and now in his final moments.

It arced in his direction.

Now!

Running hard, Clay coiled for his final pitch.

He could see Adler at bat, Wyatt squatting behind him with a baseball glove, egging him on.

Clay would never see them again.

"Ahhhh!" He yelled, lunged forward on his left leg, and let the grenade fly.

The machine gun barrel swept his way, spattering out death.

Clay saw his bullet. Impossible. No one could see a flying bullet, but he did.

And he didn't want it.

He wanted to see his wife and daughter, the girls he loved. He wanted to hear their laughter. He wanted to hold them tight.

He wanted to live.

The grenade disappeared into the dark mouth of the casemate.

The tracer fire was upon him.

"No!" Clay twisted away, threw himself forward.

Heat seared through his chest, cracking, roasting, tearing through his right side.

He fell to the ground, hands splayed before him.

An explosion rocked the earth, and he lifted his head, his mouth hot and wet.

Smoke poured out of the casemate.

Clay had succeeded. The Germans would be dead, injured, or too stunned to resist. His buddies would take the position.

"Clay! Pax!" Gene cried, high and frantic. "Medic!"

Too late for that, and Clay rested his cheek on the land beneath him.

Now that he wanted to live, he wouldn't.

Chicago

> Three muses dance, their hands entwined,
>   A circle of love, as one.
> Thalia laughs, an idyllic song
>   Of earth and fields and home.
> Calliope calls, an epic ballad
>   Of valor and heroes and might.
> Polyhymnia chants, a sacred hymn
>   Of praise and truth and faith.
> Each one unique, each one must part
>   And lift her voice alone.

Leah pushed the baby carriage down the sidewalk, unseeing. The final stanza. That wasn't what she'd wanted, what she'd planned.

It was supposed to end with the three muses dancing off together forever. Not like this.

But Callie and Polly's circle was already complete.

Greenery drew her, a park, and she wound her way down the path.

Hadn't she always prayed her sisters would be alive and healthy? They were. They had a beautiful home and doting parents. They had each other.

But they didn't have her, didn't even know they had another sister. Didn't need her.

Pain pressed on her chest, and she gulped a breath. She didn't belong, even with her own sisters.

She parked the carriage and sank onto a wrought iron bench.

What if she ran after her sisters and inserted herself into their circle?

Leah hugged her stomach and folded over her knees. What would happen? They'd be shocked to learn that they had a sister, that they'd been adopted, and that their parents hadn't told them the truth.

Questions. Anger. Tears.

What if one sister rejoiced at the news and the other didn't? Would they be divided?

A groan built in her belly and rumbled out. Mrs. Scholz was right. The girls were happy and well adjusted. Leah would bring chaos. Even if both girls embraced her one day, would it be worth the wedge she might drive between the girls and their parents?

Leah's belly contracted, and a sob ripped out. She didn't know her sisters. She only loved the idea of them, not the young ladies they were today. She hadn't been there for the late-night feedings, the measles, and the essays. Mr. and Mrs. Scholz had. They'd poured fifteen years of love into Callie and Polly—as Leah wanted them to do.

She might have a right to reunite with her sisters, but to exercise that right would only be for herself. Not for the sisters she claimed to love.

Sobs heaved through her, over and over, a sound she hadn't allowed for years. In the Jones home, crying led to a beating. In the orphanage, it led to ridicule and torment.

Now she couldn't stop. A lifetime of abandonment and loneliness and rejection poured out.

Alone. Alone. Unwelcome. Unwanted. Unloved.

Her sisters belonged. Leah didn't.

They were loved. She wasn't.

She didn't want them to share her fate. She wanted to share theirs, and she never would. Too odd. Too foreign.

Like Leah in the Bible, such an appropriate namesake, the unloved wife who yearned for love and never received it.

"Clay. Oh, Clay." All her grief smashed together. Clay wanted to die and might already be dead. If she'd been the kind of woman he could have loved, could she have given him a reason to live?

No one loved her. Not her husband. Not her sisters. Not . . .

The sound of her own cries penetrated her ears and shifted. Another cry, desperate and fearful and hiccupping.

"Helen!" Leah sprang to her feet and blinked heavy-lashed eyelids. Helen lay in her carriage, her fists flailing, her face red and warped.

"Oh, baby! My sweet girl." Leah snatched her up and clutched her to her shoulder. "I'm so sorry. I didn't mean to scare you. I didn't."

The blanket hung loose, and Leah grabbed it and dried her baby's face and her own. "You poor baby. Mama's here. Mama's sorry."

The hiccups disappeared but the cries continued, and Leah walked and rocked and cooed.

What a horrible mother she was. How could she have ignored the person who needed her most, the only person who loved her?

She stilled, her hand on her daughter's head. Yes, Helen loved her. Leah wasn't unloved.

Leah resumed the rocking and pacing. "Mama loves you. Jesus loves you."

And sweet, warm peace flowed about her. "Jesus loves me too."

She'd never truly been alone or unloved, and she never would be. "Lord, forgive me. You saw me when I was abandoned and rejected, and you stayed by my side. You're my true Father."

In the Bible, God had seen Leah too. He'd seen that Jacob didn't love her, so he opened her womb and gave her children.

Leah kissed her own gift from God. "Thank you. Thank you for giving me Helen, for sending Clay so I could keep her."

Love for her husband built inside, strong and deep. He didn't love her in a romantic way, but he loved her in the best way, protecting and giving everything he had. A true husband.

That wasn't all. She had Rita Sue, as dear as any true sister. And Mama Paxton, who loved Leah like a true mother.

Fresh moisture filled her eyes. "Oh, Lord. I've been searching for the family I lost, and I didn't see the family you gave me."

42

The pain—it hurt to breathe.

Another explosion, lower and deeper. It jostled Clay, and he cried out.

Sharp retorts in the casemate. Rifle fire?

"Position secure!" Perkovich called.

His buddies had taken it, just as in his dream, and Clay's smile dug into the dirt.

"Casualties?" Taylor yelled.

"One dead Jerry, two injured. No Rangers hurt."

"Paxton is!" Gene shouted. "Pax is down. Medic!"

"Don't—bother," Clay mumbled.

Footsteps pounded his way, and someone rolled him onto his back.

Pain carved into Clay's chest, and he groaned.

"He's alive!" Ruby grasped his shoulders. "Come on, Clay. Stay with me. Tell me what to do. You paid attention in first aid class, remember?"

"Let me go." He squeezed his eyes shut.

"Don't talk that way." Ruby ripped open Clay's field jacket. "Tell me what to do."

"Come on, Clay. Don't give up." Gene hobbled over, using his rifle as a crutch.

He had to give his buddies a task so they'd feel better. Clay lifted his head enough to see his chest. So much blood. "Check—check to see if the bullet went through."

"Sorry, pal." Ruby pushed on Clay's shoulder and hip.

It hurt like blazes, and Clay bit his lip so he wouldn't scream.

"Yeah, another hole in your back and bigger."

"Pack 'em with field dressings. Sit me upright." His breath was fast, shallow, painful.

More footsteps. Lieutenant Taylor knelt in front of him, and so did Pete Voinescu, a medic.

"Clay said to put on field dressings, sit him upright." Gene clenched Clay's shoulder.

"That's right." Pete opened his bag.

So much activity. Ruby eased Clay up to sitting and supported him. Someone tore off Clay's shirt. Packets were ripped open. Dressings pressed to his chest. Nothing—nothing had hurt worse in his life.

"My—Bible." Clay reached for his discarded shirt. "G. M.?"

"Sure, buddy." Gene dug into the pocket and pressed the Bible into Clay's hand.

With effort, Clay shoved it into a trouser pocket.

A sharp pinch in his thigh. Morphine to ease the pain and prevent shock. "Only—a quarter grain. I need—to be able to cough."

Pete's blond eyebrows arched up and under his helmet. More information than in the first aid manual, but what did it matter?

"Let's get him to Doc Block. Ruby, get between his knees, grab one leg under each arm." Pete came behind Clay and reached under Clay's armpits. "This'll hurt, Pax. Stay with me."

He lifted. Clay stifled a cry and more cries when the men ran across the pockmarked land. Why hadn't they just let him bleed out? It would've hurt a lot less.

Finally they went down steep steps into a dark concrete bunker, reeking of sweat and blood.

A flashlight shone at him.

"Corporal Paxton, shot through the chest," Pete said. "Bullet went through. Gave him a quarter grain of morphine. He said not to give him the entire half grain."

"Set him here," Dr. Walter Block said.

Pete and Ruby sat Clay on a litter, and he leaned back against the concrete, dank and cold against his bare skin.

Doc Block examined the field dressings. "Well, Paxton. What treatment options would you recommend?"

Dozens of wounded men filled the bunker. "Let me go. Help the others."

"Can't hear you, young man." He eased Clay forward to examine his back.

A dagger of pain, and he cried out. "Did you—hear that?"

The physician smiled. "Loud and clear. Now, tell me how to treat you."

"Dressings with petrolatum in case they're sucking wounds." Clay forced a deep breath. "Keep me upright or on my right side to prevent hemothorax. Get me coughing to clear secretions. Plasma if I show signs of shock."

"Do you?"

Sweat tingled on his cold face, and his respiratory rate and pulse were high. "Yes."

"Where should I place the line?"

Clay pointed to the inside of his elbow.

"Oh, so close to a perfect score. No, I'll put it in your ankle, then it won't be in the way when you go into surgery."

"Surgery?" The battalion had no surgical equipment.

296

"When we evacuate you." His voice sounded tight. "Now, cough. The morphine should be kicking in."

Clay pulled in a long, fiery breath, and he coughed it out. "Dying—dying would've hurt less."

"Yes, it would have." Something in the physician's tone told Clay dying was still an option.

He leaned back against the rough concrete. Why had he twisted away from that bullet? If he'd let it hit square in the heart, he'd already be with Jesus. No pain ever again. The half made whole.

Instead, he'd let love pull him toward life—more likely, to a painful, protracted death.

But Leah. His tingling lips bent upward. His muse. This pain, this delay in his home-going was worth it for the joy she'd brought him.

Clay bumped, and pain reverberated in his chest.

"Careful!" Gene barked.

Clay opened his eyes to a partly cloudy sky.

"First you say, 'Faster,' and now you say, 'Careful.' Can't have it both ways, pal." A voice Clay didn't recognize.

A plywood wall to his right. A rising and falling sensation. Was he in a landing craft?

Seated to his left, Gene shielded his eyes. "I want him to get to the battleship, but I want him to get there alive."

"Battleship?"

Gene grinned at him. "There you are."

Clay nodded, but the movement pulled on his chest wall and made him wince. His body felt like lead. He couldn't even move his arms. Oh, he was strapped in a basket litter under a brown blanket. "Doc Block wouldn't give up, would he?"

Gene's face clouded. "It—it's been touch and go with you all day."

"All day?" Clay only remembered a haze of pain.

"Yeah. We've been calling for reinforcements and evacuation all day, but these two LCVPs were the first boats to make it to the point. It's 1500."

"The Rangers?" His chest felt tight, his breathing compressed and rapid.

"We're holding on. We took the observation post at the tip of the point, and the LCVPs brought in sixty Rangers from Omaha. That'll help a lot." Gene grimaced at his leg. "I wanted to stay, but Doc put me on this boat. Guess I'm not much good for fighting with this leg."

"You did all right by me. More than all right." Each word cost.

Gene waved him off. "You were the hero. Rudder says you'll get a medal for it."

He wanted to shrug, but it wasn't worth the pain.

The landing craft engine noises changed, and the boat turned. Sailors in dungarees and life vests and helmets moved about and called out orders—something about heaving to.

"This man first." A sailor grabbed the end of Clay's litter. "Doc says he needs surgery."

Metallic clanks around him, and ropes swished into and out of his line of vision.

Gene leaned over. "See you on board, buddy."

Clay smiled although he wouldn't see Gene again. His symptoms indicated he was in shock and had a lot of blood in his lungs.

A jerk on the litter, and Clay winced. Sailors shouted and turned the litter in the air.

Then he rose, swinging gently, climbing the steep gray cliff of the battleship's hull. Too bad the Rangers didn't have a winch to hoist them to the top of Pointe du Hoc.

The whir of the winch stopped, the litter shuddered to a stop, and hands grabbed the litter and swung it over the side of the ship and onto the deck.

Half a dozen faces stared down at him, each capped with helmets.

"G'morning," Clay said.

A sailor laughed. "Good afternoon to you. Let's get you to sick bay."

More metallic clanks as they unhooked the litter from the ropes.

"Say, what ship is this?"

"The fightingest ship in the West—the USS *Texas*."

"My home state. Only fitting." Coming home to die.

43

Mama Paxton opened Juanita's front door and helped Leah carry the baby carriage up the steps. "Come in. I have a surprise for you."

It was far too early for news about Clay, and Leah had released her hope to be united with her sisters, leaving her both depleted and strangely replenished. "A surprise?"

Mama scooped up Helen and motioned Leah into the living room. "You have visitors."

A couple sat on the couch and stood when Leah entered.

"Mrs. Demetrios!"

"Hello, Thalia. It's good to see you again." Mrs. Demetrios clasped Leah's hand. "This is my husband, Dr. Lukas Demetrios."

"I'm pleased to meet you, Dr. Demetrios." Leah shook his hand. "You—you knew my father."

He tipped up a sad smile topped by a neat gray mustache. "A good friend and a fine scholar."

"Leah, would you like some tea?" Mama asked. "Dr. and Mrs. Demetrios, would you like some more?"

Leah managed a "no, thank you," sat in the armchair, and set her purse on the floor beside her. "I'm glad you came, Mrs. Demetrios. I rushed off yesterday, but there was so much I should have asked."

"I'm glad you gave me your address." Mrs. Demetrios cradled her teacup in her hand. "Did you find your sisters?"

"I did. They're beautiful."

A gasp, and Mama peeked back into the living room.

Leah gave her mother-in-law an apologetic look. "I stood outside their house and watched them walk to school. They are beautiful. They're happy and bright and charming, and they're close to their mother and each other. And I—I said nothing. I let them go."

"Ah, *mija*." Mama squeezed Leah's shoulder. "That was brave and wise."

Leah turned to her guests. "I may not be able to meet my sisters, but maybe you can acquaint me with my parents."

"That's why I brought this." Dr. Demetrios opened a cardboard box on the coffee table.

Over the next hour, Leah saw photos of her father at an award ceremony, of her parents dressed as Zeus and Hera for a party, and of the young parents and baby Thalia at a faculty picnic on the shore of Lake Michigan.

She heard stories of her father's exuberant teaching and her mother's sense of humor, her father's clumsiness and her mother's gift with a needle and thread, and of their love for their girls.

She cried over the article about her parents' deaths—how Althea had gotten her heel stuck in a crack in the street and had struggled to unlace her shoe, how her father saved his three daughters and shielded his wife when a car careened around the corner.

Leah held in her hands a book her father had written on Greek poetry, dedicated to his four muses.

Dr. Demetrios set newspaper clippings and photographs back into the box. "These are for you, Thalia."

"But they're yours," Leah said, even as she clutched the book. "He was your friend."

"And I will always remember him dearly." He slid the box to her. "But he was your father. These belong to you."

Leah set a tentative hand on the box. "Thank you."

"If you don't have plans tomorrow, please come to the university." Dr. Demetrios settled back on the couch. "I can show you where Georgi's office was and give you a tour."

"I'd love that. I especially want to see the library." Leah picked up her purse, pulled out the postcard, and passed it to her guests. "This is how I learned I was from Chicago. When I saw this, I remembered the library so clearly I could smell it. This is how I found you and my name and my sisters and my . . . my identity."

Mrs. Demetrios's face twisted with sweet sympathy. "I'm so glad we could help."

Leah stroked the dust jacket of her father's book.

No, her identity had never been lost. At her core, she was the same as she'd been a week earlier. Even without her birth name, without having seen her sisters, without any information on her family history, she'd always been complete.

She always would be.

USS *Texas*, OFF NORMANDY
THURSDAY, JUNE 8, 1944

Gene stood on crutches at the foot of Clay's cot lying on the deck of the battleship's crowded sick bay. "You look real good, Pax."

He found a smile for his friend.

"You didn't look so good when they took you on board." Gene tipped to the side and readjusted his crutches. "Doc says you perked right up with oxygen and some blood, and then they took you to surgery. Sure am glad."

"Me too." Clay sat propped up against a metal locker, very much alive. "How are you?"

Gene lifted his bandaged leg. "Not too bad. They're giving

me that new penicillin we keep hearing about. Doc says I'll have
a couple weeks in a hospital in England, then back to the front.
Sure hope they send me back to the Rangers."

"Hope so too."

"Remember that D Company LCA that sank? A lot of those
fellows are here too." He nodded down the row of cots lined up
like sardines. "So is Sergeant Lombardi. He's over there by the
wall. They had to take off most of his leg though."

Clay winced. "I'm sorry to hear that."

"Don't be. He says you saved his life. Right now he's real happy
to be alive. Bet you feel the same."

He should, so he smiled. But he felt . . . disembodied.

Dr. Rinehart squatted at the foot of Clay's cot. What he lacked in
hair, he made up for in smiles. "How are you this morning, Corporal?"

"See you later, Pax." Gene hobbled away on his crutches.

Clay shot a glance upward. "You sailor boys know how to wake
a man up, sir."

"Those 14-inch guns are impressive, aren't they?" Dr. Rinehart
inspected a clipboard. "How are you feeling?"

"Doesn't hurt as much as it should."

"We gave you a nerve block during surgery. You already know
why." A big toothy grin.

"So I'll breathe deeply and cough up secretions."

"Are you doing that?"

"Yes, sir." Clay deliberately took as deep a breath as he could,
his bare shoulder blades rubbing the locker vents.

"Good." He squeezed between the cots and inspected the large
gauze bandage taped to Clay's chest. "You're one lucky man. The
bullet missed the major vessels. You only have one broken rib, and
it's in the back. The initial surgery went well, and the X-rays show
no retained foreign material. In about a week, you'll have reparative surgery to close the wound. Barring any complications, you
should be back to duty in six to eight weeks."

"Complications—like infection."

Dr. Rinehart nudged Clay to lean forward, and he inspected the dressings on Clay's back. "Since there was no abdominal involvement, the risk of infection is low. With perforating thoracic—chest—wounds, the greatest risk is in the first few hours. Your prognosis is excellent."

An excellent prognosis? Clay shook his head. His dream had come true, but he was alive. What had happened? Had he failed somehow by dodging that bullet?

Dr. Rinehart eased Clay back against the locker. "Everything looks great. I'll look in on you this afternoon. In the meantime, keep doing the breathing and coughing exercises the pharmacist's mate gives you. Any questions?"

"No, sir." None the physician could answer anyway.

He felt discombobulated. What would he do with his life now that he had one? The problem with believing he had no future was that he had no plans.

His convalescence would be longer than Gene's, and they probably wouldn't return him to the Rangers. Where would they send him? Regular infantry or a support job, like in supply?

What about after the war?

Clay forced a deep breath, inhaling the beloved smells of antiseptic and gauze. If Wyatt kept his promise and paid Clay back, could he go to college?

He had a wife and daughter to support. He might be able to afford it if they all lived in one household.

Except he'd promised Leah he'd die.

Clay groaned, and he flexed and pointed his feet to prevent blood clots. Most fellows went off to war promising their wives they'd come home, but Clay had promised he wouldn't.

Leah hadn't signed up for a lifetime with him. To talk her into marrying him, he'd had to promise her—his chest collapsed with the weight of it, straining the dressings—he'd promised that if he survived, they'd get a divorce. He'd have to say he'd cheated on her to give her grounds.

No matter how much he loved her, he had to keep his word and offer that divorce.

Then he'd have two households to support. Even if Wyatt repaid him and Clay worked summers, he couldn't afford eight years of school. He'd have to get a job. Where? At Paxton Trucking? The job he'd hated? Working with Wyatt and Adler?

Reconciling with his brothers seemed less appealing now that it was actually possible. It was one thing to write words of forgiveness and another to live it out each and every day. Could he do so? Or would it be better to start over in a new town?

His pocket Bible lay on the cot beside him, and he opened it. Leah and Helen's photo had survived the mayhem, and Leah's sweet smile burrowed into his heart and made itself at home. How could he give her up?

Perhaps he could persuade her to remain married.

A laugh burst out, and he clutched his side. Even with the nerve block, he felt that.

"You okay, Pax?" the fellow on the next cot asked.

"Yeah. Yeah, I'm fine."

Persuade Leah to remain married? Fat chance. She'd barely known Clay on their wedding day, and what had he done since then to commend himself to her? Nada.

He'd whined about forgiving his brothers and resenting his parents' forgiveness. He'd wanted to die so much that he'd apparently manufactured a dream to support that wish. He was a half-breed with no job prospects.

She might even think he was mercenary, wanting to stay married just so he could afford medical school. And why would she want to be married to a college boy?

Clay closed the Bible. The kindest thing would be to set her free.

44

TULLAHOMA
TUESDAY, JUNE 13, 1944

Under her umbrella, Leah compared the address on the library postcard to the house before her, a blue-and-white Victorian in Tullahoma's nicest neighborhood across from the railroad and businesses these families had founded.

She and Mama had returned to Tullahoma yesterday, and this morning Mama had taken the train back to Kerrville. Leah's little house felt empty without Lupe Paxton.

Up on the porch, Leah lowered her umbrella and rang the doorbell. In a minute, a slender woman with graying blonde hair opened the door.

"Good afternoon, ma'am. I'm Mrs. Clay Paxton. Is Mr. Robert Mason at home?"

"He's at work." Her eyes narrowed—in suspicion? "I'm his wife. May I help you?"

"Yes, please." Leah shone her brightest smile and held out the postcard. "I'm returning a postcard addressed to him."

"A postcard?" She didn't take it.

"Yes, ma'am. Did you donate a set of encyclopedias to the Victory Book Campaign?"

"Why, yes." Mrs. Mason's posture relaxed.

306

"Thank you so much. The campaign wasn't able to use the books, so we donated them to the Coffee Children's Home. The children love having their own encyclopedia set. It's so much easier for them to do homework."

Thin lips curved in a pleasant smile. "I never would have thought of that. How wonderful."

"A child found this postcard tucked inside. I must confess I took it home because it's beautiful and reminded me of my childhood. But it doesn't belong to me, so I'm returning it."

She frowned and took Leah's offering. "It's only a postcard."

"But it belongs to your husband."

Mrs. Mason smiled at the back. "From Ricky. Oh my. Richard— he's my husband's little brother. He hasn't gone by Ricky for years. This must have been from his gallivanting days."

"I'm sure it'll be a fond memory for your husband."

She laughed, bright as the colors on the postcard. "I'm sure he won't remember, but thank you. I'm sorry, you told me your name and I don't recall it. We haven't met before."

"Mrs. Clay Paxton—Leah. I'm fairly new to town."

"I can tell from your accent." Her smile continued to grow in warmth. "Thank you. This was right kind of you."

Leah said her good-byes and departed, a warm rain pattering on her umbrella. As much pleasure as the postcard had given her, she'd received greater pleasure returning it, releasing what had never belonged to her.

Tonight she'd take the final step in releasing what *did* belong to her—her sisters. Leah planned to write Mrs. Scholz, letting her know she would respect her wishes and never contact Callie and Polly. She would record information about her parents, enclose a photo of herself with Helen, and include the Paxtons' address as well as hers. If the Scholzes should ever change their minds or the girls should raise questions, they were free to contact her. But she would never intrude.

Leah rounded the corner onto Moore Street. She would thank the Scholz family for giving her sisters a loving home, and she'd say it was enough to know her sisters were healthy, happy, and together.

It was indeed enough. Leah had the family the Lord had given her, and she'd received the extra gifts of her family history and of witnessing her sisters' happiness.

She had so much more than when she'd arrived in Tullahoma. A year ago to the day, she'd started her job at Camp Forrest. And she'd met Clay.

She breathed out another prayer for the man she loved, set her umbrella on the porch of the Bellamy home, and entered. "Rita Sue? I'm back. Thank you for watching the baby so I didn't have to take her out in the rain."

"Always a joy," Rita Sue called from the kitchen. "Let's sit a spell."

"Maybe this afternoon." Leah knelt by the blanket on the rug where Helen lay, playing with her fingers. "Hi, sweetie. Let's go home so Mama can do laundry."

"What's the hurry?" Rita Sue entered the living room. "You can't hang out your washing in this weather."

A stiffness in her friend's movements and a strain in her voice niggled inside Leah. "Is something wrong?"

Rita Sue sat on the couch and patted the cushion. "Come sit down, sugar."

Something was wrong, and Leah's blood stilled, her hands firm around her baby's warm middle. "A telegram."

A twitch of the eye confirmed the truth. "Please sit down, sugar."

Leah felt as if she were spinning, rising, looking down on the whole nation. Hundreds, thousands of telegrams were being delivered. Hundreds, thousands of lives were being shattered. Leah wasn't special. If anything, Leah was better prepared for this moment.

Then her vision narrowed and spun back to earth, to the only soldier who mattered to her. "Clay . . ."

"Come sit—"

Leah collapsed onto her backside and pulled her daughter to her chest. How could she bear this?

A rustle of movement, and Rita Sue knelt beside her and wrapped her arm around Leah's shoulder. "The Western Union boy arrived while you were out. Now, don't panic. We don't know what's inside."

Leah did. She shifted Helen onto her lap, supported by her left arm, and she took the small envelope from her friend.

With numb fingers, she opened the envelope and removed the slip of paper. A prayer, and she read the dreaded words: "REGRET TO INFORM YOU YOUR HUSBAND CPL CLAY PAXTON WAS ON SEVEN JUNE WOUNDED IN ACTION IN FRANCE STOP YOU WILL BE ADVISED AS REPORTS OF HIS CONDITION ARE RECEIVED."

That wasn't right, but each time Leah blinked, the words became clearer. Wounded . . . wounded . . . "He was wounded."

Rita Sue hugged Leah's shoulders. "Oh, sugar, I'm so sorry."

"No, no." An odd little laugh escaped. "He's only wounded. He's alive!"

Rita Sue ducked to the side and stared at Leah.

"He's alive. Thank God, he's alive." She laughed and kissed her baby's head. She didn't care if he'd lost all his limbs, been burned, disfigured, and maimed forever. Clay Paxton was alive. "He'll survive."

Rita Sue massaged Leah's shoulder. "I pray he will."

Leah tucked in her lips. True. The telegram didn't say how badly he was wounded. She had no guarantee he'd survive, but she had hope that one day he'd come home to her.

She lifted Helen and kissed her sweet-smelling cheek.

Leah could picture Clay stepping off the train, breaking out in his gorgeous smile, taking her into his arms, and kiss—

No, he wouldn't.

Leah pressed up to her knees and then to her feet. Even more clearly, she could see him in the hospital at Camp Forrest, proposing to her, assuring her he'd die in battle and promising—promising to divorce her should he survive.

She wobbled a bit, then sent a grateful smile down to Rita Sue. "Thank you. May I—may I make a call to Texas to tell his parents?"

"Of course, sugar." Rita Sue led Leah into the kitchen.

Clay would indeed come home, but not to her.

Once again, Leah would have to release someone she loved.

45

Clay eased down onto the hospital bed after a long walk around the hospital grounds. He could feel the benefits of the early post-surgical ambulation the physicians now promoted, but boy, did it take a lot out of him.

"Very good, Corporal." Lieutenant Dugoni, his nurse, winked at him. "Tomorrow we'll send you on a five-mile march."

Clay hefted his legs onto the bed and leaned back against the headboard. "I'd prefer climbing a cliff, but a march will do if that's all you've got."

The nurse laughed and straightened Clay's bathrobe over his legs. "I'll see what I can arrange. In the meantime, keep doing your exercises. You're making excellent progress."

"Thank you, ma'am." He filled his lungs, careful to keep his shoulders and pelvis straight and to not favor his wounded side. He didn't want to become a "chest cripple," permanently bent to one side as were too many veterans from World War I.

Almost three weeks had passed since the *Texas* had brought him to England and almost two weeks since he'd undergone the second, reparative, surgery at the 158th General Hospital in Salisbury. It had taken forever for him to learn that the Rangers had held Pointe du Hoc until June 8, when forces from Omaha Beach finally linked up with them.

Hearing that the Rangers had succeeded and the Allies were making progress in Normandy was a benefit of surviving.

Another benefit was being able to report Frank Lyons's confession to the military police. Now Peggy's family in Florida would have resolution, and the boyfriend of the girl in Braunton wouldn't be punished for a crime he hadn't committed.

The ward door opened, and a Red Cross worker entered the semi-cylindrical Nissen hut. The tall blonde's heels clicked on the concrete floor, and patients called out "Hiya, Red Cross" as she passed.

She stopped at the foot of Clay's bed. "Good afternoon. Are you Cpl. Clay Paxton?"

"Yes, ma'am. Good afternoon to you too."

She peered at him more closely, then grinned. "Oh, I see it. I hear it."

A curious thing to say, and he tilted his head.

She laughed and extended her hand. "Pardon me. My name is Violet Lindstrom. I'm with the American Red Cross."

He could tell by her blue-gray uniform with the Red Cross patch on the sleeve and the Red Cross pin on the garrison cap. He shook her hand. "Right nice to meet you, ma'am."

Her pretty face sobered. "I'm here on behalf of two officers who are looking for you. Your—your brothers, Adler and Wyatt."

Just like that, the "Prodigal's elder brother" part of him didn't want to be found. He cleared his throat. "They're doing fine then? After D-day?"

"Oh yes. They each had an adventure, but they're alive and well." She held out some envelopes with a hesitant look. "I've brought letters from them. They said they're very sorry for what they did to you."

Clay's eye twitched, and he took the letters. Just how much of his embarrassing life story had they shared with this stranger?

Miss Lindstrom twisted her purse strap. "They dearly wish to see you, but they'll understand if you don't want to."

Clay's brain felt full of mud. He wasn't ready, wasn't sure he'd ever be, and he set the letters on the bedside table. "I don't need to read these."

"Oh." Her eyebrows tented, and she blinked a lot. "They'll understand, but please keep the letters. Maybe someday you'll be ready."

Clay sighed and fixed his gaze on her. "That wasn't what I meant. I don't need to read the letters to know that I need to see my brothers."

"You do?" A bright smile bloomed. Miss Lindstrom seemed to be taking this case awful personally for an objective Red Cross worker. "Right now?"

"Right now? They're here?" His gaze flew to the door, but he didn't see them.

"They're waiting outside, but . . . maybe another day."

All the air and all the resistance drained out of him. "They've come a long way, haven't they?"

"In more ways than you know," she said in a soft voice.

Clay nodded to her. "I'll see them now."

"Thank you." She darted forward as if to hug him but stopped. "They'll be so happy."

Clay groaned as apprehension and anticipation battled in his heart. Three years had passed. Three years of pain and misery and division. Today it could change—or it could continue. He alone carried the key that could turn the course of his family.

Was this how Joseph had felt in Egypt, waiting for his brothers to be ushered in to his presence?

Miss Lindstrom opened the door and beckoned. Two tall blond officers appeared, one in a navy-blue uniform and one in an olive drab Ike jacket and khaki trousers—Wyatt and Adler.

Clay's chest constricted, and the apprehension crowded out the anticipation.

Miss Lindstrom pressed her hand to Adler's cheek, and he kissed her forehead.

Well, that explained why she'd taken the case personally.

His brothers stepped inside the ward and removed their caps. Slowly, cautiously, they approached, sizing him up.

Clay didn't stand as he should for officers, didn't smile as he should for family. But hadn't Joseph tested his brothers three times to see if their repentance was genuine? Nothing wrong with making his brothers squirm.

They stood at the foot of his bed, hats in hand, their faces as familiar as his own, yet changed, older . . . and etched with remorse.

That was enough squirming. "Howdy."

"Howdy," they said.

The sound of their voices unraveled his last knot of resentment.

Wyatt gestured to the letters. "I wish you had read our letters first."

"Wouldn't change anything."

His brothers winced and exchanged a glance.

Clay sighed. Why wasn't he communicating clearly? "You both have letters coming. I wrote them before D-day, before I could see for myself whether or not you were sorry—"

"We *are* sorry." Adler's gaze stretched out to him. "You have no idea how—"

Clay held up one hand, feeling very much like Joseph on his throne. "I wrote those letters to tell you I've forgiven you fully and completely. Both of you."

Wyatt's shoulders drooped. "We—we don't deserve it."

Adler hung his head. "Not one whit."

Neither did Clay deserve their forgiveness.

Words weren't enough. Clay swung his feet to the floor and pushed to standing.

Both brothers took half a step backward, as if expecting blows, then stood their ground.

Wyatt was closest. Clay clasped his oldest brother's shoulders and drilled his gaze deep into Wyatt's hesitant gray-blue eyes. Last time Clay had seen him, Wyatt had been running for his life, on his way to steal Clay's savings.

Everything buckled inside, and Clay tugged Wyatt into a tight embrace.

His brother stiffened, then sagged and hugged Clay back. "I don't—"

"No more of that. No more." He released Wyatt and turned to Adler, whose sky blue eyes widened.

Clay refused to think about how he'd last seen Adler, and he fell on his middle brother, holding him as firmly as he'd held the rope on Pointe du Hoc, as if his life depended on it, as if the life of his whole family depended on it.

"But—but—" Adler's voice sounded thick and husky. "I ruined your life."

"We both did," Wyatt said.

"My life isn't ruined." He stepped back and grabbed Adler's arm, Wyatt's arm. "It isn't. It's different, but it's good. It's very good."

Adler shook his head. "But—"

"Sit down." Clay sat on the side of the bed and patted the mattress. "I reckon officers can take orders as well as give them."

One corner of Wyatt's mouth twitched. He nudged Adler and took his seat.

"Remember the story of Joseph in Egypt?" Clay pulled his little Bible from the table. "He had every right to say his brothers had ruined his life. They sold him into slavery. He was in a pit, then in prison. Thirteen years. But you know what he said, don't you?"

Wyatt and Adler nodded with a trying-to-recall-the-verse look in their eyes.

Clay recalled it. He'd memorized it. "Joseph told his brothers, 'But as for you, ye thought evil against me; but God meant it unto good, to bring to pass, as it is this day, to save much people alive.'"

"What good could possibly . . . ?" Adler squeezed his eyes shut. Where should he start? "So much good. Saved Leah's life."

"Who's Leah?" Wyatt asked.

"My wife."

They gasped as one. "You're married?"

"And a father." Clay pulled out the well-loved photo. "Her name is Helen, and she's two months old. Aren't they the prettiest girls you've ever seen?"

"Well, I'll be," Adler said.

"Congratulations."

Clay savored the first smiles he'd seen from his brothers in three years. "Neither Leah nor Helen would be alive if you hadn't done what you did."

Wyatt's eyes stretched wide. "What happened?"

"That's a story for another day." Clay tucked the photo away. "If I'd gone to college, I wouldn't have been in the Rangers or on Pointe du Hoc. And that's where I was meant to be."

"You really climbed those cliffs." Wyatt whistled.

Clay shrugged and set aside his Bible. "Only a hundred feet tall, nothing to speak of."

His brothers laughed, and Clay joined in, then laughed harder at the wonder of it, of laughing with them again.

Adler smiled and shook his head. "Never thought this day would come."

A twinge of pain in his right side, but the laughter had been worth it. "Reckon we'll still have moments."

"Reckon so." Sobering, Wyatt gestured to the nightstand. "Please read my letter. Adler's too."

"Yeah," Adler said. "Easier to write all that than to say it, and it hurt like blazes to write."

"I will."

"I sent my check to Daddy," Wyatt said. "Three thousand dollars."

"What?" Clay gaped at him. "Three thousand? I'd only saved two."

"I charged myself interest and a fine." Wyatt pulled a notepad from the breast pocket of his white shirt. "Between that and the GI Bill, college and medical school should be about covered."

"Medical school?"

Adler leaned forward on his knees. "You still want to be a doctor, don't you?"

"I . . ." Did he dare glance in the direction of that dream? He closed his gaping mouth. "The GI Bill. I've heard the fellows talking about it, but I paid it no mind. I thought it had to do with loans."

"And education." Wyatt flipped pages in his notepad. "Roosevelt signed it a few days ago. The bill is pretty restrictive, but it seems tailor-made for you. I took notes."

An accountant to the core, and Clay leaned closer to see.

Wyatt tapped a page filled with his neat handwriting. "You get one year of benefits, plus an additional year for each year of service, up to a maximum of four years."

If Clay stayed in the service until February, that'd be two years of service—three years of benefits. He tried to make sense of the figures before him, the hope before him.

Wyatt moved his finger down the page. "Five hundred dollars a year for school expenses, plus fifty dollars a month for living expenses." Then he laughed. "No, seventy-five—you have dependents. Use the GI Bill benefits for the first few years while my check collects interest in the bank, then use the savings. If you work summers, you'll have plenty."

Clay did the math in his head. If he couldn't convince Leah to stay married to him, he'd need to work for a year or two before starting college, but . . . "I could do it."

"You'd better," Adler said. "You're meant to be a doctor. I'd be glad to help out if you need it."

They thought—both brothers thought he ought to be a physician. For three years he'd assumed they thought the profession was too good for him. Clay's throat swelled, and he coughed to clear it.

Not a half-breed. Not a half brother.

"If you don't do this . . ." Adler glared at him. "This time, I'll beat *you* up."

Out of all the misery, a laugh escaped. "I'd like to see you try."

Wyatt elbowed Adler. "You'd better do it now when he's weak from getting shot, because—hooey!—look at those arms."

"Yeah. What did they feed you in the Rangers? Better than the slop we get at the airfield."

Healing warmth flowed through his heart and lungs and veins. "I want to hear. Tell me. Tell me your stories."

46

Leah savored Clay's handwriting as she walked down Jackson Street in the balmy summer evening. Since Rita Sue was watching Helen, Leah's hands were free to hold the precious stationery.

If only she could have seen the reunion of the Paxton brothers! Clay's letter overflowed with the joy of reconciliation.

On the final page he said he'd be returning stateside for more training—although he didn't say what sort.

In his letters, he'd only told her a few details about what had happened in France—that he'd scaled the cliffs of Pointe du Hoc on D-day and had taken a bullet through the chest the next morning.

Leah pressed her hand over the scar on her chest, over a year old now. How much worse for Clay to have taken a bullet.

But something strange stood out to her. Not once since D-day had he mentioned his recurring dream, even though she'd asked about it. Had it failed to come to pass?

Then the last paragraph—how it destroyed her heart each time she read it: "I'm looking forward to seeing you and to meeting Little Miss Helen. We have a lot to talk about, you and I."

Any other wife would thrill to the thought of sweet words

murmured in her ear. But Leah knew they had to talk about lawyers and papers and alimony and other horrible things.

Leah kissed the letter and folded it. She could stop the divorce with three little words—I love you. Part of her wanted to say them, shout them, and free them from her heart.

If he knew she'd fallen in love with him, he'd feel obligated to stay married to her, honorable man that he was.

As much as she wanted him to stay, she didn't want him to stay out of obligation and honor. Manipulating him with her feelings would be as selfish as declaring herself to her sisters would have been.

Loving Clay meant releasing him, and loving God meant trusting him to provide.

Leah tucked the letter in her purse and entered the Coffee Children's Home for the board meeting. Children ran out from the dining room to greet her. She hugged them all, then sent them back to finish their homework.

Miss King, Mrs. Whipple, and Mrs. Susskind greeted Leah warmly. Mrs. Channing shook her hand, which was far warmer than her usual chilly greeting. But Mrs. Ross made a face as if Leah reeked of garbage. How very odd.

Mrs. Channing opened the meeting, and the board members ran through their reports.

When they finished, Miss King turned to Leah. "Mrs. Paxton, please tell the board about that idea you and Mrs. Sheridan discussed with me."

"Thank you." After the Chicago trip, Leah had returned to volunteering at the library and to sorting donated books. "Mrs. Sheridan is delighted with how the orphans conduct the scrap drives. She's become especially fond of Marty, who picks up her scrap each week. She asked if the older children might be interested in volunteering at the library."

Mrs. Channing's eyes stretched wide. "She wants them there?"

"Yes, ma'am." Leah forced a smile. "We'd like to start a junior librarian program. The children would help the community and also learn useful skills."

Mrs. Channing adjusted her reading glasses. "You don't need the board's permission for that any more than you did for the scrap drives. Proceed."

"Thank you." Miss King grinned at Leah.

"I have a proposal." Mrs. Whipple's face crinkled in the sweetest way. "A few months ago, Mrs. Paxton proposed a pancake breakfast."

Leah winced at the memory. "I'm—"

"Now is the time." She folded her plump hands on the table. "My friends say they never used to think twice about the children's home. But now that they're acquainted with the children through the scrap drives, they're noticing. And they're noticing a need for repairs. I hadn't seen anything, but my eyesight isn't what it used to be."

Miss King twiddled a strand of hair. "I admit we've fallen behind in maintenance."

Leah held her breath. How would Mrs. Channing and the others react?

Mrs. Whipple slid a piece of paper to Mrs. Channing. "I propose we hold a pancake breakfast and work party. Folks could paint or fix things or do yard work, and the children will cook and serve the breakfast. Thanks to Mrs. Paxton's scrap drives, folks will be happy to help."

All Leah had hoped for, and so much more. She sent Mrs. Whipple a grateful, joyful smile. At last the children were beginning to belong.

Mrs. Ross shoved back her chair. "I can't listen to this anymore."

The ladies gasped and stared at her.

Mrs. Ross stood and pointed a shaking finger at Leah. "Y'all are singing this girl's praises when she's nothing but a common thief."

The familiar words slapped Leah in the face.

"Pardon?" Mrs. Channing said.

Mrs. Ross straightened her shirtwaist dress, her reddening face clashing with the peach floral print. "When I was having my hair done, I was chatting about Mrs. Paxton's scrap drives. The lady in the next chair said we'd better watch our pennies because that girl will steal every last one of them."

Leah clutched her arms around her belly, trying to hold herself together. Oh no. It had to be someone from the boardinghouse.

Mrs. Whipple's face grew stern. "That's a strong accusation."

Mrs. Ross lifted her round chin. "Her name is Minerva Perry, and she used to rent a room to Mrs. Paxton. Kicked her out for stealing from her roommate."

"That couldn't be true," Mrs. Whipple said.

Leah's eyelids drooped shut. Would she ever be seen as anything but a dirty, thieving orphan? "My roommate did accuse me of stealing, but I never took anything from her."

"Just what a thief would say." Mrs. Ross's voice rose high. "How can we have someone like that working with impressionable young people—children already predisposed to a life of crime?"

Leah groaned. Just when she'd found someplace where she belonged, someplace where she could help other orphans belong. "I admit that I used to steal when I was younger. Growing up in the orphanage, sometimes I took things other children had lost or neglected. Or food. I told my roommate in the boardinghouse about it. When she lost twenty dollars, she accused me of taking it and told Mrs. Perry about my past. Mrs. Perry believed her. There was no way to prove the money was mine."

"An admitted thief." Mrs. Ross's voice called down judgment. "A bad influence."

Leah's head hurt it was so heavy. She'd given up her sisters for their own good. She had to give up Clay for his own good. And now she had to give up the orphans for—

"Leah . . . ?" Miss King had never used her given name before.

She peered at the orphanage director.

Miss King implored her with her eyes. "You're so good with the children."

Which was she? A bad or a good influence?

Leah sat up taller. She'd talked to Mikey about not lying about his homework and to Marty about avoiding fights. She'd helped Hattie see her skin color as beautiful. And she'd shown so many children the joy of stories.

Rightness and purpose straightened her shoulders, and she held Miss King's gaze. "I belonged to no one, and no one belonged to me. That's why I took things. I'd imagine I had a father to bring me candy and a mother to tie pretty ribbons in my hair."

"That doesn't make it right." Mrs. Ross sniffed.

Leah swept her gaze around the circle. "No, but it does mean I understand these children. I understand their desperate need to belong. I understand the ridicule and exclusion they endure. And I understand the temptations they face. But with the Lord's help, I have overcome all this. It's behind me and forgiven. I can help them overcome too. If you will, I am the very *best* person to work with these children."

Miss King smiled softly at her, and Mrs. Whipple dabbed her eyes with a handkerchief and nodded.

Still standing, Mrs. Ross tapped the table like a judge with a gavel. "I want her out, and I call for a vote. Who's with me?"

"I'm afraid I agree with Mrs. Ross." Mrs. Susskind's lips squirmed.

"I vote no," Miss King said. "I want her here, and so do the children."

"I vote no too," Mrs. Whipple said in a firm voice. "Where is your Christian mercy, ladies?"

That left Mrs. Channing, and Leah's heart plummeted. She threaded her arm through her purse strap so she could leave.

Mrs. Channing scanned the board with her steely gaze. "Let me tell you a story about Mrs. Paxton."

A story? What story could that be?

Mrs. Channing removed her reading glasses. "A few weeks ago, my daughter said Mrs. Paxton came to her house to return an old postcard tucked inside an encyclopedia they'd donated to the Victory Book Campaign—and that ended up at this orphanage."

Leah's jaw flopped open. "Mrs. Mason is your daughter?"

Mrs. Channing nodded. "That postcard was worthless, a scrap of paper long forgotten and fit only for the scrap bin. Mrs. Paxton told my Alice the postcard was lovely and reminded her of her childhood—and yet she returned it. Do those sound like the deeds of a common thief?"

"Indeed not," Mrs. Whipple said.

"Indeed not." Mrs. Channing raised her chin higher than Mrs. Ross ever could hope to. "Those are the deeds of a woman of integrity, the kind of woman we want influencing these impressionable young minds. Mrs. Ross, you're outvoted."

Leah managed to inhale and then to exhale a "thank you."

Mrs. Channing winked at her and raised half a smile. "If you can help these ruffians turn out half as well as you've turned out, we'll all be delighted."

Leah smiled back. On her way out, she'd hug the orphans with extra zest.

47

Troop transport USS *West Point*
Boston, Massachusetts
Saturday, August 5, 1944

"The Yankees are coming! The Yankees are coming!" the soldier next to Clay whooped. "One if by land and two if by sea!"

Clay grinned and leaned his elbows on the railing of the troop transport USS *West Point*. The soldier might have mixed up his quotes, but Clay felt his excitement about sailing into Boston Harbor.

The ship chugged past vessels and piers, and Boston's skyline cut a jagged line in the blue above.

When he'd sailed from New York nine months earlier, he thought he'd never see America again. Now here he was. Not just in America, but in historic Boston. If he had to wait for a train to Tennessee, he'd see the Old North Church, Paul Revere's House, and—

"Bunker Hill Monument!" A soldier pointed to the gray obelisk.

That too. Maybe the Boston Public Library for Leah's sake.

But the sooner he could get to Tullahoma, the better. Then he'd head to Kerrville, with the timing dependent on Leah. He didn't have to report to Fort Sam Houston in San Antonio until the first of September.

"First thing, I'm finding me a real American hamburger." Swee-ney, Clay's bunkmate on the voyage, rubbed his belly.

Clay's mouth watered, then even more as his thoughts drifted homeward. "Mama's chili, that's what I want." Since San Antonio was only fifty miles from Kerrville, he might be able to indulge more than once during his three-month training period.

His healing time had come. Right after he'd decided to go to college and medical school, he'd also decided to train to become a medical technician. Only fitting. Might as well spend the duration of the war doing what he was meant to do.

Maybe they'd send him back to the Rangers. Sure would be nice to work as a medic alongside Doc Block and to see his buddies. Gene had returned to the battalion. He'd promised to write, but Clay missed him.

The ship slowed as it neared an empty pier.

The Rangers' exploits on D-day were getting plenty of press, and Mama said the *Kerrville Times* had mentioned Clay's involve-ment. He resisted the urge to stroke the third stripe on his sleeve for his promotion to sergeant, or the ribbons for the Bronze Star and the Purple Heart on his chest. Every man on the beaches of Normandy deserved a shirt full of medals.

Clay pushed away from the railing. "I'm going below to get my gear. I want to be the first one off this ship."

Sweeney whistled. "Someone's in a hurry to get home to the missus."

"Yes, sir." Although not for the reason Sweeney assumed. He worked his way through the crowd of men in olive drab to the stairway.

He passed a military policeman by the doorway. Clay laughed to himself. On his last Atlantic crossing, he'd seen Adler and hadn't wanted to. On this crossing, he would have loved to have both brothers by his side.

They'd each visited him once more before he shipped out from

Liverpool. Reading their letters of apology had only deepened his forgiveness, if that were possible.

Clay trotted downstairs, then headed down the narrow passageway to the ballroom where he'd been quartered. The *West Point* could carry eight thousand troops, but on this westbound trip, only thirteen hundred men had sailed. A lot roomier.

Clay checked his duffel to make sure he'd packed everything. Leah's most recent letter lay on top, and he opened it again.

She described a work party she'd helped organize at the orphanage, a rousing success from what he could tell from her modest wording. She'd accomplished more than any fund-raiser could have—she'd helped make those orphans part of the community.

"You're an incredible woman, Leah Paxton," he murmured.

He lingered over his favorite section.

Recently I've learned that not everything in my hands is meant to stay there. Some I am meant to release, like my sisters. Although I pray we will be reunited and I will always hold them close in my heart and prayers, I have let them go.

But God has placed some things in my hands that I am meant to cling to hard, like my daughter and the orphans. I will fight for them with everything in me.

Clay folded the letter and closed his duffel. Her letter reminded him of the third chapter of Ecclesiastes, where he'd spent a lot of time recently. "A time to keep, and a time to cast away." Leah had learned the difference.

What about Clay? Did she mean to keep him or to cast him away?

He hefted his duffel over his shoulder, pausing to let a twinge of pain in his wound follow its course. He pressed a lungful of air against the pain, mastering it.

In their letters since D-day, he and Leah had skirted the topic of their marriage, but the time to speak had also come. He'd do everything he could to persuade her to remain his wife.

Clay straightened his garrison cap and made his way down the passageway, the rumbles of the giant engines working through his legs.

Leah intended to fight for Helen and the orphans, and Clay rubbed his thumb along the warmth of his wedding ring. "Well, darlin', I'm fixin' to fight for you with everything in me. Don't make me resort to dirty fighting, you hear?"

When he reached the stairs, soldiers were streaming down, grinning and chatting. Clay worked his way upstream to the deck of the former ocean liner. Even though he'd still have to wait for his group to be called to disembark, he wanted to be at the front of the line.

Outside, he filled his lungs with fresh American air. Alive.

Ever since D-day he'd been puzzling over the recurring dream. God knew everything. God knew Clay would dodge that bullet and live. So why did he send the dream?

Clay leaned against the railing. Down on the pier, men muscled thick lines into place to secure the mighty ship.

He'd been so miserable for so long, the dream had come as a relief, assuring him the misery would come to an end.

That dream had served good purposes, leading him to join the Rangers and to marry Leah. But if those were the only purposes, why hadn't the dream stopped after the wedding?

It had also made him fearless in training and in combat, but was that enough of a reason? Was he such a coward that he couldn't charge a casemate without that dream? He hoped not.

Clay gazed over the land he thought he'd never see again. All he knew was the dream had stopped, and his new life was about to begin.

328

48

Leah checked the clock hanging under the eaves at the railroad depot. It was 6:32, only three minutes until Clay's train was expected. Her stomach wriggled more than Helen did in her baby carriage.

If only she'd had more time to prepare for his arrival. He'd sent a telegram when he arrived in Boston, saying he'd be in Tullahoma as soon as the trains allowed.

Then this afternoon he'd called the Bellamy home while Leah was on her way to the orphanage. Rita Sue had called her there, and Leah had said her hellos, apologies, and good-byes, and she'd hurried home as quickly as she could push the baby carriage.

She'd rushed to make phone calls, prepare dinner, feed and change the baby, and get dressed.

"Time to meet your daddy, sweetie." Leah picked up the four-month-old and smoothed her yellow dotted swiss dress, made from remnants after Rita Sue made dresses for Luella and Sally. The girls were thrilled that Helen had a matching dress.

Leah had taken extra care with her own grooming—her hair rolled in a fashionable style under her summer hat, her lips red and her nose powdered, her grassy green suit pressed, and her cream pumps shiny. She had to look capable of caring for herself and her daughter on her own.

Bouncing Helen on her shoulder, Leah paced on the short platform and avoided glancing up the tracks toward Nashville too often.

Her heart did a little trill at the thought of seeing Clay, but she had to be careful. Everything she did and said tonight had to be just right.

She needed to—wanted to—greet him warmly as the dear friend he was. But it was vital that she conceal her love so he'd feel no guilt or concern when he went his way in the world.

A chugging sound rose to the north, and Leah spun that direction. He was coming.

Lord, help me. Clay deserved to find a woman he adored as much as Leah adored him.

The maroon-and-yellow locomotive of the Nashville, Chattanooga & St. Louis Railroad came down the tracks, steam pluming behind.

Passengers stepped out of the main waiting room and the colored waiting room, ready to board, and Leah retreated to an open spot by the white frame depot where she wouldn't be in the way.

"Chattanooga Choo Choo" played in Leah's head. With Clay's radio in the house, she was becoming familiar with popular music, but the lyrics anticipating a romantic depot reunion didn't help her state of mind.

The train stopped with a sigh of steam, and doors opened. Soldiers and civilians streamed out, but where was Clay?

Then he stepped out in uniform, as grand as an Indian chief, and he slipped on a garrison cap over his shiny black hair.

His gaze landed on her, and a grin spread, broader than any she'd seen from him.

That grin unleashed her own. Without thinking, she waved wildly. She tried to restrain herself, but it was too late.

He strode right up to her, even more handsome and bronzed and strong than she remembered. "Hello, Leah."

That voice. It wove its way deep into her heart and resonated. She swallowed hard. "Hello, Clay."

"Well." He set his hand on her shoulder, ducked down, and planted a kiss on her cheek, so fleeting, she wouldn't have known its existence but for the lingering warmth.

Her right hand had found his waist as if it had a mind of its own.

With his hand on Leah's shoulder, Clay turned to Helen. His smile changed, new and wondrous.

"Say hello to your daddy," Leah said.

Helen crowed, and Clay and Leah laughed.

Clay took Helen's hand and made a courtly bow. "Miss Helen Margarita Paxton, it is a pleasure to meet you." And he kissed that tiny plump hand.

Leah's heart melted and molded into a new shape, completely contoured around this man before her. She would never love any man as much as she loved him.

Clay released Helen's hand.

Before he could straighten up, the baby grabbed his ear and crowed again.

Clay twisted to face Leah with a comical look, and he laughed. Leah laughed too, and Helen added her adorable throaty giggle.

For one blissful moment they stood there, linked and laughing, in a perfect triangle of happiness. If only it could last.

Clay extricated himself from the baby's iron grip. "Reckon I ought to fetch my duffel. Be right back." He tipped a little salute to Leah and marched down the platform.

Leah settled Helen into her carriage for the walk home and settled her heart back into its proper place.

Clay returned with a canvas bag over his shoulder and a hesitant expression. With only a telegram and a phone message since his arrival, they'd had no opportunity to discuss accommodations.

She took the reins. "If you haven't eaten, I have dinner ready at my—your house. You do pay the rent."

"*Our* house." He opened the door to the depot for her. "You're the one who lives there."

Leah pushed the carriage through the waiting room, and Clay darted ahead to open the door on the other side.

"For tonight at least, you'll have to live there too." Leah headed south on Atlantic. "I'm afraid the house is rather small, but the hotels don't have any vacancies."

He shrugged. "All I need is a blanket and a spot on the floor. In this heat, the blanket is optional."

"Nonsense. Alice Mason just gave me her old couch. I'll sleep there and—"

"No, you don't." Clay's dark eyes crinkled with amusement. "I won't kick you out of your bed."

"But you're fresh out of the hospital."

"And the couch sounds just dandy. No arguing."

She glanced him up and down. "How are you? You look well."

His teeth shone white. "I feel great. A few twinges of pain, nothing to speak of. Remarkable, considering a bullet passed through my chest."

Leah's throat clogged. What if that bullet had hit his heart?

"They've made incredible progress in thoracic surgery since the war started," Clay said. "In World War I, a soldier with the same injury would have ended up a chest cripple, but here I am, cleared for active duty."

"That's wonderful." She turned left on Moore. "So, what are your plans? How long will you be in Tullahoma? Are you going home? You said something about more training, but you didn't elaborate."

"So many questions." His voice had a delightful teasing lilt.

"I'll spend some time here, some in Kerrville. Then on September 1, I report to Fort Sam Houston in San Antonio to train as a medic."

"A medic! But I thought you didn't want to be a medic. I know you wanted to be a physician, but—"

"Want. Not past tense anymore. I want to be a physician, and Lord willing, now it can happen." The look on his face was new to her—determined and content.

Leah stopped beside her house and studied him. "You can? Oh, Clay, that's wonderful. I want to hear all about it."

"Keep walking. Starving man." He made a darling pathetic face.

Concealing her love from him would not be easy. She rounded the corner of her house, scooped Helen out of the carriage, and unlocked the front door.

He stepped inside and took in a big breath. "Smells good, almost like . . ."

"Like your mama's chili? It is."

He turned to her, his eyes wide and unbelieving.

Leah passed him and set Helen on her belly in her playpen. Helen pushed up on her arms and stretched for her fluffy bunny.

"I'd planned to make enchiladas for your homecoming, but I didn't have time." Leah tied an apron over her suit. "Thank goodness, I'd already put the beans to soaking for chili. The recipe makes plenty."

Clay followed her into the kitchen, eyes almost closed. "You have no idea how good that smells after almost two years of Army cooking."

"Please have a seat." Leah took out two hot pads and laid them on the table. "It'll only be a minute while I set the table."

"Let me help then."

"All right. Thank you." She pulled a pan of cornbread from the oven, where it had been keeping warm. "The plates and bowls are in the cupboard."

While she brought out the chili and cornbread, Clay laid out the dinnerware. As they passed each other and worked together, it reminded her of the sweet domestic camaraderie at the Bellamy home. But this was her home. And her husband.

Leah's middle clenched. Not for long.

Clay set out silverware and nodded to the radio on the kitchen table. "I recognize that."

Because it was his, not hers. "You ought to take it with you."

"To the barracks? No place for it there." Then he glanced to the bookshelf and grinned. "Is that my violin?"

"Your parents brought a lot of your things."

He crossed the room and opened the case. "I haven't played in ages."

"I loved how you used to play for me in the hospital."

His gaze turned to her, so warm and personal, she couldn't breathe. "I could play for you tonight, if you'd like."

Oh, she'd like that very much. "Helen would love that. You ought to see. She bounces to the music on the radio. She's very fond of the Andrews Sisters."

"Is that so, baby girl?" Clay squatted beside the playpen with his violin in hand. "Wait till you hear the Paxton brothers."

"Oh?" Leah surveyed the table. If only she had butter for the cornbread, but she'd used her red ration points for lard to make refried beans for the enchilada dinner. "Do the Paxton brothers sing together?"

"We called ourselves the Gringo Mariachis." Clay stood and put his violin under his chin. "We sang, we played, we broke hearts all across Texas."

Leah untied her apron and slipped it over her head. If Wyatt and Adler were half as appealing as Clay, they'd broken many a heart.

Clay drew the bow across the strings in a discordant tone, and he made a funny face. "Now I'm breaking eardrums all across Tennessee."

Leah laughed. Had she ever seen him so . . . sunny? "Shall we eat?"

"Yes, ma'am. I'll tune her up after dinner." He put away the violin and sat at the table.

Clay said a heartfelt blessing over the food, then ate with gusto, praising her cooking and praising his mama for giving Leah the recipes and the spices.

Leah brimmed over with questions. What had happened in Normandy? What about his recurring dream? One question felt safest. "Tell me about becoming a medic—and a physician."

Clay dunked a slice of cornbread in his chili. "Wyatt paid me back and far more than he stole. That money and the benefits from the GI Bill will pay for college and medical school. I may have to work summers for Daddy, but I can afford it."

"I'm so happy for you. Your original dream is back."

"It is. In the meantime, there's no reason I can't start healing people right now. I helped in the hospital in England as part of my rehabilitation. It felt right. It's who I really am. So I'll serve as a medic for the duration, then go to college afterward."

Leah sipped from her glass of milk. "Then in eight years you'll be a physician." Dr. Clay Paxton. She could see him in a white coat warming the bell of a stethoscope in his thick hands. He would be the best doctor ever.

Clay set down his spoon and leaned back in his chair, although his bowl wasn't empty. "What do you think about all this?"

What did she think? Her heart wanted to be a part of this grand plan, but her mind knew she'd only hold him back and get in the way.

She had her own plan. When Helen started first grade, Leah would find a job so Clay wouldn't have to support her any longer. She might even be able to work as a librarian.

"Leah?" Clay's mouth turned down at the corners. "What do you think? I'd like your opinion."

She forced a smile, and then her love for him made it real. "I think it's perfect. You were meant to be a doctor. Your parents say so, and I see it too. I'm so glad you'll be able to make that dream come true."

A half smile, then Clay turned his attention to his chili.

Releasing him was for his own good. If only it didn't have to hurt so much.

49

Where was he? Clay turned his vision ninety degrees and oriented himself. Leah's house. His house.

The savory smell of chili lingered, and he smiled and sat up on the couch, the blanket discarded on the floor.

When Leah had told him she'd made Mama's chili, he'd come awfully close to taking her in his arms and kissing the daylights out of her. But that would have been the stupidest way to declare his love to a woman who had been attacked and violated by a man.

After a good belly scratch, Clay stood to do his chest and shoulder exercises.

Sounds rose from Leah's room and the adjoining nursery, with Leah using her singsong mama voice.

Clay swung his arms behind his back and held the stretch. My, Leah was beautiful, more beautiful than the year before, and more than the photograph he'd cherished.

He flexed his arms like football goalposts, pushing back over and over to strengthen his back. Why hadn't he told her she was beautiful at the depot? Instead he'd said, "Well," and pecked her cheek like a deranged chicken.

He thrust his fists in front of him and pulled back and forth as if rowing a boat. Last night he'd avoided talking about love and marriage. She'd approved of his plans for the future but hadn't said whether she wanted to be a part of them.

Clay reached his left arm overhead and leaned to the right. Why would she say anything? He'd asked in a general way, requesting her opinion on his plans. No wonder she'd looked confused. He should have been direct and clear.

Clay reversed the stretch—the painful side, pulling the scar tissue. The rest of the evening, they'd talked about his reunion with his brothers and she'd shown him the articles and photographs of her family—even her birth certificate.

He grabbed his left elbow and drew it across his chest, then repeated on the right. All of the conversation had been great, but in a friendly, brotherly-sisterly way.

Today. Today he'd tell her how he felt and ask her to give him a chance.

He rubbed his scruffy face. Not looking like a grizzly bear, he wouldn't.

Clay grabbed his toiletry kit and uniform and went into the bathroom. Soon he came out, showered, shaven, and dressed in his khaki shirt and trousers.

Now the smell of eggs and fried potatoes climbed above the smell of chili.

Leah stood at the sink, scrubbing a pan, an apron tied over a short-sleeved dress in a golden color. Her hair was down, and all he wanted to do was brush those curls aside and kiss her slender neck.

He pulled himself together. "Good morning."

"Good morning." Leah smiled over her shoulder. "Let me get your breakfast."

"Thank you." He could get used to this. Helen was propped up in the high chair, chewing on a zwieback biscuit, and he ruffled her short black curls. "Good morning to you too, missy."

She smiled around that biscuit.

Leah brought him a plate of scrambled eggs and potatoes.

"You look nice today." Oh, he had to do better than that. "Very pretty."

"Thanks." She shot him a quick smile. "I need to leave soon, but please take your time over breakfast and make yourself at home."

"You have plans?" He scooped a forkful of eggs into his mouth, fluffy and perfectly salted.

"I'm sorry." Leah grabbed a washcloth and wiped Helen's face to tiny protests. "This is my morning volunteering at the library in town. I called yesterday after I received your message, but Mrs. Sheridan didn't answer. So I really should go in."

"That makes sense." The potatoes were even better—crisp, with just a bit of chili powder.

"Come on, sweetie," Leah cooed to Helen as she extracted her from the high chair. "Ready for a fun morning with Mrs. Travers and Carrie?"

"Mrs. Travers?" Clay took a swig of coffee.

Leah walked back to her room with Helen on her hip. "She's the lady I met at church. We take turns volunteering and watching babies."

"That's right. You told me." He tried not to admire the way she walked, but she had a fine, womanly walk. Motherhood had been good to her in many ways.

"I'm taking the baby to her house," Leah called from the bedroom. "Then I'm supposed to volunteer from eight until noon, but I know Mrs. Sheridan won't mind if I leave at eleven so we can meet with the lawyer."

The lump of eggs in Clay's mouth turned icy cold. Somehow he swallowed. "Lawyer?"

Leah strode out of the bedroom with the baby, and she lifted a big bag over her shoulder. "I forgot to tell you yesterday, but I made an appointment for us at eleven. Here's his card with the address." She pulled a business card from on top of the icebox and set it next to Clay.

The eggs curdled in his stomach. "What's this about?" But he knew.

"I'm sure you'll want to start the divorce proceedings right away." She went to the door and took her purse off a hook, speaking as breezily as if she were announcing a run to the grocery and dry cleaners. "I have no idea how long it'll take, so we should get started. You have so many wonderful plans, and I know you'll want to move forward with your life."

Clay's hand froze around his fork, and his mind froze around that hated word—divorce.

Leah faced him with the serene smile he'd always loved. "I'm so happy for you. I really am. I'll see you at eleven. Good-bye."

And she was gone.

Silence flooded the house.

The remaining eggs and potatoes sat forlorn on his plate, never to be eaten.

Clay shoved back his chair and wandered around the table. She didn't want him. She liked him as a friend, but she didn't want him for a husband.

Who would?

"*Why would I want to marry Clay?*" He could still hear Ellen Hill as Daddy pleaded with her to marry Clay for the sake of her baby.

He could still see the defiance on Ellen's face, hear the contempt in her voice. "*I've always loved Adler. I never loved Clay. How could I marry a dirty Mex—*"

At least Ellen had enough sense to shut her mouth when Daddy's face turned redder than Mama's enchilada sauce. After all, Daddy had married a Mexican.

Clay punched his fist into his open hand. Whatever made him think any woman could love him? Not Ellen. Not Leah.

Except he'd never truly loved Ellen. He'd thought he was in love, but he'd only been enamored by her beauty.

Leah, on the other hand . . .

He loved Leah heart and soul.

Clay moaned and went back into the kitchen. He loved how she'd learned to make his favorite recipes. He loved the yellow checkered curtains she'd made, hanging at the window over the sink. He loved how her few dishes and pans were set in order in the cupboards.

He wandered into Leah's bedroom. He probably shouldn't have, but he did.

The bed, made so neatly it would have passed Sergeant Lombardi's inspections. And big enough for two. Not that it mattered.

He averted his eyes and stepped into the nursery, a tiny room with a crib and a chair and a dresser topped with baby things. Everything smelled clean and fresh.

Clay abandoned their private space and went back into the living room. A small bookcase contained his books and hers, with his childhood books on the bottom shelf where Helen could reach them when she was able.

His violin. His radio. A red truck with "Paxton Trucking" in Daddy's printing. The playpen with a white stuffed bunny and Clay's old teddy bear.

He turned in circles in the middle of the room—Leah, Helen, and Clay all intermingled in this home, the three of them woven together over the past year in a way he savored.

Now it would all be undone.

He plopped onto the couch and dropped his head into his hands. "No, Lord. No."

He loved her, wanted to keep her, but she didn't want him.

His fingers dug into his scalp. He could still hear her breezy voice, rejecting him. He tried to shove the words away, but they played in his ear.

"I'm sure you'll want to start the divorce proceedings right away . . . You have so many wonderful plans, and I know you'll want to move forward with your life."

Clay's eyes and his mind opened, slowly, together. Wait. She hadn't said she wanted a divorce, only that *he'd* want one, that *he'd* want to get on with his life.

He did want to get on with his life—but with her beside him.

Clay sucked in a breath through his nostrils and sat back. Regardless, they had an appointment with a lawyer at eleven. Obviously, she did want a divorce if she'd made that appointment.

He might as well get ready. No use moping around for three hours.

In his duffel he found his Ike jacket, and he fingered the ribbons over the pocket, decorations he'd earned for courage under fire. And he traced the diamond patch on the sleeve, an honor he'd worked hard to earn.

Rangers were fighters. Fighters.

Clay punched his arms through the sleeves, dressing for war.

He had one more battle to fight.

50

Leah's hand shook as she slid the book onto the shelf. The hour of quiet before the library opened had been a blessing, as she'd returned books, straightened shelves, and watched for titles misplaced by patrons.

The detailed work had kept her mind off her turmoil.

Almost.

Leah rested her forehead against the cool metal shelf. This would be the hardest day of her life. She'd had many hard days, losing loved ones, being abandoned, being attacked. But those pains had been inflicted upon her. This pain she was inflicting on herself.

Lord, help me through today. This is necessary for his future.

A clicking sound, the creak of the front door, and Mrs. Sheridan greeted the first patrons.

Leah straightened her spine and the shelf before her. She could do this. She'd done very well the night before and this morning. She'd surprised herself with how she'd told Clay about the appointment, confident and casual, despite the pain ripping her apart inside.

Clay had looked shocked that the helpless waif had become a competent woman. What a relief it must have been for him to realize she'd do fine on her own.

She would. With the Lord, she would.

Footsteps sounded in the next aisle. "Thalia?"

Clay? What was he doing there? And why had he called her Thalia?

Where there was a gap on his side of the shelf, Leah pulled out three books on her side to make a tunnel. "Clay?"

He ducked down and smiled at her through the tunnel. "Hi."

"Hi." She wasn't ready to see him, and she tried to gather her casual, confident persona.

Clay leaned his forearm on the shelf and rested his chin on his arm. "I had a different idea for our appointment with the lawyer. I think you should legally change your name."

His face was achingly close, and she eased back. Would her name change after the divorce? She knew so little about such things.

"What's your legal name?" he asked. "Leah Jones Paxton?"

"Yes." How she'd miss that name.

"That isn't who you are. Now that you have your birth certificate, you should change your name to Thalia Karahalios Paxton."

"I hadn't considered that." Her gaze drifted away, above the shelf. "Thalia Karahalios."

"Paxton. I want you to keep the Paxton."

Her gaze lowered to her wedding ring, which had imprinted itself on her finger and her heart. How kind of him to let her keep his name. "Oh. For Helen's sake."

Clay huffed out a breath and scrunched up his face. "Why am I having such a hard time communicating lately? Not just for Helen's sake. For mine."

And why was she having such a hard time comprehending lately?

His gorgeous dark gaze strengthened. "I don't want you only to keep my name. I want you to keep me."

"Keep you?"

"As your husband."

Leah inhaled sharply and pushed back from the shelf. "Clay, no. That's a bad idea."

"It's a great idea."

"No." Her head swung back and forth. "You have plans. College, medical school."

"I'd like to include you in those plans, if you're willing."

Her willingness had nothing to do with it. "We'd hold you back."

"I don't see how." His massive shoulders shrugged. "If anything, you'd make it easier."

Leah rubbed her temple. If only she could rub away his sense of obligation. "I know what you're doing. I know you feel sorry for me and you enjoy providing for me, but I'll be fine on my own. I will. The Lord is my provider. You don't have to do this anymore."

"But I want to. I—"

"No, Clay. You once dreamed of becoming a physician and marrying a woman you loved, and you lost that dream. But you deserve to become a doctor. You deserve to marry a woman you love. I won't let you lose it again. Not out of—out of *charity*." She spat out the detested word.

"Charity? Is that what you think?"

Leah shoved the books back into the gap. "I'll see you at eleven."

"Leah!"

She shoved the cart up the aisle, then down the farthest aisle from Clay, her throat tight and her chin quivering. Why was he making this difficult? Why couldn't he see this was for the best? Why did he have to be so honorable, so generous, so . . . charitable?

"Thalia Karahalios Paxton!" Clay's voice boomed from the reading area.

What on earth? Leah dashed to the end of the aisle.

Clay stood on a table— on top of a table—legs astride and fists on his hips.

She gripped a shelf for support. He looked so grand and noble, and yet adorably silly. What on earth was he doing?

He stretched his hands and a grin to her. "Thalia, my muse. Leah, my wife, my—"

"Sir!" Mrs. Sheridan marched over. "Excuse me, but I'll have to ask you to quiet down and get off the table. This is a library."

"I do apologize, ma'am." Clay turned that electrifying grin to the librarian. "But I'm not coming down until I'm finished proposing to my wife."

Proposing? To her? She gripped the shelf harder and pressed her free hand to her chest, to her tumbling, fluttering mess of a chest.

"Mrs. Paxton?" Mrs. Sheridan gave her a bewildered look. "Is this your . . . ?"

"Yes, ma'am," she whispered.

Clay swept off his garrison cap and bowed. "Sgt. Clay Paxton at your service, ma'am."

Leah gave the librarian a tiny nod to let her know she was all right, although she was anything but.

Mrs. Sheridan raised a mischievous smile and sauntered toward the office. "I'll leave y'all be."

Thank goodness there were no patrons. Leah darted to the table and gripped the back of a chair. "What are you doing up there?"

He smiled down at her. "Showing you I'm not acting out of charity."

In all the time she'd known him, she'd never known him not to make sense. "By standing on a table?"

"Look around, Leah." He gestured toward the bookshelves. "How many of these books tell of men doing heroic deeds for their ladies? I'm a Ranger. Rangers climb cliffs. You don't have any cliffs in this here library, so I climbed this table." He tapped the surface with his foot and grinned with satisfaction. "I didn't even need a rope."

Had he suffered a head injury in Normandy? "Clay, are you all right?"

"I will be when you agree to remain my wife."

Still not making sense. "I mean, are you well?"

"Am I well?" He threw his head back and laughed. Then he raised his arms and shook them like a football player who had made the winning score. "I'm alive, Leah! Alive! I want to live. I want to live a long, long life, and I want to live it with you."

Did he mean it? Was he saying what she longed for beyond longing?

His hands drifted down to his sides, and his gaze to hers. "I want to live my life with you out of love, not out of charity. I've fallen in love with you."

Leah's mouth opened, but all her words, all her beautiful words failed to come together to express the poetry in her heart. How could this man love her in return?

"I never told you what happened in Normandy."

The swerve in topic threw her off balance, and she clutched the chair tighter. "Normandy?" Her voice sounded thin and breathless.

"I needed to tell you in person." He lowered himself to sit on the edge of the table, his legs straddling the chair Leah required to support her rubbery legs, especially with his chocolate gaze at her eye level.

"I told you we climbed the cliffs," he said. "We found and disabled the German guns, blocked the road, and fended off counterattacks. But by the end of the day, I was still alive and hadn't seen a pillbox like in my dream."

"I—I'm glad you were wrong about the dream."

"I wasn't wrong." He let out a wry chuckle. "I woke up the next morning in a crater, just like in my dream. I looked over the top, and there was a gun casemate, exactly where I knew it would be. And I knew—I knew it was time."

Leah clapped one hand over her mouth.

"I volunteered." His eyes grew serious and his chin determined. "I ran up to that casemate just like in my dream and threw in my grenade. The Germans were firing a machine gun, closer and closer."

She cringed at the thought of the bullet piercing his chest.

Clay folded his hand over hers, clasped on the chair back, and his broad fingers softened her grip and worked inside until she was clasping his hand instead, clasping it for all she was worth.

"Leah—" His voice rasped, and he cleared his throat, his gaze delving deep into hers. "I saw the bullet, and I didn't want it. I wanted to see you. I wanted to see Helen. The girls I love."

Her knees threatened to give way, and her hand fell from her mouth to grip the chair.

"I twisted away, so the bullet hit here"—he took her hand and pressed it against his right chest—"instead of here." And he pressed her hand over his heart.

Leah spread her fingers wide over the hard wall of his torso, the life in him thumping against her palm. "I—I'm glad."

Clay lowered his chin and caressed her hand, her fingers, and her wedding band. "I finally figured out the dream. All this time I thought the dream was a premonition of my death, to help me prepare. To allow me to help you and the baby. To give me courage in the final moment."

Leah couldn't look in his eyes, only at the row of colorful ribbons he'd won for that courage, at the chest still breathing and beating with life. Thank goodness, with life.

"Leah, it wasn't a premonition. It was a warning."

"A warning?" She dragged her gaze up, but his head was still lowered, his brow not far from her lips.

"God sent the dream as a warning, so I'd recognize the moment when it came, so I could make a choice. And I chose. I chose hope and life and love. Because of you. Because I love you." He raised his chin.

Leah saw the truth in his eyes—the gentle strength, the vulnerable confidence, the pained joy, and the love, deep and certain. "Oh, Clay."

With a huff of breath, he pulled her hand from his chest and held it before him, turning her ring and frowning at it. "I know this is a lot to spring on you all at once. I made a promise to you. I promised if I survived, we'd get a divorce. And now I want to break that promise."

"Clay, I—" Her words clumped together and plugged her throat.

He squeezed her hand. "However, on the day I gave you this ring, I made a higher promise. I promised before God to have and to hold you for the rest of my days."

Leah's free hand floated up from the chair into the space between them, a space she wanted to close.

"I'm asking you a favor." He spoke to her hand. "I love you and want to stay married to you, but that isn't what you agreed to. Could you do me the favor of holding off that divorce for a while? Maybe till I've finished my three months of training? If by then you know for sure you don't want me for your husband, then I'll go through with it. No fussing. But first, please let me try to win your heart."

The chair that had been her dearest help was now her most exasperating hindrance. She shoved it aside.

Clay raised those warm, dark eyes, his brows high.

Just when she needed words most, she had none. She stepped into the space between his knees, gripped his lapels, and pressed her face to his shoulder.

"Hey, now." He set his hands on her waist. "What's all this about?"

"You already have it," she mumbled into the soft wool of his jacket. "My heart. You can't win what already belongs to you."

His chest lifted a bit. "You don't mean . . . ?"

"Oh, a fine poetess I am." She worked one arm over his shoulder, and she clutched the back of his warm neck. "The most beautiful moment of my life. I should be breaking forth in a sonnet to tell you how much I love you, how very long I've loved you, and how very happy I am, and how I love being your wife. And that long life of yours—I want to be with you for all of it, every single day."

He was still, so very still. Then his arms circled her waist, and he drew her closer. "Well, darlin'. It might not rhyme, but you got your point across."

She had? She stood up straight, and the nearness of him stole her breath. Nearer than she'd ever seen him, except that fleeting moment at their wedding when he'd . . . Her gaze dropped to his lips—sure and smiling and so very fine.

Those lips moved. "Reckon I should ask you out on our first date."

Something new floated inside her, light and playful. "After a year of marriage? A year and three days?"

"I missed our anniversary? All the more reason to take you out." He shrugged, making her aware of the breadth of his shoulders. "I was hoping if I took you someplace nice, I might get a good-night kiss."

A fog swirled inside, heady and delicious. Leah glanced to the side and raised one shoulder, hoping she looked coy. "On our first date? Really, Sergeant."

"Unless . . ." His thumb made circles on her lower back. "Unless I could talk you into a kiss right now."

"In the library?" She gazed around the unusually empty space.

"No one's here." His face pressed to her cheek. "Besides, we're married."

The fog settled into all her limbs, dissolving them, and she leaned into him for support. "You did just come home from war."

"I did." His breath tingled on her jaw. "And that kiss I gave you yesterday? That was about the worst homecoming kiss ever. I can do better." His mouth slid over her cheek.

This time she was prepared and tilted her head in the right direction.

Oh, but how unprepared she was. At the touch of his lips, everything in her fell apart then came together in a new way, one with him, melded with him, she belonging to him and he belonging to her.

Their first kiss had given her a glimpse of what the poets wrote about, but this one was poetry they wrote together, silently singing in a meter all their own.

"A lifetime of this," she murmured against his lips.

"I won't mind getting a kiss like that every night."

"Starting tonight."

Clay's eyes widened, and hers did too. They shared a house. As man and wife. A man and wife deeply in love with each other.

"Um." Clay mashed his lips together. "Maybe I should—it'll make you more comfortable if I find someplace else to sleep while I'm in town."

Leah stroked his strong cheekbones and knew without a doubt where she wanted him to sleep. "In the—in the orphanage we always slept two, even three to a bed. Sleeping alone feels strange to me. Lonely."

He squeezed his eyes shut. "Leah . . ."

"I'm not saying . . . we don't have to . . . you know." She squirmed around the words she couldn't say.

"Sweetheart." Clay leaned his forehead against hers. "I know what—that man did to you. I don't want to hurt you, to rush things. I love you enough to wait, however long it takes."

"I know." His hair was smooth and soft under her fingers. "I trust you. I trust you completely."

He kissed her nose. "We'll take things slowly, I promise."

The nose wasn't enough, and she kissed his lips. "Don't go somewhere else tonight. Please? Last night I felt safe. I slept so well—knowing you were close."

Clay pulled back a bit and searched her face, his eyes round. "If you put it that way."

She bit her lip, at once shy and completely comfortable. "Will you join me?"

"Yes, ma'am." He didn't even hesitate. Then he laughed. "Now I really need to take you someplace nice for dinner."

"Ahem." Someone cleared a throat across the room.

Leah sprang out of Clay's arms.

Mrs. Sheridan laughed. "No need to jump, Mrs. Paxton. However, we do have patrons outside waiting to come in."

"You kept them out?" Leah smoothed her hair. Oh dear—her lipstick would be a mess.

"Sergeant, when did you come home?" the librarian asked.

"Last night, ma'am."

Mrs. Sheridan pointed over her shoulder with her thumb. "Y'all, get out of here. And Mrs. Paxton, I don't want to see you for days and days."

Clay grinned and jumped off the table. "I've been in the Army long enough to know an order. Come on, Leah." He grabbed her hand and marched toward the door.

"But I haven't finished . . ." She gestured to her cart—oh, where had she left it?

"I'll finish." Mrs. Sheridan held out Leah's purse. "Off with you."

Leah scampered after Clay, barely managing to grab her purse.

On the sidewalk they passed a few people waiting to enter the library, and Clay kept up his brisk pace.

Leah laughed, her hand entwined with his and her feet struggling to keep up. "Where are you off to in such a hurry?"

"To live, my little wife. To live!" Clay spun to her, grabbed her in his arms, and lifted her off her feet. Right in downtown Tullahoma in sight of everyone.

But Leah could only see the love in her husband's face.

He set her on her feet and rocked her in a circle, her first dance and the sweetest she could imagine. "It's our time to live. Our time to laugh, our time to dance, our time to love."

"Our." No finer word graced the English language. "And here I find where I belong."

Epilogue

Kerrville, Texas
Monday, December 24, 1945

Clay smoothed Mama's embroidery on his white mariachi outfit and the extra strips of fabric Leah had sewn into the sleeves and sides to accommodate Ranger muscles.

He hadn't worn the outfit for four and a half years, since the day his brothers had run away. Now they were all home.

He trotted down the stairs inside the Paxton home in Kerrville. Mariachi music drifted in from the front lawn where the clan was gathering for the annual Paxton-Ramirez Christmas Eve barbecue.

So why did he hear male voices in Daddy's study?

Daddy, Wyatt, Adler, and Reginald Fairfax, Wyatt's British father-in-law, sat chatting. Daddy smiled up at him. "Howdy, son."

Clay leaned against the doorjamb. "It's Christmas Eve, the war is over, and you fellows are talking business."

Adler shrugged. "I can't think of a better way to celebrate."

"Pull up a chair, Clay." Daddy gestured to an empty seat. "This concerns you too."

"You can't make me work at Paxton Trucking. I start at the

355

University of Texas next month." He gave his father a teasing look, but he sat.

"You're still a part owner." Daddy grinned. "And it's Paxton Freight Company now."

"Paxton Freight . . . ?" Since he'd arrived home a few days before, he'd heard an awful lot of business talk from these four—which he'd successfully avoided.

"When I thought I'd never be able to come home—" Adler lowered his chin, and his Adam's apple bobbed.

Clay gripped his hands together. Even with forgiveness, regrets remained. "Go on."

Adler cleared his throat. "I came up with a business idea—Air Cargo Express Shipping, ACES for short."

"A great idea," Daddy said. "Air shipping is the future, and the military will have a lot of surplus planes for sale."

Adler leaned his elbows on his knees. "After I decided to come home, I didn't give ACES a second thought."

"But we did." Wyatt lifted a clipboard. "It's a smart way for our company to grow."

Clay frowned at his oldest brother. "I thought you and Dorothy were going to stay in England and work for Fairfax & Sons."

"It was a fine plan." Mr. Fairfax's British accent sounded out of place in the Texas Hill Country. "However, Wyatt had difficulty obtaining permission to reside in England, and the new Labour government plans to nationalize many areas of commerce. My company might not be viable for long."

"I'm sorry to hear that, sir."

"But America is brimming with opportunity." Had Daddy ever looked so happy? "Dorothy is welcome in the US as a war bride, and Reg will have both family and a job, so he'll probably be welcome too. I'll pull some strings and make it happen."

Wyatt flipped a page on the clipboard. "The first of the year, we'll set up Paxton Freight Company here in Kerrville. Daddy will be in charge and will still run the trucking business. Adler will set up ACES."

"We want to base ACES in Salina, Kansas, Violet's hometown. We'll stay in Kerrville a while to let Timmy get used to living with me and his new mama." Adler smiled with a newlywed glow. He and Violet had gotten married in Salina at the beginning of December with the whole Paxton family in attendance.

"Reg will be in charge of setting up branches at our hubs, starting in Salina, partnering with other regional trucking companies or buying them." Daddy clapped Mr. Fairfax on the back.

The Englishman stiffened but smiled. Maybe Clay ought to loan Daddy his serviceman's guide to Britain to teach his father about English reserve.

"A company this big will need a full-time accountant." Wyatt raised a satisfied smile. "I'll never have to leave my office again."

Adler sent Clay a mischievous look. "All we need is a company physician."

"Not on your life. I just want to be a small-town family doctor." Clay stood. "Y'all should wrap this up. If Mama hears y'all talking business while there's a party outside . . ."

Daddy whistled. "We'd better vamoose."

Clay headed outside and stood on the big wraparound porch with his brothers. Dozens of family members circulated on the big lawn under the oaks and honey locusts, and the smell of Mama's cooking and Daddy's barbecue threaded into his lungs.

It was good to be home.

The previous August, Leah had come with him to Kerrville and stayed with his parents while he was at Fort Sam Houston. Whenever he could get leave, he took it. Those had been sweet, sweet months.

In December he'd shipped overseas to join the Rangers again, and he'd followed them into Germany and Czechoslovakia, celebrating V-E Day with Gene Mayer at his side.

When he shipped overseas, Leah had returned to Tullahoma to help at the orphanage and the library. She'd also worked with the librarian at Camp Forrest to arrange the donation of the library's collection to the town after the base closed. That meant the little town library would need a larger building.

Leah had passed her part of the project to Rita Sue, because in January, Clay and Leah were moving to Austin, to a little place of their own. He couldn't wait.

"Daddy!" Helen toddled across the lawn in a red dress with a red bow tied in her black curls. She flopped onto the bottom porch step and crawled up. Hard to believe she'd be two in April.

"Hello, my little jingle bell." Clay scooped her up and kissed a sticky cheek. "Are you having fun?"

She nodded and bounced in his arms. "Moo! Moo!"

"Yes, music." Pawpaw, Uncle Emilio, and other Ramirez uncles and cousins played rollicking mariachi music on Daddy's makeshift stage under a honey locust.

"Tee-tee!" Helen squealed and pointed at Timmy, who was running up with a sprig of blond hair waving above his head. How Helen adored her three-and-a-half-year-old cousin.

"Hi, Uncle Clay. Hi, Uncle Wy. Hi . . . Daddy." The little boy stopped short of the father he'd only known through letters and photos until recently.

"Howdy, buckaroo." Adler squatted in front of him. "Want to fly?"

"Yippee!" Timmy jumped up and down, then scrambled onto Adler's back.

Helen leaned out of Clay's arms. "Me! Me! Me!"

Timmy frowned. "Not her."

"Yes, her." Adler reached for Helen. "But she'll go in the cargo hold. You're the pilot this time. Then we'll switch."

"Yay!"

Clay relinquished his daughter. "Remember, she's cargo, not a bomb to drop."

"I think I can remember that." He winked at Clay and clutched the little girl to his belly. "Time for takeoff." Off he ran with two giggling children.

Wyatt shook his head. "Here I am, the oldest and the last to have kids."

"Not for long." Clay nudged him. "Am I right?"

Wyatt glanced across to the tables, where his pretty redheaded wife was setting out food with Violet. Dorothy's waist was a lot thicker than when Clay had met her in England. Wyatt put a finger to his lips. "Don't say anything till we make our announcement, you hear?"

"Better make it soon before her belly makes the announcement for you."

Wyatt punched Clay in the shoulder and laughed. "Come on, let's get tamales."

They moseyed across the lawn toward the food tables.

Mama and Leah came out of the side door of the house carrying trays, Leah wearing a red suit and a little round red hat. Leah called out something, and Dorothy and Violet turned to her and laughed.

Now that Leah had a family, she was doing her best to welcome her new sisters-in-law into the fold.

Leah turned to him as if she felt his gaze, and her smile took his breath away. How was it possible for her to get more beautiful each day?

She set down her tray and placed one hand on her flat stomach. She'd just found out she was expecting again. It was a boy, she insisted, and his name was William Walter Paxton.

William after Daddy, and Walter for Dr. Walter Block, who had been killed by shrapnel from German artillery when the Rangers were battling for Bergstein, Germany, in December 1944. Right before Clay had arrived. The whole battalion had mourned for Doc Block, a fine physician and an even finer man.

The mariachi music stopped, and Pawpaw lifted his guitar. "It took a war to bring my grandsons together again, but here they are, three of the finest heroes you've ever seen. On the sea, in the air, and on the ground."

Clay rolled his eyes to Wyatt, but his usually modest brother smiled with appropriate pride. Across the lawn, Adler set down the two children, avoiding everyone's stares, not like the boy who'd thrived on adulation as the star of the Kerrville High baseball team.

The war had done more than bring them together. It had changed them all.

"Here they are!" Pawpaw said. "The Gringo Mariachis, together again."

The tamales would have to wait.

Clay headed up to the wooden stage. He plopped his sombrero on his head and unpacked his violin and bow, while Adler pulled out his trumpet and Wyatt his guitar.

"Merry Christmas, y'all," Wyatt said from under his broad white sombrero. "We're going to play 'Las Mañanitas.'" His voice flickered out at the end.

Some of the faces before them looked hopeful, some looked leery, and some downright hostile. As family, they all knew what Wyatt and Adler had done.

"We're ready," Clay said in a firm voice to his brothers. *Uno, dos, tres.*"

He drew his bow across the strings, Wyatt began strumming, and Adler put the trumpet to his lips.

The music picked up confidence, even though they'd had little time to practice. Each instrument added its own flavor and strength, blending and weaving together.

Adler lowered his trumpet, and they sang, their voices merging and climbing into the cool air. The familiar Spanish rolled off Clay's tongue.

They watched each other as they played, keeping tempo in silent communication.

Clay's heart swelled to fullness. In the future, moments of tension would arise between them, maybe even arguments. But nothing—nothing—could rip them apart again.

At the back of the crowd, Daddy stood with his arm around Mama, who wiped her face with a hankie. Both faces were wild with emotion.

This barbecue was a feast thrown for their three prodigal sons.

Three. Clay might not have run away, but he'd been lost in a pit. And that pit had been partly of his own making. But he was out now, home for good, and joy welled up through his violin and his voice.

He'd been through a dark season. A time to lose what he'd treasured. A time to mourn his lost dreams. A time of war.

Now he lived in a new season. A time to heal, not just bodies but his family and his own heart. A time to keep and to love. And today, a time to laugh and dance.

Prayers of thanks floated up to the heavens. Only the Lord could turn the seasons. Only the Lord could put the shards of his life and his family back together into something stronger and more beautiful than before.

Wyatt, Adler, and Clay struck the final chord in unison, and the crowd applauded, their faces grinning or teary-eyed or hesitant, but each transformed.

With his bow in one hand and his violin in the other, Clay draped his arms over the shoulders of his brothers. His *whole* brothers. And they bowed as one.

His throat constricted. Not only had his forgiveness been the key to restoring his family, but it was the key to his brothers becoming accepted in the community again.

After the applause died, Pawpaw stepped onto the stage. "Dinner is served."

Wyatt and Adler each gave Clay a glance full of meaning.

"It's good," Wyatt said. "It's good to be back together."

It certainly was. "Hurry up, or Uncle Emilio will eat all the tamales."

"No kidding." Adler poked Wyatt. "Race you."

Off they ran, and Clay laughed. Some things would never change.

As much as he loved tamales, he had something better in mind. Despite Leah's height, Clay had no trouble picking her out. She crossed the stream of the crowd, her face glowing just for him.

"That was the most beautiful thing I've ever seen." She hugged him tight.

Clay pressed a kiss to her soft curls.

Leah tipped up her face, her glistening eyelashes the only hint of tears. "I love you so much."

He enjoyed this game they played. "Not as much as I love you."

"I love you more than libraries."

"Ah, you always say that." He smacked her on the lips. "I love you more than—"

"I love you more than all the books in all the libraries in all the world."

Clay's words evaporated, and he swallowed at the radiance of her gaze. "That's a whole lot."

She pressed up on her toes for a kiss.

He whipped off his sombrero, held it as a shield from busybodies, and kissed her soundly. No book, no library could express the wonder and passion and joy he felt for his wife. Thank goodness she gladly accepted kisses in lieu of poetry.

She pulled away, plucked his sombrero out of his hand, and set it back on his head. "There. Very handsome."

Clay eyed the second-floor window of their bedroom. Maybe no one would miss them . . .

Leah snuggled up. "Oh, Clay, this is the best Christmas I've ever had."

"Me too." He rocked her in a circle until he could no longer see that tempting window.

"Even with all the mariachi music, I can only think of 'Hark! the Herald Angels Sing.'"

"Why is that, my little poetess?" How he loved her musings.

"The third verse. 'Hail the heav'n-born Prince of Peace! Hail the Sun of righteousness! Light and life to all He brings, Risen with healing in His wings.' That's what the Lord has done in our lives, in our family—light, life, healing, peace."

"So true." Across the lawn, Daddy and Mama were directing people in line, Wyatt plopped a tamale onto Dorothy's plate, and Adler carried two plates to a blanket on the lawn while Violet carried Timmy.

"Did you know 'Paxton' means 'town of peace'?" Leah said.

"Mm-hmm. Now it's finally true." Clay gave her a little kiss, then nuzzled in her hair and took in the sight of his family. All together, all determined, all forgiving, and all forgiven.

The time for peace had come.

Dear Reader,

On a cool and blustery summer day in 2007, my family visited Pointe du Hoc in Normandy, France. Our young children ran whooping through the giant craters, and my husband and I stared down the sheer cliffs in awe, picturing the men of the US 2nd Ranger Battalion climbing under German fire. Clay's story began to form on that day.

The 2nd Ranger Battalion was a real unit, and the details of their training and combat were drawn from the historical record. While Clay and the men in his platoon are entirely fictional characters, many of the real Rangers appear in this story—Lt. Col. James Earl Rudder, Capt. Walter Block, Capt. Dean Knudson, Lt. James Eikner, 1st Sgt. Leonard "Len" Lomell, and Staff Sgt. Jack Kuhn.

Companies D, E, and F of the 2nd Ranger Battalion became legendary on D-day when they climbed the cliffs of Pointe du Hoc, found and disabled the guns, and fended off counterattacks for two full days until relieved on June 8. The remaining three companies, plus the 5th Ranger Battalion, fought horrific battles on Omaha Beach, where Brig. Gen. Norman Cota gave the command that later became the Ranger motto—"Rangers, lead the way!"

I hope you enjoyed some of the details on pregnancy and baby care in the early 1940s. I found several "Mother's Books" from the era, which were fascinating and slightly scary in parts (daily sunbaths for infants, anyone?). While official advice has changed—

and will continue to change—the love of a mother for her child remains through all generations.

In Tullahoma, all locations and businesses are real, with the exception of the fictional Coffee Children's Home and the characters' homes, but all townspeople are entirely fictional.

One "too coincidental to be real but really happened" moment occurred in the story. The 2nd Ranger Battalion and the US 357th Fighter Group actually sailed to Britain on the same ship on the same day. When history hands you something like that on a platter, you take it.

I hope you enjoyed reading about D-day on the ground. If you missed the first two books in the series, please join Wyatt at sea in *The Sea Before Us* (2018) and Adler in the air in *The Sky Above Us* (2019).

If you're on Pinterest, please visit my board for *The Land Beneath Us* (www.pinterest.com/sarahsundin) to see pictures of Tullahoma, England, Pointe du Hoc, Rangers, 1940s libraries, 1940s maternity and baby wear, and other inspiration for the story.

Acknowledgments

What a privilege and an honor it is to finish my fourth series. I have been blessed to have had the same editors (Vicki Crumpton and Kristin Kornoelje), same agent (Rachel Kent), and many of the same marketing and publicity experts for all twelve books. I'm thankful for each of you and for all you do, and I'm thrilled that we'll be able to work together in the future.

Thank you to reader friend Corinne Reynolds, who contributed the name Gene Mayer in the pre-order campaign for *When Tides Turn*. Corinne said, "I'd love to name a character after my grandfather, Gene Mayer, who served during the occupation of Japan at the end of WWII. He passed away a few years ago, but I would be delighted to honor his memory in this way."

Thank you to writer friend Janice Laird, who sent me tons of resources on Camp Forrest and Tullahoma. I appreciate your friendship.

Many thanks to Katherine VonWert of the Coffee County Lannom Memorial Public Library in Tullahoma, Tennessee, for fielding my questions about the library in Tullahoma during World War II.

One of the greatest joys in my research for this story was wandering into the historic Couch's store in Tullahoma. There I met

Candy Couch, great-granddaughter of the founder, "Daddy Billy." For well over an hour, Candy told stories upon stories, showed me historical photos, and told me what was what in town. Many of her tidbits found their way into this novel—but not nearly as many as I would have liked! Of course, I had to work the store into my story.

And thank you to my readers! I appreciate your messages, prayers, and encouragement. Please visit me at www.sarahsundin.com to leave a message, sign up for my email newsletter, read about the history behind the story, and see pictures from my trips to England, Normandy, and Tullahoma. I hope to hear from you.

Discussion Questions

1. The actions of the US 2nd Ranger Battalion on Pointe du Hoc on D-day have fascinated many. Were you familiar with this event? What did you learn from Clay's experiences on D-day?

2. "Books are weapons in the war of ideas" was the motto of the Victory Book Campaign in World War II. The VBC and the Armed Services Editions are credited with creating a generation of readers. What interested you about Leah's experiences in a base library and with the VBC? How have you seen this motto to be true?

3. Clay firmly believes he will die soon. How does this affect the decisions he makes, for better or worse? Would you like to know how much time you had left? Would it change how you live?

4. More than anything, Leah longs for family and belonging. How does this drive everything she does? How does this desire shift as the story progresses? What do you think of her insight in the last line of chapter 41? In our fractured society, have you found family in unusual places?

5. Clay sees parallels between his life and the biblical story of Joseph. What similarities do you see? Are there any biblical characters you're drawn to? What is it about their stories that you relate to or draw strength from?

6. Leah tells Clay, "Words make delightful playthings. They cost nothing, they never wear out, and no one can ever take them away from you." Do you have a hobby that gives you the same joy as poetry gives Leah?

7. Throughout the story, Clay is torn between his natural desire to heal and his need to go to combat. What do you think of his struggle? Do you think he makes the right decision at the end of the book?

8. Leah has trained herself to respond to pain by focusing on the good. How does this help her cope? How does her attitude help Clay? Could there be negative consequences of relying on this coping technique?

9. Clay believes he's forgiven his brothers, then comes to realize his forgiveness stops at the surface. What did you think of his journey toward forgiveness and reconciliation? Did his insights spark any realizations in your life? They certainly did in mine!

10. When Leah volunteers with the orphans, she enjoys being on the giving end of charity for once. How does her volunteer work cause her to grow? What do you think of her declaration that her background makes her the best type of person to work with orphans?

11. What did you think about the pain Will and Lupe Paxton experience due to their sons' sins and estrangement? Do you agree with how they act toward their three sons? Would you have done anything differently?

12. The story of the Prodigal Son plays out in each novel in the Sunrise at Normandy series. When Clay realizes he's the

Prodigal's elder brother, how does this affect his relationship with his brothers? Have you ever been the "elder brother"?

13. Leah's lifelong dream has been to find her sisters, but she faces an ethical decision when she finds them. Do you agree with the choice she makes? Why or why not? Did the old attitudes toward orphans and adoption surprise you?

14. "To every thing there is a season, and a time to every purpose under the heaven" (Eccles. 3:1). How does Clay's acceptance of this help him weather unpleasant seasons—and embrace pleasant ones? Have you experienced this in your life?

15. Leah has worn a lot of negative labels as an orphan, many of which she believes. Over the course of the story, this changes. Have you ever been assigned labels? Do you accept them or reject them?

16. If you read *The Sea Before Us* and *The Sky Above Us*, what did you think about the continuation of Wyatt's and Adler's stories?

Sarah Sundin is the bestselling author of *The Sea Before Us* and *The Sky Above Us*, as well as the WAVES OF FREEDOM, the WINGS OF THE NIGHTINGALE, and the WINGS OF GLORY series. Her novel *The Sea Before Us* received the 2019 Faith, Hope, and Love Reader's Choice Award, *When Tides Turn* and *Through Waters Deep* were named to Booklist's "101 Best Romance Novels of the Last 10 Years," and *Through Waters Deep* was a finalist for the 2016 Carol Award and won the INSPY Award. In 2011, Sarah received the Writer of the Year Award at the Mount Hermon Christian Writers Conference.

During WWII, her grandfather served as a pharmacist's mate (medic) in the US Navy and her great-uncle flew with the US Eighth Air Force. Sarah and her husband have three adult children—including a sailor in the US Navy! Sarah lives in northern California, and she enjoys speaking for church, community, and writers' groups. Visit www.sarahsundin.com for more information.

Nothing but Love Could Heal the Wounds of War . . .

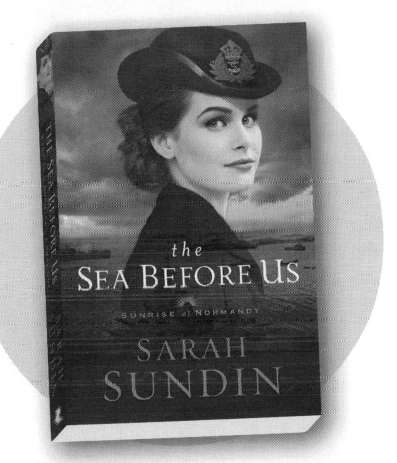

As D-day approaches, American naval officer Lt. Wyatt Paxton is teamed up with Dorothy Fairfax, a British officer. Once they piece together family and reconnaissance photos to map Normandy, will Wyatt's bombardment plans destroy what Dorothy loves most?

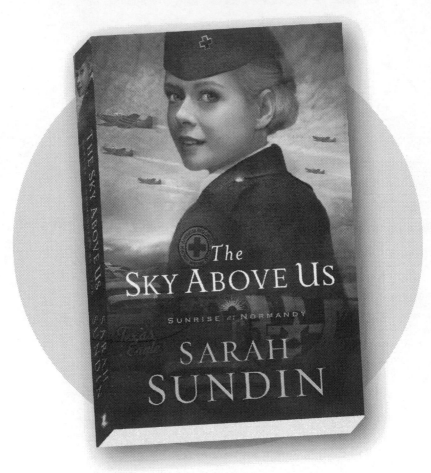

WAR IS COMING.

Can love carry them through the rough waters that lie ahead?

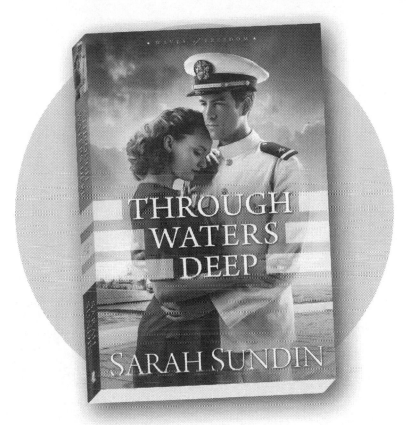

In 1941 as America teeters on the brink of World War II, Mary Stirling and Ensign Jim Avery work together to expose a saboteur. Will the dangers they encounter draw them together or tear them apart?

In a time of sacrifice, what price can one put on true love?

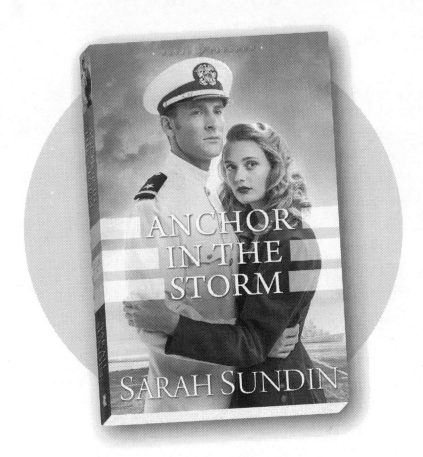

World War II pharmacist Lillian Avery is determined to ignore the attention of Ensign Archer Vandenberg, but will that change when she's forced to work with him on a dangerous case?

In a time of war, sometimes battles take place in the heart.

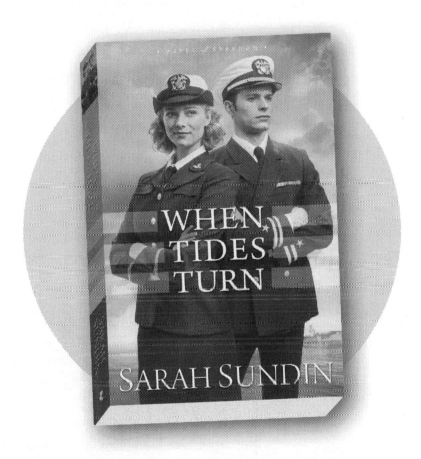

A fun-loving glamour girl. A no-nonsense naval officer. Only a war could bring them together. What happens next will change their lives.

"A gripping tale of war, intrigue, and love."

—*RT Book Reviews* review of
A Memory Between Us

"Sarah Sundin seamlessly weaves together emotion, action, and sweet romance."

—*USA Today's* Happy Ever After blog

GET TO KNOW

SARAH SUNDIN

★ ★ ★

To Learn More about Sarah,
Read Her Blog, or See
the Inspiration behind the Stories
Visit

SARAHSUNDIN.COM

Printed in the United States
By Bookmasters